Dear Reader,

Miami is my home. I'm from here, grew up here and still live here! Miami itself went quickly from being a small Southern town to being a massive international destination. We are like a mini United Nations. The best remedy to ease the insanity of a crowded city—a day trip into the wilderness of the Everglades or down to the Keys.

I love both. Every once in a while, whether I need to or not, I head out west on the Tamiami Trail toward Naples. On the trail, you'll encounter our parks, airboat facilities and a number of Miccosukee Indian camps and the best pumpkin bread you'll ever taste. As well as mosquitos, snakes and more, of course, but also some of the most beautiful birds in the world and wildlife to take your breath away.

Have we found bodies in barrels in the Everglades? Yes. Such a wilderness may be tempting to many criminals, as you'll see in my first Harlequin Intrigue, *Law and Disorder*. But we have fine rangers and experienced guides to bring you through this strange wonderland, one of the very few places on earth where you'll find both the American alligator and the American crocodile.

Heading south, you'll find the Biscayne entrance to Everglades National Park. And when you've explored there, you can keep heading south...all the way down to Key West. There you'll find one of the largest collections of Victorian homes in the US, built during the golden age of salvage, when, per capita, Key West was head and shoulders above the rest of the country! You'll also find incredible water sports, and history that ranges from pirate days to the Civil War and on to cigars and so much more. Hey, how many other places can you find a story about a man who lived with a corpse for seven years and a woman who died and had written on her tombstone "I told you I was sick"?

I sincerely hope you'll enjoy this little bit of South Florida.

Heather Graham

New York Times and *USA TODAY* bestselling author **Heather Graham** has written more than a hundred novels. She's a winner of the RWA's Lifetime Achievement Award and the International Thriller Writers' Silver Bullet. She is an active member of International Thriller Writers and Mystery Writers of America. For more information, check out her website: theoriginalheathergraham.com. You can also find Heather on Facebook.

Visit the Author Profile page
at Harlequin.com for more titles.

New York Times and USA TODAY Bestselling Author

HEATHER GRAHAM

LAW AND DISORDER &
IN THE DARK

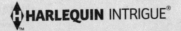

HARLEQUIN INTRIGUE®

ISBN-13: 978-0-373-83902-5

Law and Disorder & In the Dark

Recycling programs for this product may not exist in your area.

CONTENTS

For Kathy Pickering, Traci Hall and Karen Kendall

Great and crazy road trips

Florida's MWA and FRA...

And my magnificent state, Florida

LAW AND DISORDER

CHAPTER ONE

DAKOTA CAMERON WAS stunned to turn and find a gun in her face. It was held by a tall, broad-shouldered man in a hoodie and a mask. The full-face rubber mask—like the Halloween "Tricky Dickie" masks of Richard Nixon—was familiar. It was a mask to denote a historic criminal, she thought, but which one?

The most ridiculous thing was that she almost giggled. She couldn't help but think back to when they were kids; all of them here, playing, imagining themselves notorious criminals. It had been the coolest thing in the world when her dad had inherited the old Crystal Manor on Crystal Island, off the Rickenbacker Causeway, between Miami and South Beach—despite the violence that was part of the estate's history, or maybe because of it.

She and her friends had been young, in grammar school at the time, and they'd loved the estate and all the rumors that had gone with it. They hadn't played cops and robbers—they had played cops and *gangsters*, calling each other G-Man or Leftie, or some other such silly name. Because her father was strict and there was no way crime would ever be glorified here—even if the place had once belonged to Anthony Green, one of the biggest mobsters to hit the causeway islands in the late 1940s and early 1950s—crime of any kind was seen as very, very bad. When the kids played games here, the coppers and the G-men always won.

Because of those old games, when Kody turned to find the gun in her face, she felt a smile twitching at her lips. But then the large man holding the gun fired over her head and the sign that bore the name Crystal Manor exploded into a million bits.

The gun-wielder was serious. It was not, as she had thought possible, a joke—not an old friend, someone who had heard she was back in Miami for the week, someone playing a prank.

No. No one she knew would play such a sick joke.

"Move!" a husky voice commanded her.

She was so stunned at the truth of the situation, the masked man staring at her, the bits of wood exploding around her, that she didn't give way to the weakness in her knees or the growing fear shooting through her. She simply responded.

"Move? To where? What do you want?"

"Out of the booth, up to the house, now. And fast!"

The "booth" was the old guardhouse that sat just inside the great wrought-iron gates on the road. It dated back to the early years of the 1900s when pioneer Jimmy Crystal had first decided upon the spit of high ground—a good three feet above the water level—to found his fishing camp. Coral rock had been dug out of nearby quarries for the foundations of what had then been the caretaker's cottage. Over the next decade, Jimmy Crystal's "fishing camp" had become a playground for the rich and famous. The grand house on the water had been built—pieces of it coming from decaying castles and palaces in Europe—the gardens had been planted and the dock had slowly extended out into Biscayne Bay.

In the 1930s, Jimmy Crystal had mysteriously disappeared at sea. The house and grounds had been swept up by the gangster Anthony Green. He had ruled there for years—until being brought down by a hail of bullets at his club on Miami Beach by "assailants unknown."

The Crystal family had come back in then. The last of them had died when Kody had been just six; that's when her father had discovered that Amelia Crystal—the last assumed member of the old family—had actually been his great-great-great-aunt.

Daniel Cameron had inherited the grandeur—and the ton of bills—that went with the estate.

"Now!" the gun wielder said.

Kody was amazed that her trembling legs could actually move.

"All right," she said, surprised by the even tone of her voice. "I'll have to open the door to get out. And, of course, you're aware that there are cameras all over this estate?"

"Don't worry about the cameras," he said.

She shrugged and moved from the open ticket window to the door. In the few feet between her and the heavy wooden door she tried to think of something she could do.

How in the hell could she sound the alarm?

Maybe it had already been sounded. Crystal Manor was far from the biggest tourist attraction in the area, but still, it *was* an attraction. The cops were aware of it. And Celestial Island—the bigger island that led to Crystal Island—was small, easily accessible by boat but, from the mainland, only accessible via the causeway and then the bridge. To reach Crystal Island, you needed to take the smaller bridge from Celestial Island—or, as with all the islands, arrive by boat. If help had been alerted, it might take time for it to get here.

Jose Marquez, their security man, often walked the walled area down to the water, around the back of the house and the lawn and the gardens and the maze, to the front. He was on his radio at all times. But, of course, with the gun in her face, she had no chance to call him.

Was Jose all right? she wondered. Had the gunman already gotten to him?

"What! Are you eighty? Move!"

The voice was oddly familiar. Was this an old friend? Had someone in her family even set this up, taunting her with a little bit of reproach for the decision she'd made to move up to New York City? She did love her home; leaving hadn't been easy. But she'd been offered a role in a "living theater" piece in an old hotel in the city, a part-time job at an old Irish pub through the acting friend who was part owner—and a rent-controlled apartment for the duration. She was home for a week— just a week—to set some affairs straight before final rehearsals and preview performances.

"Now! Get moving—now!" The man fired again and a large section of coral rock exploded.

Her mind began to race. She hadn't heard many good things about women who'd given in to knife- or gun-wielding strangers. They usually wound up dead anyway.

She ducked low, hurrying to the push button that would lower the aluminum shutter over the open window above the counter at the booth. Diving for her purse, she rolled away with it toward the stairway to the storage area above, dumping her purse as she did so. Her cell phone fell out and she grabbed for it.

But before she could reach it, there was another explosion. The gunman had shot through the lock on the heavy wooden door; it pushed inward.

He seemed to move with the speed of light. Her fingers had just closed around the phone when he straddled over her, wrenching the phone from her hand and throwing it across the small room. He hunkered down on his knees, looming large over her.

There wasn't a way that she was going to survive this! She thought, too, of the people up at the house, imagining distant days of grandeur, the staff, every one of which adored the house and the history. Thought of them all…with bullets in their heads.

With all she had she fought him, trying to buck him off her.

"For the love of God, stop," he whispered harshly, holding her down. "Do as I tell you. Now!"

"So you can kill me later?" she demanded, and stared up at him, trying not to shake. She was basically a coward and couldn't begin to imagine where any of her courage was coming from.

Instinctual desperation? The primal urge to survive?

Before he could answer there was a shout from behind him.

"Barrow! What the hell is going on in there?"

"We're good, Capone!" the man over her shouted back.

Capone?

"Cameras are all sizzled," the man called Capone called out. She couldn't see him. "Closed for Renovation signs up on the gates."

"Great. I've got this. You can get back to the house. We're good here. On the way now!"

"You're slower than molasses!" Capone barked. "Hurry the hell up! Dillinger and Floyd are securing the house."

Capone? As in "Al" Capone, who had made Miami his playground, along with Anthony Green? Dillinger—as in John Dillinger? Floyd—as in Pretty Boy Floyd?

Barrow—or the muscle-bound twit on top of her now—stared at her hard through the eye holes in his mask.

Barrow—as in Clyde Barrow. Yes, he was wearing a Clyde Barrow mask!

She couldn't help but grasp at hope. If they had all given themselves ridiculous 1930's gangster names and were wearing hoodies and masks, maybe cold-blooded murder might be avoided. These men may think their identities were well hidden and they wouldn't need to kill to avoid having any eye witnesses.

"Come with me!" Barrow said. She noted his eyes then. They were blue; an intense blue, almost navy.

Again something of recognition flickered within her. They were such unusual eyes...

"Come with me!"

She couldn't begin to imagine why she laughed, but she did.

"Wow, isn't that a movie line?" she asked. "*Terminator*! Good old Arnie Schwarzenegger. But aren't you supposed to say, 'Come with me—if you want to live'?"

He wasn't amused.

"Come with me—if you want to live," he said, emphasis on the last.

What was she supposed to do? He was a wall of a man, six-feet plus, shoulders like a linebacker.

"Then get off me," she snapped.

He moved, standing with easy agility, reaching a hand down to her.

She ignored the hand and rose on her own accord, heading for the shattered doorway. He quickly came to her side, still holding the gun but slipping an arm around her shoulders.

She started to shake him off.

"Dammit, do you want them to shoot you the second you step out?" He swore.

She gritted her teeth and allowed the touch until they were outside the guardhouse. Once they were in the clear, she shook him off.

"Now, I think you just have to point that gun at my back," she said, her voice hard and cold.

"Head to the main house," he told her.

The old tile path, cutting handsomely through the manicured front lawn of the estate, lay before her. It was nearing twilight and she couldn't help but notice that the air was perfect—neither too cold nor too hot—and that the setting sun was painting a palette of colors in the sky. She could smell the salt in the air and hear the waves as they splashed against the concrete breakers at the rear of the house.

All that made the area so beautiful—and, in particular, the house out on the island—had never seemed to be quite so evident and potent as when she walked toward the house. Jimmy Crystal had not actually named the place for himself; he'd written in his old journal that the island had seemed to sit in a sea of crystals, shimmering beneath the sun. And so it was. And now, through the years, the estate had become something glimmering and dazzling, as well. It sat in homage to days gone by, to memories of a time when the international city of Miami had been little more than a mosquito-ridden swamp and only those with vision had seen what might come in the future.

She and her parents had never lived in the house; they'd stayed in their home in the Roads section of the city, just north of Coconut Grove, where they'd always lived. They managed the estate, but even in that, a board had been brought in and a trust set up. The expenses to keep such an estate going were staggering.

While it had begun as a simple fishing shack, time and the additions of several generations had made Crystal Manor into something much more. It resembled both an Italianate palace and a medieval castle with tile and marble everywhere, grand columns, turrets and more. The manor was literally a square built around a center courtyard, with turrets at each corner that afforded four tower rooms above the regular two stories of the structure.

As she walked toward the sweeping, grand steps that led to the entry, she looked around. She had heard one of the other thugs, but, at that moment, she didn't see anyone.

Glancing back, she saw that a chain had been looped around the main gate. The gate arched to fifteen feet; the coral rock wall that surrounded the house to the water was a good twelve feet. Certainly not insurmountable by the right law-enforcement troops, but, still, a barrier against those who might come in to save the day.

She looked back at her masked abductor. She could see nothing of his face—except for those eyes.

Why were they so…eerily familiar? If she really knew him, if she had known him growing up, she'd have remembered who went with those eyes! They were striking, intense. The darkest, deepest blue she had ever seen.

What was she thinking? He was a crook! She didn't make friends with crooks!

The double entryway doors suddenly opened and she saw another man in its maw.

Kody stopped. She stared at the doors. They were really beautiful, hardwood enhanced with stained-glass images of pineapples—symbols of welcome. Quite ironic at the moment.

"Get her in here!" the second masked man told the one called Barrow.

"Go," Barrow said softly from behind her.

She walked up the steps and into the entry.

It was grand now, though the entry itself had once been the whole house built by Jimmy Crystal when he had first fallen in love with the little island that, back then, had been untouched, isolated—a haven only for mangroves and mosquitos. Since then, of course, the island—along with Star and Hibiscus islands—had become prime property.

But the foyer still contained vestiges of the original. The floor was coral rock. The columns were the original columns that Jimmy Crystal had poured. Dade country pine still graced the side walls.

The rear wall had been taken down to allow for glass barriers to the courtyard; more columns had been added. The foyer contained only an 1890's rocking horse to the right side of the double doors and an elegant, old fortune-telling machine to the left. And, of course, the masked man who stood between the majestic staircases that led to the second floor at each side of the space.

She cast her eyes around but saw no one else.

There had still been four or five guests on the property when Kody had started to close down for the day. And five staff members: Stacey Carlson, the estate manager, Nan Masters, his assistant, and Vince Jenkins, Brandi Johnson and Betsy Rodriguez, guides. Manny Diaz, the caretaker, had been off the property all day. And, of course, Jose Marquez was there somewhere.

"So, this is Miss Cameron?" the masked man in the house asked.

"Yes, Dillinger. This is Miss Cameron," Barrow said.

Dillinger. She was right—this guy's mask was that of the long-ago killer John Dillinger.

"Well, well, well. I can't tell you, Miss Cameron, what a delight it is to meet you!" the man said. "Imagine! When I heard that you were here—cuddle time with the family before the final big move to the Big Apple— I knew it was time we had to step in."

The man seemed to know about her—and her family.

"If you think I'm worth some kind of ransom," she said, truly puzzled—and hoping she wasn't sealing her own doom, "I'm not. We may own this estate, but it's in some kind of agreement and trust with the state of Florida. It survives off of grants and tourist dollars." She hesitated. "My family isn't rich. They just love this old place."

"Yeah, yeah, yeah, Daddy is an archeologist and Mom travels with him. Right now they're on their way back from South America so they can head up north with their baby girl to get her all settled into New York City. Yes! I have the prize right here, don't I?"

"I have no idea what you're talking about," Kody told him. "I wish I could say that someone would give you trillions of dollars for me, but I'm not anyone's prize. I'm a bartender-waitress at an Irish pub who's struggling to make ends meet as an actress."

"Oh, honey," Dillinger said, "I don't give a damn if you're a bad actress."

"Hey! I never said I was a *bad* actress!" she protested. And then, of course, she thought that he was making her crazy—heck, the whole situation was making her crazy—because who the hell cared if she was a bad actress or a good actress if she wasn't even alive?

Dillinger waved a hand in the air. "That's neither here nor there. You're going to lead us to the Anthony Green stash."

Startled, Kody went silent.

Everyone, of course, had heard about the Anthony Green *stash*.

Green was known to have knocked over the long-defunct Miami Bank of the Pioneers, making off with the bank's safe-deposit boxes that had supposedly contained millions in diamonds, jewels, gold and more. It was worth millions. But Anthony Green had died in a hail of bullets—with his mouth shut. The stash was never found. It had always been suspected that Anthony Green—before his demise—had seen to it that the haul had been hidden somewhere in one of his shacks deep in the Everglades, miles from his Biscayne Bay home.

Rumor followed rumor. It was said that Guillermo Salazar—a South American drug lord—had actually found the stash about a decade ago and added a small fortune in ill-gotten heroin-sales gains to it—before he, in turn, had been shot down by a rival drug cartel.

Who the hell knew? One way or the other, it was supposedly a very large fortune.

She didn't doubt that Salazar had sold drugs; the

Coast Guard in South Florida was always busy stopping the drug trade. But she sure as hell didn't believe that Salazar had found the Green stash at the house, because she really didn't believe the stash was here.

Chills suddenly rose up her spine.

If she was supposed to find a stash that didn't exist here...

They were all dead.

"Where is everyone?" she asked.

"Safe," Dillinger said.

"Safe where?"

No one answered Kody. "Where?" she repeated.

"They're all fine, Miss Cameron."

It was the man behind her—Barrow—who finally spoke up. "Dillinger, she needs to know that they're all fine," he added.

"I assure you," Dillinger continued. "They're all fine. They're in the music room."

The music room took up most of the left side of the downstairs. It would be the right place to hold a group of people.

Except...

Someone, somewhere, had to know that something was going on here. Surely one of the employees or guests had had a chance to get out a cell phone warning.

"I want to see them," she said. "I want to see that everyone is all right."

"Listen, missy, what you do and don't want doesn't matter here. What you're going to do for us matters," Dillinger told her.

"I don't know where the stash is. If I did, the world would have known about it long ago," she said. "And, if you know everything, you surely know that history says Anthony Green hid his bank treasure in some hut somewhere out in the Everglades."

"She sure as hell isn't rich, Dillinger," Barrow said. "Everything is true—she's taken a part-time job because what she's working is off-off Broadway. If she knew about the stash, I don't think she'd be slow-pouring Guinness at an old pub in the city."

Dillinger seemed annoyed. Kody was, in fact, surprised by what she could read in his eyes—and in his movements.

"No one asked your opinion, Barrow," Dillinger said. "She's the only one who can find it. I went through every newspaper clipping—she's loved the place since she was a kid. She's read everything on Jimmy Crystal and Anthony Green and the mob days on Miami Beach. She knows what rooms in this place were built what years, when any restoration was done. She knows it all. She knows how to find the stash. And she's going to help us find it."

"Don't be foolish," Kody said. "You can get out now. No one knows who you guys are—the masks, I'll grant you, are good. Well, they're not good. They're cheap and lousy masks, but they create the effect you want and no one here knows what your real faces look like. Pretty soon, though, walls or not, cops will swarm the place. Someone will come snooping around. Someone probably got something out on a cell phone."

She couldn't see his face but she knew that Dillinger smiled. "Cell phones? No, we secured those pretty quickly," he said. "And your security guard? He's resting—he's got a bit of a headache." He shook his head. "Face it, young lady. You have me and Barrow here. Floyd is with your friends, Capone is on his way to help, and the overall estate is being guarded by Baby Face Nelson and Machine Gun Kelly and our concept of modern security and communication and, you know, we've got good old Dutch—as in Schultz—working it all, too. I think we're good for a while. Long enough for you to figure out where the stash is. And, let's see, you are going to help us."

"I won't do anything," she told him. "Nothing. Nothing at all—not until I know that my friends and our guests are safe and that Jose isn't suffering from anything more than a headache."

Not that she'd help them even then—if she even could. The stash had been missing since the 1930s. In fact, Anthony Green had used a similar ruse when he had committed the bank robbery. He'd come in fast with six men—all wearing masks. He'd gotten out just as fast. The cops had never gotten him. They'd suspected him, but they'd never had proof. They'd still been trying to find witnesses and build a case against him when he'd been gunned down on Miami Beach.

But her demands must have hit home because Dillinger turned to Barrow. "Fine. Bring her through."

He turned to head down the hallway that led into the music room—the first large room on the left side of the house.

It was a gorgeous room, graced with exquisite crown molding, rich burgundy carpets and old seascapes of famous ports, all painted by various masters in colors that complemented the carpet. There was a wooden dais at one end of the room that accommodated a grand piano, a harp, music stands and room for another three or four musicians.

There were sofas, chairs and love seats backed to all

the walls, and a massive marble fireplace for those times when it did actually get cold on the water.

Kody knew about every piece in the room, but at that moment all she saw was the group huddled together on the floor.

Quickly searching the crowd, she found Stacey Carlson, the estate manager. He was sixty or so with salt-and-pepper hair, old-fashioned sideburns and a small mustache and goatee. A dignified older man, he was quick to smile, slow to follow a joke—but brilliant. Nan Masters was huddled to his side. If it was possible to have platonic affairs, the two of them were hot and heavy. Nothing ever went on beyond their love of Miami, the beaches and all that made up their home. Nan was red-haired, but not in the least fiery. Slim and tiny, she looked like a cornered mouse huddled next to Stacey.

Vince Jenkins sat cross-legged on a Persian rug that lay over the carpet, straight and angry. There was a bruise forming on the side of his face. He'd apparently started out by fighting back.

Beside him, Betsy Rodriguez and Brandi Johnson were close to one another. Betsy, the tinier of the two, but by far the most out-there and sarcastic, had her arm around Brandi, who was nearly six feet, blond, blue-eyed, beautiful and shy.

Jose Marquez had been laid on the largest love seat. His forehead was bleeding, but, Kody quickly saw, he was breathing.

The staff had been somewhat separated from the few guests who had remained on the property, finishing up in the gardens after closing. She couldn't remember all their names but she recalled the couple, Victor and Melissa Arden. They were on their honeymoon, yet they'd just been in Texas, visiting the graves of Bonnie Parker and Clyde Barrow in their separate cemeteries. They loved studying old gangsters, which was beyond ironic, Kody thought now. Another young woman from Indiana, an older man and a fellow of about forty rounded out the group.

They were all huddled low, apparently respecting the twin guns carried by another man in an identity-concealing mask.

"Kody!" Stacey said, breathing out a sigh of relief. She realized that her friends might have been worrying for her life.

She turned to Dillinger. "You'd better not hurt them!"

"Hurt them?" Dillinger said. "I don't want to hurt any of you, really. Okay, okay, so, quite frankly, I don't give a rat's ass. But Barrow there, he's kind of squeamish when it comes to blood and guts. Capone—my friend with the guns—is kind of rabid. Like he really had syphilis or rabies or something. He'd just as soon shoot you as look at you. So, here's my suggestion." He paused, staring Cody up and down. "You find out what I need to know. You come up to that library—and you start using everything you know and going through everything in the books, every news brief, every everything. You find that stash for me. Their lives depend on it."

"What if I can't find it?" she asked. "No one has found this stash in eighty-plus years!"

"You'd better find it," Dillinger said.

"Help will come!" Betsy said defiantly. "This is crazy—you're crazy! SWAT teams aren't but a few miles away. Someone—"

"You'd better hope no one comes," Dillinger said. He walked over to hunker down in front of her. "Because that's the whole point of hostages. They want you to live. They probably don't give a rat's ass one way or the other, either, but that's what they're paid to do. Get the hostages out alive. But, to prove we mean business, we'll have to start by killing someone and tossing out the body. And guess what? We like to start with the big-mouths, the wise-asses!"

He reached out to Betsy and that was all the impetus Kody needed. She sure as hell wasn't particularly courageous but she didn't waste a second to think. She just bolted toward Dillinger, smashing into him with such force that he went flying down.

With her.

He was strong, really strong.

He was up in two seconds, dragging her up with him.

"Why you little bitch!" he exclaimed as he hauled his arm back, ready to slam a jaw-breaking fist into her face.

His hand never reached her.

Barrow—with swift speed and agility—was on the two of them. She felt a moment of pain as he wrenched her out of Dillinger's grasp, thrusting himself between them.

"No, Dillinger, no. Keep the hostages in good shape. This one especially! We need her, Dillinger. We need her!"

"Bitch! You saw her—she tackled me."

"We need her!"

The hostages had started to move, scrambling back, restless, frightened, and Capone shoved someone with the butt of his gun.

Barrow lifted his gun and shot the ceiling.

Plaster fell around them all like rain.

And the room went silent.

"Let's get her out of here and up to the library, Dillinger. Dammit, now. Come on—let's do what we came here to do!" he insisted. "I'm into money—not a body count."

Kody felt his hand as he gripped her arm, ready to drag her along.

Dillinger stared at him a long moment.

Was there a struggle going on? she wondered. A power play? Dillinger seemed to be the boss, but then Barrow had stepped in. He'd saved her from a good beating, at the least. She couldn't help but feel that there was something better about him.

She was even drawn to him.

Oh, that was sick, she told herself. He was a crook, maybe even a killer.

Still, he didn't seem to be as bloodthirsty as Dillinger.

Dillinger stepped around her and Barrow, heading for the stairs to the library. Barrow followed with her.

"Hey!"

They heard the call when they had nearly cleared the room.

She turned to see Capone standing next to Betsy Rodriguez. He wasn't touching her; he was just close to her.

He moved his gun, running the muzzle through her hair.

"Dakota Cameron!" he said. "The world—well, your world—is dependent on your every thought and word!"

She started to move toward him but Barrow stopped her, whispering in her ear, "Don't get them going!"

She couldn't help herself. She called out to Capone. "You're here because you want something? Well, if you want it from me, step the hell away from my friend!"

To her surprise, Dillinger started to laugh.

"We've got a wild card on our hands, for sure. Come on, Capone. Let's accommodate the lady. Step away from her friend."

From behind her, Barrow added, "Come on, Capone. I'm in this for the money and a quick trip out of the country. Let's get her started working and get this the hell done, huh? Beat her to pieces or put a bullet in her, and she's worthless."

"Miss Cameron?" Dillinger said, sweeping an elegant bow to her. "My men will behave like gentlemen—as long as your friends let them. You hear that, right?"

"I can be a perfect gentleman!" Capone called back to him.

"Tell them all to sit tight and not make trouble—that you will manage to get what we want," Barrow said to her.

She looked at him again.

Those eyes of his! So deep, dark, blue and intense!

Surely, if she really knew him, she'd recognize him now.

She didn't. Still, she couldn't help but feel that she did, and that the man she knew wasn't a criminal, and that she had been drawn to those eyes before.

She shivered suddenly, looking at him.

He didn't like blood and guts—that's what Dillinger had said.

Maybe he was a thief, a hood—but hated the idea of being a murderer. Maybe, just maybe, he did want to keep them all alive.

"Hey!" she called back to the huddled group of captives. "I know everything about the house and all about Anthony Green and the gangster days. Just hold tight and be cool, please. I can do this. I know I can do this!"

They all looked at her with hope in their faces.

She gazed at Barrow and said, "They need water. We keep cases of water bottles in the lower cabinet of the kitchen. Go through the music room and the dining room and you'll reach the kitchen. I would truly appreciate if you would give them all water. It will help me think."

But it was Dillinger who replied.

"Sure," he said. "You think—and we'll just be the nicest group of guys you've ever met!"

CHAPTER TWO

NICK CONNOLLY—KNOWN as Barrow to the Coconut Grove crew of murderers, thieves and drug runners who were careful not to share their real names, even with one another—was doing his best. His damned best.

Which wasn't easy.

Nick didn't mind undercover work. He could even look away from the drugs and the prostitution, knowing that what he was doing would stop the flow of some really bad stuff onto the city streets—and put away some really bad men.

From the moment he'd infiltrated this gang three weeks ago, the situation had been crazy, but he'd also thought it would work. This would be the time when he could either get them all together in an escape boat that the Coast Guard would be ready to swoop up, or, if that kind of maneuver failed, pick them off one by one. Each of these guys—Dillinger, Capone, Floyd, Nelson, Kelly and Schultz—had killed or committed some kind of an armed robbery. They were all ex-cons. Capone had been the one to believe in Nick's off-color stories in an old dive bar in Coconut Grove, and as far as Capone knew, Nick had been locked up in Leavenworth, convicted of a number of crimes. Of course, Capone had met Nick as Ted—Ted Johnson had been the pseudonym Nick had been using in South Florida. There really had been a

Ted Johnson; he'd died in the prison hospital ward of a knife wound. But no one knew that. No one except certain members of the FBI and the hospital staff and warden and other higher ups at the prison.

None of these men—especially "Dillinger"—had any idea that Nick had full dossiers on them. As far as they all knew, they were anonymous, even with each other.

Undercover was always tricky.

It should have been over today; he should have been able to give up the undercover work and head back to New York City. Not that he minded winter in Miami.

He just hated the men with whom he had now aligned himself—even if it was to bring them down, and even if it was important work.

Today should have been it.

But all the plans he'd discussed with his local liaisons and with Craig Frasier—part of the task force from New York that had been chasing the drug-and-murder-trail of the man called Dillinger from New York City down through the South—had gone to hell.

And the stakes had risen like a rocket—because of a situation he'd just found out about that morning.

Without the aid, knowledge or consent of the others, for added protection, Dillinger had kidnapped a boy right before they had all met to begin their takeover of the Crystal Estate.

It wouldn't have mattered who the kid was to Nick— he'd have done everything humanly possible to save him—but the kidnapped boy was the child of Holden Burke, mayor of South Beach. Dillinger had assured them all that he had the kid safely hidden somewhere— where, exactly, he wasn't telling any of them. They all knew that people could talk, so it was safer that only he

knew the whereabouts of little Adrian Burke. And not
to worry—the kid was alive. He was their pass-go ace
in the hole.

That was one thing.

Then, there was Dakota Cameron.

To be fair, Nick didn't exactly know Kody Cameron
but he had seen her—and she had seen him—in New
York City.

And the one time that he'd seen her, he'd known immediately that he'd wanted to see her again.

And now, here they were. In a thousand years he'd
never imagined their second meeting would be like this.

No one had known that Dillinger's game plan ended
with speculation—the vague concept that he could kidnap Dakota, take her prisoner—and *hope* she could find
the stash!

Dillinger planned the heists and the drug runs; he
worked with a field of prostitution that included the
pimps and the girls. He had South American contacts.
No one had figured he'd plan on taking over the old
Crystal Estate, certain that he could find a Cameron
family member who knew where to find the old mob
treasure.

So, now, here he was—surprised and somewhat anxious to realize that the lovely young brunette with the
fascinating eyes he'd brushed by at Finnegan's on Broadway in New York City would show up at the ticket booth
at a Florida estate and tourist attraction.

Craig Frasier, one of the main men on the task force
Director Egan had formed to trace and track "Dillinger,"
aka Nathan Appleby, along the Eastern seaboard, spent
a lot of time at Finnegan's. The new love of his life was

co-owner, along with her brothers, of the hundred-and-fifty-year-old pub in downtown Manhattan.

Nick and Kody Cameron had passed briefly, like proverbial ships in the night, but he hadn't had the least problem recognizing her today. He knew her, because they had both paused to stare at one another at the pub.

Instant attraction? Definitely on his part and he could have sworn on hers, too.

Then she'd muttered some kind of swift apology and Craig's new girlfriend, who'd come over to greet them, explained, "That's Kody Cameron. She's working a living theater piece with my brother. Sounds kind of cool, right? And she's working here part-time now, making the transition to New York."

"What's living theater?" Nick had asked Kieran Finnegan.

"Kevin could tell you better than me," she had explained, "but it's taking a show more as a concept than as a structured piece and working with the lines loosely while interacting with the audience as your character."

Whatever she did, he'd hoped that he'd see her again; he'd even figured that he could. While Kieran Finnegan actually worked as a psychologist and therapist for a pair of psychiatrists who often came in as consultants for the New York office of the Bureau, she was also often at Finnegan's. And since he was working tightly with Craig and his partner, Mike, and a cyber-force on this case, he'd figured he'd be back in Finnegan's, too. But then, of course, Dillinger had come south, met up with old prison mates Capone, Nelson, Kelly, Floyd and Schultz, and Nick—who had gone through high school in South Florida and still had family in the area—had been sent down to infiltrate the gang.

The rest, as the saying went, was history.

Now, if Dakota Cameron saw his face, if she gave any indication that she knew him, and knew that he was an FBI man...

They'd both be dead.

And it didn't help the situation that she was battle ready—ready to lay down her life for her friends.

Then again, there should have been a way for him to stop this. If it hadn't been for the little boy who had been taken...

He had to find out where the kid was. Had Dillinger stashed him with friends or associates? Had he hidden him somewhere? It wasn't as hard to hide somewhere here as one would think, with the land being just about at sea level and flat as a pancake. There were enough crack houses and abandoned tenements. Of course, Nick was pretty sure Dillinger couldn't have snatched the kid at a bus station, hidden him wherever, and made it to the estate at their appointed time, if he had gone far.

But that knowledge didn't help much.

Nick's first case when he'd started with the Bureau in the Miami offices had been finding the truth behind the bodies stuffed in barrels, covered with acid and tossed in the Everglades.

He refused to think of that image along with his fear for the child; the boy was alive. Adrian Burke wouldn't be worth anything in an escape situation if he was dead.

Nick wiped away that thought and leaned against the door frame as he stood guard over Kody. Capone was now just on the other side of the door.

Like the entire estate, the library was kept in pristine shape, but it also held an air of fading and decaying elegance, making one feel a sense of nostalgia. The floors were marble, covered here and there by Persian throw rugs, and built-in bookshelves were filled with volumes that appeared older than the estate itself, along with sea charts and more.

Kody Cameron had a ledger opened before her, but she was looking at him. Quizzically.

It seemed as if she suspected she knew him but couldn't figure out from where.

"You're not as crazy as the others," she said softly. "I can sense that about you. But you need to do something to stop this. That treasure he's talking about has been missing for years and years. God knows, maybe it's in the Everglades, swallowed up in a sinkhole. You don't want to be a part of this—I know you don't. And those guys are lethal. They'll hurt someone…kill someone. This is still a death penalty state, you know. Please, if you would just—"

He found himself walking over to her at the desk and replying in a heated whisper, "Just do what he says and find the damned treasure. Lie if you have to! Find something that will make Dillinger believe that you know where the treasure is. Give him a damned map to find it. He won't think twice about killing people, but he won't kill just for the hell of it. Don't give him a reason."

"You're not one of them. You have to stop this. Get away from them," she said.

She was beautiful, earnest, passionate. He wanted to reassure her. To rip off his mask and tell her that law enforcement was on it all.

But that was impossible, lest they all die quickly.

He had to keep his distance and keep her, the kidnapped child and the others in the house alive.

Capone was growing curious. He left his post at the

archway and walked in. "Hey. What's going on here? Don't interrupt the woman, Barrow. I want to get the hell out of here! I've done some wild things with Dillinger, but this is taking the cake. Makes me more nervous than twenty cartel members in a gunboat. Leave her be."

"Yeah. I'm going to leave her be. And she's going to come up with something," Barrow said.

He'd barely spoken when Schultz came rushing in. While Capone knew how to rig a central box and stop cameras and security systems, Schultz was an expert sharpshooter. He was tall and thin, not much in the muscles department, but Nick had seen him take long shots that were just about impossible.

"News is out that we're here," he said. "Cops are surrounding the gates. I fired a few warning shots and Dillinger answered the phone—told them we have a pack of hostages. You should see them all out there at the gates," he added, his grin evident in his voice. "They look like a pack of chickens. Guess they're calling for a hostage negotiator. Dillinger is deciding whether to give them a live one or a body."

Kody Cameron stood. "They give him a body and I'm done. If he gives them one body, it won't make any difference to him if he kills the rest of us."

"And just how far are you getting, sweet thing?" Schultz asked, coming close to her. He reached out to lift the young woman's chin.

Nick struggled to control himself. Hell, she wasn't just a captive. Not just someone he had to keep alive.

She worked for Finnegan's. She was connected to Kevin Finnegan and Kieran Finnegan—and therefore, to Craig Frasier.

And he noticed her the first time he'd ever seen her. Known that he'd wanted to see her again.

He'd never imagined it could be in this way.

For a moment he managed to keep his peace. But, damn her, she just had to react. Schultz cradled her face and she stepped back and pushed his hand away.

"Hey, hey, hey, little girl. You don't want to get hurt, do you? Be nice."

Nick stepped up, swinging Schultz around.

"Leave her alone, dammit. We're here for a reason."

"What? Are you sweet on her yourself?" Schultz asked him, his tone edgy. "You think this is merchandise you keep all for yourself?"

"I'm not merchandise!" Kody snapped.

"I want her to find what Dillinger wants, and I want to get the hell out of here!" Nick said. He was as tall as Schultz; he had a lot more muscle and he was well trained. In a fair fight, Schultz wouldn't stand a chance against him.

There were no fair fights here, he reminded himself. He had to keep an even keel.

"Leave her alone and let her get back to work," he said. "Get your mind on the job to be done here."

"Shouldn't you be up in one of the front towers?" Capone asked Schultz. "Isn't that your job in all this?"

Schultz gave them all a sweeping and withering glare. Then he turned and left.

Capone was staring at Nick. "Maybe you should get your mind on the job, too, Barrow," he suggested.

"And you," Nick added softly.

Capone continued to stare at him.

It went no further as Dillinger came striding into the

room. He ignored Capone and Nick and walked straight to the desk and Kody.

"How long?" he asked her.

"How long? You're asking me to do something no one has managed in decades," Kody said.

"You're got two hours," Dillinger said. "Two hours. They're bringing in a hostage negotiator. Don't make me prove that I will kill."

"I'm doing my best," Kody said.

"Where's the phone in this room?" Dillinger asked.

"On the table by the door, next to the Tiffany lamp," Kody said.

"What the hell is a Tiffany lamp?" Dillinger demanded, leaning in on Kody.

"There. Right there, boss," Nick said, pointing out the elegant little side table with the lamp and the white trim-line phone. He walked over to it and saw that the volume was off.

"Ready for calls," he told Dillinger.

"Good. We'll manage it from here. Capone, get on down and help Nelson with the hostages. Schultz is in the eagle's seat in the right tower. Floyd's in the left. And we've got our good old boy, our very own private Machine Gun Kelly, in the back. Don't trust those hostages, though. I'm thinking if we have to get rid of a few, we'll be in better shape."

"No, we won't be," Nick said flatly. "You hurt a hostage, it tells the cops that they're not doing any good with negotiation. We have to keep them believing they're getting everyone back okay. That's the reason they'll hold off. If they think we're just going to kill people, they'll storm us, figuring to kill us before we kill the hostages. That's the logic they teach, trust me," Nick told Dillinger.

Dillinger shrugged, looking at the phone. "Well, we'll give them a little time, if nothing else. So, Miss Cameron, just how are you doing?"

Dakota Cameron looked up and stared at Dillinger, then cocked her head at an angle. "Looking for a needle in a haystack?" she asked. "I'm moving some hay out of the way, but there's still a great deal to go. You do realize—"

"Yes, yes," Dillinger said impatiently. "Yes, everyone has looked for years. But not because their lives were at stake. You're holding so many precious souls in your hands, Miss Cameron. I'm just so sure that will help you follow every tiny lead to just where the treasure can be found."

"Well, I'll try to keep a clear head here," she said. "At the moment, my mind is not hampered with grief over losing anyone, and you really should keep it that way. I mean, if you want me to find out anything for you."

Nick wished he could have shut her up somehow; he couldn't believe she was taunting a man who was half-crazy and holding the lives of so many people in his hands.

He had to admire her bravado—even as he wished she didn't have it.

But Dillinger laughed softly beneath his mask.

"My dear Miss Cameron, you do have more balls than half the men I find myself working with!" Dillinger told her. "Excellent—if you have results. If you don't, well, it will just make it all the easier to shut you up!"

She wasn't even looking at Dillinger anymore. She'd turned her attention back to the journal spread open before her.

"Let me work," she said softly.

Dillinger grunted. He took a seat in one of the chairs by the wall of the library, near the phone.

Nick walked to the windows, looking out at the gardens in the front of the house, the driveway and—at a distance—the wall and the great iron gates that led up to the house.

More and more cars were beginning to arrive—marked police cars, unmarked cars belonging to the FBI and other law-enforcement agencies.

He wondered how Dillinger could believe he might get out of this alive.

And then he wondered just how the hell any of them were going to get out alive.

The phone began to ring. Dakota Cameron jumped in her chair, nearly leaping from it.

Nick nearly jumped himself.

Dillinger rose and picked up the phone. "Hello? Dillinger here. How can I help you? Other than keeping the hostages alive... Let's see, how can you help me? Well, I'll begin to explain. Right now, everyone in the house is breathing. We have some employees, we have some guests... What we want is more time, really good speed boats—cigarettes or Donzis will do. Now, of course, we need a couple because a few of these good people will be going with us for just a bit when we leave. We'll see to it that you get them all back alive and well as long as we get what we want."

Nick wished he was on an extension. He wanted to hear what was being said.

He saw Dillinger nod. "How bright of you to ask so quickly! Yes, there is a missing child, too, isn't there? An important little boy—son of a mayor! Ah, well, all children are important, aren't they...? Mr. Frasier? Ah!

Sorry, Special Agent Frasier. FBI. They've brought in the big guns. Let's go with this—right now, I want time. You give me some time and you arrange for those boats. To be honest, I'm working on a way to give you back that kid I scooped up. Not a bad kid, in the least. I liked him. I'd hate for him to die of neglect, caged and chained and forgotten. So, you work on those boats."

Nick saw Dakota Cameron frown as she'd heard the name Frasier. Not that Frasier was a rare name, but Kody was good friends with Kevin Finnegan and therefore friends with his sister Kieran—and so she knew Craig. She had to be puzzled, wondering first if he was indeed the same man a friend was dating and, if so, what he was doing in South Florida.

She looked up from her ledger. She was staring at Dillinger hard, brows knit in a frown.

A moment later Dillinger set the receiver back in the cradle. He seemed to be pleased with himself.

"You kidnapped a child?" she asked.

"I like to have a backup plan," Dillinger said.

"You have all of us."

"Yes. But, hey, maybe nobody cares about any of you. They will care about a kid."

"Yep, they will," Nick interrupted. "But I think they need to believe in us, too. Hey, man, you want time for Miss Cameron to find the treasure, the stash, or whatever might be hidden? If we're going to buy that time, we need to play to them. I say we give them the security guard. He needs medical attention. Best we get him out of here. An injured hostage is just a liability. Let's give him up as a measure of good faith."

"Maybe," Dillinger said. He looked at Kody. "How are you doing?"

"I'd do a lot better if you didn't ask me every other minute," she said. "And," she added softly, "if I wasn't so worried about Jose."

"Who the hell is Jose?" Dillinger asked.

"Our security guard. The injured man," Kody said.

Dillinger glanced restlessly at his watch and then at the phone. "Give them a few minutes to get back to me."

He walked out of the room, leaving Nick alone with Kody.

"How *are* you doing?" he asked her.

She shrugged and then looked up at him. "So far, I have all the same information everyone has had for years. Anthony Green robbed the bank, but the police couldn't pin it on him, couldn't make an arrest. He wrote in his own journal that it was great watching them all run around like chickens with no heads. Of course, it wouldn't be easy for anyone to find the stash. What it seems to me—from what I've read—is that he did plan on disappearing. Leaving the country. And he was talking about boats, as well—"

She broke off, staring at the old journal she was reading and then flipping pages over.

"What is it?" Nick asked.

She looked up at him, her expression suddenly guarded. He realized that—to her—he was a death-dealing criminal.

"I'm not sure," she said. "I need time."

"You've got time right now. Use it," he said.

"We need to see some of the hostages out of here—returned to safety," she said firmly. "In good faith!"

They were both startled by the sound of a gunshot. Then a barrage of bullets seemed to come hailing down on the house.

A priceless vase on a table exploded.

Nick practically flew across the room, leaping over the desk to land on top of Kody—and bring her down to the floor.

The barrage of bullets continued for a moment—and then went silent.

He felt her move beneath him.

He looked down at her. Her eyes were wide on his as she studied him gravely. He hadn't just been intrigued, he realized. He hadn't just wanted to see her again.

He'd been attracted to her. Really attracted.

And now...

She was trembling slightly.

He leaped to his feet, drawing her up, pulling her along with him as he raced down the hall to the stairs that led to the right tower where Schultz had been keeping guard.

Nick was pretty damned certain Schultz—a man who was crazy and more than a little trigger happy—had fired the first shots.

"What the hell are you doing?" he shouted.

As he did so, Dillinger came rushing along, as well. "What the hell?" he demanded furiously.

"I saw 'em moving, boss. I saw 'em moving!" Schultz shouted down.

The phone started ringing. Nick looked at Dillinger. "Let me take it. Let me see what I can do," he said.

Dillinger was already moving back toward the library. Nick followed, still clasping Kody's hand.

When they reached the library, Dillinger stepped back and let Nick answer the phone.

"Hello?" Nick said. "This is Barrow speaking now. We don't know what happened. We do know that you responded with the kind of violence that's going to get someone killed. Seriously, do you want everyone in here dead? What the hell was that?"

"Shots were fired at us," a voice said. "Who is this?"

"I told you. Barrow."

"Are you the head man?"

Nick glanced over at Dillinger.

"No. I'm spokesman for the head man. He's all into negotiation. What we want doesn't have anything to do with a bunch of dead men and women, but that's what we could wind up with if we don't get this going right," Nick said.

"We don't want dead people," the voice on the other end assured him.

"We don't, either," Nick said.

"Barrow. All right, let's talk. I think everyone got a little panicky. No one wants anyone to die here today. We're all working in the same direction, that being to see that everyone gets out alive. Okay?"

Nick knew who was doing the negotiating for the array of cops and FBI and law enforcement just on the other side of the gates.

He was speaking with Craig Frasier. Nick was glad the FBI and the local authorities had gotten it together to make the situation go smoothly. He knew Craig; Craig knew him. There was so much more he was going to be able to do with Craig at the other end.

"How are they doing on my boats?" Dillinger asked, staring at Nick.

"We're going to need those boats," Nick said. He needed to give Craig all the information he could about the situation, without making Dillinger suspicious, and he wanted, also, to maintain his position as spokesman for Dillinger.

"Yes, two boats, right?" Craig asked.

"Good ones. The best speedboats you can get your hands on. Now, we're not fools. You won't get all the information you need to save everyone until we're long gone and safe. But, right now, we're going to give you a man. Security guard. He's got a bit of a gash on his head. We're going to bring him out to the front and we'll see that the gate is opened long enough for one of you to get him out. Do you understand? The fate of everyone here may depend on this nice gesture on our part going well."

He knew that Craig understood; Nick had really just told him the guard had been the only one injured and that he did need help.

"No one else is hurt? Everyone is fine?"

Craig had to ask to keep their cover. But Nick knew the agent was also concerned for Dakota Cameron. That the Cameron family owned this place—and that Kody was down here—was something Craig must have realized from the moment Dillinger made his move.

"No one is hurt. I'm trying to keep it that way," Nick assured him, glancing over at Dillinger.

Dillinger nodded. He seemed to approve of how Nick handled the negotiations. There was enough of a low-lying threat in Nick's tone to make it all sound very menacing, no matter what the words.

"That's good. Open the gate and we'll get the man. There will be no attempts to break in on you, no more bullets fired," Craig said.

Nick looked at Dillinger. *Yes?* he mouthed.

Dillinger nodded. "Keep an eye on her!"

As he hurried out, Kody stood and started after

him, then paused herself, as if certain Nick would have stopped her if she hadn't. He held the phone and stared at her, wishing he dared tell her who he was and what his part was in all this.

But he couldn't.

He couldn't risk her betraying him.

He covered the mouthpiece on the house phone. "Don't leave the room."

"Jose Marquez…" she murmured.

"He's really letting him go," Nick said.

She walked over to him suddenly. He was afraid she was going to reach for the mask that covered his face.

She didn't touch him. Instead she spoke quickly. "You're not like that. You could stop this. You have a gun. You could—"

"Shoot them all down?" he asked her.

"Wound them, stop this—stop them from killing innocent people. I'd speak for you. I'd see that everyone in court knew that people survived because of you."

She was moving closer as she spoke—not to touch him, he realized, but to take his gun.

He set the phone down and grabbed her roughly by the wrists.

"Don't pull this on anyone else. Haven't you really grasped this yet? They're trigger happy and crazy. Just do as they say. Just find that damned stash!"

Something in her jaw seemed to be working. She looked away from him.

"You found it already?" he said incredulously. "You have, haven't you? But that's impossible so fast!"

She didn't confirm or deny; she gave no answer. He heard a crackle on the phone line and put it back to his ear. As he did so, he looked out the windows.

Dillinger, wielding a semiautomatic, was leading out two hostages carrying Jose Marquez. They brought him close to the gate, Dillinger keeping his weapon trained on them the entire time.

They left Jose and walked back into the house.

Dillinger followed them.

A second later the gate opened. Police rushed in and scooped up the security guard. They hurried out with him.

The gates closed and locked.

"Barrow! Barrow? Hey, you there?"

"Yes," Nick replied into the phone.

"We have the security guard. We'll get him to the hospital. What about the others? Do they need food, water?"

Kody was staring at him. He heard footsteps pounding up the stairs, as well.

Dillinger was back.

"Sit!" he told Kody. "Figure out what we need to do in order to get our hands on that stash."

To his surprise, she sat. She sat—and had the journal up in her hands before Dillinger returned to the room.

"Well?" Dillinger said to Nick.

Nick spoke into the phone. "We've given you the hostage in good faith. We really would like to see that all these good folks live, but, hey, they call bad guys bad guys because…they're bad. So back away from the gates and start making things happen. What about our boats?"

"I swear, we're getting you the best boats," Craig said.

"I want them now," Dillinger said.

"We need you to supply those boats now," Nick said, nodding to Dillinger and repeating his demand over the phone. "We need them out back, by the docks, and then we need you and your people to be far, far away."

"The boats will be there soon," Craig told Nick.

"Soon? Make that six or *seven* minutes at most!" he said.

He hoped Craig picked up on the clue. Stressing the word told him there were seven in this merry band of thieves.

"Don't push it too far!" Nick added. "Maybe we'll give you to ten or *eleven* minutes to get it together, but... well, you don't want hostages to start dying, do you?"

Easy enough. That told him there were eleven hostages, including Dakota Cameron, being held.

Dillinger looked at Nick and nodded, satisfied.

"We've got one of the boats," Craig said. "How do I get my man to bring it around and not get killed or become a hostage himself?" he asked.

"One boat?"

"So far. Getting our hands on what you want isn't easy," Craig said. "If we give you that one boat, what do we get?"

"You just got a man."

"We could find a second boat more quickly if we had a second man—or woman," Craig said.

They had to be careful; the negotiator's voice carried on the land line.

Of course, Craig Frasier knew that. He would be careful, but Nick knew that he had to be more so. Dakota could hear Craig, as well.

"Please," she said softly, "give them Stacey Carlson and Nan Masters. They're older. They'll just be like bricks around your neck when you need hostages for cover. Please, let them leave."

"Please," Dillinger said, mimicking her plea, "find what I want to know!"

"I might have," Kody said very softly.

"You might have?"

"Give the cops two more hostages. Give them Stacey and Nan," she said. "I'll show you what I think I've figured out once you've done that. Please."

Dillinger looked at Nick. "Hey, the lady said please. Let's accommodate her. Get on the phone and tell them to get the hell away from the gate. We'll give them two more solid, stand-up citizens." His eyes narrowed. "But I want my boats. Two boats. And I want them now. No ten minutes. No eleven minutes. I want them now!"

He looked at Kody. She was staring gravely at him.

"We have a present for you," he told Craig over the phone. "Two more hostages. Only we want two boats. Now. We want them right now."

"And if we don't get those boats soon..." Dillinger murmured.

He looked over at Kody.

And his eyes seemed to smile.

CHAPTER THREE

"IT'S DONE. HE'S let them go. Three of the hostages. Your security man, Marquez, and the manager and his assistant."

Kody looked up from the journal she'd been reading.

Concentration had not been an easy feat; men were walking around with guns threatening to kill people. That made her task all the more impossible.

But it was Barrow who had walked in to speak with her. And the news was good. Three of her coworkers were safe.

And she was sure it was Craig Frasier out there doing the negotiating with them on the phone. Craig Frasier. From New York. In Miami.

But then, at Finnegan's, Kieran had been saying that Craig was going on the road; they'd been tracking a career criminal who'd recently gotten out of prison and was already starting up in NYC, and undercover agents in the city had warned that he was moving south.

Dillinger?

Was Craig Frasier here in Miami after Dillinger?

The masked man with the intense blue eyes was staring at her. She schooled her expression, not wanting to give away any of her thoughts or let on that she knew the negotiator and might know about their leader.

"So what happens now?" she asked. Capone was once

again standing just outside the library, near the arched doorway to the room. He was, however, out of earshot, she thought, as long as they spoke softly.

"We need getaway boats. And, of course, Anthony Green's bank haul stash. How are you doing?" Barrow asked her.

How the hell was she doing?

Maybe—*maybe*—with days or weeks to work and every bit of reference from every conceivable source, she might have an answer. So far she had found some interesting information about the old gangster, Miami in the mob heyday, and even geography. She'd gone through specs and architectural plans on the house. But she was pretty sure she'd been right from the beginning—the stash was not at the house on Crystal Island. It was in the Everglades—somewhere.

To say that to find something in the Everglades was worse than finding a needle in a haystack was just about the understatement of the year. The Everglades was actually a river—"a river of grass," as one called it. On its own, it was ever-changing. Man, dams, the surge of sugar and beef plantations from the middle of the state on down, kept the rise and flow eternally moving, right along with nature. There were hammocks or islands of high land here and there. The Everglades also offered quicksand, dangerous native snakes and now, sixty-thousand-plus pythons and boas that had been let loose in the marsh and swamps, not to mention both alligators and, down in the brackish water, crocodiles, as well.

Great place to hide something!

"Well?" Barrow asked quietly.

"I don't think the stash is here," she said honestly. "Anthony Green talks about having a shack out in the

Everglades. My dad and his University of Miami buddies used to have one. They went hunting—they had their licenses and their permits to take two alligators each. But usually they just went to their shack, talked about school and sports and women—and then shot up beer cans. The shacks were outlawed twenty or thirty years ago. But that didn't mean the shacks all went down, or that some of the old-timers who run airboat rides or tours off of the Tamiami Trail don't remember where a lot of them are."

"So, the stash is in one of the old cabins," Barrow murmured. "But you don't know which—or where." He hesitated. "A place like Lost City?"

Kody stared at the man, surprised. Most of the people she knew who had grown up in the area hadn't even heard about Lost City.

Lost City was an area of about three acres, perhaps eight miles or so south of Alligator Alley, now part of I-75, a stretch of highway that crossed the state from northwestern Broward County over to the Naples/Ft. Myers area on the west coast of the state. It was suspected that Confederate soldiers had hidden out there after the Civil War, and many historians speculated that either Miccosukee or Seminole Indians had come upon them and massacred them all. Scholars believed it had been a major Seminole village at some point—and that it had been in use for hundreds of years.

But, most important, perhaps, was the fact that Al Capone—the real prohibition era gangster—had used the area to create his bootleg liquor.

She hesitated, not sure how much information to share—and how much to hold close.

Then again, she didn't have a single thing that was solid.

But...

It was evident he knew the area. Possibly, he'd grown up in South Florida, too. With the millions of people living in Miami-Dade and Broward counties alone, it was easy to believe they'd never met.

And yet, they had.

She knew his eyes.

And she had to believe that, slimy thief that he was, he was not a killer.

Yes, she had to believe it. Because she was depending on him, leaning on him, believing that he was the one who might save them—at the least, save their lives! She had to believe it because...

It wasn't right.

But, when she looked at him. When he spoke, when he made a move to protect one of them...

There was just something about him. And it made her burn inside and wish that...

Wish that he was the good guy.

"Something like that," she said, "except there's another version of the Al Capone distillery farther south. Supposedly, Anthony Green had a spot in the Everglades where he, too, distilled liquor. Near it, he had one of the old shacks. The place is up on an old hammock and, like the Capone site, it was once a Native American village, in this case, Miccosukee."

"You know where this place is?" Barrow asked her.

"Well, theoretically," she said with a shrug. "Almost all the Everglades is part of the national parks system, or belonging to either the Miccosukee or the Seminole tribes. But from what I understand, Anthony Green had his personal distillery on a hammock in the Shark Valley Slough—which empties out when you get to the Ten Thousand Islands, which are actually in Monroe County. But I don't think that it's far from the observation tower at Shark Valley. There's a hammock—"

Kody stopped speaking when she noticed him staring down at one of the glass-framed historic notes she had set next to the Anthony Green journal she'd been cross-referencing.

"Chakaika," he said quietly.

She started, staring at him when he looked up and seemed to be smiling at her.

"A very different leader," he said. "Known as the 'Biggest Indian.' He was most likely of Spanish heritage, with mixed blood from the Creek perhaps, or another tribe that had members flee down to South Florida. Anyway, he was active from the center of the state on down—had his own mix of Spanish and Native American tongues and traded with other Native Americans, but seemed to have a hatred for the whites who wanted to ship the Indians to the west. He attacked the fort and he headed down to Pigeon Key, where he murdered Dr. Henry Perrine—who really was, by all historic record, a cool guy who just wanted to use his plants to find cures for diseases.

"Anyway, in revenge, Colonel Harney disguised himself and his men as Native Americans and brought canoes down after Chakaika, who thought they could not find him in the swamp. But they found a runaway slave of the leader's who led them right to the hammock where the man lived. They didn't let him surrender—they shot him and his braves, and then they hanged him. And the hammock became known as Hanging People Kay.

I know certain park rangers believe they know exactly where it is."

Kody lowered her head, keeping silent for a minute. Her parents had been slightly crazy environmentalists. She knew all kinds of trivia about the state and its history. But while most people who had grown up down here might know the capital and the year the territory had become a state or the state bird or motto, few of them knew about Chakaika. Tourists sometimes stopped at the museum heading south on Pidgeon Key where Dr. Henry Perrine had once lived and worked, but nothing beyond that.

"Chakaika," he said again. "It's written clearly on the corner of that letter."

"Yes, well…they found oil barrels sunk in the area once," she murmured. "They were filled with two of Anthony Green's henchmen who apparently fell into ill favor with their boss. I know that the rangers out there are pretty certain they know the old Green stomping grounds—just like they know all about Chakaika. The thing is, of course, it's a river of grass. An entire ecosystem starting up at Lake Kissimmee and heading around Lake Okeechobee and down. Storms have come and gone, new drainage systems have gone in… I just don't know."

"It's enough to give him," Barrow said. "Enough to make him move."

Kody leaned forward suddenly. "You don't want to kill people. You hate the man. So why don't you shoot him in the kneecap or something?"

"And then Capone would shoot us all," Barrow said. "Do you really think that I could just gun them all down?"

"No, but you could—"

"Injure a man like that, and you might as well shoot yourself," he told her. "And, never mind. I have my reasons for doing what I'm doing. There's no other choice."

"There's always a choice," Kody said.

"No," he told her flatly, "there's not. So, if you want to keep breathing and keep all your friends alive, as well—"

Dillinger came striding in. "So, Miss Cameron. Where is my treasure?"

"Dammit! Listen to me and believe me! It's not here, not in the house, not on the island," she told him. She realized that while she was speaking fairly calmly, she was shivering, shaking from head to toe.

It was Dillinger and Barrow in the room then.

If Dillinger attacked her, what would Barrow do? Risk himself to defend her?

There certainly was no treasure at the house—other than the house itself—to give Dillinger. She'd told him the truth.

"So, where is it?" he demanded.

Thankfully he didn't seem to be surprised that it wasn't in the Crystal Manor.

"I have no guarantees for you," she said. "But I do have a working theory. This letter," she said, pausing to tap the historic, framed note that had been hand-penned by Anthony Green, "refers to the 'lovely hammock beneath the sun.' It was written to Lila Bay, Green's favorite mistress. In summary, Green tells her that when he's about on business and she's missing him, she should rest awhile in the hammock, and find there the diamond-like luster of the sun and the emerald green of the landscape."

"What's that on the corner?" Dillinger demanded suspiciously.

"It's the name of a long-ago chief or leader who was killed there. I think it was a further reference for Green when he was trying to see to it that Lila found the stash from the bank," Kody said.

Dillinger stood back, balancing the rifle he carried as he crossed his arms over his chest and stared at her.

"So, my treasure is in an alligator-laden swamp— along with rattlers, coral snakes, cottonmouths and whatever else! And we're just supposed to go out to the swamp and start digging in the saw grass and the muck?" Dillinger said.

"I'm still reading his personal references," Kody said. "But, yes. I can't put this treasure where it isn't. I'm afraid I'd falter and you'd know me for a liar in an instant."

"And you think you can find this treasure in acres of swamp land?" he asked.

Everything in Kody seemed to recoil. She shook her head. "I'm not going into the swamp. I don't care about the treasure or the stash. You do. I mean, I can keep reading and give you directions, all kinds of suggestions, but I—"

"Come on, Dillinger," Barrow said. "She'd be a pain in the ass out in the swamp!"

Dillinger turned to stare at Barrow. "She's going with us, one way or the other."

"What?" Barrow asked.

"Did you think I'm crazy? No way in hell we're leaving here without a hostage. We'll take Miss Cameron here for sure. I can't wait to see her dig in the muck and the old gator holes until she finds the diamonds and the emeralds! Come on, Barrow, you can't be that naive. They're not going to just give us speedboats. They're going to have the Coast Guard out. They're going to be following us. Now, I'm not without friends, and I'm pretty damned good at losing people who are chasing me, but...hey, you need to have a living hostage." He turned to Kody. "And, of course, Miss Cameron, if you're going to send us on a wild-goose chase, you have to understand just how it will end for you."

The house line began to ring again.

Dillinger looked at Barrow. "Get it! See if they have my boats for me now. You!" He pointed a finger at Kody. "You figure it out—or you will be the one in the snake and gator waters!"

Kody looked down quickly at the journal she was reading. She prayed he couldn't see just how badly she was shaking.

She knew local lore. She'd walked the trails at Shark Valley. She'd driven out from the city a few times just to buy pumpkin bread at the restaurant across from the park.

But she'd never camped in the Everglades. She'd never even gotten out of her car on the trail once it had grown dark.

Tramping out in alligator- and snake-infested swamps? No way.

"Get the line," Dillinger told Barrow again when the phone continued to ring.

Barrow answered.

"Where are the boats? We're doing our best to make sure that this works but you need to start moving on your end. And, be warned—no cops, no Coast Guard, no nothing coming after us!" he said.

He looked over at Dillinger. "He's getting us a pair of Donzi racers."

"That will do," Dillinger said. "As long as he starts getting it done. As long as he backs off some."

"You keep your men in check—I mean stay back," Barrow said to the person on the other end of the line.

Barrow covered the phone with his hand. "He swears they won't fire unless they're fired on. You've made that clear to the others, Dillinger, right? I don't want one of those trigger-happy psychos getting me killed."

"Hey, we fire on them, they fire back," Dillinger said with a shrug. "Like the saying goes, no one lives forever. If they shoot, they take a chance on killing a hostage!"

Barrow politely relayed Dillinger's threat. Then he walked out of the room, leaving Kody alone with Dillinger.

She kept telling herself that Craig was out there. He was playing a careful game, all that any man could do when hostages were involved.

Did Craig know she was in there? Of course, she knew him, she'd had meals with him and Kieran and the Finnegan family, and they'd talked about her home in Miami and the estate on Crystal Island with all its mob ties...

She blinked, determined that she not give anything away.

Dillinger just looked at her and tapped his fingers on the desk. "We need you, Miss Cameron. Isn't that nice? As long as you're needed, you know that you'll live. Remember that."

Then Dillinger, too, walked out of the room.

Kody looked around, wondering what was near her that might possibly be used as a weapon.

Nothing.
Nothing in the room stood up to a gun.

NICK STOOD WITH Dillinger in the ballroom—the large stretch on the left side of the house that connected two of the towers. Crown moldings and silk wallpaper made the room a work of real, old-artisan beauty, but, at the moment, it felt empty and their soft-spoken conversation seemed to echo loudly with the acoustics of the room.

"You played us all," he told Dillinger. "You made us all think that coming here was the job—that there was something here we'd be taking. In and out. Quick and easy. Round up people as a safety net and then get the hell out."

"I said the house was the key to great riches!" Dillinger said. "And this is an easy gig. We have some scared people. We have the cops keeping their distance at the gate. The guard is going to be okay. At worst, he'll have some stitches and a concussion. So, Barrow, don't be a pansy. You know what? I'm not so fond of the killing part myself. But, hell, when a job needs to be done..." He let Nick complete the thought himself.

Instead, Nick went on the offensive. "If Miss Cameron is right, we've got to go south from here and then west into the Everglades. Donzi speedboats aren't going to take us in to where we need to be. I don't think you planned this out."

"You don't think?" Dillinger said, tapping Nick on the forehead. "You don't think? Well, my friend, you're wrong. I know where Donzis won't take us—and I know where airboats will take us! I've done lots of thinking."

"This isn't an in and out!" Nick snapped.

"No. But the reward will be worth the effort."

So, Dillinger had known all along that what he'd wanted wouldn't be found on the property. And he had other plans in the works already. Who else was in on it? Any of the men? None of them? Was Dillinger so uptight and paranoid that he hadn't trusted a single person in their group?

Nick was pretty sure he was doing a decent job of maintaining his cover while giving his real coworkers as much information as possible. Craig and their local FBI counterparts and law enforcement knew how many men were in the house—and how many hostages remained. He hadn't been able to risk a call to Craig—other than those he made as Barrow. While the agent didn't know the who, how or where, he now knew Dillinger had expected he'd have to leave the house to find his treasure. Would he assume that he'd be heading out to the Everglades, given the legends?

Dillinger had to have people lined up and waiting to help him. As he'd said, to get where they wanted to go, a Donzi would be just about worthless. They'd need an airboat.

Dillinger had no doubt been playing this game for the long run from the get-go.

It was still crazy. There was no real treasure they were taking from the house. There was just information—a major league *maybe* on where treasure might be found.

Dillinger was, in Nick's mind, extremely dangerous. He was crazy enough to have taken a house—a historic property—for what might possibly have been found in it.

And while none of them had even so much as suspected Dillinger would go off and do something like kidnap a child, he had done so—and been smug when he'd let them all know that he had the child for extra leverage.

The kid changed everything. Everything.

Nick couldn't wait for that moment when Dillinger was off guard and the others were in different places and he could take him down and then wait for the others. He couldn't risk losing Dillinger—not until he knew where the man was holding the little boy.

First thing now, though, Nick knew, was to get them all out of the house—alive.

Then he'd just have to keep Dakota Cameron—and himself—alive until Dillinger somehow slipped and told them where to find little Adrian Burke. Then he'd have to get himself and Kody away from Dillinger and whoever the hell else he had in on it and—

Baby steps, he warned himself.

"Here's the thing—we haven't done anything yet, not really," he told Dillinger. "Okay, assault—that's what they can get us on. They don't understand what we're doing, why in God's name we've taken this place, why we've taken hostages…and they really don't have anything. What you really want—what we all want—is the Anthony Green bank-job treasure. They just promised that they're getting the boats—that they'll be here right away. The young woman whose family owns this place is still reading records and I do think she's gotten something in two hours that no one else thought of in decades. Not that it doesn't mean we'll be digging in the muck forever but… I really suggest that you let more hostages go," Nick said.

"I don't know," Dillinger said. "Yeah, maybe…maybe we should get rid of that one woman—the one with the mouth on her. She might be stupid enough to attempt something."

"Good idea. Here's the thing—the hostages are weakening us. We have the hostages in the front and the front towers covered, and you've proven you have sharpshooters up there who will pick off men and happily join in a gunfight. But, with everyone moving around and everything going on, we are missing a man for sound protection in back. I'm afraid they'll eventually figure that out. Let go a few more hostages, and we'll be in a better position to control the ones we do keep."

Dillinger seemed to weigh his words.

Then they heard shots—individual rat-a-tats and then a spray of gunfire.

Dillinger swore, staring at Nick. "What the hell? What the bloody hell?"

"I guarantee you, the cops and the Feds were clean on that," Nick snapped. "One of your boys just went crazy with a pistol and an automatic."

He raced down the length of the room to the stairs to the tower. He was certain the first shots had come from that direction.

Another round of gunfire sounded. Nick ran on up the stairs.

Schultz was there, spraying rounds everywhere.

"What the hell is the matter with you?" Nick shouted.

The man was wielding a semiautomatic. He had to take great care.

Schultz gave him a wild-eyed look before he turned back to the window. Nick made a flying leap at him, hitting him in his midsection, bringing him down.

The semiautomatic went flying across the floor.

Nick rose, ready to yell at Schultz. But the man was staring up at him with swiftly glazing eyes. He was dead. A crack police marksman had evidently returned the spray of bullets with true accuracy.

"Hey, Barrow! Schultz!" Dillinger shouted from below.

Nick inhaled. He stood and went to the stairs.

"You brought in an idiot on this, Dillinger!" he called down. "They've taken down Schultz. The idiot just went crazy and the police returned his fire. A sharpshooter got him. We need to play for a little time while those boats get here. We need to let more of the hostages go—now. If they figure out just how weak we are in numbers, they might storm the house."

"They do, and everybody dies!" Dillinger swore.

"Don't think with your ass, Dillinger. We can pull this off if no one else acts like we're in the wild, wild, West! I want to live. I didn't come in on a frigging suicide mission! We came here for something. We need to keep calm and figure out the best way to get it. Let me offer up more hostages."

"The girl almost has it. We can grab up whatever journals and all she's using and take the boats. I want them now!"

"The boats are coming. Let me free a hostage!" Nick pleaded.

Dillinger was quiet for a minute. "Yeah, fine. Just one."

"Two would be better. There's a young couple down there—"

"No, only one of them. And tell the cops if another one of our number dies, they'll have all dead hostages. One way or the other!" Dillinger snapped. "Schultz is dead," he reminded Nick. "We should retaliate. Kill someone—not let them go."

Nick hurried along the hall back to the library, Dillinger close at his heels.

The phone was already ringing when they reached the room.

Dakota Cameron remained behind the library desk.

Her face was white, but rather than afraid she looked uneasy. Guilty of something.

For the moment Nick ignored her. He picked up the phone. Once again Craig was on the other end and they were going to play their parts.

"What happened?" Craig asked.

"Your people got a little carried away with fire," Nick said. "We now have a dead man. We should kill a hostage."

"No. The boats are coming. And your man started the firing. He was trying to kill people out here. Our people had to fire back."

"Do it again, the hostages die."

"We don't want to fire."

"Yeah, well, we have anxious people up here carrying semiautomatic weapons. But just to prove that we can keep our side of a bargain, we're going to give you another hostage. Then we want the boats."

"Yes, all right. That can be done."

"We'll have someone for you, so watch the gate. No tricks or someone will die."

"No tricks," Craig said.

Nick hung up. Dillinger was looking at him.

"Okay, we give them a hostage," Nick said. "Or two."

"Two? I said—"

"Two. We'll give them the sassy girl—Betsy, I think her name is—and then a guest. All right?"

"Fine. Do it," Dillinger said.

"You want me out there?" Nick asked.

"Yes, you, Mr. Diplomacy. Get out there."

Nick was surprised. "You're leaving her alone upstairs?" he asked.

"No." Dillinger looked over at Kody, smiled and headed over to her. "I'll be close. But just to be careful..." He reached into his pocket and pulled out police-issue plastic cuffs.

"Miss Cameron, one wrist will do. We just need to see that you don't leave the desk. I can attach you right here, to the very pretty little whirligig in the wood," Dillinger said.

Nick was relieved to see that Kody offered him her left wrist and just watched and waited in silence as he secured it to the desk. She didn't protest; she didn't cause trouble. She was probably just glad they were letting another hostage free.

But Nick didn't trust her. She was a fighter.

"Miss Cameron, you have all the clues, clues that are like a road map, right? You know what we need to do?" Dillinger asked her.

"I have an area. I have an idea," Kody said.

"Don't lie to me," Dillinger said.

She shook her head. "I told you—no guarantees. This treasure has been missing for decades. I believe I know where you can dig, but whether it's still there or not, I don't know. Even the earth shifts with time."

"I knew you could find it, my dear Miss Cameron!"

"Me? How did you even know I'd be here? I don't even live here anymore. I live in New York," Kody said.

"Oh, Miss Cameron. Of course, I checked out my information about the stash, the house—and you. It was possible but I doubted that the treasure would be in the house. I knew that you were here. I knew how much you loved this old house...and, yeah, I knew you'd be leaving soon. So it was time to act." He shrugged, as if he was done explaining. "Now let me get rid of your big-mouthed friend. You help me, I help you. That's the way it works."

Dillinger turned and looked at Nick.

Nick gritted down hard on his teeth.

Yeah, they'd all been taken on this one. Dillinger had known damned well that he hadn't gotten them all to take the house for the treasure.

They'd taken the house for Dakota Cameron.

Because Dillinger believed that she was the map to the treasure.

"Get going, Barrow. Do it. I'll be watching from the top of the stairs. I mean, I really wouldn't want to leave Miss Cameron completely alone," Dillinger said.

Nick headed on out and down the sweeping marble stairs to the first floor.

He was loath to leave the upstairs, especially now that Schultz had been killed. He was afraid Dillinger would lose all logic in a frenzied moment of anger and start shooting.

But he had no choice. And Dillinger needed Kody Cameron. He wouldn't hurt her.

Dillinger was at the top of the stairs.

Watching Kody.

Watching Nick.

And there was nothing to do but play out the man's game...

And make it to the finish line.

CHAPTER FOUR

CAPONE AND NELSON were with the hostages when Nick arrived in the living room. The group of them was still huddled together.

The group, at least, was a little smaller now.

"You," he said quietly, pointing at the tiny woman who had given them the hardest time. "What's your name?"

"What's it to you?" she demanded.

He fired his gun—aiming at a mirror on the wall.

It exploded. He waited in silence.

"Betsy Rodriguez!" the young woman answered him.

"Thank you," he told her. "Come on."

"What?" she asked.

"Come on. You're going out."

"Me. Just me?"

"No," he said and pointed to another young woman. She appeared to be in her mid- to late-twenties; she was clinging to the arm of the man beside her. They were a couple. It was going to be hard to split them up.

But it was what Dillinger wanted.

"You," he said to the young woman.

"Us?" she asked. As he'd expected, she didn't want to be separated from the man she was with.

"No. Just you," he said softly.

The young woman began to sob. "No," she said stubbornly. "No, no, no!"

"Please, miss," Nick said. "Honestly, none of us wants any of you dead. Help me try to see that no one does wind up dead."

"Go, Melissa, please go," the dark-haired man who was with her said. "Go!" he told her. "Please. I need to know that you're all right."

"Victor, I can't leave you," the woman—whom he now knew to be named Melissa—said.

Melissa hugged the man she had called Victor. He pulled away from her, saying, "You can and you must."

"How touching! How sweet!" Capone said.

"Nauseating!" Nelson agreed. He walked over as if about to strike one of them with the butt of his gun.

Nick moved more quickly, walking through the huddled crowd to reach Melissa and pull her to her feet. He looked down at Victor as he did so. There was something cold and hateful in the man's eyes. Cold, hateful—and oddly calm.

The guy was a cop! Nick thought. Some kind of a cop or law enforcement. He just knew it. He also knew the man wasn't going to cause trouble when he couldn't win.

Nick thought about the situation quickly. It would be good to have another cop around—except this guy didn't know that he was FBI and he could easily kill Nick thinking he was with the bad guys—which he was, by all appearances.

He reached down and grasped the man's arm.

"Victor, you're coming, too."

The man stood and looked at him. "No, don't take me. Take the young woman who is one of the guides here. She's very scared. I'm scared—just not as scared," Victor said.

Nick liked him.

He wished he could keep him around, that they were in a situation where they could trust one another.

They weren't.

"No, I think we're going to let you lovebirds go together. I don't want my friends here becoming nauseated."

"Hey!" Nelson said. "He told you to go. You don't want us shooting up your lovey-dovey young wife, do you?"

Staring at Nick with a gaze that could cut steel, Victor took his wife's arm and started out of the room, followed by Betsy Rodriguez and then Nick.

He had to be careful now. Dillinger was watching from upstairs and Nelson was following him out to the porch.

Nick walked out toward the gate, making his way slightly past Betsy Rodriguez. He came as close to Victor as he dared and spoke swiftly.

"Cop? Please, for the love of God, tell me the truth," Nick said urgently.

Victor stared at him and then nodded.

"Tell Agent Frasier that the main man plans to get out to the Everglades, down south of the Trail, near Shark Valley. Keep his distance. Watch for men abetting along the way."

It was all he dared say. He shoved the man forward, shouting to the assembled police, agents and whoever else at the gate, "Get the hell back! Take these three—and remember, sharpshooters have a bead on you and inside there are a few guns aimed at the skulls of a few hostages."

Craig Frasier stepped forward, his hands raised, showing that he was unarmed.

"No trouble! And boats will show up at the docks almost as we speak. But what's the guarantee for the rest of the hostages?"

"You'll find them once we're gone. Most of them," he added quietly. "But we need assurances that we won't be followed. Get too close and— Well, just keep your distance."

He stepped back behind the gate and locked it again.

Betsy Rodriguez and Melissa went running toward officers who were waiting to greet them with blankets.

Only Victor held back a moment, nodding imperceptibly to Nick.

"Wait!" Craig called. "I need more…more on the hostages to give you the two boats."

"As soon as I can see them from the back, I'll bring out a few more," he promised.

"I'll be here. Waiting."

Nick nodded gravely. He turned and headed back toward the house.

As he'd suspected, Capone had waited and watched from the porch.

Nelson was with the rest of the hostages. Dillinger was still upstairs and Floyd and Kelly would be manning the towers.

He doubted that anyone other than himself and Dillinger knew Schultz was dead. Dillinger wouldn't have shared that news, fearing the others might have wanted revenge.

Dillinger only wanted one thing: the treasure.

Capone walked with him through the grand foyer and into the music room. "Good call, by the way, on getting rid of that cop," Capone said.

Nick looked at him; Capone was no idiot. "You saw that, too?"

"Yep. That kind of guy is dangerous. We don't want any heroes around here, you know."

"No heroes," Nick agreed. He shook his head. "I've got to admit—it's got me a little worried. Getting out of here, I mean." He hesitated. A man really wouldn't want to be bad-talking an accomplice in an evil deed. "I kind of thought that Dillinger was sure what he wanted was here. I guess he had the idea we might be heading someplace else to find it all along—and that's why he took the kid. More leverage."

"Yeah, I'm figuring that's the leverage he's using to get us all out of here. Do the cops even know he's the one who took the boy?" Capone asked. "You know, I've done some bad things, but I've never hurt a kid. That's why he didn't tell us. Hell, even in prison, the men who hurt, kill or molest kids are the ones in trouble. I'd never hurt a kid!"

"Nor would I—and probably not our other guys, either, but who knows. And I don't know if the cops know that Dillinger took the boy yet, but I'm figuring they do. And if they find the kid…"

"If they find the kid, we may all be screwed," Capone said.

"Do you know where he stashed him?"

Capone shrugged. "He didn't tell me. Dillinger isn't the trusting kind. Let's just hope he knows what the hell he's doing."

Nick nodded.

He really hoped to hell he knew what he was doing himself.

KODY HAD A letter opener.

Not just any letter opener, she told herself. This was a letter opener that was now considered a historic or collectible piece. It was fashioned to look like a shiv—the same kind of weapon often carried by Anthony Green and his thugs. They'd been sold at almost every tourist shop in Miami right after Green had been gunned down on the beach.

Now, they were rare. And collectible.

And she had slid the one the property had proudly displayed on the library desk into the pocket of her jeans.

Yep, she thought, a letter opener. Against automatic weapons. Still, it was something.

Maybe it would help once they got to the Everglades. She didn't imagine it would do much against a full-size alligator if one came upon her while she was trying to find the place in the glades where Anthony Green might have hidden his stash—or even one of the thousands of pythons. But at least it was something.

She looked up as Dillinger came striding back into the room.

"How are you doing?" he asked her.

She stared back at him. "Um, just great?" she suggested.

He laughed softly. "You are something, Miss Cameron. You see, I do know what I'm doing. I know that you know what you're doing. See, if you were to go on-line and Google yourself, you'd find some of your acting pages or your SAG page or whatever it is, and you'd find some promo pictures and play reviews and things like that. But when you keep going, you find out that you were quite the little writer when you were in college and that you did a feature for the school paper on the mob in Miami. You'd already done a lot of studying up on Anthony Green—and why not? Your dad inherited this place! Now, of course, I know you're not rich, that he runs it all in a trust. But I knew that if anyone knew how to get rich, it would be you. As in—if anyone could find the stash, it would be you."

Kody tried not to blink too much as she looked back at him. The man wasn't just scary. He was creepy. He was some kind of an intellectual stalker—and knew things about her that she'd half forgotten herself. It was terrifying to realize he'd really gone on a cyber-hunt for her—and that he'd found far more than most people would ever want to find.

Her skin seemed to crawl.

"I keep telling you this—there's no guarantee. Most people who have studied Anthony Green and Crystal Island and even the mob in general have believed that Green stashed his treasure out in the Everglades. I think I've found verification of that—and that's all," she said.

"But you know just about where. Everyone has looked around Shark Valley—but you know more precisely where. Because you also studied the Seminole Wars, and you loved the Tamiami Trail growing up—and made your parents drive you back and forth from the east to the west of the Florida peninsula all the time."

"I didn't make them," Kody protested, noting how ridiculous her words were under the circumstances. "And you really are counting on what may not exist at all."

"The stash exists!"

"Unless it was found years ago. Unless it's sunk so deep no one will ever find it. Oh, my God, come on! Criminals have written volumes on people killed and tossed into the Everglades, criminals through time who never did a day of time because the Everglades can hide just about anything—and anyone! I can try. I can try with everything I've learned now that I've been put to the fire, and everything that I know from what I've heard and what I've read through the years. But—"

She broke off. He was, she was certain, smiling—even if she couldn't exactly see his face.

"That's right," he said softly. "Bodies have disappeared out there. You might want to remember that."

"Maybe you should remember not to threaten people and scare them and make them totally unnerved when you want them to do calculated thinking!" she countered quickly.

He held still, quiet for a minute. "It will be fun when we reach the peak, Miss Cameron. It will be fun," he promised.

Ice seemed to stir and settle in her veins.

It would be fun...

He meant to kill her.

And still, she'd play it out. Right now, of course, because many lives were resting on her managing to keep this man believing...

And then, of course, because her life depended on it.

Barrow came striding into the room, his blue eyes blazing from his mask. As they lit on her, she felt the intensity of their stare and once again she had a strange feeling that she'd been touched by those eyes before.

"We're closing in on time to go. What are you going to need here, Miss Cameron?" he asked. Then he turned to Dillinger. "I'd wrap up whatever books and journals she wants to take. We'll be getting wet, getting out of here in speedboats."

"Well, what do you need, Miss Cameron?" Dillinger asked.

Barrow had walked over to the windows that looked out over the water.

"They're coming now," he said.

Dillinger walked over to join him. "They've stopped about a mile out."

"I'll give them a few more people and they'll bring the boats in to the docks. Their people will clear the area and we'll leave the last of the hostages on the dock for them," Barrow said.

"Not good enough," Dillinger said. "We need at least a couple of them with us."

"All right, how's this? We let three go. We take two with us—and leave them off once we're a safe distance away."

"I say when it's a safe distance. And if they follow us, the hostages are dead," Dillinger said flatly.

"I'm telling you, hostages will be like bricks around our necks once we start moving," Barrow said.

"Let the guests go. There are a couple of people who work here left—keep them," Dillinger said.

Kody jumped up. "If you're taking them, let me talk to my friends. The guides who work here. Let me talk to them. It will make it easier for you."

Dillinger pulled out a knife. For a moment she thought that Barrow was going to fly across the room and stop him from stabbing her.

But he didn't intend to stab her.

He cut through the plastic cuffs that held her to the desk.

"Go down. I'll warn our guys in the turrets about what's going on," he said.

Barrow caught Kody by the arm. She wanted to wrench free but she didn't. She felt the strength of his hold—and the pressure of her shiv letter opener in her pocket.

She glanced at him as they headed down the stairs.

"This isn't the time," he said.

"The time for what?"

"Any kind of trick."

"I wasn't planning one, but if I had, wouldn't this be the right time—I mean, before we're in a bog or marsh and saw grass and Dillinger shoots me down?"

Those blue eyes of his lit on her with the strangest assessment.

"Now is not the time," he repeated.

She looked away quickly. The man put out such mixed signals. He didn't like blood and guts, yet he didn't want any escape attempts.

He headed with her into the music room where they joined Capone and Nelson.

"You, you, and you!" he said, pointing out the two male and the one female guests.

They stood, looking at one another anxiously. Kody was amazed at how clearly she remembered their names now. The men were Gary Goodwin and Kevin Dean. The woman was Carey Herring.

"No, no, no! They're getting out—and we're not!"

Kody turned quickly to see that Brandi Johnson, her face damp with tears, was looking at the trio who was then standing.

She left Barrow's side, hurrying over to the young woman. "It's okay. It's okay, Brandi," she said. She squeezed the girl's hand and then pulled her close, talking to her and to the young man with the thick glasses at her side. "Brandi, Vince, we're all going to be together. We're going to be fine. Don't you worry. They need us."

"I'm good, Kody. I'm good," Vince told her. She smiled at him grimly. She really loved Vince; he was as smart as a whip and loved everything about his job at the estate. He had contacts that he seldom wore and he was a runner—a marathon runner. He'd told her once that he liked to look like a nerd—which, of course, he was, in a way—because nerds were in.

He would be good to have at her side. Except...

She was very afraid that Brandi was right; they were the ones who would end up dead.

But not now. Right now, she was still needed. All she had to do was to make sure that Dillinger believed they could all be important in finding his precious Anthony Green treasure.

"Come on, you three, it's your lucky day," Barrow said quietly to the guests. "Let's go."

Kody stayed behind with the two guides, taking their arms in hers. "Just hang tight with me," she whispered to a trembling Brandi.

"Stop it. Move away from each other," Nelson told them.

"She's scared!" Kody informed him. "We're not doing anything. She's just scared."

Barrow—who almost had the three being released out the door—paused and looked back. "They're okay, Nelson. Trust me." He turned to Kody. "No tricks at this moment in time, right?"

She met those eyes and, for whatever reason, she had a feeling he was giving her advice she needed to heed. "No tricks."

ALL THE WAY to the gate, the young woman who was being set free looked back at Nick, tripped and had to grasp someone to keep standing.

"We're almost at the gate," Nick told her. "Look, it's all right. You're going!"

"Someone is going to shoot me in the back!" she whispered tearfully.

"No, you're safe. You're out of here."

When he got the gate open, Craig Frasier raised his arms to show that he was unarmed then stepped forward to accept the hostages.

As he did so, they heard a short blast of gunfire.

"What the hell!" Nick muttered, spinning around furiously. The angle meant the shot had come from one of the towers—and it hadn't been aimed at one of the hostages, him or Craig.

The shot had been aimed at the sky.

Dillinger. He'd headed up to one of the towers himself.

He leaned out over the coral rock balustrade to shout out to the FBI.

"We've got three young people left. They will die if you don't back off completely. You follow us, they die. It's that simple. Do you understand?"

Craig pushed the three hostages through the gate, then stepped back from the fence, lifting his hands. "We aren't following. How do we get the last three?" he shouted.

"We'll call you. Give Barrow there a number. If

we get out safe and sound, they'll be safe. Even deal.
Got it?"

Craig reached into his pocket and handed Nick his
card. Nick shoved the card into the pocket of his shirt.
Barely perceptible, Craig nodded. Then he shouted
again, calling out to Dillinger, "You have someone else.
The boy that was kidnapped this morning. When are you
going to give us the boy?"

For a moment Dillinger was silent. Then he spoke.

"When I'm ready. When you keep your word. When
you get these hostages back, you'll know how to find
the boy."

"Give us the boy now—in good faith. He's just a
kid," Craig said, looking at Nick for some sign. But Nick
shook his head. So far, he hadn't gotten Dillinger to say
anything.

"Kids are resilient!" Dillinger called. "You keep your
word, you get the kid."

Craig looked at Nick again. Nick did his best to silently convey the fact that he knew it was imperative
they keep everyone alive—and that he figured out where
Dillinger had stashed Adrian Burke before it was too
late.

The cop—Victor Arden—had apparently repeated
word for word what Nick had said earlier. Craig knew
what Nick knew so far; they wouldn't have to follow
the Donzis at a discreet distance. Dillinger would take
his band the sixty-plus miles from their location there
on the island down and around the peninsula, curving
around Homestead and Florida City, to Everglades National Park.

Every available law-enforcement officer from every
agency—Coast Guard, U.S. Marshals, State Police,

Rangers, FBI, Miccosukee Police and so forth—would be on the lookout. At a distance.

While that was promising, the sheer size of the Everglades kept Nick from having a good feeling. Too many people got lost in the great "river of grass" and were never seen again.

He needed to actually speak with Craig—without being watched or heard.

"The boats are docking now in back," Craig told him. "How will my men get back?" He looked up at the tower and raised his voice. "If they're assaulted in any way—"

A shot was fired—into the sky once again.

And Dillinger spoke, shouting out his words. "They just walk off onto the dock. You stay where you are. My friend, Mr. Barrow there, is going to walk around and bring them to you. You know that I have sharpshooters up here in the towers. No tricks. Hey, if I'm going to die here today, everybody can die here today!"

"We don't want anyone to die," Craig said.

"So, my boats best not run out of gas," Dillinger said. "Fix it now...or a hostage dies, I guarantee you."

"You're not going to run out of gas. You have good boats, in sound working order," Craig promised him. "My men will leave the boats' keys in the ignitions, and give Barrow here backups. As soon as my men are safely off the property, we'll all back away."

"Go get 'em, Barrow!" Dillinger shouted.

Nick backed away from the fence and then turned to follow the tile path around the house and out to the back. He traversed the gardens to the docks.

There were two Donzis there, both a good size, both compact and tight. They were exactly what Dillinger had wanted.

Two men, Metro-Dade police, Nick thought, leaped up onto the dock as they saw Nick. They eyed him carefully as he came to meet them. He figured they knew his undercover part in this, but they would still carry out the charade for his safety.

He reached for the keys then he pretended to jerk the two men around and push them forward. He lowered his head and spoke softly. "Tell Frasier and the powers that be to concentrate south of Shark Valley. Around Anthony Green's old distillery grounds."

"Gotcha," one of the men murmured, turning back to look at Nick and raise his hands higher, as if trying to make sure Nick wouldn't shoot him.

"They're after Green's treasure?" the second man asked, incredulous. "Asses!" he murmured. "Everyone is still…okay?"

"Yeah. I'm trying to keep it that way," Nick said. He fell silent. They had come closer to the house on the path. In a few steps they'd be turning the corner to the front. He couldn't risk Dillinger so much as looking at his lip movement suspiciously.

He got the two men to the gate, opened it and shoved them out.

He carefully locked the gate again, looking at Craig.

There was no shout and there were no instructions from the tower. Dillinger, he knew, had already moved on. He'd have gotten what books and materials Dakota Cameron was using and he'd have headed on down and out.

Nick walked backward for a few minutes and then headed back into the house.

As he'd expected, it was empty.

He went through the music room, checked the courtyard and made his way through the vast back porch to look out to the docks.

The cons were already on their way to the boats with the hostages. Dillinger himself was escorting Kody Cameron.

Nick reached the docks just as Dillinger was handing out boat assignments.

Nelson, Capone, Kelly and the young woman, Brandi Johnson, were to take one boat.

Dillinger would take the second with Floyd, Vince and Kody Cameron.

And Barrow, of course.

"Barrow, move it!"

"No!" Brandi cried, trying to break free from Capone to reach Kody and Vince. "No, please, no. Please don't make me be alone, please…"

"You don't need to be alone. I can shoot you right here," Dillinger said.

"Then you can shoot me, too!" Kody snapped. "You let her come with us or you let me go with her, one or the other!"

"I should shoot you!" Dillinger flared, gripping Kody by the front of her tailored shirt.

"Hey!" Barrow stepped in, extracting Kody from Dillinger's grip—a little less than gently—and staring down Dillinger. "Eyes on the prize, remember? Can we get out of here, dammit! Let's go while the going is good. Vince, just go with the nice Mr. Nelson, nice Mr. Capone, and nice Mr. Kelly, please. Brandi—Miss Johnson, step aboard that boat, please!"

Everyone seemed to freeze in response to his words to Dillinger for a minute.

Then Dillinger ripped off his cheap costume shop mask and glared around at everyone.

Nick had his hand on Kody's arm. He could feel the trembling that began.

Now they all knew what Dillinger looked like. They could identify him. Until now, the hostages weren't at much of a risk.

Now they were.

"What are you doing?" Capone began.

"What's the difference?" Dillinger spat. "Who cares? We'll be long gone, and we'll leave these guys in the Everglades. By the time they're found—if they're found—we'll be gone."

The others hesitated and then took off their masks.

And Barrow had no choice. He took off his mask and stared at Kody—praying.

The instant he pulled it off, he detected the flare in her eyes.

She recognized him, of course. Knew that she knew him…immediately. He'd always had the feeling she'd suspected he was familiar, but now that she could see his face, she was certain.

But from the look of confusion that overtook her face, he knew she couldn't place him exactly. And if she did figure it out, he'd have to pray she was bright enough to not say anything. She had to be. Both their lives depended on it.

"Let's get going!"

Nick moved them along, hopping into the front Donzi himself without giving Dillinger a chance to protest.

Dillinger followed, allowing his changes.

Nick turned the key in the ignition, shouting back

to Capone after his boat roared to life, "You good back there?"

"She's purring like a kitten!" Capone called to him.

Nick led the way. He looked anxiously to the horizon and the shoreline. He skirted the other islands, shot under the causeway, joining the numerous other boats.

There was no way to tell which might be pleasure boats and which might be police. He had to trust in Craig to see that law enforcement got in front of them, that officers would be in the Everglades to greet them.

He drove hard for forty-five minutes. The day was cool and clear; under different circumstances, it would have been a beautiful day for boating.

Dillinger suddenly stood by him at the helm. "Cut the motor!" he commanded.

"I thought you wanted—"

"Cut the motor!"

Nick did so. "What are you doing?"

"See that fine-looking vessel up there? Not quite a yacht, but I'd say she's a good thirty feet of sleek speed."

"Yeah, so?"

"We're taking her."

"Ah, come on, Dillinger! She's not the prize," Nick protested.

The second Donzi came up next to them. "That one?" Kelly shouted to Dillinger.

"Looks good to me," Dillinger shouted back.

Nick realized they'd come up with this game plan while he'd been working with the hostages.

"No," Nick said. "No, no, this isn't good."

"What are you, an ass?" Dillinger asked him. "You don't think the cops won't be looking for these Donzis soon enough? Even if they know we have hostages—even they know I took the kid. We're taking that boat!"

Kelly was already moving his boat around the larger vessel. He started shouting. A grizzly-looking fellow with bright red skin and a captain's hat appeared at the rail. "What the hell are you carrying on about, boy?" he demanded.

Kelly lifted his semiautomatic and pointed it at the old man. "Move over, sir! We're coming aboard!"

"Son of a bitch!" Nick roared. He kicked his vessel back into gear, flooring it on a course toward the second Donzi.

Kelly turned to him, gun in hand.

"What the hell is the matter with you?" Nick demanded of Kelly.

"What the hell is the matter with *you*?" Dillinger asked him.

"We're not killing the old bastard," Nick said, snapping his head around to stare at Dillinger. "We're not doing it. I am not risking a death penalty for you stupid asses!"

Huddled together in the seat that skirted the wheel, Kody and Brandi Johnson were staring at him.

For the moment, he ignored them.

They were safe for now.

The old man wasn't.

Not giving a damn about damage or bumpers, Nick shoved the Donzi close to the larger vessel; she was called *Lady Tranquility*.

Nick found a hold on the hull and lifted himself up and over onto the deck. The old man just stared at him, shaking his head. "You think I'm grateful? You think

I'm grateful you didn't kill me? You're still a thug. And you should still be strung up by the heels."

"You got a dinghy of any kind?" Nick asked, ignoring him.

"Yeah, I got a blow-up emergency boat."

"This is an emergency. Blow it up and get the hell out of here!" Nick said.

By then, he heard Dillinger yelling at him again. Floyd was coming up on board, using a cleat the same way Nick had, and Dillinger was pushing Kody upward.

He helped Floyd on, and Kody, and then Brandi.

"Get him in his inflatable dinghy and get him out of here!" Nick urged Floyd.

Floyd stared at him. Then he shrugged and grabbed the old man. "Let's do it, you old salt. Let's do it."

"Make sure he stays the hell away from the radio!" Dillinger ordered, crawling up onto the deck at last. "Come on, get on up here!" Dillinger called to the men in the second Donzi.

Nick left them at the bow, heading toward the aft. He got a quick look down the few stairs that led to the cabin. Seemed there was a galley, dining area, couches—and a sleeping cabin beyond.

The storage was aft; the old man had gotten his inflatable out.

Floyd was keeping an eye on him. "Hurry it up, geezer!" Floyd commanded.

Nick took a quick look down into the cabin and toyed with the idea of using the radio quickly. He made it down the steps, but heard movement above.

"Who the hell does he think he is?" Nick heard. It was Kelly—and he was furious that Nick had stopped him. "Like he thinks he's the boss? Well, the pansy sure as hell isn't my boss!"

Nick looked up the stairs and saw Kelly's gun aimed at the old man again.

Nick couldn't shoot but he couldn't let the man die. His hand reached out for the nearest weapon—a frying pan that hung on a hook above the galley sink. He grabbed it in an instant and aimed it at Kelly's head.

His aim was good—and the old frying pan was solid. Kelly stumbled right to the portside and over the deck and into the water.

Floyd stared at him.

"We're not killing anyone!" Nick snapped.

Floyd shrugged and turned to the old man. "Better get in that boat, then, mister. If he's alive, Kelly will be coming back meaner than hell."

Nick looked at Floyd.

Floyd wasn't a killer, he realized.

Good to know.

Of course, Floyd wasn't a model of citizenry, either.

It was still good to know that in this number, there was at least one more man who didn't want the bay to run red with blood.

"Hey, Barrow!"

It was Dillinger shouting for him. He hurried around to the front.

"Get her moving!" Dillinger said.

"Aye, aye, sir," Nick said. He hurried back to the helm, set the motor and turned the great wheel.

A minute later Dillinger came and stood by him. "Hey, where the hell is Kelly?"

Nick tensed. "I think he went for a swim." Dillinger was silent.

"Hmm. At this point, good riddance." Dillinger shrugged and then turned toward the cabin. "Well, I'll bet the old guy didn't know much about fine wine, but there's bound to be some beer aboard. You know the course, right? Hold to it. We'll be around the bend to some mangrove swamps I know and love soon enough."

Dillinger left him, heading down to the cabin.

Nick spared a moment to take stock. This mission was definitely not going the way they'd planned when he'd signed on to go undercover. But he was playing the hand he'd been dealt. He had no other choice.

At least they were down to three hostages. Dakota Cameron, Brandi Johnson and Vince Jenkins.

And down to four cons. Nelson, Capone, Floyd and Dillinger.

And, of course, there was still a kidnapped boy out there…

And they were heading for the Everglades. Where, soon enough, the winter sun would set.

CHAPTER FIVE

"GOD, IT'S DARK!" Brandi whispered to Kody.

"Yes, it's dark," Kody whispered back. She wasn't sure why they were whispering. She, Vince and Brandi were the only ones down in the cabin. They were hardly sharing any type of useful secrets.

Above them, on deck, were their captors. Men she could see clearly now.

Dillinger, the oldest and the craziest in the group, had a lean face with hollow cheeks, and eyes that darted in a way that made her think of a gecko. Floyd was almost as much of a "pretty boy" as his borrowed gangster name implied. Nelson, also whipcord-lean, tense, reminded her of a very nervous poodle. Capone was muscular and somewhat stout, with brown eyes and chubby cheeks.

And Barrow.

Yes, she knew him. She knew his face. She recognized him.

From where? She still couldn't pinpoint just when she'd seen him before. So how could she possibly be so certain they had met? But she was.

Why did she feel a strange sense of attraction to him, as if he were some kind of an old friend, or an acquaintance, or even someone she had seen and thought…

I need to know him.

"Where are we? Do you think we're still in Florida?"

Brandi asked. "I mean…we're on the water, I know that, but we're not really moving anymore. I don't think. Or we're going really slow."

"We're right off the tip of the peninsula," Vince said. "Kind of out in the swamps that would make us really hard to find. But, in truth, a pretty cool place, really. You know crocodiles usually hang out in salt water, and alligators like fresh water, but here, we have both—yeah, both. Alligators and crocodiles. 'Cause of the way the Everglades is like a river of grass, you got the brackish thing going…"

Brandi was staring at him in horror.

Kody set a hand on his arm. "Come on, all three of us grew up here. I know I've been to Shark Valley a couple of dozen times. The wildlife is just there—snakes and alligators in the canals and on the trails—and people don't bother them and they don't bother people. We're going to be fine," she told Brandi.

"They're going to leave us out here, aren't they?" she asked, tilting her head to indicate the men on the deck.

"Don't be silly," Kody said.

"Yeah, don't be silly," Vince said. "They're not going to leave us—not alive anyway."

Brandi let out a whimper; Kody pulled her in close and glared at Vince.

"Sorry!" he whispered. "But, really, what do you think is going on?"

"I don't know," Kody admitted.

Vince looked over at her, obviously sorry he'd been so pessimistic when Brandi was barely hanging in.

"I've come down this way a lot," he said. "Hop on the turnpike and take it all the way down to Florida City, hop off, take a right and you get to the Ernest F.

Coe Visitor Center, or head a little farther west and go to the Royal Palm Visitor Center and you can take the Anhinga Trail walk and see some of the most amazing and spectacular birds ever!"

Brandi turned and looked at him sourly. "Birds. Yep, great. Birds."

Vince looked at Kody a little desperately.

"Let me see what's going on," she whispered.

She left her position at the main cabin's table and inched her way to the stairs.

As she did so, she heard a long, terrified scream. She ran up the few stairs to reach the deck and paused right when she could see the men. Vince and Brandi came up behind her, shoving her forward so that she nearly lost her balance as the three of them landed on the highest step.

"What the hell?" Dillinger demanded angrily.

Yeah, what the hell? Kody wondered.

The boat's lights cast off a little glow but beyond that the world seemed ridiculously dark out on the water. Except, of course, Kody realized, the moon was out—and it was high up in the sky, bathing in soft light the growth of mangroves, lilies, pines and whatever else had taken root around them.

Kody wasn't a boater, or a nature freak. But she did know enough to be pretty sure they were hugging a mangrove shoreline and that the boat they were on had basically run aground—if that was what you called it when you tangled up in the mangrove roots.

And now it appeared that Nelson was heading back to the boat across the water, walking—or rather running— on water. He wasn't, of course. He was moving across submerged roots and branches and the build-up of sediment that occurred when the trees, sometimes in conjunction with oyster beds, formed coastlines and islands.

"What the hell are you doing, running like a slimy coward?" Dillinger thundered. "Where the hell is Capone?"

"Back there… We were shining the lights and trying to see around us but it's pitch-dark out here. We were a few feet apart. We kept flashing the lights, trying to attract your friend who is supposed to come help us, just like you told us… There was a huge splash, a huge splash, can't tell you how it sounded," Nelson said. He held a gun. He was shaking so badly, Kody was afraid he'd shoot somebody by accident. He worked his jaw and kept speaking. "I saw…I saw eyes. Like the devil's eyes. I heard Capone scream…it was…it was…not much of a scream…a choking scream… It's out there. A monster. And it got him. It got Capone."

"You mean you two were attacked by the wildlife and you just left Capone out there to fight it alone? You have a gun! No, wait! You don't just have a gun—you have an automatic!"

"I couldn't see a damned thing. I couldn't shoot—I couldn't shoot. I could have hit Capone."

"You left Capone!" Dillinger said.

Nelson stared back at him. "Yeah, I left Capone. He was—he was being eaten. He was dead. Dead already. There wasn't anything I could have done."

Kody heard a shot ring out. She saw Nelson continue to stare at Dillinger as if he was in shock. Then, he keeled over backward, right over the hull of the boat, gripping his chest as blood spewed from it.

He crashed into the water.

And Brandi began to scream.

Dillinger spun around. "Shut her up!" he ordered. He was still holding his smoking gun.

Kody was ice cold herself, shaking and terrified. She turned to Brandi and pulled her against her, begging, "Stop, Brandi. Stop, please!"

Vince caught hold of Brandi, pulling her back down the stairs to the cabin, out of harm's way.

There was silence on deck then.

Barrow, Floyd and Dillinger—and Kody—stood there in silence, staring at one another.

"He was one of us!" Floyd said.

"He wasn't one of us!" Dillinger argued. "He let a pre-historic monster eat Capone, eat my friend." He swore savagely and then continued. "Capone was my friend. My real friend. And that idiot led him right into the jaws of a croc or gator or whatever the hell it was!"

"I don't think it was his fault," Floyd said. "I mean—"

Dillinger raised his gun again. Barrow stepped between the two men, reaching out to set his hand on the barrel of Dillinger's gun and press it downward.

"Stop," Barrow said. "Stop this here and now. What's happened has happened. No more killing!"

Dillinger stared at Barrow. Maybe even he saw Barrow as the one voice of sanity in the chaos of their situation.

But, Kody realized, she was still shaking herself. Cold—and shaking so badly she could hardly remain on her feet.

She shouldn't be so horrified; the two dead men were criminals. Criminals who had been threatening her life.

But it was still horrible. Horrible to think that a man had been eaten alive. Horrible to have watched a man's face as a bullet hit his chest, as he splashed over into the water...

"I never heard such a thing," Floyd murmured as if speaking to himself. "An alligator taking a full-grown man like that."

"Maybe that idiot Nelson panicked too soon and Capone is still out there?" Dillinger asked.

Kody jerked around, startled when she heard Vince speaking from behind her.

"In the Everglades, alligator attacks on humans are very rare. I think the worst year was supposed to be back in 2001. Sixteen attacks, three fatal. You know all those things you see on TV about killer crocodilians are usually filmed in Africa along the Nile somewhere. Crocs are known to be more aggressive, and of course, we do have them here, but... Capone is a big man...not at all usual." He spoke in a monotone; probably as stunned as she was by the events in the last few minutes.

"Someone has to look," Dillinger said. "The airboat is still due. Someone has to look, has to find Capone. Has to make sure..."

No one volunteered.

"Go," Dillinger told Barrow.

"What about the hostages? Three of them and three of us," Barrow noted.

Kody had to wonder if he was worried about Dillinger managing the hostages—or if he was afraid for the hostages.

"I've got the hostages," Dillinger said. "Floyd is here with me. We're good. Go on, Barrow. You're the one with the steel balls—get out there. Find Capone. See if—"

"Alligators drown their victims. They twist them

around and around until they drown them," Vince offered.

Kody gave him a good shove in the ribs with her elbow.

He fell silent.

Luckily, Dillinger hadn't seemed to have heard him.

Barrow had.

He suddenly turned and pointed at Vince. "Right, you know a fair amount, so it seems. You come with me."

Kody could feel Vince's tension. Huddled behind him, Brandi whimpered.

Kody had to wonder if Barrow hadn't told Vince to come with him because he was afraid for Vince—afraid that Vince would say something that would send Dillinger into a fit of rage again.

"Um…all right," Vince said.

He looked at Kody, his eyes wide with fear. But then, as he stared at her, something in him seemed to change. As if, maybe, he'd realized himself that Barrow was actually trying to keep them all alive. He smiled. He crawled on past her up the rest of the cabin steps and out onto the deck.

Barrow was already crawling over the hull.

"There's a good tangle of roots right here," Barrow said. "Watch your step, and cling to the trees this way. Dillinger!"

"Yeah?" Dillinger asked.

"The boat's spotlight—throw it in that direction," Barrow said.

"Yeah, yeah, should have done that before."

Kody heard some splashes. For a few minutes she could see Barrow leading, Vince following, and the two men walking off into the mangrove swamp. Then they disappeared into the darkness of the night.

Everything seemed still, except for the constant low hum of insects...

And the occasional sound of something, somewhere, splashing the water.

Victim or prey.

"THEY REALLY DON'T," Vince said, his voice still a monotone as he followed Nick across the mangroves, slipping and sliding into several feet of water here and there. "Alligators, I mean. They don't usually attack people. We're not a good food supply. And since the python invasion down here, gators don't get big enough anymore."

"Tell that to the alligators," Nick murmured. He didn't know what the hell had happened himself. It was unlikely that a man Capone's size had been taken down by an alligator, but it wasn't impossible.

And he didn't know who the hell Dillinger was supposed to be meeting, but it was someone coming with an airboat.

Dillinger had taken over at the helm once they'd headed around the tip of the peninsula; Nick had known that he'd force them to come aground. But Dillinger had a one-track thing going with his mind. There'd been no stopping him.

Now, of course, he'd taken Vince with him to keep him alive. Dillinger was trigger happy at the moment.

Nick had been stunned himself when Dillinger had gunned down Nelson without blinking. They were all at risk. What he really needed to do was to take Dillinger down. Take him out of the equation altogether—no matter what it took.

But what about the boy? Adrian Burke. Where was the child? Only Dillinger knew.

Then again, what about the hostages?

Dillinger seemed to get even crazier the deeper they got into the Glades. Did Nick risk Vince, Brandi and Kody in the hope of saving a child who might be dead already by now?

"Help!"

He was startled to hear someone calling out weakly.

"Hey…for the love of God, help me. Please…"

The voice was barely a whisper. It was, however, Capone's voice.

"I hear him!" Vince said.

"Yeah, this way," Nick murmured.

He was startled when Vince suddenly grabbed him by the arm, so startled, he swung around with the Smith & Wesson he was carrying trained on the man.

"Whoa!" Vince said. "I guess you are one of them!"

"What?"

"You, uh, you've kept us alive a few times. I thought that maybe you were a good guy, but, hey…never mind."

Nick said nothing in response. He couldn't risk letting Vince in on the truth. The man talked too much. Instead, he turned, heading for the sound of Capone's weak voice.

Nick came upon him in a tangle of mangrove roots. Capone seemed to be caught beneath branches and roots that had actually tangled together.

"We thought a gator got you," Vince said.

"Gator? That Nelson is an idiot!" Capone said. "The branch broke, splashed down and pinned me here like a sitting duck. If there is some kind of major predator around… " He paused, looking up at Nick. "My leg is broken. I won't be able to make it to...wherever it is exactly that Dillinger wants to go. You gotta help me somehow, Barrow. You gotta help me. He'll kill me if I'm useless. Dillinger will kill me!"

Nick hesitated but Vince didn't.

"No, no, he likes you!" Vince said. "He just shot that other guy—Nelson—for leaving you!"

"He shot Nelson?" Capone demanded, staring at Nick.

"Yeah," Nick said quietly.

He reached down. First things first. He had to get Capone out of the mire he was tangled in.

There was a sudden fluttering sound as Nick lifted a heavy branch off the man. He had disturbed a flock of egrets, he saw. A loud buzzing sounded; he'd also attracted a nice swarm of mosquitos.

Vince swore, slapping at himself.

"Help me!" Nick snapped.

Vince went to work, slapping at his neck as he did so. "Amazing. Amazing that people actually came and stayed to live in these swamps."

He rambled on but Nick tuned him out. He was too busy detangling Capone.

When they lifted off the last branch and pile of brush, Capone let out a pained cry.

"My leg," he wailed. He looked at Nick desperately. "What the hell do I do? He'll kill me. No, no, we have to kill him, Nick. We have to kill him before he kills all of us."

"We can't just kill him, Capone," Nick said.

"Why the hell not? The hostages are free or with us. Once we kill him—"

"We don't know who he has coming. He made plans for this. Someone is bringing an airboat here. We're stuck, if you haven't noticed. And this may be a national park, but if you've ever spent any time in the Everglades, you know that we could be somewhere where no one will ever find us."

"We have guns."

"And he's got a kid stashed somewhere, too, Capone. A little kid."

"I know. He made sure we all knew. I'm sorry about the kid but—"

"I won't tell him that you wanted to kill him," Nick said firmly.

Capone stared at him and nodded.

"Yeah. Okay. But you watch. He's going to want to kill me."

"I can see that you're left behind. On the boat. The one we stole from that poor old man. Someone will come upon it eventually," Nick said.

"You can make that happen?"

Nick shrugged. "I can try. If you stay behind, it'll probably be the cops who find you. But, hey, these guys might speak nicely for you when it comes to sentencing."

Capone suddenly pulled back and shot him a look. "You're a cop!"

Nick didn't miss a beat. "I swear I am not a cop." Without a moment's hesitation he called to Vince for help lifting Capone.

With Capone shrieking in pain, they got the man up on his one good leg.

Just as they did, they heard the whirr of an airboat and saw a blinding light flood the area.

Sleeping birds shrieked and fluttered and rose high in flight.

Nick noticed the glassy eyes of a number of nearby gators; they'd been hidden in the darkness.

The sound of one engine sputtered and stopped; a second did so just a moment after.

Two airboats had arrived.

"Hey, are you having trouble?" someone shouted.

Nick couldn't see a thing; he was blinded.

But he didn't have to. He knew this had to be Dillinger's associate, whoever he had been waiting for to bring him the airboat.

"Broken leg!" Nick shouted.

The light seemed to lower. He saw the first airboat and a second airboat in back.

A man jumped off the first one and came sloshing through the water. He was quickly followed by another. Both men were tall and muscular and quick to help support Capone.

"Where's Dillinger?" the older of the two, a man with dark graying hair and a mustache and beard to match, asked Nick.

"Back at the boat we took this afternoon," Nick said.

"Cops have been looking for that ever since the old man who owned her got picked up by a Coast Guard vessel about an hour ago."

"You gotta ditch it," the younger man said. He looked just like the older man.

Father and son, Nick figured.

"Everyone is all right?" the older one asked, sounding nervous.

"Do I look all right?" Capone moaned.

"I meant…"

"The hostages are all alive. We've had a few difficulties," Nick said. "There—ahead, there's the boat!"

"Dillinger!"

Dillinger looked over the bow as Nick, Vince, Capone and the two unnamed newcomers came along, nearing the boat.

"Capone!" Dillinger cried. "I knew it. I just knew you weren't dead. You're too damned mean for any alligator to eat!" He frowned then, realizing how heavily Capone leaned upon the men at his sides. "What happened?" he asked darkly.

"We've brought you an airboat—just as you asked," the older of the men shouted.

"Good. How will you get back?" Dillinger asked.

"We've got a second boat. We'll get out of here and back to our business," the older man said.

"All right, go."

"We're even then, right?" the older man demanded. "We did what you wanted."

"Yep. You did what I wanted. Head to the old cemetery in the Grove. Find the grave of Daniel Paul Allegro. Dig at the foot. You'll find what you want. You've evened the score enough, so go," Dillinger said.

"How do I know that the papers are there?" the older man asked.

"You're going to have to trust me. But I've always been good to my word," Dillinger said.

The man with the graying dark hair and beard looked at Nick. "If you would help us…?"

"Yes, of course," Nick said. He took Capone's arm and wrapped it around his shoulder. The night was cool but Capone was still sweating profusely.

The men who had brought the airboat nodded and walked away.

Nick watched as they left, water splashing around them as they returned to the second airboat.

They'd owed Dillinger; he'd been holding something over them. Now all they wanted was to get away as quickly as possible, get to a graveyard and dig something up.

What hold could Dillinger have had on the men?

It didn't matter at the moment. What mattered was the fact that one man was dead and Capone couldn't move an inch on his own.

"My leg is broken!" Capone shouted up to Dillinger. "I'm in bad shape. I tripped, fell, Nelson went running off…"

Dillinger started swearing. "We've got to get you up here." He paced the deck, grabbing his head, swearing. "Floyd! Floyd, get up here, help!"

Floyd appeared on deck, looking around anxiously. He saw Capone. "Hey, you're alive!"

"Well, somewhat," Capone said.

It wasn't easy, but with help from Floyd and Vince, they got Capone onto the boat.

Nick crawled over the hull.

By then, Kody and Brandi had pillows and sheets taken from the boat's cabin stretched out and ready on the deck. In a few minutes, they had Capone comfortably situated. Vince had noted a broken plank caught up in a nearby mangrove. He hurried to get it and, between them all, they splinted Capone's leg.

"He needs medical care," Kody said.

"He can't go slogging through the Everglades, up on the hammocks, through the saw grass and the wetlands," Nick agreed quietly.

"I'll make it! I'll make whatever!" Capone said. "Don't...don't..."

"He thinks you're going to kill him," Vince told Dillinger.

"What?" Dillinger asked. He truly looked surprised.

"I'm like a lame horse," Capone said quietly.

Kody had been kneeling on the deck by him. She stood, retreated down the steps for a minute, and came back with a bottle of vodka.

"This will help," she said.

"I killed Nelson for leaving you, because we don't turn on each other," Dillinger said. He looked at his friend and reassured him.

"Then you have to leave me," Capone said, looking at Dillinger and taking a long swig of the vodka. He sighed softly, easing back as the alcohol eased some of his pain. "I swear there's nothing I will tell them. There's nothing I can tell them. I don't even know where you're going. Just leave me."

"You'll do time. You know you'll do time," Dillinger told him.

"Yes, yes, I will. But I may live long enough to get out," he said. "If I try to go with you..."

Dillinger thought about his words. He lowered his head. After a long moment he nodded.

He walked over to the big man on the ground, leaned down and embraced him.

Then he jerked up, his gun trained on the others.

"He stays. We go," he said.

Nick was startled when Kody spoke up. "You can't leave him, not like this."

"Miss Cameron," Nick said, trying to step in, trying to stop whatever bad things her words might do to Dillinger's mind.

"He needs help. Look," Kody said, determined. "Brandi is screaming and scared and freaking us all out. She needs to be picked up as soon as possible. And Capone here needs help. Leave the two of them. Capone still has his gun, and Brandi isn't a cruel person. They have enough supplies on the boat to get them through the night okay. I say we leave them both." She turned to Dillinger. "That leaves five of us. Five of us in good health and good shape and not prone to hysterics in any way. We can make it."

Dillinger stared back at her. Nick barely dared to breathe.

Dillinger smiled. "You are quite something, Miss Cameron. I think you might have something. All right! Get supplies together. We leave Capone and little Miss Cry Baby here. Actually, Blondie, you really were starting to get on my nerves. Let's do it."

"You want to move deep into the Everglades by night?" Vince asked Dillinger.

"Well, hell, yes, of course!" Dillinger said. "The cops or someone will be around here very soon. We've got to get deep into the swamp and the muck and the hell of it all before the law comes around. Darkness, my boy! Yes, great. Into the abyss! Indeed, into the abyss!"

CHAPTER SIX

THE AIRBOAT WAS a flat-bottomed, aluminum-and-fiberglass craft with the engine and propeller held in a giant metal cage at the rear. Dillinger prodded everyone in.

Kody recalled the two men who had come to deliver the boat. They hadn't looked like bad men.

Once again she asked herself, *So what did bad men look like?*

Why didn't Barrow look like a bad man? Was he a good man—somehow under the influence of real criminals because he was between a rock and a hard place? He had a child somewhere being held, perhaps. Somehow, he was being coerced…either that, or she was simply being really drawn to someone really, really bad—and she couldn't accept that!

She had a hard time understanding what was going on with any of the men. She wished she could close her eyes and open them to find out that everything that had happened had occurred in her imagination.

But it was real. Too real.

At least she was grateful that Dillinger had listened to her and left both Capone and Brandi behind.

Alive.

As she was. For now…

Amid the deafening sounds of the motors she looked out into the night.

It was dark. Darker than any darkness Kody had ever known before. There was a haze before her to the north, and she knew the haze she saw was the light that illuminated the city of Miami and beyond up the coast.

But it was far away.

Out here Kody had no concept of time. She realized suddenly that she was tired, exhausted. It had to be getting close to the middle of the night. It seemed they'd been moving forever, but, of course, out here, that didn't mean much. Unless you were a ranger or a native of the area, each canal, new hammock and twist and zig or zag of the waterways seemed the same. The glow of gator eyes—caught by the headlights of the airboat— was truly chilling.

And despite it all, she'd nearly drifted to sleep twice. Vince had caught her both times.

Suddenly the whirr of the airboat stopped. She jerked awake—as did Vince at her side.

"Where are we?" Vince murmured.

Kody didn't know. But as she blinked in the darkness, Barrow and Floyd jumped out of the airboat and caught hold of the hull, pulling it—with the others still aboard—up on a hammock of higher, dry land. The lights still shone for a moment, long enough for Kody to see there was a chickee hut before them. It was the kind of abode the Seminole and Miccosukee tribes of Florida had learned to use years before—built up off the ground, open to allow for any breeze, and covered with the palms and fronds that were so abundant.

She was still staring blankly at the chickee hut when

she realized Barrow had come back to the airboat—and that he had a hand out to assist her from her chair.

She was so tired that she didn't think; she accepted his hand. And she was so tired that she slipped coming off the airboat.

He swept her up quickly. Instinctively she wound her arms around his neck.

It felt right; it felt good to hold on to him…

She wanted to cry out and pull away. And she didn't know why she felt with such certainty that he would protect her and that he'd keep her from harm.

He set her down on dry ground. "Hop on up. I'm going to light a fire," he said, indicating the chickee hut.

It was just a few feet off the ground. Vince was already there. He offered her an assist up and she took it.

There was nothing in the little hut—nothing at all. But it was dry and safe, Kody thought. Floyd was up on the platform with them and he indicated that the two of them should sit. "Make yourselves as comfortable as you can. Grab what sleep you can. This isn't exactly the Waldorf but…"

Kody took a seat in the rear of the chickee hut and Vince followed her. She could hear Dillinger and Barrow talking, but they kept their argument low and nothing of it could be heard.

Vince shook his head. "What the hell?" he murmured.

Kody reached for his hand and squeezed it. "Hey. We're going to be okay."

"Yeah."

"Just follow directions and you'll be okay," Floyd said.

They were both silent. Then Vince spoke, as if he just had to have something to fill the silence of the night.

"Did you know that Alexander Graham Bell led the team that created the first airboat?" Vince asked idly as they sat there. "And it was up in Nova Scotia? The thing was called the *Ugly Duckling*. Cool, huh? The things are useful down here—and on ice for rescues. Go figure."

"Sure, cool," Kody agreed. "I had not known that," she said lightly.

"Alexander Graham Bell, huh, go figure!" Floyd said.

Kody thought Floyd was just as interested in what the others were saying as she and Vince were. He kept trying to listen. He had his gun on his lap—ready to grab up—but Kody was getting a different feeling from the man than she had earlier. Somehow, right now, he didn't seem as dangerous.

Floyd inched closer. "Do you really think you can find this treasure stash Dillinger thinks you can find?" he asked, looking first at Kody and then on to Vince. "I guess I never knew the guy. I mean, I hope you can find that treasure. Seems like the only one who can kind of keep Dillinger in check right now is Barrow, but even then…" His voice trailed. He squinted—as if squinting might make him hear more clearly.

Kody glanced at Vince and then at Floyd. "I don't know. I mean…we're following a written trail. Things change. The land out here changes, too." She hesitated and then asked, "Do you think he's going to kill us all?"

Floyd shrugged. "Hell, I don't know. I actually wish I was Capone! Yeah, they'll get him. Yeah, he'll go to jail. But he won't die out here in this godforsaken swamp!"

"Why don't you just shoot him?" Vince asked. "You just shoot Dillinger dead when he least expects it. Kody and I disappear until we can get help. You disappear into the world somewhere, too. You don't want to hurt us, and we won't turn you in. The three of us—we live."

Floyd hesitated, looking away. "Dillinger won't do it—he, um, he won't kill us."

"He might! Why take a chance?" Vince said.

Floyd smiled. "Don't kid yourself. I could never out-draw Barrow. I could never even take him by surprise." He lifted his shoulders in a hunch and then let them fall. "If I could...no. You've got to be careful, toe the line! Barrow is freaked out that Dillinger kidnapped that kid. Barrow can't take the kid thing and I think he's pretty sure the boy is stashed somewhere and he'll wind up dying if we don't get the truth from Dillinger. He won't do anything until Dillinger gives up the kid, and now that we're out here... I don't know how in hell that's going to happen."

Kody swatted hard at an insect, her mind racing. "If the police just got their hands on Dillinger, they could make him talk."

Floyd shook his head. "Dillinger's real name is Nathan Appleby. I'm not supposed to know any of this. None of us is supposed to know about the others. But I was at this place Dillinger was staying at in the Grove one day and I found some of his papers and then I looked up anything I could about him. He served fifteen years of a life sentence up north. He and some other guys had kidnapped a white-collar executive. He wouldn't give up the guys he was working with to the cops—or the old crack house where they were holding their hostage. The hostage wound up dying of an overdose shot up into his veins by the people holding him. Nathan's gang on that one did get away with the money. But one of them betrayed Nathan. That guy wound up in the Hudson River.

"See, that's just it—he holds things over on people. Like the guys who brought the airboat. He had papers on them, I'm willing to bet, which would have proven the older man's—the dad's, I'm pretty sure—illegal status here in the USA. And, I'm willing to bet, when Nathan gets what he wants here, he's got some other poor idiot he's blackmailing somehow to have a mode of transportation available for him that will get him out of the country. Not so hard from here, you know. He can get to the Bahamas or Cuba damned easily, and move on from there."

Kody had been so intent on Floyd's words that she didn't hear or see Dillinger approaching until Vince nudged her. She turned to see that Dillinger and Barrow had come up on the platform. She wasn't sure if Dillinger had heard what Floyd had been saying.

"What's going on here?" Dillinger asked.

"I'm telling them that they'd be crazy to try to escape," Floyd said. "Nowhere to go."

"I don't believe you," Dillinger said. There was ice in his voice. He raised his gun.

Kody wasn't sure what might have happened if she hadn't moved, and she wasn't the least sure of what she was doing.

She was just very afraid that Dillinger was about to shoot Floyd.

She rolled off the ledge of the chickee hut and landed down on the ground of the little hardwood hammock they had come upon.

And she began to run.

He wouldn't fire at her, would he? Dillinger wouldn't fire at her!

She heard a shot. It was a warning shot, she knew. It went far over her head.

And she stopped running. She couldn't see anything at all, except for large shadowlike things in the night, created by the weak moonlight that filtered through here and there. She tried to turn and her foot went into some kind of a mud hole. She stood for a moment, breathing deeply, wondering what the hell she had done—and what the hell she could do now.

She could hide and maybe they wouldn't find her.

"Kody."

She heard her name spoken softly. It was Barrow. She turned but she couldn't see him.

"Stay where you are," he whispered. "Don't move."

She stood still, puzzled, afraid—and lost.

And then she understood. At first it sounded as if she was hearing pigs rooting around in a sty. Then she realized the sound was a little different.

She felt Barrow's hand on her upper arm, at the same time gentle and firm. He jerked her back, playing a light over the muck she'd just stepped into.

And right there in the mud hole she saw a good-size group of alligators. They weren't particularly big, but there were plenty of them gathered together on the surface of the mud.

She froze and her breath stalled in her throat.

"Come on!" he said, pulling her away.

With his urging, she managed to move back. She realized she had come fairly far—the chickee hut and the fire Barrow had built were a distance ahead through a maze of brush and trees. She knew then that this was the opportunity she'd been waiting for. She turned to Barrow.

"He's going to kill everyone and you know it," Kody said.

"I don't intend to let him kill everyone," he said. "You have to believe me."

He looked directly into her eyes then and, in the light of the flashlight, she saw his face clearly. She wasn't sure why, but at that moment she remembered where and when she had seen Barrow before.

In New York City. She and Kevin had been walking out of Finnegan's. He'd been telling her that he had a secret new love in his life, and he was very excited. And she had been laughing and telling him she was glad she was all into her career and the move to New York, because she didn't have anyone who resembled a love—new or old—in her life at all.

And that's when she'd plowed into him. Run right into him. He'd been there with another man—Craig Frasier. Of course, she knew Craig Frasier because she knew his girlfriend Kieran Finnegan.

They paused to look at one another, both apologizing and then...

She'd thought instantly that he felt great, smelled great, had a wonderful smile, and that she wanted to find out more about him. She'd hoped he wasn't married, engaged or dating, that she'd be able to see him and...

Then Kevin had grasped her arm and they'd hurried on out and...

Her mind whirled as the memories assailed her.

"You're FBI!" she said.

His hand on her arm tensed and he pulled her closer. "Shh!"

"All along, you're FBI. You could have shot him dead several times now. We're here, out in the true wilds, the Everglades where even the naturalists and the Native Americans and park rangers don't come! You could have shot him, you—"

"Shh! Please!"

"You didn't say anything to me! Not a word," Kody told him. She was shaking, furiously—and still scared as could be.

"I couldn't risk it," he said.

"But I recognize you—"

"It took you a while," he said. "Look, if you'd recognized me and it had shown, and Dillinger had known, or Schultz, or even one of the others, we could all be dead now. I just infiltrated this gang not long ago. It should have been easy enough. We should have gotten into the house. I should have been able to design a way in for the cops and the FBI, but…there's a little boy out there. Dillinger kidnapped a kid. I have to get him to tell me where he's holding that boy."

She stared at him, sensing his dilemma, because she herself felt torn.

On the one hand, her desire to survive was strong.

And on the other hand, she couldn't let an innocent child die.

"You've had opportunities to tell me," she said. "I could maybe help."

"How?"

"You're forgetting—he believes he needs me. He thinks I know all about Anthony Green and the stash of riches from the bank heist Green pulled off years and years ago. Maybe he'll talk to me. Maybe he will—you don't know!"

"And maybe he won't. And maybe he'll figure out that Vince is really more up on history than you are and that he needs him—and doesn't need you. Dammit, I'm trying to keep everyone alive," Barrow said to her.

Barrow. His real name was Nick. Nicholas Connolly. Now she remembered clear as day.

She remembered everything. She'd asked Kieran and Craig about him later, and they'd told her his name— and what he did!

"You're on some kind of a team with Craig Frasier. He's the one you've been talking to all along on the negotiations," Kody said.

"A task force. And, yes. Our task force has followed Dillinger—actually, Nathan Appleby—from New York on down. And now...we've got to stop him here. But we've seen what he's capable of. We have to find that boy before Nathan knows that he's trapped." He was staring at her and he let out a long breath.

"What do we do?" she whispered. "He's—he's crazy. Even Floyd thinks he's crazy. He shot and killed one of his own men!"

"We go back. We make it through the night," he told her. "There's nowhere to go out here. We're north of the tip of the peninsula and south of Tamiami Trail and the Shark Valley entrance up that way. A mile here is like a hundred miles somewhere else. The chickee is the safest place to be for the night." When she shivered, he added, "One of us will be on guard through the darkness."

She looked at him.

He was right about one thing.

She didn't want to just walk into the darkness of the Everglades.

Vipers, constrictors and crocodilians, oh, my.

"Okay," Kody said quietly. "Okay. So we go back. Morning comes. We head to what I believe to be the area where Anthony Green had his distillery, his Everglades hideout. And what happens if I can't find the treasure he wants? What happens if you can't find the boy?"

"I have to believe that we'll get what we need—that somewhere in all this, Dillinger will trust me and that I can get him talking. And if not, I pray that the cops and the FBI and everyone else working the kid's disappearance will find a clue. One way or the other, I will see to it that you and your friend, Vince, are safe by tomorrow morning. I got information to Craig. They know where to go. They'll have a very carefully laid ambush for tomorrow. We just have to get to that time."

Kody nodded dully. Okay. She'd go back.

He suddenly pulled her into his arms; she swallowed hard, looking up at him, seeing the emotion conflicting in his eyes.

"I'll keep you safe!" he vowed. "I'll keep you safe!"

"I know!" she whispered, hoping there was more courage in her voice than she felt.

"I have to make this look real," he told her.

She felt the muzzle of his gun against her back. "Of course."

Dillinger was standing by the edge of the chickee hut ledge when they returned—watching for them.

"My dear Miss Cameron! Foolish girl. Where were you going to go?" he asked.

"She's not going anywhere. She's going to be by my side from here on out," Barrow—or, rather, Nick Connolly—told him.

"Let's hope not. It's getting late. We could all use a little sleep. Oh, but, please, don't go thinking that my fellows are sweet on you, Miss Cameron, or that if I sleep, you can run again," Dillinger said. "I wake at a whisper in the wind. You will not pull things over on me.

"Not to mention…the coral snake doesn't have much of a mouth span, but the bite can be lethal. There are pygmy rattlers out there and Eastern diamondbacks. And the cottonmouth. Nasty, all of them. Not to mention the pythons and boas. But, since I'm being honest here, I haven't heard of anyone being snuffed out by one of them yet. There are the alligators and the crocs—mostly alligators where we are right now, but, hey, if you're going to get mauled or eaten by an alligator or a croc, do you really care which one?"

"I'm not going anywhere," Kody said. "You scared me. You scared me worse than the thought of a snake or an alligator or whatever else might be out here." She inhaled air as if she could breathe in courage. So far, it seemed to work with him. "You have to stop. You got mad at your own man for nothing. You—you shot one of your own men."

"He betrayed the brotherhood," Dillinger said.

"I want us all to live. You want Vince and me to find your treasure. So quit scaring everyone so much and we'll find your treasure."

Dillinger smiled and glanced at Barrow where he stood right behind her.

"This one is a little firecracker, isn't she?" Dillinger asked.

"And you need her," Barrow said softly. "And you do have your code of honor, Dillinger. None of these people has betrayed anyone, so let's just let them be. Meanwhile it's you, me and Floyd taking turns on guard. We'll get some sleep."

"Sure," he said. "Floyd, there's some water and some kind of food bars on the airboat. Go get 'em."

"On it, boss," Floyd said.

Kody realized that she was desperately parched for water—and that she was starving, too.

Barrow—Nick—walked around her, leaped up onto the platform and then reached a hand down to help her up.

She accepted it.

And when Floyd came with the water and power bars, she gratefully accepted those, as well.

After she ate, she found herself curling into a little ball on the wooden platform. Vince was to her one side. Nick was to her other side, leaning against one of the support poles.

"I'll take the first hours," Dillinger said. "Floyd, you're up next."

Hours later, Kody realized she had fallen asleep. She opened her eyes and Nick was still by her side, sitting close beside her, awake, keeping guard. She could feel his warmth, he was so close, and it was good.

The night had been cold, and she was scared, but she'd slept, knowing Nick Connolly remained at her side.

She looked up at him. His eyes were open and he was watching her. She was startled to feel a flood of warmth streak through her.

Of course, she remembered now when she had initially met him. Her reaction had been quite a normal one for a woman meeting such a striking man. He was really attractive with his fit build and dark blue, intense eyes. She'd had to hurry out that night at Finnegan's, but she'd thought that maybe she'd see him again.

Then life, work and other things had intervened.

And now…

He was good, she thought. Good at what he did. He had kept all the hostages alive so far. He had gotten many of them to safety.

He was still a very attractive man. Even covered in Everglades' mud and muck. With his broad shoulders and muscled arms he looked like security. Strength. And she was so tempted to draw closer to him, to step into the safe haven of those arms…

What was she thinking? This had to be some kind of syndrome, she told herself. Kieran Finnegan would be able to explain it to her. It was a syndrome wherein women fell in love with their captors.

No, she wasn't in love. And he wasn't really a captor. He was as G-man and he worked with Craig Frasier!

"You okay?" he whispered.

She nodded.

"I will get you out of this."

"Yes…I believe you."

He nodded grimly.

"Vince? Is Vince all right."

"Right now? He's quite all right. Take a look."

Kody rolled carefully to take a look at Vince. He was actually snoring softly.

She turned back to Nick. She nodded and offered him a small, grim smile.

"Hey! You're up, Barrow!" Dillinger suddenly called out.

"Yep, I'm on it," Nick called back to him.

He stood. Kody saw that he'd never let go of his gun, that it was held tightly in his hands.

It would be so easy! So easy for Nick just to walk over

and shoot the man who was holding them all hostage, threatening their lives.

But she saw the way that Dillinger was sleeping. His gun in his lap.

The man even slept with his damned eyes open!

Kody didn't sleep again. She watched as the sun came up. It was oddly beautiful. The colors that streaked the sky were magnificent. Herons and cranes, white and colorful, flew to the water's edge. Then nature called.

She stood and saw that Floyd and Dillinger and Nick were all up. Nick had gone over to kick the fire out. There was little preparation to be made for them to move on, but they were obviously ready to go.

She cleared her throat.

"I…I need a few moments alone," Kody said. "I need privacy."

"Don't we all," Dillinger said.

"I'm serious. I need to take a little walk. As you've pointed out, there's really nowhere for me to go. I insist. I mean it, or you can shoot me now!"

Dillinger started to laugh. "Okay, Barrow, take Miss Cameron down a path. Give her some space—but not too much. You seem to be good at hunting her down, but we're ready to move on and I don't want to waste any time."

"Yeah, fine," Nick said.

"Don't worry. Hey, I'm fine right here!" Vince said. "It's a guy thing, right? No one cares about my privacy, huh?"

They all ignored Vince.

"Go. Move! There's a trail there," Nick told her.

She walked ahead of him, aware that Dillinger was watching. Nick kept his gun trained on her.

A great blue heron stood in her way. The bird looked at her a moment and then lifted into flight. It was beautiful…and it was all so wrong.

Fifty feet out and into the trees, she turned and told Nick, "I really need privacy. I won't go anywhere, I swear."

"Scream bloody murder if you need me," he said and stopped.

She'd really only need a few seconds—what they used to call *necessary* seconds for the nonexistent facilities out here—but she was one of those people who absolutely needed to be alone.

The hammock was riddled with what they called gator holes—little areas of mud and muck dug out by gators when they tried to cool themselves off in summer. It was winter now, but the holes remained. One was full of water and she dared dip her hands in, anxious to pretend she was dealing with something that resembled normalcy and hygiene.

She looked up, ready to rise—and a scream caught in her throat.

She was staring at a man. He had coal-dark eyes and long dark braids, and he was dressed in greenish-brown khaki jeans and a cotton shirt. He was, she knew, either Miccosukee or Seminole, and he was capable of being as silent as a whisper in the air.

He quickly showed her a badge and brought his finger to his lips. "Tell Nick that Jason Tiger is here," he said softly. Then he disappeared back into the brush by the gator hole.

He might never have been there.

CHAPTER SEVEN

"JASON TIGER," KODY SAID, whispering as she returned to Nick. "He showed me his badge!"

Instead of taking her by the arm to lead her back, Nick reached down and pretended to tie his shoes. "Tiger?" he said. He didn't know why he needed the affirmation. If Kody had said the name, she had certainly seen the man.

His heart skipped a beat.

He silently sent up a little prayer of thanks.

He'd known Jason Tiger from years before, when they'd both attended the same Florida state university. Neither of them had been FBI then. Since then he'd seen Jason only once, just briefly, right before he'd gone undercover.

The name Tiger signified one of the dominant clans of the Miccosukee. Jason had been proud to tell him that his family clan was that of William Buffalo Tiger, who was just recently deceased, and had been the first elected tribal chairman when the Miccosukee had been recognized as a tribe in the 1960s. Jason knew the Everglades as few others. He'd been recognized by the FBI for the contributions he'd made in bringing down murderers and drug lords—those who had used what Jason considered to be the precious beauty and diversity of the Everglades to promote their criminal activities.

If Kody had seen Jason Tiger, they were going to be all right.

Jason would be reporting to Craig and the county police and the tribal police and every other law enforcement officer out there.

It was good.

It was more than good; it was a tremendous relief. Jason was out there and Nick wasn't working this alone anymore.

He stood and grabbed her arm. "All right." He nodded, knowing that was all the reassurance he could give her right now. Just fifty feet away, he felt Dillinger looking their way.

He held her arm tighter as they returned to the chickee. He couldn't show the relief he was feeling. He didn't dare defy Dillinger as yet—not until they knew the whereabouts of the boy. And still, the lives of Kody and Vince were at stake.

Kody wrenched free from his hold as they neared the airboat. He wasn't prepared. She managed the feat easily.

She walked over to Dillinger. He followed closely, ready to intervene.

"I don't care about the money or your treasure or whatever," she told him. "I'm more than willing to help you find it and you are just welcome to it. But if you want my help—or Vince's help—you better tell us where that little boy is. You kidnapped a kid. We've been out overnight now. That little boy is somewhere terrified, I imagine. Let him go, and I will dig from here until eternity to find the treasure for you."

Nick realized he was holding his breath, standing as tense as steel—and ready to draw on Dillinger or throw himself in front of Kody Cameron.

But Dillinger laughed softly.

He stared at Kody, obviously amused. "Wow. Hey, Vince, is that true? You don't care about yourself, right? You'll work yourself to the bone for me—if I tell you where the kid is, right? Yeah, Vince, you ready to throw your own life away for a kid you've never seen?"

Vince didn't answer. He pushed his glasses up the bridge of his nose, looking nervous.

"Okay, Miss Cameron, you want to know where the kid is? He's up in the northwest area, an abandoned crack house that's ridiculously close to the fancy new theater they've got up there north of the stadium. So, there's your kid. Yeah, it's probably getting bad for him. He was a pain in the ass, you know. I had to tie him up and stuff a gag in his mouth. So, I'm going to suggest you find this treasure for me as quickly as possible. Then I'll leave you where—if you're lucky—some kind of cop will find you before the wildlife does. And you can tell the cops where to look. You happy now?"

For a moment the air seemed to ring with his words. And then everyone and everything was silent, down to the insects.

"Yes, thank you!" Kody snapped at last, and she hurried past Dillinger, ready to hop aboard the airboat.

Dillinger studied Nick for a long moment. Nick was afraid he was on to something.

Then Dillinger smiled. "I will get what I want!" he said softly.

"I'm sure you will. I have to tell you, I'm confused. What the hell is the idea with the boy? I mean, we're in the Everglades. The boy is in an abandoned crack house."

"If they find us—not an impossible feat, even out

here—I may need to use that boy to get free," Dillinger said.

"You have hostages."

"And by the time we find the treasure, we may not," Dillinger said. He shook his head, swearing. "Here we are, end of the road, the prize in sight. And I'm down at the finish line with you and Floyd, the two most squeamish crooks I've come across in a long career."

"I told you, I'm not in this to kill people. I never was. I like the finer things in life. I've been around, too. You can survive without killing people," Nick said. "I'm also against the jail terms or the needle that can come with killing people."

"Ah, well, they can only stick a needle in once," Dillinger said. "And we've already killed people, haven't we?"

"You killed Nelson. I sure as hell had no part in that. The hostages... Thanks to me, we're not going to die because of them."

"Ah, but you did kill Schultz, didn't you?" Dillinger accused him. "It's so obvious, my friend. You've got a thing for the woman. Schultz was getting too close. You took care of him, huh?" Barrow asked, his grin broad— eerie and frightening—as he stared at Nick.

And Nick was good at this, the mind game— delving into the psyche of criminals, following the trails of sick minds.

But he wasn't sure about Dillinger. Nick had studied this man. But, right now, he wasn't sure.

"You'll never really know, will you?" he asked Dillinger quietly, and he was pleased to see a worried frown crease the man's brow. Dillinger didn't know; the man really didn't know if Barrow would go ballistic on him or not.

Pull a trigger—or not.

It was good. It was very good to keep Dillinger off guard.

"Thing is, no one has any idea who killed old Schultz. You shot Nelson in front of the hostages. Oh, yeah, so you don't intend that Dakota and the young man should live, right? Well, start thinking anew. I'll help make sure you get the hell out of here. But you aren't killing that girl. You've got it right. I've got a thing for her. And she's coming with me."

"And then what, you idiot?" Dillinger demanded angrily. "You're going to just keep her? Keep her alive? You will rot in jail, you idiot."

"You'll be long gone—what will you care?"

"She'd better find what I want, that's all I've got to say. You want her alive? She'd better find it."

Nick looked at the ground and then shook his head as he looked back up at Dillinger. "You want to know if I can be a killer? Touch a hair on her head. You'll find out."

"Really?" Dillinger said, intrigued.

"Yeah. Really."

With that he shoved his way past Dillinger and headed toward the airboat.

In minutes, it seemed that they indeed flew, the craft moving swiftly across the shallow water and marshes of the Everglades.

"Such an interesting place," Dillinger said, "this 'River of Grass!' If one wants to be poetic, I mean. Imagine Anthony Green. Out here, in pretty good shape. But he's out of ammunition and there are a dozen deadly creatures you can encounter in every direction—with no real defense. Imagine being here. Deserted. Alone. With nothing."

Kody didn't answer him or even respond, even though Vince looked at her nervously, apparently praying she had some clue as to what they were doing.

They'd traveled for hours until she'd told them to stop. Now she held a map unfolded from the back page of one of the journals. She pointed in what she truly hoped was the right direction. "Anthony Green's illegal liquor operation was out here, right on this hammock. When he had the place, he had workstations set up—chickees. But there was a main chickee where he set up a desk and papers and did his bookkeeping."

"Obviously, not here anymore, right?" Dillinger asked, eyes narrowed as he stared at her.

"You're sure this is the right place?" Floyd asked her.

"I'm not *sure* of anything," Kody said. "I know that there were four chickees and all the parts for having a distillery. I'm thinking that they were set about the hammock in a square formation, with the 'cooking' going on right in the middle by the water. Remember, land floods and land washes away. But I do think that we have the right hammock area…" She paused and looked over at Vince. "Right?"

"The Everglades is full of hammocks," Vince murmured. "Hardwood hammocks, with gumbo limbo trees, mahogany and more, and there are pine islands. Unless you really know the Everglades, it can all be the same."

"My sense of direction isn't great," Kody said. "But I believe that we did follow the known byways from the southern entrance to the park and that, if we were to continue to the north, we would come upon Shark Valley and Tamiami Trail. Naturally, we've really got to hope that this was the hammock. But—"

"Great," Floyd murmured. "We have to hope!"

Kody ignored him. "Okay, so, the heating source they used was fire, but anything they might have used to create fire would have been swallowed up long ago into nature. But Green had a massive stainless-steel still and a smaller copper still—a present to Green from the real Al Capone—and other tools that were made of copper or stainless steel. If we can find even the remnants of any of the containers, we'll know we're in the right place."

"This is ridiculous," Floyd told Dillinger. "Even if we find a piece of stainless steel, how are we going to find out where the chickees were? This has been an idiot's quest from the get-go, Dillinger!"

The way Dillinger looked at Floyd was frightening.

Floyd quickly realized his mistake and lifted a hand. "Sorry, man. I just don't see how we're going to find this."

"There is hope," Kody said quickly. "There are notes in Anthony Green's journal about his chickees. He didn't intend that his operations be washed away in a storm. Each one of the chickees was built with pilings that went deep into the earth. If we see any sign of pilings or of the remnants of a still, we'll know we're in the right place."

"Well, we know what we need to do." Nick stepped forward, defusing the tension and getting the group to focus on the task at hand. "We need to all start looking. Span out over the hammock, but be careful. There are snakes that like to hide in the tall grasses. Vince and

Kody, you stay to the center and see if you can find remnants of a still. Floyd, you and Dillinger, try the upper left quadrant over there. I'll head to the right. We're looking for any one of the sections where the workmen's chickees might have stood."

It was like looking for a needle in a haystack. Time passed. Decades. There were so few of them; there was so much ground to cover.

"Let's cover each other, crossing positions around here," Vince suggested to Kody.

She looked at him, smiled and nodded. He was a good guy, she thought. Afraid, certainly, but doing his best to be courageous when it didn't look good at all for them.

Vince didn't know that "Barrow" was FBI. She longed to tell him but she wasn't sure if that would be wise. Vince could still panic, say something.

"We're going to be okay," she told him.

"Yeah. We're going to have to make a break for it somehow," he told her. "Do you realize that if we really find this stash—oh, so impossible!—Dillinger will kill us?"

"Maybe he'll let us go," Kody said.

"He killed one of his own men!"

"Yes, but that man deserted one of his friends. Maybe he does have some kind of criminal code of honor," Kody said.

Vince shook his head. "We have to get out of here," he said.

"But what is your suggestion on how?" Kody asked. "We're in the center. The three guys with guns can focus on us in a matter of seconds."

"Two of them won't kill us—neither Floyd nor Barrow," Vince said, his voice filled with certainty. "We just have to watch out for Dillinger."

"Who has an automatic weapon," Kody murmured. "We might be all right, Vince. Help will be on the way."

Vince let out a snort. "Yeah. Help. In the middle of the Everglades."

"Okay, so, to us it's a big swamp. But there are people who know it well, down to each mangrove tree, just about. It's going to be okay."

"Hey!" Dillinger suddenly called. "Are you two working out there?"

"Yes!" Kody shouted.

"Anything?" Nick asked.

Kody turned, hearing Nick's voice behind her. He was walking in quickly toward where they stood.

But before he could speak, Vince stood and stared at her, shaking his head, a look of desperation in his eyes. "We're going to die. If we just stay here, we're going to die. I'd rather feed a gator than take one of that asshole's bullets. I'm sorry, Kody."

He turned, ducking low into the high grasses, and began to run.

"What the hell?" Dillinger shouted.

He began to fire.

Nick threw himself on top of Kody, bringing her down to the damp, marshy earth. The gunfire continued and then stopped.

"Now, take my hand. Run!" Nick told her. He had her hand; he was pulling her. He came halfway to his feet and let go with a spray of bullets.

Then, hunched low, and all but dragging her behind him, he started to run.

Kody was stunned; she had no idea where they were

going or why they had chosen that moment to leave. Vince had wanted to run...

Where was he?

Had he been shot?

What about Floyd? Was he shooting at them along with Dillinger?

Kody just knew that, for the moment, they were racing through a sea of grass and marsh. Her feet sank into mush with their every movement. Grass rose high around her, the saw grass tearing into her flesh here and there.

"Low! Keep low!" Nick told her.

Keep low and run? So difficult!

She could still hear Dillinger firing, but the sound was nowhere near as loud as it had been.

While Kody had no idea where they were running to, apparently Nick did. She felt the ground beneath her feet harden. They had come to a definite rise of high hammock ground, possibly a limestone shelf. She was gasping for breath and tugged back hard on Nick's hand.

"Breathe. Just breathe!" she gasped out.

And he stood still, pulling her against him as she dragged in breath after breath.

Suddenly the sound of gunfire stopped.

Now they could hear Dillinger shouting. "You're a dead man, Barrow! You're dead. I'll find you. And I'll let you watch me rip your pretty little pet to shreds before I kill you both. You're an ass. If the cops get you, you'll face a needle just like me!"

Nick remained still, just holding Kody.

"You can come back! You, too, Floyd! You can come back and we'll find the treasure, and we'll go on, free as the birds. I know where to go from here. I've got friends, you know that! They'll see that we get out of here safely. We can be sipping on silly drinks with umbrellas in them. Hey, come on now. Barrow, just bring her on back. I won't kill her, I promise. I just want that damned treasure!"

Nick held still and then brought his finger to his lips. He started to walk again—away from the sound of Dillinger ranting.

As they moved, though, they could still hear the man. "Vince! You idiot. Why did you run? I wouldn't have killed you. I just need the knowledge that you have. You're going to die out here. You have no way back in. I'm your way back in. Floyd! Oh, Floyd. You'd better be running. You are such a dead man. Such a namby-pamby dead man. I will find you. I will see that you die in agony, do you hear me? You are dead! You're all dead! I will find you!"

Only when Dillinger's voice had grown fainter did Kody dare to speak. "What the hell was that? What just happened? You said that a child would die. That—"

"Jason Tiger is out here," Nick said. "I'm going to get you to him as quickly as possible, and then I'll try to find your friend Vince."

"But the child. The little boy…"

"Adrian Burke," Nick said, smiling at her. He was studying her with a strange mixture of awe and disbelief. "Jason was still out there when we took off this morning. I met up with him earlier, looking for the pilings. Jason overheard Dillinger give up the boy's location. He got a message through to Craig Frasier and the local cops. They searched all the buildings in the area that Dillinger mentioned and they found the little boy. He's safe."

"Oh, my God! Really?" Kody asked. She wasn't sure if she believed it herself. She was so relieved that she felt ridiculously weak—almost as if she would fall.

"They found him—because of me confronting Dillinger?" she asked incredulously.

"Yep." He looked uncomfortable for a minute. "I should have trusted you," he said softly. "I should have trusted in you earlier."

"I'm just—I'm just so grateful!"

"Me, too. The kids…finding kids. It's always the hardest!"

She was still standing God-alone-knew-where in the middle of deadly wilderness, and it would be wise not to fall. She blindly reached out. Nick caught her hands, steadying her.

"I have to get back around to where I can leave you with Jason Tiger," he told her. "Then I can look for your friend."

"There was so much gunfire," Kody said. "But Vince… Vince is smart. There's a chance he made it." She paused, as if to reassure herself, then said, "He was determined to escape. He was certain that Dillinger would have killed us."

Nick was quiet.

"He would have killed us," Kody said.

"Most likely. Come on. We're on solid ground here, and I think I know where I'm going, but I haven't worked down here in Florida for years."

"You worked here—in Florida?"

"I did. I'm from Florida."

"Ah. But…you know Craig?"

"I work in New York City now," he told her. "I often work with him there. I've been on a task force with

Craig and his partner. We've been following Dillinger—
Nathan Appleby—all the way down the coast. I was
the one who had never been seen, and I know the
area, so I fit the bill to infiltrate. Especially once we
knew that Dillinger was down here. That he was forming a gang and pulling off narcotic sales, prostitution,
kidnapping…murder."

She was really shivering, she realized.

But it wasn't just fear. The sun was going down.

A South Florida winter was nothing like a northeast-
ern winter, but here, on the water, with the sun going
down, it was suddenly chilly. She was cold, teeth chat-
tering, limbs quaking. And he was watching her with
those eyes of his, holding her, and he seemed to be a
bastion of heat and strength. She didn't want to lean on
him so heavily. They were still in danger—very real,
serious danger. And yet she felt ridiculously attracted
to him. They'd both been hot, covered in swamp water,
tinged with long grasses…

She was certain that, at the moment, her hair could
best be described as stringy.

Her flesh was burned and scratched and raw…

And she was still breathing!

Was that it? She had survived. Nick had been a captor at first, and now he was a savior. Did all of that mess
with the mind? Was she desperate to lean on the man because there was really something chemical and physical
and real between them, or was she suffering some kind
of mental break brought on by all that had happened?

She never got the chance to figure out which.

"Come on," he urged her.

And they began to move again, deep into the swamp.

She felt his hand on hers. She felt a strange warmth sweeping through her.

Even as she shivered.

THEY WEREN'T IN a good position, but once Vince had suddenly decided to run, there had been no help for it.

Nick couldn't have gone after Vince and brought him down and go on pretending he was still part of Dillinger's plan. If he'd brought Vince back to Dillinger, the man would have killed Vince.

There had been nothing else to do but run then. Now all he could do was hope that Vince was smart enough to stay far, far away from Dillinger. And while Nick hadn't seen Floyd disappear, it was pretty clear from Dillinger's shouting that he'd used the opportunity to get away, as well.

It was one thing to be a criminal. It was another to be a crazed murderer.

Hurrying along at his side, Kody tugged at his hand, gasping.

"Wait, just one minute. I just have to breathe!" she said.

And Kody breathed, bending over, bracing her hands on her knees, sweeping in great gulps of air.

Nick looked around anxiously as she did so. Naturally, Dillinger had seen the direction in which they had run.

Nick believed he knew the Everglades better than Dillinger, at any rate. But, even then, he was praying that Jason Tiger had been watching them, that Tiger had followed him after they had spoken.

"You…you think that Vince will be okay?" Kody asked him.

"He's smart. He needs a good hiding place and he needs to hole up. Dillinger has studied the Everglades on paper, I'm sure. Though he was hoping that the treasure might have been at the mansion, he thought that it might be out here. He had communication going with men who owed him or needed him. I'm sure he has someone coming out here for him soon. But he's not a native. Vince is, right? He seems knowledgeable."

Kody stared at him. "He's knowledgeable. I'm knowledgeable. But this? We're on foot in the swamps! Oh, please! Who is at home out here and knows what they're doing—except for the park rangers and maybe some members of the local tribes and maybe a few members of the Audubon Society. Dillinger was right—we don't know what we're doing out here."

"But Jason Tiger does," Nick reminded her gently.

"Oh! But where is he?"

"He's been watching, I'm sure. He'll find us. Don't worry. Ready?"

She nodded. He grabbed her hand again and hurried in a northwesterly direction, hoping he had followed the directions he'd received from Jason Tiger.

He'd been out in the Everglades often enough. His dad had brought him out here to learn to shoot, and his grandfather had kept a little cabin not far from where they were now. But most of what he knew about the Everglades he'd learned from a friend, Jimmy Eagle. Jimmy's dad had been a pilot from Virginia but his mom had been Miccosukee.

One of the most important things he'd ever learned from Jimmy was that it was easy to lose track of where you were, easy to think one hammock was another. Waterways changed, and there could be danger in every step for the unsuspecting.

He heard a bird call and stopped walking, returning the call.

A moment later Jason Tiger stepped out onto the path, almost as if he had materialized from the shrubs and trees.

"Right on the mark," he told Nick. "Miss Cameron, excellent."

Kody flushed at the compliment.

"I was excellent at running," she murmured. "But…" She paused, looking at Nick and telling him, "Your expression when you came toward me…it was so… determined."

"I was trying to let you know that we'd be able to do something," Nick told her. "I was going to let you know that Jason had found me while I was looking for the pilings of Anthony Green's distillery operations."

"And Vince chose that moment to run," Kody murmured.

"You think he's alive?" Jason Tiger asked Nick.

"I think it's possible."

"I'll get you to the cabin, then I'll look," Jason said.

"I wanted Kody safe with you," Nick said. "As long as Kody is safe, I can go back out and search until I find Vince—and Floyd. Floyd deserves jail time, but he doesn't deserve a bullet in the back from Dillinger."

"This way," Jason Tiger said.

He led them through a barely discernible trail until they came to the water.

He had a canoe there.

"Hop in," he told them.

Nick steadied the craft and gave Kody a hand. He

stepped in carefully himself. Jason hopped in after, shoving his oar into the earth to send them out into the water.

They were in an area of cypress swamps; the trees grew here and there in the water. Egrets, cranes and herons seemed to abound and fish jumped all around them. Nick saw a number of small gators, lazy and seeking the heat of the waning sun.

The sun was going down, he realized. Night was coming again.

Jason drew the canoe toward the shore and then leaped out. Nick did the same, helping to drag the canoe up on the shore.

He wasn't sure what he was expecting, but not the pleasant cabin in the woods he and Kody saw as they burst through the last thick foliage on the trail.

It wasn't any kind of chickee. It was a log cabin, on high ground.

Nick looked at Jason Tiger, who seemed amused.

"There are a lot of houses out here. A lot on tribal lands. We're not completely living in the past, you know. Hey, guys, if it were summer, there's even an air conditioner. Everything here is run on a generator," Jason told them.

"Wow, so, there are a lot of these out here? For the Miccosukee and Seminole?" Kody asked.

Jason laughed. "No. Actually, this one belongs to the United States government. A lot of drug traffic goes through here."

Jason had a key; he used it, letting them into the cabin. It was rustic, offering a sofa in worn leather, a group of chairs, a center stove and a few throw rugs.

"There are bedrooms to the right and left. Hot showers are available—naturally, we ask you to conserve water. I have lots of coffee and power bars and other food."

"You live out here?" Kody asked him.

"When I need to. When we're watching the flow of illegal drugs through the area. I work with a newbie, Sophia Gray, and when she's in residence, she uses the second bedroom. You'll find clean clothing there, Miss Cameron. Anyway, I've been in touch with Special Agent Frasier and the police. We are actually on the edge of National Park land. You're at a safe house. You'll be fine, and we'll have you out of here by morning," Jason told Kody. "And now…"

"I need to get back out there," Nick said. "Find Vince first…and hope that I can find Floyd, as well."

"And Dillinger," Kody said. "He's still out there. He has to be stopped. I think that he really is crazy—dangerously crazy."

"Yes, and Dillinger," Nick said. "And, yes, he is crazy. Functionally crazy, if you will, and that makes him very dangerous." His tone softened as he added directions. "You stay here and obey anything Jason says, and stay safe."

"Of course," Kody said.

"Wait, this is backward. You need to watch over Miss Cameron," Jason said. "I'll see if I can find your friend, Vince, and the others."

"I can't ask you to take on my case," Nick said.

"You have to ask me. I know these hammocks and waterways like the back of my hand. You don't. I'll find them." When Nick was about to protest, he added, "I'm right, and you know that I'm right. I'm better out here than you are, no disrespect intended."

Nick was quiet for a moment and then lowered his head. "All right," he said.

"You're still armed?" Jason asked Nick.

Nick reached for the little holster at his back and the Glock there. "I am armed."

"All right, then. I'm going to head right back out. My superiors at the FBI know this place. We're remote, but they'll get here."

"I should go out with you—"

"But you won't," Jason told him.

Nick nodded. "You're right. You're far better for this job than me."

He felt Kody's fingers slip around his arm. "I'm sorry. You could both go if it weren't for me. Honestly, I know how to lock a door. I can watch out for myself here."

"No way. You're a witness who can put Dillinger away forever," Jason said.

"He's right. We can't risk you."

"Great. Because I'm a witness," Kody murmured.

Jason smiled at them both. "You're okay here for the moment. Take showers, relax. You were both amazing. Miss Cameron, you behaved selflessly, with great courage, and Special Agent Connolly, you're the stuff that makes the Bureau the place to belong. So, take this time. Sit, breathe… Hey, there's real coffee here."

"Thanks, Jason," Nick murmured.

Kody stepped over to Jason and took his hand, shaking it. "Thank you! And the child…the child is really all right?"

"Yes. Thanks to you, they knew where to search. He's safe and sound."

"I'm so glad," Kody murmured.

Jason nodded then and headed to the door. "Lock

up," he told Nick. "Not that I'm expecting you'll have any company, but—"

"You just never know," Nick finished for Jason. He offered him a hand, as well. "Thank you, my friend."

"We're all in this together," Jason assured him.

When he left, Nick locked the door.

Kody was heading toward the kitchen. "Coffee!" she said. "Food."

"Yes."

"He's an agent. You're an agent." She spoke while searching the cabinets.

"Yes."

"But you didn't know him before?"

"Yes."

"He's from here and you're from here."

Nick laughed softly. "A lot of people are from here. But, yes—Jason and I went to college together," he said.

"It's ironic, isn't it, that I saw you in New York City? Never here," she said.

He grinned at that. "Millions of people live in this area. I don't suppose it's odd in any way that people from South Florida never met. It's just odd that we wound up here together in this way after we did see each other in New York. I was probably a few years ahead of you in school. I went to Killian—and then on to the University of Florida. I was in Miami-Dade Homicide…and then the FBI," Nick told her. "And, for the last ten months or so, I've been on the task force with Craig. For the last few weeks, I've been undercover as Barrow."

"Incredible," she murmured.

"Not really."

She stared at him a moment longer and then smiled.

And he thought that she really was beautiful—a perfect ingénue for whatever play it was she was doing.

She walked over to him.

"Well, I'm alive, thanks to you," she murmured.

"It's my job," he said. "It never should have gone this far. I should have been able to stop Dillinger at the mansion. I should have—"

He suddenly remembered the day she'd brushed by him at Finnegan's. He knew then he would have liked to have met her. Now…

They were safe—relatively safe, at any rate. They'd come far from Dillinger and his insanity. Jason Tiger was a great agent who knew this area and loved it, knew the good, the bad and the ugly of it, and would find and save Vince and Flynn if anyone could.

He would have given so much to smile, think they were back, way back before any of this, imagine that they'd really met, gone out…that he could pull her into his arms, hold her, feel her, kiss her lips…

But Nick was still an agent.

He was still on duty.

"Should have what?" she asked softly.

"Should have been able to finish it all earlier," he said softly.

She still held the bag of coffee. He took it gently from her fingers and headed into the kitchen to measure it out. In no time, he heard the sound as it began to perc.

She still stood in the living room of the cabin, looking out. He saw that she walked to the door to assure herself it was locked. She turned, probably aware that he was studying her.

"Windows?" she asked with a grimace. "I'm usually not the paranoid type."

"They've got locks, I'm sure," Nick said. He crossed the room to join her at the left window to check.

It was impossible.

They'd been crawling around in fetid swamp water, muck and more. Yet there was still something sweet and alluring in her scent.

She looked at him. Her face was close, so close. Her lips...so tempting.

Get a grip! he told himself.

"We should check them all," she said.

"That's a plan. Then all we need fear is a raccoon coming down the chimney," he said, grinning at her.

They checked and double-checked one another, close and closer. He headed to each of the two bedrooms. Simple, rustic, charming, clean...

Equipped with beds.

"This is good, right?" Kody asked him, tugging at the left bedroom window. It was evidently Jason Tiger's room. It was neat as a pin, but there were toiletries on the dresser and some folded clothes on the footrest.

"Yeah." Nick double-checked the window. "One more room," he said.

In the second room, the guest room, he could almost smell the scent of crisp, cool, cotton sheets.

Kody checked a window; he walked over to her.

How the hell could her hair still smell like some kind of subtle, sweet shampoo?

"Good, right?" she asked.

He inhaled the scent. "Yep, excellent."

"And you're still armed?" she asked.

"I am. Glock in the holster at the back of my belt."

"Then it's good. It's really all good. We aren't in any danger."

Nick arched a brow.

They weren't in any danger?

He was pretty sure he was in the worst danger he'd been in since he'd started on his undercover odyssey.

Because she was danger.

Because he was falling into love/lust/respect/admiration...

And he was an agent.

And she was the bartending actress he was duty-bound to protect.

And yet the mind could be a cruel beast at times. No matter what the circumstances, no matter what their danger, his position, her position, he couldn't help but believe there was a future. And in that future they were together.

Or was that just his mind teasing him?

For the moment he needed to shape up and damn the taunting beast of a voice within him that made him picture her as she headed for the shower.

CHAPTER EIGHT

CLEAN!

There was nothing like the feeling of being clean.

Kody could have stayed in the shower forever, except, of course, she knew the water was being heated by a generator. Special Agent Nick Connolly certainly deserved his share of the water.

And Vince was still out there, somewhere. Was he safe? He surely knew more about the Everglades than Dillinger, but just living in the area and knowing history and geography did not ensure survival. There were just too many pitfalls. Crocodilians, snakes, insects—and, of course, a madman running around with a gun.

And what about Floyd?

Floyd was a criminal but not a killer; he had never wanted to hurt them.

She couldn't help but be worried about them both.

She had to believe that Jason Tiger would find Vince. Meanwhile, Vince was smart enough to watch out for sinkholes, gator holes and quicksand. He knew which snakes were harmful and which were not. He probably even had a sense of direction. He would head straight for the observation tower at Shark Valley—and the Tamiami Trail. He was going to be okay.

Hair washed, flesh scrubbed, Kody emerged from the shower. A towel had been easy to find in the bathroom.

She hesitated when she was dry, feeling as if she was somewhat of an invader as she headed to the dresser and found clothing that belonged to Jason Tiger's "newbie" associate. "Forgive me," she murmured aloud, finding panties and a bra and then a pair of jeans and a tailored cotton shirt.

When she returned to the living room, Nick was sipping coffee at the little dining table that sat between the kitchen and the living room. He'd obviously showered; his hair was wet and slicked back. She couldn't help but notice the definition of his muscles in a borrowed polo shirt and jeans. She met his eyes, so beyond blue, and she felt such a tug of attraction that she needed to remind herself they were still in a perilous position.

And that Nick had been her captor—who had turned into her savior.

There was surely a name for the confusion plaguing her!

"Hey," he said softly.

"Hey."

"Feel better?"

"I feel terrific," she told him. "Clean. Strong. Okay—still worried."

"Jason will find Vince," he assured her.

She nodded and pulled out a chair to join him at the table. "What are you doing?" she asked him.

He swept an arm out, indicating the maps on the table. "I'm following your lead. This map was created by a park ranger about ten years ago. Now, of course, mangrove islands pop up here and there, water washes away what was almost solid. You have your hardwood hammocks and you have areas where the hardwood hammocks almost collide with the limestone shelves. From what I'm seeing here and where we've been, I'm convinced that we were in the right place. Anthony Green's still sat on a limestone shelf."

"Where we were today, I'm pretty sure," Kody agreed.

"Exactly. Well, on this map, the ranger—Howard Reece—also made note of the manmade structures he found, or the remnants thereof. Kody, you were right, I believe." He paused and pointed out notations on the map. "There are the pilings for different chickee huts he had going there. Back quarter—that's the one where Anthony Green did his bookkeeping. So, if you're right, that's where we'll find the buried treasure."

"If it does exist," she said.

"I believe that it does."

"And you want to go find it—now?"

He laughed softly. "Nope. I want to stay right here now. Stay right here until you're picked up by my people and taken to safety. Then I want to help Jason Tiger and the forces we'll get out here to find Vince and Floyd. And then, at some point, get the right people with the right equipment out here to see if we're right or wrong."

She nodded and bit into her lower lip.

He reached out, laying his hand over hers where it rested on the table. "I know that you're worried. It will be okay. Jason will find Vince, and, I hope, Floyd."

"What if he can't find them? What if he can't find either of them?" Kody asked.

"He will." The conviction with which he spoke the words sank into her, giving her hope. "For now," he said, "let's find something to eat. There's not a lot of food here, nothing fresh, but there are a lot of cans and, as Jason said, power bars."

"There's soup," Kody said, pointing to a shelf in the kitchen area.

"Anything sounds good. Want me to cook for you?"

"You mean open a can?"

"Exactly."

Kody laughed. "Yes, I'd love you to open a can for me."

The both rose. Nick dug around for a can-opener. Kody found bowls, spoons and even napkins. She set the table.

"Nice," Nick told her.

"Well, we want to be civilized, right?"

"I don't know. I could suck the stone-cold food out of a can right now, but, hey, you're right. Heated is going to be better."

She smiled. It was an oddly domestic scene as they put their meal of soup and crackers together. Jason kept a hefty supply of bottled water at the cabin, and the water tasted delicious.

"So, when you're not playing the part of a thug and holding up historic properties, what are you doing?" Kody asked as she ate.

"I'm with the same unit as Craig Frasier—criminal investigation," Nick told her. "New York City is my home office. The man you know as Dillinger was carrying out a number of criminal activities in New York that included extortion and murder. He served time. He should have served more time, after. The cops had arrested him again a few years ago on an armed robbery, but the one witness was found floating in the East River. Then he started to move south, so we followed his activities. And as I said, I was a natural to slide into the gang he was forming down here."

"And you like your work?" Kody asked. "I know that Craig likes his work and his office."

"I love what I do. It feels right," he said. "What about you—what do you do when you're not guarding the booth? Ah, yes! Acting. And you're friends with Kevin Finnegan." He was quiet for a minute. "Well, this is just rude, but what kind of friends?"

She laughed. "Real friends. We've struggled together on a number of occasions. We met on the set of a long-running cop show that we both had a few short roles on." She grinned. "He was the victim and I was the killer once in the same episode. And we've gone to some of the same workshops together. But, trust me, we were never anything but friends."

"Kevin is a good-looking, great guy," Nick said.

"That he is," she agreed. "And it's cool to have a friend like him for auditioning and heading out and trying to see what's going on. We were both accepted to a really prestigious class once because we could call on one another right away and work together. We decided long ago that we'd never ruin what we had by dating or becoming friends with benefits, or anything like that." She hesitated, flushing. That was way too much information, she told herself. "And, by the way, Kevin is in love. It's even a secret from me, it's such a hush-hush thing. I hope it works out for him. I do love him—as a friend."

"Nice," he murmured.

He was watching her, his eyes so intense she looked away uncomfortably.

She rose uneasily, afraid it sounded as if she was determined he know she wasn't involved with Kevin. She wandered closer to the stove and nervously poured more coffee into her cup. "So. What happens now? I mean,

Jason Tiger has been in contact with Craig and the FBI and the local police, right? They'll be out soon, right?"

"They'll be out soon," he agreed. "We're just in an area where there is no easy access. But they'll get here. Why don't you try to get some sleep? You have to be exhausted."

"I'm fine, really. Well, I'm not fine. I'm worried about Vince. I just wish—"

"Jason Tiger is good. For all we know, he might have found Vince by now."

"Right," she murmured. She smiled at him. "I can't believe that I didn't know you right away. I mean, it's not as if we got to know one another that night at Finnegan's. But you do have a really unusual eye color and…"

"I was afraid that you'd recognize me," he said quietly. "That, naturally, you would call me out, and we would all be dead."

"Yes, well…"

"I just wasn't that memorable," he said, a slight smile teasing his lips.

"Oh, no! I had been thinking…"

"Yes?"

Kody flushed, shaking her head.

"You know what I was thinking?" he asked.

"What's that?"

"I was thinking that it was a damned shame that I was on this assignment, that I never had asked you out, that I was meeting you as an armed and masked criminal."

"Oh," she said softly.

He stood and joined her by the stove. Stopping close to her, he touched her chin, lifting it slightly.

"What if it had been different? What if we'd met

again in New York and I'd asked you to a show...to dinner? Would you have said yes?"

Kody was afraid her knees would give way. She was usually so confident. Okay, so maybe being under siege, kidnapped at gunpoint and still trapped in a swamp was making her a little too emotional. She was still shaky. Still caught by those eyes. And she was attracted to him as she couldn't remember being attracted to anyone before.

"Yes," she said softly.

He smiled, his fingers still gentle on her chin. He moved toward her and she could almost taste his kiss, imagine the hunger, the sweetness.

Then there was a pounding on the door.

Dropping his hands from her chin, he moved quickly away from her, heading to the door.

"It's Tiger!" came a call.

Nick opened the bolt on the door. Jason Tiger was there with Vince. Vince was shaking.

And bleeding.

"Oh, get in, get in! Sit him down. I'll boil water. Is an ambulance coming? Can an ambulance come?" Kody demanded.

Nick took Vince's weight, leading him to a chair. Apparently both men were adept at dealing with wounds. Nick had Vince's shirt ripped, while Jason went for his first-aid box.

Kody did set water to boil.

"It's just a flesh wound," Nick said.

"We'll get it cleaned, get some antiseptic on it," Jason murmured.

Nick took the clean, hot towel Kody provided and in

moments they discovered he had been right; it was just a flesh wound.

"Dillinger didn't shoot you?" Kody asked.

Vince looked up at her with a shrug. "I tripped on a root. Scratched myself on a branch."

"Oh," she said, relieved, sliding down to sit in one of the chairs.

"Floyd?" Nick asked Jason Tiger.

"No sign of him—nor have I been able to find Dillinger. The airboat is where it was. He hasn't taken off from where you were, by the old distillery."

Vince suddenly turned and grabbed Nick's arm. "You weren't one of them. You're not a crook."

"No," Nick said, hunkering down and easing himself from Vince's hold. There wasn't time to give him the background of his undercover investigation right now. They had to find Dillinger. "You were smart—and lucky. When Dillinger started shooting, you went down low. But he is still out there. As long as he's out there, other people are in danger. Did you see him again? Did you hear him stalking you?"

Vince looked from Nick to Jason and then at Nick again. "I think he chased me through half of the hammock. Then he was gone."

"I didn't see him," Jason said.

Nick stood. "All right." He looked over at Jason Tiger. "This time, I think it's me. I think that I need to go," he said.

Tiger nodded.

"You're going out there again?" Kody asked him.

"Yes, we need to stop Dillinger and, hopefully, find Floyd alive."

He turned, heading out of the little cabin in the

swamp. Even as he did so, they heard shouts. Kody hurried to the door behind Jason.

An airboat had arrived; it bore a number of men in khaki uniforms.

Men with guns.

They were going after the killer in the swamps.

"Kody!"

One of the men, she saw, was hurrying toward her. It was Craig Frasier. He caught her up in a hug.

"Thank God. Kieran and Kevin have been going insane, they've been so worried about you. Not to mention your family. We'll get you home. We'll get you back to safety."

She gave him a hug back. Craig was truly an amazing man. Kody was happy that he and Kieran Finnegan were together—and happy that he was a good friend to Kevin and all of the Finnegan family.

She was grateful to know him, and everyone involved with Finnegan's on Broadway.

He was there for her.

She and Vince were safe.

And yet, at that moment—right when she was surrounded by law enforcement—she felt bereft.

Nick was gone. He was off with the teams of officers that had come out to find Dillinger and Floyd.

EMTs had arrived with the officers; they were looking at Vince's wounds. They were asking her if she was all right.

Soon, she was escorted onto an airboat. And before she knew it, she was back on the Tamiami Trail, headed toward downtown Miami and to the home in the Roads section of the city, just north of Coconut Grove, where she had grown up. A policewoman came with her, took her statement and promised to watch her house through the night—just in case Dillinger found his way to her before they were able to find Dillinger.

And there was nothing left to do except watch the television to see how the rest of it all began to unfold.

DILLINGER WAS OUT THERE. He was determined to get the treasure, and so, Nick was certain, he had to have stayed in the general area where they had been.

Law enforcement had fanned out, but by the time they reached the hammock again, the airboat that Dillinger had extorted from the men he had been blackmailing was gone. He was off, somewhere.

The forces that had come out for the search were from Miami-Dade and Monroe counties, Florida Highway Patrol, the U.S. Marshal's Office and the FBI.

But, as the hours went by, they found nothing.

Nick was about to give it up himself when he determined one more time to search the original hammock. The grasses grew high there, and a twisted pattern of pines might hide just about anything along the northern edge of the hammock.

He came out alone and stood in the center, as still as he could manage. And that was when he was certain he heard movement. He cautiously took a step, and then another, and drew his weapon and gave out a warning. "FBI. Show yourself, hands above your head."

Floyd emerged out of the grass. He was shaking visibly.

"I don't want to die. I don't want to die. They can lock me up, but I don't want to die."

"You're not going to die. But you are under arrest."

"Barrow. You," Floyd said. "I should have known

you were a cop. I mean, I don't like blood and guts. But you…? Wow. I should have guessed it. It's cool. It doesn't matter. Get me in. Protect me. He was running around here crazy. Dillinger, I mean. He wants me dead. He wants you dead more but…" He shook his head as he stepped forward. "Get me out of here. Quickly. He'll shoot me dead right here in front of all of you, he just wants me dead so badly."

"All right, all right," Nick said, and cuffed the man. He caught him by the elbow and hurried back toward the airboat where other officers were waiting. "Come on, we'll get you in. You'll be safe."

"Did you get him? Did you get Dillinger?" Floyd asked.

"Not yet."

"You have to get him."

"Yes, we know."

But while Floyd was brought in, and they worked through the night, there was no sign of Dillinger to be found.

When morning dawned, he was still on the loose.

KODY SIPPED COFFEE and watched the news.

She should have slept, but she hadn't.

Her parents had arrived as soon as humanly possible, of course. They'd been worried sick about her, and she understood.

They'd nearly crushed her. Her mother had cried. Her father had cursed the day he'd discovered he'd been related to the Crystal family. Emotions had soared and then, thankfully, fallen back to earth and she had finally managed to make her parents behave normally once again.

She'd gotten a call from Mayor Holden Burke. He'd nearly been in tears as they had spoken. He'd been told by the police that it had been her courage against the kidnappers that had led to his son being found. She'd told him how grateful she was that the boy, Adrian, was alive, and she'd begged him not to do anything publicly for her—she wanted it all to remain low key.

"Yes, but I hear you're an actress—don't you want the publicity?" he'd asked.

She'd laughed. "No, I want to create characters and read well for auditions and, of course, get great reviews," she told him. "The only publicity I want is for great performances. As far as my home goes… I just worry."

"Oh, trust me," he assured her, "more people than ever will want to tour the house now. And I will thank you with my whole heart and remain low key."

When she hung up, she'd smiled, glad of a new friend.

She needed to sleep.

But hours later she was back up, staring at the television. She wanted to hear about Nick.

Every local channel and even the national channels had covered the news.

Nathan Appleby, aka Dillinger, was still on the loose. The FBI had been on his trail for nearly a year, from the northeast down to the far south. Thanks, however, to the combined efforts of various law-enforcement groups, the hostages taken at the Crystal Manor were safe, as were those who had been forced to accompany the criminals. Three of the gang had been killed; their bodies had been recovered by the Coast Guard and the Miccosukee police.

Dillinger, however, was still at large. The local populace was advised that he was armed and extremely dangerous.

There was nothing said about Nick Connolly.

"Hey!"

She had been sitting in the living room, quietly watching the television. She turned to see that her father was already up, as well.

She smiled and patted the sofa next to her. He came and sat with her.

"The manhunt continues?" he asked.

"Here's the thing. Dillinger manipulates people. The men who brought him the airboat—they weren't bad. I mean, I don't think they would ever want to hurt anyone. Dillinger put them into a desperate situation, like he does with everyone."

With an arm around her shoulders, her father said, "I didn't want you moving to New York. And I didn't want to stop you. You have to follow your dreams, and you're responsible and...well, now I'm glad you're going to be in New York—far, far away from wherever the Anthony Green stash might be. I thank God that you were rescued. I can't imagine what your mom and I would have gone through if we had made it home and...and you hadn't been found."

"I'm very thankful."

"You don't ever have to work at that awful mansion again—under any circumstances!"

"Dad, the house wasn't at fault. I love the old house and the history—and we don't throw it all away because of a very bad man. They will find him."

He nodded. "I know. For your mom and me, you're everything, though. We thought it was tough when you decided to move to New York, when you landed the role and you got the part-time gig at Finnegan's. But...you were safer there."

"None of us can ever expect something like what happened, Dad. Anywhere. Bad people exist everywhere."

"I know," he told her quietly. "Because of New York, though, you already knew that FBI man who brought you home."

"Craig Frasier. Yes, I know him through Kieran Finnegan, who is Kevin's sister. You met Kevin—I introduced you to him when we were in an infomercial together."

"Right."

"His family owns the pub where I'll be working part-time. And you will love it when you come up," Kody assured her father.

"And he's the one who saved you?"

Kody shook her head. "No. That was Nick."

"They haven't even mentioned a Nick on the news, you know."

"I know. He was working undercover. But... " Her voice trailed.

"Well, if he weren't all right and still working this thing, you'd be hearing about a dead agent," her father said.

"Dad!"

"Am I right?"

"Yes, you're right."

She leaned against his shoulder. "Don't blame the house on Crystal Island, Dad. Don't stop loving it. Don't stop caring about it. If we do that, we let the bad guys win, you know."

"Very nobly said," her father told her, a slight smile

twisting his lips. "But...I say screw all noble thoughts when it comes to your safety!"

"Dad!"

"Not really. I just want them to catch that guy!"

Kody agreed.

And she longed to hear that Nick Connolly was fine, as well.

TWO DAYS LATER there were still a number of officers searching through the miles and miles that encompassed the enormous geographical body known as the Everglades.

Nick was no longer among them.

The chase now would fall to the men who knew the area.

He spent a day being debriefed and a day on paperwork. That was part of it, too.

He was going to be given a commendation. Thanks to his work, according to Director Egan via a video conference, a kidnapped child had been found and not a hostage had been harmed.

In his debriefing, Nick was determined that the agency understand it had been Dakota Cameron who had gotten the information out of Nathan Appleby and that Jason Tiger had been the one to convey it to the police and the FBI back in Miami. He was told that Kody had completely downplayed her role in the entire event, hoping that life could get back to normal.

He, too, would stay out of the public eye. It didn't pay, in his position, to have his face plastered on newspapers across the country.

Floyd—aka Gary Forman—had told the police everything he knew about Dillinger, the gang and the various enterprises that Dillinger had been into. What seemed surprising to Nick at the end of it all was that Dillinger was an amazing crook. The man had worked with a scope that Nick, even as part of the gang, had merely been able to guess about.

Sitting with Craig Frasier in the Miami Bureau offices, he shook his head and said, "Why did the man become so obsessed with a treasure that may not exist? If he stayed away from Crystal Island, he could still be fronting all his illicit operations."

"Who says he isn't? The man is still out there," Craig reminded him.

"So he is. But he's known. His face is known. The thing is, of course, that he does use people."

"Exactly. He may well be deep in Mexico now, on an island somewhere—or headed for the Rockies. No one knows with a man like that."

"True," Nick said. "There was just something about him and that treasure. He was obsessed, like an addict. He still means to get that treasure somehow."

"Well, Jason Tiger and the local Miccosukee police as well as the FBI and city and county police are still on it."

"Yes," Nick murmured. "Good people. And still…I don't feel right. I don't feel that we should be turning it over now. You and me—we followed Nathan Appleby all the way down the east coast. I was the one chosen to go undercover."

"Something that is completely blown now, of course—albeit in the best way."

"Yes. It doesn't feel right, though."

"And we're due on a plane back to New York tomorrow. It's over for us. I thought you'd be glad. I know that you didn't mind and accepted the undercover—but, it's also damned good to get out of it."

"I am ready, I don't mind doing what's needed, but you're right—there's a time you're ready for out. There's always the point where you may have to give yourself away or commit a criminal act. And then you have guys like Nathan Appleby—guys who kidnap kids and don't give a damn if they live or die, as long as the act gives them their leverage. I am glad it's over. I just wanted it to be over with Nathan Appleby behind bars."

"We don't win every time. We try our best. That's what we do."

Nick stood and grinned at Craig. "Tomorrow, hmm. What time?"

"Plane leaves at 11:00 a.m."

"I'll be there."

"And tonight?"

"Tonight…I want to stop by and see a girl. I want to pretend that months and months haven't gone by and that I just saw her say hi to you and smile at me as she left a restaurant."

"And?"

Nick laughed softly. "And, hopefully, I'm going on a date."

CHAPTER NINE

AN ICONIC POP singer died. An earthquake rattled Central America. A boatload of refugees made landfall just south of Homestead, and a rising politician threw his hat into the ring for a vacated senate seat.

Given all that, the news about the assault on the historic mansion on Crystal Island at last died down.

Kody had spent hours with her folks, assuring them she was fine. She had made arrangements for them to fly to New York when the show opened, and she'd told them about her apartment, her part-time job and her friends, especially the Finnegans. She told them about the four siblings who owned the pub. How Declan was the boss and Kieran was a clinical psychologist and therapist who often worked with the police and the FBI. How Danny was a super tour guide and would take them around and, as they knew, Kevin was an actor.

It was all good.

She went back out to the mansion. She and her coworkers and friends who had been taken hostage hugged and cried and did all the things that survivors did. She was somewhat surprised to discover that none of them was leaving.

"I just don't see it happening again," Vince said.

"You don't give in to violence," Stacey Carlson told her.

Nan Masters, his supportive assistant, as always,

smiled. "Stacey does not give in. He hires more security. That's the way we roll."

Jose was still in the hospital, but doing well.

Brandi was fine, as well—traumatized, but fine.

Kody felt relieved and almost happy when she left them. Everything was perfect.

She'd called Craig; he'd assured her that Nick Connolly was fine. They were all disappointed, of course, that they hadn't been able to find Nathan Appleby.

Her parents were still at a board meeting, seeing to the trust, when Kody came back from the mansion and turned on the news.

Yes. The story had already fallen to the back burner.

The doorbell rang as she was staring at the television.

When she looked through the peephole, her heart skipped a beat. It was Nick.

She instantly thrust the door open.

"Hey! You're supposed to be cautious!" he began.

He was barely able to speak. She threw her arms around him, holding him fiercely.

"Um, cautious…or not!" he said, looking down into her eyes, half detangling himself and half sweeping her closer. And he just looked at her and then his mouth touched down on hers and he kissed her.

Her mouth parted and she tasted the sweet heat of his lips and tongue. The warmth swept into her limbs, magical and wonderful, and causing her to tremble. He lifted his mouth from hers, searching out her eyes.

"You're okay," she said as if she needed him to confirm it.

"Yes. And you?"

"Absolutely fine, thank you. I… You're here. Thank you. I mean, thank you for knowing that I would be worried about you. And thank you for letting me know that you're okay."

"That's not why I'm here," he said. "Although I'm grateful to know that you were worried."

"Of course," she murmured. "So, why are you here?"

"Ah, yes. Well, you're not being held by a demonic kidnapper anymore. I'm not working undercover. In fact, I'm free until tomorrow, when I fly back to New York. I'm here to ask you to dinner. This is your family home, though, I understand. Should I ask your folks, too?"

"No! Oh, don't get me wrong. I love them dearly. But I don't need their approval to tell you this. I would love to go to dinner with you. That would be great. Where should we go?"

"I'm staying at the Legend, the new place on the bay. They have a chef who just won the grand prize on a reality show," he said with a rueful smile. "Want to try it?"

"Yes. Give me one minute." She started into the house, leaving him on the steps, then went back to invite him in. Gathering her wits, she ran to the kitchen counter to leave a note for her parents so they wouldn't worry, grabbed her purse and headed back. He smiled, watching her.

"What?" she asked.

"I was nervous coming here to ask you out, and I can see you're nervous, too. But we shouldn't be so nervous. We know each other, right? We slept together—kind of—in a hut."

"Yes…but it's different now, huh?"

He offered her his arm. She took it and then headed down the walk to his rental car, a black Subaru. He opened the door for her; she slid in.

"They still haven't found Dillinger—Nathan Appleby?" she asked.

"No. It's amazing that he's managed to disappear the way he has—and yet, not. He has such a network going. He had a way to reach someone who got him out—or got him into hiding in the Everglades, one or the other."

"But you're going home, right?"

"Yes. I wouldn't be useful anymore undercover. He knows me. Craig Frasier is heading back, too. The operation will be handled from here now. Every agency down here is on the lookout."

"You don't sound happy about it," Kody said.

"I'm not. I hate it when we haven't finished what we started out to do. Dillinger has been a step ahead of us down the eastern seaboard. I'm not happy, but…" He shrugged, glancing over at her. "But you're heading to New York City, too, right?"

"The play opens in a few weeks."

"Living theater?" he asked. "I mean, isn't most theater living? Not to sound too ignorant or anything, but…"

Kody laughed. "Interactive would be a better description. It's been done before in a similar manner. We're doing a Shakespeare play, except that it all takes place on different floors within an old hotel. I love what we're doing. It's never the same thing, different every night. Basically, we are the characters. We work with the script and draw people in from the audience. And the audience moves from place to place while we have our scenes in which we work."

"I can't wait to see it."

"You'd really come?"

"Sure. We can have FBI night at the theater."

"Very amusing."

"I'm serious. I'm sure that Craig and Kieran will come, and Craig's partner. And once I'm home, I'm hoping to be paired again with my old partner, Sherri Haskell."

"Ah, Sherri."

"Married to Mo."

"I didn't ask."

"Yes, you did."

Nick drew up to valet parking and they left the car behind.

He caught Kody's hand, hurrying up the planked ramp that led out to the bay and along the water. The moon was a crescent, dozens of stars were shining and the glow of lights from the hotel and restaurant on the water was magical.

"Florida will always be home," Nick said.

"Always," Kody agreed. He pulled her into his arms and he kissed her again, and she thought that, indeed, it was all magic. She couldn't remember when she had met someone who made her feel this way, when she had longed for just such a touch and just such a kiss.

He drew away from her and leaned against the rail, just holding her, smoothing her hair, looking out on the water.

"You have a room?" she asked softly.

"That's a leading question, you know."

"Yes, I know."

He studied her eyes. "Room service?"

"That would be lovely."

He caught her hand again and led her to the elevator. When he opened the door to his room, she went straight to the large window that looked out on the night.

"Sorry, there's no balcony. Not on taxpayers' money,"

he said. "However, it is much better than the place I had before, when I was hanging with Dillinger's gang."

She turned to look at him.

"It wouldn't matter to me where you stayed," she said.

He strode to her, taking her into his arms. She drew the backs of her fingers down his face. He kissed her again, his fingers sliding to the zipper at the back of her dress. She allowed it to slip from her body.

"I wasn't… I'm not really prepared," he told her. Then he laughed. "I'm sure I can be—there're a dozen stores nearby."

"I'm on the pill," she told him.

"I'm not— There's no one else at the moment?" he asked.

She shook her head. "I've been working on the play, on the move…on life. But I've always been an optimist."

He laughed at that, pulled her closer. And he slid from his jacket, doffed his holster and gun, and kissed her neck and throat while she struggled with the buttons on his shirt. Still half dressed, they fell back on the bed. He kissed her again and then again, and stared down at her, and she reached up to him, drawing him back and tugging at his belt and his waistband.

Rolling, mingling passionate kisses with laughter, they finally stripped one another completely and lay breathlessly naked together, frozen for a moment of sweet anticipation and wonder. Then they tangled together again, seeking to press their lips upon one another's flesh here and there. He rose above her, staring down at her, straddled over her, and she reached for him, amazed that however it had come about, they were here together, and she was simply grateful.

He kissed her lips, her throat, and his mouth moved

HEATHER GRAHAM   167

along her body, teasing her flesh. She lay still for a moment, not even breathing, swept up by the sensation. He caressed and teased, lower and lower, until she could stay still no longer, and she arched and writhed and rolled with him, and allowed her lips and tongue to tease in turn, bathing the length of him in kisses until breathless, they came together at last. He moved within her slowly at first. Their eyes were locked as the pace of their lovemaking began to increase, bit by bit, to a fever pitch.

Outside, the stars shone on the water. A breeze drifted by. The night was beautiful and, for Kody, these were intricate and unbelievable moments in which the world was nothing but stars, the scent of shimmering seawater and the man who held her.

Their climax was volatile and incredible, and holding one another in sweet aftershocks seemed just as wonderful. And then whispering and laughing and talking—and wondering if they should indeed order room service or just let the concept of dinner go—seemed as natural as if they had known one another forever.

"So there's been no one in your life for a long time?" he asked her.

"Not in a long time. I do love what I do. Rehearsals are long and hard—then there is the part-time work, as you know. And you?"

"Long hours, too. But I was engaged. To a designer."

"A designer?"

"Marissa works for a major clothing line. She wants her own one day."

"What happened?"

"Off hours, not enough time…we drifted apart. I have nothing bad to say about her. We just—we just weren't meant to be. Being with an agent isn't easy. Takes someone who understands that time is precious and elusive."

"It's a give and take," Kody said softly. She hoisted up on an elbow and smiled down at him. "I had a similar problem with my last ex. Gerard."

"Ah. And what happened to him?"

Kody hesitated. "He met a teacher. She didn't work a second job to pay for the privilege of doing her main job. She just had much better hours."

"I'm sorry."

"I introduced him to the teacher," Kody said. "He was a good guy. I wasn't right for him."

"You think we might be right for each other?" Nick asked softly.

"I just… I hope," Kody said.

"Hmm. What made you…care about me?"

"Your ethics."

"As a crook?"

She laughed. "You wouldn't hurt people. That mattered. And you?"

"Well, there's nothing wrong with the way you look, you know," he teased.

"Ah. So it's all physical attraction, then?"

"And your courage, determination and attitude," he said.

She laughed softly. "For me it was your eyes. I knew your eyes. And I knew you, because of your eyes."

He smiled and pulled her down to him again. And what started as a kiss developed into another session of lovemaking.

By the time they finished, Kody jumped up after looking at her watch. "Oh! I have to go back. My parents… I mean, I was just home here to tie up loose ends. My mother and father are already a bit crazy."

"Say no more. I'll get you home right away," Nick promised.

They dressed quickly. "I really did intend to wine and dine you with a sumptuous meal," Nick said, his hand at the small of her back as they left the room and headed down.

"We'll both be in New York. There are tons of fabulous restaurants there, too, you know. I mean, I am assuming that we'll see one another in New York? Or is that maybe too much of an assumption? I was really worried about myself, you know. I was attracted to you—when you were with Dillinger. You weren't a killer—I knew that much…well, my feelings did make me question myself."

He smiled, holding her hand tight.

"Time is precious and elusive," he said. "I will gratefully accept any you can give me in the city—especially with your show starting."

"I'll find time," she promised. "I'm partial to old, historic restaurants."

"I know a great pub. I think we both get a discount there, too," Nick teased.

"A great pub!" she agreed.

The valet brought Nick's car. Kody glanced at her watch again. It was nearly 1:00 a.m. She was surprised that her mother or her father hadn't called her yet. Maybe they were happy she was out with an FBI agent.

The distance between the hotel and her parents' home wasn't great; she was there within minutes.

Nick walked her to the door.

"I'll really see you in New York?" she murmured.

He pulled her into his arms. "You will see me. You'll see so much of me..."

She moved into his kiss. The wonder of the night seemed to settle over her like a cloak. She was tempted to walk into her house and check on her family—and then just tell them she was off to sleep with her FBI agent before he had to get on his plane.

Kody managed to gather a sense of decorum.

"I should meet your parents," Nick said. "But I guess you shouldn't wake them up."

"Probably not the best idea," she agreed. "You'll meet them. They're coming up for opening night."

They kissed again. It seemed all but impossible to stop—to let him drive away.

But, finally, he broke away. "Kody, I..."

"Me, too," she said softly.

Then she slipped into the house, closed the door behind her and leaned against it. A sense of euphoria seemed to have settled over her.

She was walking on air.

But as she moved away from the front door, the lamp above her father's living room chair went on.

"Dad," she murmured.

Then she fell silent.

And she dead-stopped.

It wasn't her father, sitting in his chair.

It was Nathan Appleby—aka Dillinger.

NICK HEADED DOWN to the rental Subaru but paused as he reached the car. He looked up at the sky. It really was one of the most fantastic winter nights in Miami. Stars brilliant against the black velvet of the sky, a moon that seemed almost to smile in a half curve and a balmy temperature of maybe seventy degrees.

He would always love South Florida as home. There was nothing like it—even when it came to the Everglades with all its glory, from birds of uncanny beauty, endangered panthers—and deadly reptiles.

It would always be home to both of them, even as it seemed they both loved New York City and embraced all that could be found there. Actually, Nick had never cared much which office he was assigned to; he was just glad to be with the Bureau. Even if they didn't win every time.

Nathan Appleby was still out there.

But the hostages were safe. The hostages were alive. It was out of his hands and, after tonight, he could say that it had ended exceptionally well. The future loomed before them.

He turned the key in the ignition and drove out onto the street. His phone rang and he glanced at the Caller ID. It was Kody. He answered it quickly. "Hello?"

At first there was nothing. He almost hung up, thinking maybe she had pocket dialed him.

Then he heard Kody's voice. "You know me, Mr. Appleby. You know that I won't help you unless I'm sure others are safe. And this time, you have my parents. Do you really think that I'll do anything for you, anything at all, when I'm worried about their safety?"

"Right now, Miss Cameron, they are alive. You know me. I don't care a lot whether people live or die. You get that treasure for me and your parents live. It's that simple."

Nick quickly pulled the car to the side. He hadn't gone more than a block from the Cameron house. He cursed himself a thousand times over.

They had underestimated Nathan Appleby. They hadn't comprehended the depth of his obsession, realized that he would risk everything to find the Anthony Green treasure.

Appleby had known everything about the Crystal Island mansion, about Anthony Green. It was only natural that he should have known where the Cameron family lived, only natural that he had made his way out of the Everglades and into the city of Miami—and on to the Cameron house.

"You left Adrian Burke bound and gagged in an abandoned crack house," Nick heard Kody say. "I need to know where my parents are—that they will be safe. That's the only way I help you."

"Okay, here it is. They are not in a crack house. They're out on a boat belonging to some very good friends of mine. Now, you help me and I get the treasure, I make a call and they go free. If you don't come with me—nicely!—I call and they take an eternal swim in Biscayne Bay. Oh, and added insurance—if they don't hear from me every hour, your parents take a dive."

"I'll go with you. But what guarantee do I have?"

"You don't have any guarantees. No guarantees at all. But…I can dial right now. Mommy and Daddy do love the water, right?"

"Do you mind if I put sneakers on?" Kody asked. "They beat the hell out of sandals for scrounging around in the Everglades!"

TORTURE WAS ILLEGAL.

But Nick still considered slipping into the Cameron house and slicing Nathan Appleby to ribbons in order to force him to tell the truth about Kody's parents.

But there were inherent dangers—such as Appleby getting a message through to the people holding Kody's parents, Kody herself protesting, and a million other things that could go wrong—along with torture being illegal. Appleby had said he had to make a call once an hour. The man was mean enough, manic enough, to die before making a call.

Nick didn't want to give up the phone; he couldn't reach Craig or anyone else unless he did hang up the phone.

He knew where Appleby would take Kody.

"Let's go!" he heard Appleby snap. "Ditch the purse— you have a phone in there, right? Ditch the purse now!"

The line was still open but nothing else was coming from it. Nick hung up quickly and called Craig.

"We'll get the Coast Guard out in the bay along with local police," Craig said as soon as Nick apprised him of the situation. "We'll find them. Swing by for me at the hotel. We'll head out together. They'll alert Jason Tiger and he'll see that everyone out there is watching and ready."

"We know where they're going," Nick said.

"How damned crazy can that man be? He intends to dig in the swamp all night by himself?"

"He's not alone. He has Kody."

NATHAN APPLEBY MADE Kody drive.

Her own car.

She wasn't sure why that seemed to add insult to injury.

She didn't know how he'd gotten to her house; she hadn't seen a car, but then, he might have parked anywhere on the street.

Wherever he had come from, he had come to her house and kidnapped her parents. They were out somewhere in the bay. He'd come prepared; he had two backpacks—one she was certain she was supposed to be carrying through the Everglades. He'd managed all this with the news displaying his picture constantly and every law-enforcement agent in the city on the lookout for him.

He kept his gun trained on her as they drove, held low in the seat lest someone note that she was driving under stress.

Not that there were that many people out. Miami was truly a city that never slept, but here, in the residential areas that led from her home close to downtown and west toward the Everglades, there were few cars on the road.

"I'm not sure how you think I'm doing this. I mean, honestly? I don't know how I'm doing this. I've only ever dropped by the Everglades by daylight. I'm pretty sure there are gates or fences or something when you get to the park entrances," Kody said.

"We won't be taking a park entrance," he told her.

"What? You just happen to have friends with access driveways?" she asked, unable to avoid the sarcasm.

"I happen to know where to go," he said.

Kody checked the rearview mirror now and then, but she couldn't tell if any of the cars she saw behind them were following her or not.

She was fairly certain she had gotten a call out—that she'd managed to dial Nick's number without Appleby noting what she was doing as they'd spoken. Then, of course, he'd made her leave her purse.

But he'd never looked at the phone. He didn't know what she had done…

If, of course, she had actually done it.

She had, she assured herself.

They passed the Miccosukee casino where lights were still bright and the parking lot abounded with cars.

Then, as they continued west, there were almost no cars.

Businesses advertising airboat rides seemed to creep up on them. The lights were low and the darkness out there at night seemed almost surreal.

Kody had been driving nearly an hour when Appleby picked up his phone.

"My parents?" she asked.

"Yes, Miss Cameron. I'm making sure they'll be just fine."

Someone answered on the other end.

"Everything is good," he said. And he smiled at Kody and hung up. "Just keep on helping me and we'll be fine."

"You need more than just me," she said. "This is the kind of project you need a host of workers to accomplish. We have to find the pilings. We think we know that he buried the stash at the corner of the main chickee, but we're not sure. And how deep? Exactly where? We need more people to look."

"Maybe," he told her.

"Just how many friends do you have? And do you really trust these people? Okay, so I've seen you in action. You extorted an airboat from people who were forced to help you. But remember, people you bribe and threaten just might want to bite back, you know," Kody told him.

"Would you bite back?" he asked her.

"If you keep threatening my parents, I promise you, I'll bite back!"

"Not if you want them alive. And slow down!"

Kody slowed down. She had no idea what he was looking for. If she were to turn to the right at the moment, she'd wind up in a canal. Not a pleasant thought. If she turned to the left, as far as she could see, there was nothing but soupy marsh. They were, she knew, near Shark Valley, but it was still ahead of them on the trail by a mile or two.

"Here," he said.

"Where's 'here'?" Kody demanded.

"Slow down!"

She slowed even more and glanced in the rearview mirror.

There were no lights behind them.

She wasn't being followed. Her heart seemed to sink.

"Right there!" Appleby told her. "See there? See the road? And don't get any ideas. You sink us in a canal or a bog out here, your parents die. Oh, and you die, too. So, drive, and drive carefully."

"Do you know how pitch-dark it is out here?" Kody demanded.

"Do you know that's why they give cars bright lights?" Appleby retorted.

Kody grated her teeth. She turned to the left and slowly, carefully, followed the dirt road Appleby had indicated. It seemed to head into nothing but dense green grass and it slowly disappeared.

"That's good," Appleby said. "Here. This is fine. It's as far as we go by car, my dear."

She's already been dragged through the swamp. She'd spent a night in a chickee. She'd walked, not knowing if she'd disturb a rattler or a coral snake, or if she'd step on a log that turned out to be an alligator. She shouldn't have been so terrified.

And yet she was.

Appleby shoved his gun into his waistband and tossed her a backpack. "Get your flashlight," he commanded her.

She found a large flashlight in the pack along with water, a folded shovel, a pick and a power bar.

They might have been on a planned hike or tour into the wilderness!

"Turn your light on," he said.

She did so, as did he. The flashlights illuminated great circles of brush and grass and trees. "There," he said.

Where?

And then she saw an airboat before them.

"Let's go!" he said.

She took a step; the ground was no longer solid.

She stepped into swamp and prayed she wasn't disturbing a cottonmouth.

It was only a few steps to the airboat. She was grateful to climb aboard it.

And then Appleby was with her, the motor was revving and they were moving deeper into the abyss of the night.

"I WILL BE there when they arrive," Jason Tiger assured Nick. "I'll have Miccosukee police with me. They know how to hide in the night. We'll be on it, I promise."

"But don't approach until we're out there," Nick said. "We're trying to find her parents. We'll be behind them. We have a ranger meeting us to take us out to the hammock. We'll take the first miles by airboat and then switch to canoes so that we're not heard."

"We won't approach. Unless, of course, we see that Miss Cameron is in imminent danger."

"Of course," Nick agreed.

Nick spoke with Tiger as he waited for Craig to join him. He hung up just as his teammate joined him in the car.

"You know, I keep thinking about this," Nick said.

"We haven't thought of anything but for days now," Craig said grimly.

"No. I mean the timing. I went to Kody's house at 8:00 p.m. Her mom and dad were still out—at a board meeting. We came to the hotel. We were at the hotel about three hours or so. That would mean that Appleby got to her house, either charmed or laid a trap for her parents when they returned, and then found someone to threaten who had a boat, and got Kody's mom and dad out on the boat. At least, that's what he told Kody."

"And?" Craig asked him. "Ah. Yeah, timing. You don't think that he really got them out on a boat. We have the Coast Guard out, but, of course, there are so many boats out there. And they can search for the Cameron couple. Thing is…"

"There are hundreds of boats out on the water. It's dark, and the bay stretches forever, and boats move," Nick said. He shook his head. "But I don't think they're on a boat."

"Where do you think they are?"

"Somewhere near the house," Nick said. "I can't look, though. I have to get out there. I have to get out there as quickly as possible. I know what Kody was doing, where she was looking, what she believed. I need—"

"To be there. I get it. Drop me at the Cameron house.

I'll find her parents, if they are anywhere near the house," Craig said firmly.

Nick nodded. "Thank you."

"It's a plan, my friend. It's a good plan. I'll get some help out to the house with me. If Mr. and Mrs. Cameron are anywhere near, we'll find them. And, if they're on the water, the Coast Guard will find them. Appleby knows Kody. He knows that she'll do anything he says as long as she's worried about her parents."

"We're ahead of him by one step this time," Nick said. "He didn't know that she got a call through on her phone, that I heard what went on between them. As far as he knows, we don't have a clue that Kody has been taken, that he has her out in the Everglades."

"She's really the right stuff," Craig said lightly.

She's perfect! Nick thought, and it felt as if the blood burned in his veins.

He knew he probably shouldn't be on the case now. Because he would kill, he would die, to see that she was safe. And that was just the way it was.

CHAPTER TEN

THE AIRBOAT DRIFTED onto the marshy land just before the rise of the hammock.

Kody's heart sank when she thought about the impossibility of the task before them. People had known about the Anthony Green stash forever. Scholars had mused and pondered on it.

They'd agreed that the treasure was in the Everglades.

Where bodies and more had disappeared since the coming of man.

"Get your pack. We'll head straight back," Appleby told her. "That bastard G-man had it down right, just before everything went to hell, before your silly friend freaked out and ran. You know, this could have all been over. We could have found the treasure. I'd have left you out here, where one of those rangers or Miccosukee police would have found you.

"Yep. It could have all been over. You know, letting that man in was the only mistake I made," Appleby said, and shrugged. "He talked a good story—he pulled it off. He acted as if he could be tough when needed." He grinned at Kody. "Maybe that's why you two hit it off so well. Two actors, cast in different roles in life."

Appleby laughed, amused by his observation. "Okay, let's go. Get back there. We're going to find the site of the pilings, and we're going to start digging."

"Don't you think that this is a little crazy?" Kody asked him. "The local police know that you were here, the FBI know that you were here…they'll have someone out here."

"Why would they have someone out here?"

"It was a crime scene!"

Appleby laughed. "They looked for me here. They didn't find me here. They've moved on. They're checking the airlines and private planes. They're going to be certain that I've fled the area. They won't be looking for me here. So let's get started."

"This is ridiculous. It's dark. I can step on a snake. You can step on a snake. I saw gator holes back there. You could piss off a gator—"

"Yep. So let's hurry. Over here. That's where your lover boy seemed to be when all hell broke loose. And he was going by your determination."

It was insane. Maybe by daylight. Maybe with a dozen people digging and working…

"It could be worse," Appleby said.

"Really?"

"It could be summer." Appleby laughed and swatted his neck. "If it was summer, the mosquitos would be unbearable."

Every step in the night was torture. At least, once they had moved in from the edges of the hammock, the ground was sturdy, a true limestone shelf.

It was difficult to get a bearing in the darkness. While the stars remained in the sky, the glow of the flashlights only illuminated circles of light; large, yes, but not large enough. She heard the chirping of crickets and, now and then, something else. Something that slunk into the water from the land. Something that moved through the trees. There were wild boars out here, she knew. Dangerous creatures if threatened. There were Florida panthers, too. Horribly endangered, and yet, if one was there, and threatened...

She kept walking, searching the ground, a sense of panic beginning to rise within her as she thought about the hopelessness of what she was doing. And then she came upon an indentation in the earth. She paused and shone her light down.

The dry area of the heavy pine piling would have eroded with time. But beneath the limestone and far into the water, the wood had been preserved.

She'd found it.

A piling that indicated the corner of the main chickee where, decades ago, Anthony Green had maintained the Everglades "office" for his illicit distillery.

She looked up; Appleby was staring at her.

"Time to dig!"

"WE'VE BEEN WATCHING HER. She has been safe," Jason Tiger told Nick. "You don't see them, but there are three men with me, watching from different angles. Oliver Osceola is in a tree over there—he's closest. Appleby has kept his gun out, so we've been exceptionally careful not to be seen or to startle him in any way." He was quiet for a minute. "We have a sniper. A good one. David Cypress served three tours of duty in the Middle East. If we need—"

"We need to keep watching now. My partner is searching for Kody Cameron's parents. She'll throw herself in front of him, if she's worried about what will happen to her folks." The burning sensation remained with Nick, something that he fought—reminding himself over and over again that he was a federal agent, responsible to his calling. He would make every move the way a federal agent would—and that included killing Appleby point-blank if necessary to save a civilian.

The time taken to reach the hammock deep in the Everglades behind Shark Valley had seemed to be a lifetime.

He was here now.

He could see Appleby and Kody.

"All right, we're ready," Jason Tiger said. "You call the shots."

Nick nodded and ducked low into the grass. He kept as close to the ground as he could, making his way around to the area where Kody and Appleby were standing. He came close enough to hear them speaking.

"That's it! Now dig. It's there somewhere! You see! Ah, you were such a doubter, Miss Cameron! Dig! We have found it."

Kody was trying to assemble a foldable spade.

"You need to make a phone call," she said.

"I need you to dig."

"Make the call. It's been an hour again. I mean it— make the call."

"What if I just cut you up a little bit, Miss Cameron?"

"Then you'd have to dig yourself," Kody told him. "Make the call."

"You want me to make a call? Fine, I'll make a call."

Appleby pulled out his phone. He placed a call. He appeared to be speaking to someone.

But Nick wondered if there was actually anyone on the other end.

Had the man really taken Kody's parents out on a

boat somewhere? Did he have new accomplices watching over them, actually ready to kill?

Or had Nick been right? Were they somewhere near their own home?

Still a safe distance, hunkered low in the rich grasses, Nick put a call through to Craig. "Anything yet?"

"No. But we have search-and-rescue dogs on the way. We're going to find them. What's going on at your end? Have you found Kody and Appleby?"

"We have them. Jason Tiger has had them in sight. We're good here. Just…just find Kody's parents."

As he spoke he heard the dogs start to bay. They were on to something. He suddenly found himself praying that Craig and the men and the dogs weren't going to find corpses. The corpses of two people he had never met.

"Bones," Craig said over the phone.

"Bones?"

"And a little gravestone. For JoJo, a little dog who died about a decade ago."

"Oh, lord. Craig—"

"Hold up. We've got something. The dogs are heading across the street. There's a park over there. I think he has them in the park, Nick. Right back with you!"

KODY DIDN'T TRUST APPLEBY. She knew the man really didn't care if people lived or died.

She wondered with a terrible, sinking feeling if her parents weren't already dead. If Appleby hadn't come into the house, waited for them and shot them down in cold blood…

"I want to talk to my mother," she said.

"What?"

"I want to talk to my mother. I want to know that she's

alive. I don't believe you and I don't trust you. And this is sick and ridiculous, and if I'm going to continue to search and help you, I want to know that my mother is alive!" Kody said determinedly.

"Do you know what I could do, little girl?" Appleby asked her. "Do you have any idea of what I could do to you? Let me describe a few possibilities. Your knee-caps. You can't imagine the pain of having your knee-cap shot out. I could shoot them both—and then leave you here. Eventually birds of prey and other creatures would come along and then the fun would really start. They would eat you alive. Slowly. They're very fond of soft tissue, especially birds of prey. They love to pluck out eyes…you can't begin to imagine. With any luck, you'd be dead by then."

Kody wasn't about to be swayed. "I want to talk to my mother."

"You can't talk to your mother."

"Why not? Is she dead? If she's dead, I don't give a damn what you do to me."

"She can't talk because there isn't anyone with her to hand her a phone!"

"I thought she was being held on a boat by people who would kill her."

"She's alive and well, Kody. Okay, maybe not so *well*, but she is alive. She's just tied up at the moment."

"Tied up where?"

"Does it matter? She can't talk right now." Appleby let out a growl of aggravation. "She can't talk. I knocked them out, left them tied up. They're alive, Kody."

"How do I trust you?"

"How do you not? You don't have a choice. Start moving. The longer you take, the more danger there is for your mom and dad."

"Maybe you've never even had them!" Kody said.

Appleby grinned. "Mom. Her name is Elizabeth, nickname Beth. She's about five feet, six inches. A pretty brunette with short, bobbed hair. Dad—Daniel. Six-two, blue eyes, graying dark hair. Yep, not to worry, Kody, dear, I do know the folks."

Kody managed to snap her shovel into working condition. For a moment she stared at Appleby, then she studied the ground and jumped back.

"What?" Appleby demanded.

"Snake."

"It will move."

"Yes, I'm trying to let it. It's a very big snake."

"It's just a ball python," Appleby said. "Someone's pet they let loose out here. Damn, but I hate that! People being so irresponsible. They've ruined the ecosystem."

Kody stared at him. He hadn't minded shooting an accomplice at close range. But he was worried about the ecosystem.

Thankfully, the snake at her feet was a non-native constrictor instead of a viper.

She swallowed hard.

The snake was gone.

She started to dig.

"TELL ME YOU'VE got something!" Nick whispered to Craig.

"Yes! We've got them. They were left under the bridge at the edge of the park. They couldn't twist or turn a lot or they'd have been in a canal. But we have them. We have them both. Elizabeth and Daniel Cameron are safe."

"Roger that. Thank you," Nick said. He clicked the phone closed, then inched through the grass and rose slightly, giving a signal to Jason Tiger to hold for his cue.

Kody suddenly let out a little cry, stepping backward.

"What?" Appleby demanded.

"Another snake…it's a coral snake. A little coral snake, but they can be really dangerous."

"No, that's not a coral snake. It's just a rat snake. Rat snakes are not poisonous."

"'Red touch yellow, kill a fellow. Black touch yellow, friend of Jack,'" Kody said, quoting the age-old way children were taught to recognize coral snakes from their non-venomous cousins.

"Yeah! Look, black on yellow!" Appleby said.

"No, red is touching yellow!"

"You want to get your nose down there and check?" he demanded.

"I am not touching that snake!" Kody said.

Appleby made a move. Nick could judge the man's body motion, the way that he crouched. He was getting ready to strike out.

And that was it.

Nick went flying across the remaining distance between them.

Appleby spun around, but he never knew Nick was coming, never saw what hit him. Nick head-butted the man, bringing him down to the ground.

The man's gun went flying.

They could all hear the popping sound as it was sucked into the swamp.

Appleby made no effort to struggle. Nick had raised

a fist; Appleby just stared at him. He started to laugh. "You won't do it, will you? Pansy lawman. You won't do it. In fact..."

Nick didn't listen to the rest; he was already rising. Jason Tiger and his men were coming in to take the prisoner.

He looked over at Kody, who was standing there, shaking. She hadn't moved from her position; she was just staring at him.

Then she flew at him, her fists banging against his chest. "Nick! You idiot, he has my mom and dad. He's going to kill my mom and dad. He'll never tell us—"

"That's right! They'll die!" Appleby chortled.

Nick caught Kody's hands. He turned and glanced at Appleby. "No, actually, Dan and Beth are just fine. They're being checked out at Mercy Hospital as we speak, but I imagine they'll be home by the time Kody and I manage to get back in."

Kody went limp, falling against him. "Really?"

"Really," he said.

He started to lead her back toward the police boat that had brought him to the hammock.

"Thank you!" she whispered.

"You did it, you know. Getting the call through. If you hadn't managed that, no one would have known. You did it, Kody."

She looked up at him. "I called the right guy, huh?" she said softly.

He kissed her lightly, holding her close, and heedless of who might see.

Appleby let out a horrendous scream. "It got me! It got me! Son of a bitch, it got me! Help, you've got to get

me help, fast. You have to slice it, suck the poison out...
It got me. You bastards, do something!"

"Oh, I don't know," Jason Tiger said. "David, did you
see the snake?"

"Had to be a rat snake."

With Appleby supported between them, Jason Tiger
and David Cypress walked by them. Jason Tiger winked.
Rat snake, he mouthed to Nick.

And Nick grinned.

Yep...

Let Appleby do a little wondering, after what he had
done to others.

The winter's night was nearly over. Morning's light
was on the way. And with it, Nick felt, all good things.

It was done. Case over, the way he liked it.

Appleby would rot beyond bars.

And Kody was safe, in his arms.

"'HE HATH, MY LORD, of late made many tenders of his
affection to me!'"

Beyond a doubt, Dakota Cameron made the most
stunning Ophelia that Nick had ever seen.

The play was definitely different; not that, until now,
he'd really been an expert on plays.

He was learning.

But even with what he knew, *Hamlet Thus They Say*
was a different kind of show. Of course, Kody was beyond stupendous and Nick could hear the buzz among
the people around him.

It was going to be a hit.

There was no real curtain call; the play just continued
for four hours each night. There was no intermission. It
was "living theater."

And it was FBI night.

Craig was there with Kieran. Mike, Craig's partner, was there. Nick had been glad to learn that he would be repartnered with Sherri Haskell, and she was there with her New York City cop husband, Mo.

Director Egan had even come out for the night.

They waited in front of the theater for the last of the attendees to leave.

"I can't believe that they didn't break character—not once!" Kieran said, smiling at Nick. "Okay, so, actually, I can't believe you disappear, Kody goes home to settle some things, and you come back a duo, having caught a man who held a spot on the Ten Most Wanted list—and found a treasure that's been missing for decades."

"Ah, but we didn't find the treasure!" Nick told her.

"I think you did."

Nick laughed softly, looking at Craig. "Poor Ophelia, going mad for love! I think Craig and I did a bit of the same. The county, the federal government and the Miccosukee Tribe all got together—and that's when they found the treasure. None of us stayed because, as we know, the FBI is a commitment—and because the show must go on. That's a commitment for Kody.

"We stayed in Miami just long enough for her to spend a day with her parents. Then we all had to be back up here. But, yes, Kody's research and logic led those forces to the stash. They had to dig pretty deep. I don't think that Nathan Appleby would have managed to get it all out. He might have found some pieces, though. It had been buried in leather cases, and they were coming apart. But, yes, the stash was filled with gold pieces—South African—and emeralds, diamonds, you name it."

"What will happen with it all?" Kieran asked.

"I understand some of the pieces will wind up in a museum. Some will go to the state and some will wind up helping to keep the Crystal Manor going. It will be part of the trust that runs the place—along with Kody's family. And speaking of Kody's family..." He paused, waving as Daniel and Beth Cameron exited the theater. Nick drew them over and introduced them to those in their group they hadn't met already.

Of course, on arrival in the city, they'd been brought to Finnegan's and feted with stout from excellent taps and the world's best shepherd's pie.

"Wow. And you're FBI, too?" Daniel asked Sherri.

"Yes, sir. I am."

"Well, our girl will be hanging around with a good crowd," Daniel told his wife.

"Yes, certainly," Beth Cameron said, but she looked a little puzzled.

"Is anything wrong?" Nick asked her.

"No, no, of course not. I'm not so sure that I get it. I mean, living theater, or whatever it is. I'm used to the actors just...acting on stage. I've never talked with the actors before during a performance," she said. "But, of course, Kody and Kevin were wonderful!"

Kieran laughed. "Yes, they were. They were both wonderful."

"She talked to me—but as if she didn't know me!" Daniel said.

"Well, she doesn't know you. Not as Ophelia," Nick explained.

"Yes, yes, of course. She's playing a role. I guess. I mean, of course. It's just strange," Beth said. She sighed. "She has a beautiful voice. Maybe it will be a musical next. Oh, look!" she murmured, catching Nick by the hand. "There—do you know who that is?"

Nick looked. No, he didn't.

"That's Mayor Holden Burke. With his little boy, Adrian. And his wife, Monica."

The man, next to the boy who appeared to be about nine, noted Beth just as she was whispering about him.

He waved and came over, catching the hands of his wife and son so they would join him. Adrian Burke was carrying a large bouquet of flowers.

Beth introduced people all around.

"We're so grateful," he said, and his wife nodded, looking around. "You're the agents who were involved?"

"Craig and I were down there," Nick said. "But, like I said in my debriefing, in all honesty, Kody was the one who got Nathan Appleby to say where Adrian was being held. And an agent down in South Florida, Jason Tiger, got the information back to the city."

The cast door opened and the actors were all coming out. There was a round of applause that sounded up and down the street.

Nick saw Kody, and saw that she was searching through the crowd.

Looking for him, he thought. He waved and then watched her chat and smile with grace and courtesy as she spoke to fans and signed programs.

"Excuse us," Mayor Burke said.

Nick realized, as the mayor and his family approached Kody, that she'd never actually met them.

She took the flowers from Adrian, hugged him and planted a kiss on his cheek. She was hugged by the mayor and his wife.

The three left then, waving to the others.

And, finally, the crowd around the performers had just about thinned out.

He, Kody's parents, the Finnegans and the extended FBI family made their way over to the group, congratulating the actors. Nick bypassed everyone, going directly to Kody and taking her in his arms.

Her kiss was magnificent. Her eyes touched his with promise. She was filled with the excitement and adrenaline of opening night; she was also anxious, he knew, for their time together.

But first, of course, they all made their way to Finnegan's for a late-night supper and a phenomenal Irish band.

And, at last, it was time for him and Kody to leave.

In his company car they saw her parents to their hotel in midtown. Then they headed for his apartment.

When they'd first returned to the city a few weeks ago, they'd kept both apartments. That had proved to be a total waste. They both worked, and worked hard, but their free time was spent together.

When a night bartender at Finnegan's was about to lose his lease—his apartments were being turned into condos—Kody offered her apartment to him, and so, just last week, she had made the official move into Nick's place.

It was simply the best accommodation: a full bedroom, an office, a parlor, two baths. Plus it was situated right on the subway line that connected Finnegan's and the FBI offices and midtown.

Kody, of course, had already made some changes, and Nick loved them.

There were posters on the wall—show posters and band posters—and there was artwork, as well. Seascapes, mostly, from Florida, and paintings from New York City, too.

One of his favorite pieces they had bought together down in the Village. It was a signed painting of the Brooklyn Bridge.

"A new artist—who will be a famous artist one day," Kody had said. "And if not, it's still a brilliant painting and I love it."

She was, he thought, everything he needed.

Life, as he saw it, was too often grim. But Kody looked for the best, always. And she saw the best that way. She showed it to him, as well.

"So, what did you think of the play? What did you really think?" she asked when they stepped into the apartment, alone at last.

"I loved it," he said.

"Really?"

"I really did. But I do believe you have to have the right cast for that kind of theater. Your cast is truly amazing. Powerful performers—they all engaged the audience."

"I don't think my mom saw it that way."

Nick laughed. "She admitted to a bit of confusion."

"But you really thought that it was good?" she asked.

"I, like the critics, raved!"

She flew into his arms, kissing him. "Are you a liar?" she asked.

"No!"

She laughed. "Doesn't matter," she said. "You were there for me, on FBI night."

"I'll come to the show whenever I can."

"You don't have to. It's okay. We'll settle in and we'll figure it all out—the time, the FBI, the theater..."

"I know we will," he told her. And he kissed her again, shrugging out of his jacket as he did so. It had been a chilly night. Kody was in a heavy wool coat and it, too, hit the floor.

She kicked off her shoes, their lips never parting.

Nick suddenly dipped low and swept her off her feet. She laughed as she looked up at him.

"It's been a dramatic night. Thought I should be dramatic, too."

"You really are quite the actor. You know, down in Florida when I first saw you, I really thought you were a bad guy."

"But not really. You said you knew I wasn't a killer."

"You played the part very well."

"Thank you. If the law-enforcement thing fails…"

She touched his face gently, studying his eyes. "It won't. You love what you do, and you're very good, and I would never want anything different for you."

"Nor would I change a thing about you," he told her huskily.

She smiled.

They headed into the bedroom and Nick laid Kody carefully upon the sheets, kneeling beside her. He kissed her lips again, but she was impatient and rose against him, crawling over him, straddling him, while she tore away her clothes.

"Ah, my lady! Wait, I have a surprise for you," he said.

She laughed softly. "And I have a surprise for you! I can wait for nothing." And she shoved him down. She lay against him, teased his shoulders, chest and abdomen with her kisses as she tugged at his clothing, entangled them both in it, and laughed as they finally managed to strip down completely. She whispered to him, touching him, making love to him with a combination of tenderness and fierceness that drove him wild.

It was later, much later, when he lay sated and incredulous, cradling her to him, his chin atop her head, that she said, "You told me you had a surprise for me."

"Ah, yes!"

He got out of bed and Kody sat up to watch him, curious as he left the room.

He'd never been with an actress before.

This one, he knew he would love all his life. Therefore, he had figured, he would get it right.

He plucked the champagne from the refrigerator and prepared the ice bucket.

The plate of chocolate-covered strawberries was ready, as well.

Along with the long-stemmed roses. And a tiny box.

He swept up the bucket, the plate balanced atop it, the roses in his mouth. And he walked back into the bedroom.

Kody cried out with delight, clapping her hands.

"Oh, but you are perfect! Perfect! Roses, chocolate-covered strawberries, champagne—and a naked FBI guy! What more could one want?"

They both burst into laughter.

And he joined her in the bed.

They popped the cork on the champagne, laughed as it spilled over. They shared the strawberries and Kody smelled the roses and looked at him seriously.

"I love you so much," she whispered. "Is it…is it all right to say that? I tend to speak quickly, rashly, sometimes. I mean…well, you know. I probably could have gotten myself or someone else killed back in Florida if you weren't you. If you hadn't been undercover. If—"

He pulled her into his arms. "I wouldn't have you any other way at all. I love that you said what you did. I love you. And…"

He realized he was terribly nervous. He might be a well-trained agent, but his fingers were trembling as he reached for the little box.

Kody took the box, her eyes on his. She opened it and stared in silence.

His heart sank. "It's too soon, too much," he murmured. "I—"

She threw her arms around him, and kissed him, and kissed him, and kissed him.

"Is that a yes?"

"Yes!" She laughed. "Not even I am that good an actress!"

He took the ring and slipped it on her finger. "Since we're living in sin…?"

"This kind of love could never be a sin," she assured him.

"You're really so beautiful…in every way," he told her.

She smiled—a mischievous smile. "With the pick-up line you gave me in Florida, who would have thought that we would wind up here!"

"Go figure," he agreed.

He kissed her and lay her back on the bed.

"Go figure," he repeated.

And he started kissing her again and again…

It was, after all, opening night. For the show.

And for the rest of their lives.

* * * * *

IN THE DARK

To Mary Stella, with lots of love.
To both the Dolphin Research Organization
and the Theater of the Sea, with thanks.

PROLOGUE

ALEX NEARLY SCREAMED as her foot hit the shell. She choked down the sound just in time but still stumbled, and that was when she fell.

She'd missed the shell, running in the dark. As she lay there, winded from landing hard on the sand, she damned the darkness. In just another few hours, it would be light.

In just a matter of minutes, the eye of the storm would have passed and the hundred-mile winds of Hurricane Dahlia would be picking up again. And here she was, lying next to the water, completely vulnerable.

She rolled quickly, gasping for breath, ready to leap back to her feet. She didn't dare take the time to survey the injury to her foot, as the constant prayer that had been rushing through her mind continued. Please, just let me reach the resort. Please...

A thrashing sound came from the brush behind her.

The killer was close.

She would have to run again, heading for the safety of the resort. Or would even that be safety now?

She needed to reach the resort without being seen, needed to reach the lockbox behind the check-in, where the Smith & Wesson was kept. She was almost certain no one else had taken the gun.

Move! She silently commanded herself. What was she waiting for?

There was no one who could help her, no one she could trust.

She had to depend on only herself, no matter how desperately she wanted to believe in at least one man....

It was then that, so near that she could recognize him despite the darkness, she saw Len Creighton, prone on the sand.

Another body, she thought, panic rising in her. Well, she had wondered where he was. And now she knew. He was lying facedown on the sand, a trickle of blood running down his face. The wild surf was breaking over his legs where he lay surrounded by clumps of seaweed. Already, little crabs were scouring the area, carefully eyeing what they hoped would be their next meal.

She choked back a scream. Above her, the clouds broke. Pale light emerged from the heavens.

And that was when the first man exploded from the bush.

"Alex!" he called. "Get over here."

He stood there, panting for breath, beckoning to her, eyes sharply surveying the area. And he was carrying a speargun, one that had been used on some living creature already—blood dripped from the tip. "Alex, you've got to trust me. Come with me now—quickly."

"No!"

He spun on a dime at the sound of the second voice.

A second man. This one carrying a Glock, which was aimed at the first man.

"Alex, come to me. Get away from him," the newcomer insisted.

The men faced off, staring, each one aware of the weapon the other was carrying.

"Alex!"

This time, she wasn't even sure which man spoke. Once she had trusted them both. One, she had loved before. The other had so nearly seduced her heart in the days just past.

"Alex!"

There was what appeared to be a dead man at her feet. A co-worker. A friend. She should be down on her knees, attempting to find life, however hopeless that might be. But one of the two men facing her was a killer. She couldn't look away. Seconds ticked by, and she stood frozen in place.

Her heart insisted that it couldn't be either man.

Especially not him.

She couldn't think. She could only stand there and stare, eyes going from one man to the other, everything within her soul screaming that neither one of them could be a killer.

But one of them was.

She could feel the ocean lapping over her feet. She knew these waters so well, like the back of her hand.

So did they.

No, not these waters. Not this island. She knew it as few other people could.

There was only one thing she could do, even though it was insanity. The storm might have passed for the moment, but the sea was far from placid. The waves were still deadly. The currents would be merciless.

And yet...

She had no other choice.

She turned to the sea and dove into it, and as she

swam for her life, she realized that a few days ago, she wouldn't have believed this.

That was when it had all begun. Just days ago.

She felt the surge of her arms and legs as she strove to put distance between herself and the shore.

Something sped past her in the water. A bullet? A spear?

People always said that in the last seconds of some-one's life, their entire past rushed before their eyes.

She wasn't seeing that far back.

Just to that morning, by the dolphin lagoon, when she had found the first body on the beach.

The one that had disappeared.

CHAPTER ONE

"THE MAIN THING to remember is that here at Moon Bay, we consider our dolphins our guests. When you're swimming with them, don't turn and stalk them, because, for one thing, they're faster than you can begin to imagine, and they'll disappear on you in seconds flat. And also, they hate it. Let them come to you—and they will. They're here because they're social creatures. We never force them to interact with people—they want to. Any animal in the lagoon knows how to leave the playing arena. And when they choose to leave, we respect their desire to do so. When they come to you naturally, you're free to stroke them as they pass. Try to keep your hands forward of the dorsal fin. And just stroke—don't pound or scratch, okay?"

Alex McCord's voice was smooth and normal—or so she hoped—as she spoke with the group of eight gathered before her. She had done a lot of smiling, while she first assured the two preteen girls and the teenage boy, who looked like a troublemaker, that she wasn't angry but they would follow the rules. A few of her other smiles had been genuine and directed at two of the five adults rounding out the dive, the father of the boy and the mother of the girls.

Then there were her forced smiles. Her face was beginning to hurt, those smiles were so forced.

Because she just couldn't believe who was here.

The world was filled with islands. And these days the world was even filled with islands that offered a dozen variations of the dolphin experience.

So what on earth was David Denham doing here, on her island, suddenly showing an extraordinary curiosity regarding her dolphins? Especially when his experiences must reduce her swims to a mom-and-pop outing, since he'd been swimming with great whites at the Great Barrier Reef, photographed whales in the Pacific, fed lemon sharks off Aruba and filmed ray encounters in Grand Cayman. So why was he here? It had been months since she'd seen him, heard from him or even bothered to read any of the news articles regarding him.

But here he was, the ultimate ocean man. Diver, photographer and salvage entrepreneur extraordinaire. Six-two, broad shoulders bronzed, perfect features weathered, deep blue gaze focused on her as if he were fascinated by her every word, even though his questions made it clear he knew as much about dolphins as she did.

She might not have minded so much, except that for once she had been looking forward to the company of another man—an arresting and attractive man who apparently found her attractive, as well.

John Seymore, an ex–navy SEAL, was looking to set up a dive business in the Keys. Physically, he was like a blond version of David. And his eyes were green, a pleasant, easygoing, light green. Despite his credentials, he'd gone on her morning dive tour the day before, and she'd chatted with him at the Tiki Hut last night and found out that he'd signed on for the dolphin swim, as well. He'd admitted that he knew almost nothing about the creatures but loved them.

She'd had a couple of drinks…she'd danced. She'd gone so far as to imagine sex.

And now…here was David. Distorting the image of a barely formed mirage before it could even begin to find focus. They were divorced. She had every right to envision a life with another man, so the concept of a simple date shouldn't make her feel squeamish. After all, she sincerely doubted that her ex-husband had been sitting around idle for a year.

"They're really the most extraordinary creatures in the world," Laurie Smith, one of Alex's four assistants, piped up. Had she simply stopped speaking, Alex wondered, forcing Laurie to chime in? Actually, Alex was glad Laurie had spoken up. Alex had been afraid that she was beginning to look like a bored tour guide, which wasn't the case at all. She had worked with a number of animals during her career. She had never found any as intelligent, clever and personable as dolphins. Dogs were great, and so were chimps, but dolphins were magical.

"You never feel guilty, as if the dolphins are scientific rats in a lab—except, of course, that entertaining tourists isn't exactly medical research."

That came from the last member of the group, the man to whom she needed to be giving the most serious attention. Hank Adamson. He wasn't as muscled or bronzed as David and John, but he was tall and lithe, wiry, sandy-haired, and wearing the most stylish sunglasses available. He was handsome in a smooth, sleek, electric way and could be the most polite human being on earth. He could also be cruel. He was a local columnist, and he also contributed to travel magazines and tour guides about the area. He could, if he thought it was justified, be savage, ripping apart motels, hotels, restaurants, theme parks and clubs. There was something humorous about his acidic style, which led to his articles being syndicated across the country. Alex found him an irritating bastard, but Jay Galway, manager of the entire Moon Bay facility, was desperate to get a good review from the man.

Adamson had seemed to enjoy the dive-boat activities the day before. She'd been waiting for some kind of an assault, though, since he'd set foot on the island. And here it was.

"The lagoon offers the animals many choices, Mr. Adamson. They can play, or they can retire to their private area. Additionally, our dolphins were all born in captivity, except for Shania, and she was hurt so badly by a boat propeller that she wouldn't have survived in the open sea. We made one attempt to release her, and she came right back. Dolphins are incredibly intelligent creatures, and I believe that they're as interested in learning about our behavior as we are in theirs." She shifted focus to address the group at large. "Let's begin. Is there any particular behavior you've seen or experienced with the dolphins you'd like to try again?"

"I want to ride a dolphin," the boy, Zach, said.

"The fin ride. Sure, we can start with that. Would you like to go first?"

"Yeah, can I?"

She smiled. Maybe the kid wasn't a demon after all. Dolphins had a wonderful effect on people. Once, she'd been given a group of "incorrigibles" from a local "special" school. They'd teased and acted like idiots at first. Then they'd gotten into the water and become model citizens.

"Absolutely. One dolphin or two?"

"Two is really cool," David said quietly, offering a slight grin to the boy.

"Two."

"Okay, in the water, front and center. Fins on, no masks or snorkels right now," Alex said.

The others waited as the boy went out into the lagoon and extended his arms as Alex indicated. She signaled to Katy and Sabra, and the two dolphins sleekly obeyed the command, like silver streaks of light sliding beneath the water's surface.

Zach was great, taking a firm hold of each fin and smiling like a two-year-old with an oversize lollipop as the mammals swam him through the water, finishing up by the floating dock, where they were rewarded as they dropped their passenger. Zach was still beaming.

"Better than any ride I've ever been on in my life!" he exclaimed.

"Can I go next?" one of the girls asked. Tess. Cute little thing, bright eyes, dark hair. Zach had been trying to impress her earlier. Tess opted for one dolphin, and Alex chose Jamie-Boy.

One by one, everyone got to try the fin ride. John Seymore was quieter than the kids, but obviously pleased. Even Hank Adamson—for all his skepticism and the fact that he seemed to be looking for something to condemn—enjoyed his swim.

Alex was afraid that David would either demur—this was pretty tame stuff for him—or do something spectacular. God knew what he might whisper to a dolphin, and what a well-trained, social animal might do in response. But David was well-behaved, looking as smooth and sleek as the creatures themselves as he came out of the water. The only irritating thing was that he and John

Seymore seemed to find a tremendous amount to talk about whenever she was busy with the others. Then, during the circle swim, David disappeared beneath the surface for so long that the two parents in the group began to worry that he had drowned.

"Are you sure he's all right?" Ally Conroy, Zach's mother, asked Alex.

"I know him," Alex told the woman, forcing another of those plastic smiles that threatened to break her face. "He can hold his breath almost as long as the dolphins."

David surfaced at last. Macy, the staff photographer, just shrugged at Alex. They made a lot of their research funding by selling people photos of their dolphin experiences, but Alex and Macy both knew David didn't need to buy any photos.

At that point, David and John began talking quietly in the background, as Alex got the others going on their chance for dolphin hugs and smooches. She couldn't hear what the two men were saying, but she was annoyed, and became more so when Hank Adamson joined the conversation. She found them distracting, but had a feeling she'd look foolish if she were to freak out and yell at the lot of them to shut up. It looked like a little testosterone party going. They were probably chatting about diving—in a manly way, of course.

Why did it bother her so much? David was out of her life. No, David would never be out of her life.

The thought was galling. She had been able to see that the relationship wasn't working, that time wasn't going to change the facts about him, her or the situation. And they had split. She didn't regret the decision.

It's just that he was here again now, when she had a lovely minor flirtation going on, the most exciting thing she'd experienced since the divorce. And just because the object of her current affections seemed to be getting on with David as if they were long-lost friends…

"Hey," Zach whispered to her, his eyes alight, "those guys aren't paying any attention. The girls and I could sneak in and take their hugs, huh?"

She would have loved to agree. But no matter what it looked like Hank Adamson was doing, he was a reporter. One whose writing could influence the fate of Moon Bay. She had to play fair.

"I'd love to give them to you and the girls, but it wouldn't be right."

"Zach, you can take my place."

She hadn't known that David had broken away from his conversation.

She stared at him. "The girls would want an equal opportunity."

"Hey, I'll give up my time." That, amazingly, came from Hank Adamson. He grinned at Alex. "It's cool watching the kids have fun. Don't worry—you're getting a good write-up."

"I'll give up my hug, too," John Seymore told her, shrugging, a dimple going deep.

"Another round for the youngest members of the group, then," she said.

Finally the time was up. Alex went through her spiel about returning flippers, masks, and snorkels, telling the group where they could rinse off the brine and find further information on dolphins before heading off for whatever their next adventure might be.

John gave her a special smile as he stopped to thank her. "I was figuring I'd do it again, maybe check out a time when the groups weren't full. I don't have a thing in the world against hugs. Even from a dolphin."

She smiled in return, nodding.

"I think I have an in with the dolphin keeper," he added softly.

"You do," she assured him.

He turned, walking off. David had been right behind him. He'd undoubtedly heard every word. Now his dark blue eyes were on her enigmatically. She wished he wasn't even more appealing soaking wet, that thatch of impossibly dark hair over his forehead, bronzed shoulders gleaming. She wished there wasn't such an irresistibly subtle, too-familiar scent about him. Soap, cologne, his natural essence, mingled with the sea and salty air.

"Nice program you've got going," he said. "Thanks."

Then he walked away. He didn't even shake her hand, as the others had. He didn't touch her.

She felt burned.

"Thanks," she returned, though he was already too far away to hear her.

"You okay?"

Alex whirled. Laurie was watching her worriedly.

"So hunky-dory I could spit," Alex assured her, causing Laurie to smile.

Then her friend cocked her head, set her hands on her hips and sighed. "Poor baby. Two of the most attractive men I've seen in a long time angling for your attention, and you look as if you've been caught in a bees' nest."

"Trust me, David is not angling for my attention."

"You should have seen the way he was looking at you."

"You were reading it wrong, I guarantee you."

Laurie frowned. "I thought the divorce went smoothly."

"Very smoothly. I don't think he even noticed," Alex told her ruefully. She lifted a hand in vague explanation. "He was in the Caribbean on a boat somewhere when I filed the papers. He didn't call, didn't protest…just sent his attorney with the clear message to let me do whatever I wanted, have whatever I wanted…. I was married, then I wasn't, and it was all so fast, my head was spinning."

"Well, that certainly didn't mean he hated you."

"I never said he hated me."

"Well…want my advice?"

"No."

Laurie grinned. "That's because you've never been to a place like Date Tournament."

"What?"

"I told you I was going the other day," Laurie said impatiently. "It's that new club in Key Largo. They've been doing it all over the country. You go, and you keep changing tables, chatting with different people for about ten minutes each. The idea isn't bad. I mean, there are nice guys out there, not just jerks. Some are heart-broken—like me. And some are just looking. Imagine, the perfect person for me could walk by me in a mall, but we'd never talk. We never see someone and just walk up and say, 'Hey, you're good-looking, the right age, are you straight? Attached? Do you have kids? Do you like the water? We wouldn't last a day if you didn't.' So at Date Tournament, you at least get to meet people who are looking for people. Sexual preference and marital status are all straightened out before you start. You're not stuck believing some jerk in a bar who says he's sin-gle, gets more out of the night than a girl set out to give, then apologizes because he has to get home before his wife catches him."

Alex stared at her blankly for a minute. Laurie was beautiful, a natural platinum blonde with a gorgeous smile, charm and spontaneity. It had never really occurred to Alex that her friend had the least difficulty dating. Living at Moon Bay seemed perfect for Alex. She had her own small but atmospheric little cottage, surrounded by subtropical growth—and daily maid service. There was the Tiki Hut off the lagoons for laid-back evenings, buffets in the main house for every meal, a small but well-run bookstore and every cable channel known to man. She thought ruefully that just because she had been nursing a wounded heart all this time, she'd had no reason to think the others were all as happy with celibacy as she was.

She arched an eyebrow, wishing she hadn't spent so much time being nearly oblivious to the feelings of others.

"So...how was your evening at Date Tournament?"

"Scary. Sad," Laurie said dryly. "Want to hear about it?"

"Yes, but I want to get away from here first," Alex said. She could see across the lagoon, and the Tiki Hut was beginning to fill up for cocktail hour. Fishing parties returning, those who'd been out on scuba and snorkeling trips coming in, and those who had lazed the day away at the beach or the pool. She could see that Hank Adamson was talking to her boss, Jay Galway, head of operations at Moon Bay, and he was pointing toward the dolphin lagoons.

She didn't want to smile anymore, or suck up to Adamson—or defend herself. They were also standing with a man named Seth Granger, a frequent visitor, a very rich retired businessman who had decided he wanted to become a salvage expert. He signed up for dives and swims, then complained that they weren't adventurous enough. Alex had wished for a very long time that she could tell him not to go on the dives when he didn't enjoy the beauty of the reefs. Their dives were planned to show off the incredible color and beauty to be found on the only continental reef in the United States, not for a possible clash with modern-day pirates. Nor were they seeking treasure.

Well, if he wanted to talk about salvage or adventure, he could pin David down one night. They deserved each other.

Jay Galway seemed to be trying to get her attention. She pretended she didn't notice.

"Let's go to the beach on the other side of the island, huh? Then you can tell me all about dating hell," she said to Laurie.

"Mr. Galway is waving at you," Laurie said, running to catch up as Alex took off down the beach. "I think he wants you."

"Then move faster," Alex told her.

She turned, pretended she thought that James was just waving, waved back and took off at a walk so brisk it was nearly a run.

The dolphin lagoons were just around the bend, putting them on the westward side of the island rather than on the strip that faced the Atlantic. There were no roads out here from what wasn't even really the mainland, since they sat eastward of the Middle Keys. A motorboat regularly made the twenty-minute trip from the island to several of the Keys, and a small ferry traveled between several of the Keys, then stopped at the island, five times a day. Moon Bay had only existed for a few years; before its purchase by a large German-American firm, it had been nothing more than a small strip of sand and trees where locals had come to picnic and find solitude.

The western side was still magnificently barren. White-sand beaches were edged by unbelievably clear water on one side, and palms and foliage on the other. Alex loved to escape the actual lodge area, especially at night. While their visitors were certainly free to roam in this direction, mercifully, not many did once it turned to the later portion of the afternoon. Sunbathers loved the area, but by now they were baked, red and in pain.

It was close to six, but the sun was still bright and warm. Nothing like the earlier hours, but nowhere near darkness. The water was calm and lazy; little nothing waves were creating a delicate foam against the shoreline that disappeared in seconds. The palms rustled behind them as they walked, and the delightful sea breeze kept the heat at bay.

Alex glanced up at the sky. It was a beautiful day, glorious. All kinds of tempests might be brewing out in the Atlantic or down in the Gulf somewhere, but here, all was calm and perfect. The sky was a rich, powdery blue, barely touched by the clouds, with that little bit of breeze deflecting the ninety-degree temperature that had slowly begun to drop.

Alex came to a halt and sat down on the wet sand. Laurie followed suit. The identical tank tops they wore—the words Moon Bay etched across black polyester in a soft off-white were light enough that Alex almost shivered when the breeze touched her damp arms. She had little concern for her matching shorts—they were made to take the sand, sun and heat with ease. It was comfortable clothing, perfect for the job, and not suggestive in the least. This was a family establishment.

A great place to run after a bad marriage, with everything she needed: a good job doing what she loved, water, boats, sand, sun, privacy.

Too much privacy.

And now…David was here. Damn him. She wasn't going to change a thing. She was going to do exactly what she had planned. Shower, dress nicely, blow-dry her hair, wear makeup…sip piña coladas and dance at the Tiki Hut. Flirt like hell with John Seymore. And ignore the fact that every single woman in the place would be eyeing David.

Over. It was over. They had gone their separate ways….

"Well?" Laurie said.

"I'm sorry. What?"

"Do you want to hear about Date Tournament? Or do you just want to sit here, me quietly at your side, while you damn yourself for divorcing such a hunk?"

"Never," Alex protested.

"Never as in, you never want to hear about Date Tournament, or never as in…what, exactly? You are divorced, right?"

"Of course. I meant, I'll never regret what I did. It was necessary."

"Why?"

Alex was silent. Why? We were going different ways? We didn't know one another to begin with? It was as simple as…Alicia Farr? No, that was ridiculous. It was complex, as most such matters were. It was his needing adventure at all costs, her needing to be a real trainer. It was...

"Oh my God!" Laurie gasped suddenly, staring at her. "Was he...he was abusive?"

"No! Don't be ridiculous."

"Then...?"

"We just went different ways."

"Hmph." Laurie toed a little crab back toward the water. "Whatever way he was going, I'd have followed him. But then, I've had the experience of Date Tournament, which you haven't—and which I thought you wanted to hear about."

"I'm sorry. I'm being a horrible friend. I'm in shock, I think. Having this lovely time with John Seymore, and then...up pops David."

"So what?"

"It's uncomfortable."

"But you and David are divorced, so what are you worried about? Enjoy John Seymore. He's a hunk, too. Not like anyone I met at Date Tournament."

"There must have been some nice guys."

"If there were, I didn't happen to meet them. Now let's get back to your love triangle."

Alex grinned. "There is no love triangle. Let's get back to you. You're gorgeous, bright, sweet and intelligent. The right guy is going to come along."

"Doesn't seem to be too much wrong with Mr. John Seymore. Did you know he's an ex-navy SEAL? But there you go. Apparently, when my right guy comes along, he wants to date you."

Alex arched an eyebrow, surprised. "I hadn't realized that...that..."

"You hadn't realized 'that' because there was no

'that' to realize. I hadn't even talked to the guy until today. Then there's your ex-husband."

"He's certainly a free agent."

"He's your ex. That's a no-no."

"I repeat—he's a free agent."

"One who sends you into a spiral," Laurie noted.

"I'm not in a spiral. It's just that…I was married to him. That makes me…I don't know what that makes me. Yes, I do. It makes me uncomfortable."

"You never fell out of love with him."

"Trust me—I did. It's just that…"

"All you've had for company since your divorce has been a bunch of sea animals?" Laurie suggested, amused.

"Neither one of us has dated in…a very, very long time," Alex agreed.

Laurie sighed glumly, setting her hands on her knees and cupping her chin in them. "Think it might be due to the fact that we've chosen to live on a remote island where the tourists are usually married, and the staff are usually in college?"

Alex laughed. "Maybe, but you'd think…sun, boats, island—fishing. Oh, well."

"What do you mean, oh well? At least there's excitement in your life. You've got the triangle thing going. Husband, lover."

"Ex-husband and new acquaintance," Alex reminded her.

"Ex-husband, new almost-lover. Vying for the same woman. And you know guys. They get into a competition thing. What a setup for jealousy and…"

Her voice trailed off, and she stared wide-eyed at Alex, like a doe in the headlights.

"Oh my God!" Laurie gasped.

She stared at Alex in pure horror. Alex frowned. "What? Come on, Laurie. Believe me, it's not that serious. You think that they'll get into some kind of a fight? No, never. In our marriage…David just didn't notice. Didn't care. I can't begin to see him decking someone—and sure as hell not over me."

"Oh my God," Laurie breathed again.

"Laurie, it's all right. Nothing is going to happen between David and John."

Laurie shook her head vehemently and slowly got to her feet, pointing. "Oh God, Alex. Look!"

For a moment, Alex couldn't quite shift mental gears. Then she frowned, standing up herself.

"What?" she said to Laurie. She grasped her friend's shoulders. "Laurie, what in the world is it?"

Laurie pointed. Alex realized that Laurie hadn't been staring at her at all during the last few moments—she had been staring past her.

She spun around.

And that was when she saw the body on the beach.

CHAPTER TWO

"I'VE READ ABOUT YOU," John Seymore told David. "In the scuba magazines. That article on your work with great whites...wow. I've got to admit, I'm astounded to see you here. This place must seem pretty tame to you. It's great to get to meet you."

"Thanks," David said.

Seymore seemed pleasant. He was good-looking, well-muscled probably naturally, since he'd said he hadn't been out of military service long. Despite his surfer-boy blond hair and easy smile, there was a rough edge about him that betrayed age, maybe, and a hard life. David had a feeling his military stories would be the kind to make the hair rise on the back of the neck. Just as he had a feeling that, no matter how pleasant the guy might seem, he had a backbone of steel.

They'd started talking during the swim, and when Seymore had suggested a quick drink at the Tiki Hut, David had been glad to comply. He was interested in what would bring a man of John Seymore's expertise to such a charming little tourist haven.

"I know the people here," David told John. "The guy managing the place, Jay Galway, is a part-time thrill seeker. He's been on a few of my excursions over the years. I like coming here, but this is the first time I've stayed. The cottages are great. A perfect place to chill, with all the comforts of home, but you feel as if you're off somewhere in the wilds. What about you?"

"I know the water pretty well, but I've never had any fun with it. I've been out on the West Coast. I left the military...and, I'm afraid, a painful divorce."

"So you retired from the military," David said. "Living a life of ease, huh?"

Seymore laughed. "I did pretty well with the military, but not well enough to retire the way I'd like to. But my time is my own. I'm doing consulting work now. Because of my work in the service, I made some good contacts. But I needed a break, so I found this place on the Web. Seemed ideal, and so far, it has been."

Seymore was leaning on the bar, looking across the lagoon. Everyone was gone, but Seymore was staring as if someone was still there. Someone with features so delicately and perfectly proportioned that she was beautiful when totally drenched, devoid of all makeup, her hair showing touches of its radiant color despite the fact that it was heavy with sea water.

Despite himself, he felt a rise of something he didn't like. Anger. Jealousy. And an age-old instinct to protect what was his. Except that she wasn't his anymore.

He had no rights here, and when he had first seen Alex this morning, after the initial shock in her eyes had died away, they had been narrowed and hostile each time they had fallen on him.

He lowered his head for a moment. You were the one who filed the papers, sweetie. Not a word to me, just a legal document.

I didn't come here because of you, he thought.

Okay, that was a lie. There had been no way he wouldn't show once Alicia's message had whetted his curiosity. He had come expecting to find Alicia Farr, even though, after he had returned her call and not heard back, warning signals had sounded in his mind. He wasn't surprised that she wasn't here, but he was worried.

And now he was feeling that age-old protective-instinct thing coming to the fore with Alex again—whether he did or didn't have the right to feel it. He told himself it was only because he was already on edge over Alicia. And anyway, maybe nothing was going on here. Maybe Alicia had made other arrangements and gone off on her own.

Or maybe someone was dead because of something going on here.

Unease filled him again.

Whatever had happened between Alex and him, the good and the bad, he couldn't help the tension he was feeling now. Especially where his wife was concerned. Ex-wife, he reminded himself. He wondered if he would ever accept that. Wondered if he would ever look at her and not believe they were still one.

Ever fall out of love with her.

Impatience ripped through him. He hated fools who went through life pining after someone who didn't want them in return. He hadn't pined. His life hadn't allowed for it.

That didn't mean that she didn't haunt his days, or that he didn't lie awake at night wondering why. Or that he didn't see her and feel that he would go after any guy who got near her. Or that he didn't see her, watch her move, see her enigmatic blue-green eyes, and want to demand to know what could have been so wrong that she had pushed him away.

All that was beside the point now. Yes, he had come

here to meet Alicia. But he had come to meet Alicia because of Alex.

And now he was going to find out what was going on. Alex, of course, would believe that he was here only to find Alicia, to share in whatever find she had made. In her mind, he would be after the treasure, whatever that might be. Wanting the adventure, the leap into the unknown. No, she would never believe his main reason for being here was her, to watch over her, not when the danger wasn't solid, visible....

"Well," David murmured, swallowing a long draft of beer before continuing. "So you had a bad breakup, huh? They say you've got to be careful after a bad divorce. You know, watch out for rushing into things."

"Yeah, well," John told him, a half grin curving his lips, "they also say you've got to get right back on the horse after you fall off. Besides, I've been divorced about a year. You?"

"The same. About a year."

John Seymore studied him, that wry, half smile still in place. "I admit it. That's half the reason I wanted to buy you a drink. I know you were married to our dolphin instructor. Her name and picture were in one of the articles I read. I guess I wanted to make sure I wasn't horning in on a family reunion."

David could feel his jaw clenching. Screw Seymore. Being decent. Man, he hated that. He leaned on the counter, as well, staring out across the lagoon. "We split up a year ago," he said simply. "Alex is her own person."

What the hell else could he say? It was the truth. He could only hope his bitterness wasn't evident. Yet, even as the words were out of his mouth, he felt uneasy. He was, admittedly, distrustful of everyone right now, but this guy was suspicious of him, too. Here was an ex–navy SEAL, a man who knew more about diving than almost anyone else out there, at a resort where the facilities were great for tourists, but…a man with his experience?

A thought struck him, and he smiled. He was an honest man, but maybe this wasn't the time for the truth.

"Well," he said, "as far as she knows, she is, anyway."

"What does that mean?" Seymore asked him.

David waved a hand dismissively. "That's one of the reasons I'm here. There's a little technicality with our divorce. I wanted to let her know, find a convenient time for us to get together with an attorney, straighten it all out. But, hey…" He clapped a hand on Seymore's shoulder. "It's fine. Really. I think I'll go take a long hot shower. I'm beginning to feel a little salt encrusted. Thanks for the beer."

Seymore nodded, looking a little troubled. "Yeah, I…I guess I'll go hit the shower, too."

"My treat next go-around," David said. Then he set down his glass, turned, and left the Tiki Hut.

It was definitely a body. Alex and Laurie could both clearly see that, despite the seaweed clinging to it.

Alex started to rush forward, but Laurie grabbed her arm. "Wait! If she's dead, and you touch her, we could destroy forensic evidence."

"You've been watching too much TV," Alex threw over her shoulder as she pulled free.

But she came to a halt a few feet from the body. The stench was almost overwhelming. It was a woman, but she couldn't possibly be alive. Alex could see a trail of long blond hair tangled around the face.

She had to be sure.

Turning, taking a deep breath and holding it, Alex stepped forward and hunched down by the woman. She extended a hand to the throat, seeking a pulse. A crab crawled out of the mound of seaweed and hair, causing her to cry out.

"What?" Laurie shouted.

"Crab," Alex replied quickly. Bile rumbled in her stomach, raced toward her throat. She gritted her teeth, swallowed hard and felt the icy coldness of the woman's flesh. No pulse. The woman was dead. Alex rose, hurrying back to Laurie.

"She's dead. I'll stay here, you go for help."

"I'm not leaving you here alone with a corpse."

"Okay, you stay, I'll go."

"You're not leaving me here alone with a corpse!"

"Laurie—"

"She's dead. She's not going anywhere. We'll both go for help."

"Yes, but what if someone…what if a child comes out here while we're gone?"

"What?" Laurie demanded. "You think I'm going to throw myself on top of a corpse to hide it? There's nothing we can do except hurry."

"I'm not afraid to be alone with a corpse."

"You should be. What if the person who turned her into a corpse is still around here somewhere?"

Alex felt an uneasy sensation, but it was ridiculous. She shook her head. "Laurie, she's drifted in from… from somewhere else. She's been in the water awhile."

"Maybe. Neither one of us is an expert."

"Laurie, that…stink takes a while to occur."

"Let's just hurry. We won't be long, and she won't go anywhere."

"All right, then, let's go."

They tore back along the path they had taken and minutes later, neared the Tiki Hut. Laurie opened her mouth, ready to shout.

Alex clamped her hand over it. "No!"

Laurie fought free. "Alex! Did you touch that corpse with that hand? Maybe she died of some disease."

Alex had to admit she hadn't thought of such a possibility. She winced, but said, "We can't just start shouting about a corpse. We'll cause a panic."

She scanned the Tiki Hut. The mothers who had been on the swim earlier were there—the teens were evidently off somewhere else. She would have liked to see John Seymore. Since he was an ex–navy SEAL, he would surely know how to handle the situation.

She would even have liked to see David, Mr. Competence himself. Cool, collected, a well of strength in handling any given situation.

"Let's find Jay," she said.

She caught Laurie by the elbow, leading her past the Tiki Hut and along the flower-bordered stone pathway that led to the lobby of the lodge. They burst in, rushing to the desk. Luckily, no one was checking in or out. Len Creighton was on duty. Thirtyish, slim, pleasant, he smiled as he saw them, and then he saw their panic and his smile faded.

"Len, I need Jay. Where is he?"

Len cast a glance over his shoulder, indicating the inner office.

She headed straight back.

Jay wasn't there.

"He's not here," she called.

"I'll page him."

His voice was smooth as silk, hardly creating a blip against the soft music that always played in the lobby.

Moments later, Jay Galway, looking only slightly irritated, came striding across the lobby.

He was tall and lean, with sleek, dark hair, expressive gray eyes and a thin, aesthetic face. Patrician nose. His lips were a bit narrow, but they added to the look almost of royalty that he carried like an aura about him. She really liked her boss. They were friends, and he had always been ready to support her in her decisions, even if he didn't agree with them. She'd known him before she'd come to work here. In fact, he'd called her about the job when he'd heard about the divorce.

He paused in front of the counter, perfect in an Armani suit, and stared at her questioningly.

"What on earth is this all about?" he demanded.

He was still a short distance away from her, and a few guests had just come in and were heading in their direction.

"I need to talk to you. Alone." She glanced meaningfully at Len.

"I hide nothing from Len."

Alex glanced at Len and wondered if there was more going on between the two men than she knew. Not that she cared, or had time to worry about it now.

"There's a body on the beach," she said very softly.

"A body," echoed Laurie, who was standing behind her.

He stared at her as if she had lost her mind. "This is Florida, honey. There are a lot of bodies on the beach."

Alex groaned inwardly. "A dead body, Jay."

"A dead body?" Len exclaimed loudly.

They all stared at him. "Sorry," he said quickly.

Jay gave his full attention to her at last, staring at her hard, his eyes narrowing. His focus never left her face, but he warned Len, "Shut up. I mean it. That reporter is around somewhere. All we need is him getting his nose into this."

Alex stared back at him, aghast. "Someone is dead, Jay. It's not a matter of worrying about publicity. Will you call the sheriff's office—please?"

"Right. Len, call the county boys and ask them to send someone out. Someone from homicide."

"Homicide?" Laurie murmured. "Maybe she just... drowned."

"It still needs to be investigated," Alex said, still staring at Jay. His behavior puzzled her. They had no idea who the dead woman might be, where she had come from, or even if there was a murderer loose in paradise, and he seemed so blasé.

Finally he said, "Show me."

"Let's go."

Len started to follow, but Jay spun on him. "You're on duty. And you," Jay warned Alex, "make it look as if we're taking a casual stroll."

"Jay, honestly, sometimes—"

"Alex, want to cause a panic?" Jay demanded.

"Sure. Fine. We're taking a casual stroll."

They left the lobby, Alex leading, Jay behind her, Laurie following quickly. They took the path through the flowers, passed the Tiki Hut—which seemed unusually quiet for the time of day—and around the lagoon area.

"Alex, slow down. We're taking a stroll, remember?" Jay said.

She looked back, still moving quickly. "Jay, we're in

shorts and you're in an Armani suit, about to get sand in your polished black shoes. How casually can we stroll?"

He let out a sound of irritation but argued the point no further.

They reached the pristine sand beach. The temperature was dropping, the sweet breeze still blowing in.

Alex came to a halt. Jay nearly crashed into her back. As if they were a vaudeville act, Laurie collided with him.

"What the hell?" Jay demanded.

"It's gone," Alex breathed.

"What's gone?" Jay demanded.

"The body."

Laurie was staring toward the thatch of seaweed where the corpse had lain. She, too, seemed incredulous. "It—it is gone," she murmured.

Without turning, Alex could feel the way that Jay was looking at her. Like an icy blast against the balmy summer breeze, she could feel his eyes boring into her back.

She didn't turn but ran down the length of the beach, searching the sand and the water, looking for any hint as to where the body had been moved.

"What, Alex?" Jay shouted. "You saw a corpse, but it rolled down the beach to catch the sun better?"

She stopped then, whirling around.

"It's moved," she said, walking back to where Jay stood.

"Your corpse got up and walked?"

She exhaled impatiently. "Jay, it was here."

"Really, Jay, it was," Laurie said, coming to her defense.

They all turned at the sound of a motor. A sheriff's

department launch was heading their way. Nigel Thompson, the sheriff himself, had come.

Usually Alex liked Nigel Thompson. He looked just the way she figured an old-time Southern sheriff should look. He was somewhere between fifty and sixty years old; his eyes were pale blue, his hair snow-white. He was tall and heavy, a big man. His appearance was customarily reassuring.

He tended to be a skeptic.

A skeptic when rowdy, underage kids told their stories. A skeptic when adults who should have known better lied about the amount they had been drinking before a boating accident. He was never impolite, never skirted the law, but he was tough, and folks around here knew it.

He cut the motor but drew his launch right up to the beach. Hopping from the craft, he demanded, "Where's this body?"

Jay looked from Nigel to Alex.

"Well?" he asked her.

She lifted her chin, grinding down hard on her teeth. She looked at Nigel. "It was right here," she said pointing.

He looked from the sand and seaweed to her. "It was there?"

"I swear to you, it was right there."

He looked at Alex, slowly arching an eyebrow. "Alexandra, I was just about to sit down to dinner when the call came in. Tell me this isn't a joke or a summer prank."

"Had to have been a prank—and Alex fell for it," Jay said. He didn't sound angry with her, but he did sound aggravated.

"I'm here now," Nigel said, looking at Alex. "So tell me what you saw."

"A sunbather who thought it was one hell of a joke to fool someone into thinking she was dead," Jay said.

"She was dead," Alex said. "Nigel, you've known me for years. Do I make things up?"

"No, missy, you don't," the sheriff acknowledged. "But there is no body," he pointed out.

"It was here, right here. I got close enough to make sure she was…I touched her. She was dead," Alex asserted with quiet vehemence.

"She sure looked dead," Laurie offered.

Alex winced inwardly, aware her friend was trying to help. But her words gave the entire situation an aura of doubt.

"She was dead," Alex repeated.

"Cause of death?" Nigel asked her.

"I didn't do an autopsy," she snapped, and then was furious with herself.

"There was nothing that suggested a cause of death?" Nigel asked patiently.

She shook her head. "If she had washed up with a rope around her neck, I didn't see it. I'm sorry, I've dealt with dead dolphins, but I never interned at the morgue," Alex told him. "But I know a corpse when I see one."

"So you've seen lots of corpses?" Jay asked.

"I've seen enough dead mammals, Jay." She looked at Nigel. "I swear to you that there was a dead woman here, tangled in seaweed."

He sighed, looking at the sand and the water, then back to her. "No drag marks, Alex. She wasn't pulled into the bushes."

"She was here," Alex insisted stubbornly.

"Alex, I'm not saying this is what happened, but isn't it possible that someone was pulling a prank?"

"No," she said determinedly.

"So…what did happen? Why isn't she here?"

"I don't know. I thought she was far enough out of the water, so I don't think the waves could have pulled her back out… I think someone came and moved her."

"They were quick," Nigel commented.

"I'm telling you, she was here. Isn't there a way you can check? It will be dark soon. Can't you spray something around, see if there are specks of blood in the seaweed or on the sand anywhere? Better yet, take samples. Get more men out here and make certain that the only tracks around came from Jay, Laurie and myself?"

"There could be dozens of tracks around, and it wouldn't mean anything. The beach is accessible to all the staff and every guest," Nigel told her.

"Surely there's something you can do," Alex said.

"I can see if a body turns up again," he told her quietly. "Seriously, Alex. The most likely scenario is that the woman wasn't dead. Maybe she was unconscious but came to while you were up at the lodge. One of you should have stayed here."

Alex glared at Laurie.

Laurie looked back at her defensively. "Hey, how could I know that a corpse could get up and walk away?"

"A corpse can't get up and walk away," Jay interjected impatiently. "Unless the person you saw was not a corpse."

"We're going in circles here," Alex told him.

"This is ridiculous," he told her. "You pull me out here, make me ruin my good Italian shoes, drag Nigel away from his supper…because you saw someone passed out. Maybe someone in need of help, who you left. Or, more likely, someone playing a joke. A sick joke, yes. But a joke, and you fell for it."

Alex lifted her hands in exasperation. "All right, fine. There's nothing I can say or do to make you believe me. Nigel, I'm sorry about your supper. I owe you one. I'm going to take a shower."

"Wait a minute," Nigel said. "I'm not ignoring this. I'll make a check on passengers who took the ferry over today, and, Jay, you check your guest lists. We'll make sure that everyone is accounted for."

Alex stood in stony silence.

"Alex, that's all I can do since there's no body," Nigel said patiently. "We're not New York, D.C., or even Miami. I don't have a huge forensic department or the manpower to start combing every strand of seaweed, especially since the tide is coming in. Alex, please. I'm not mocking you. It's just that there is no body." He turned to Jay. "Get busy on the paperwork, Jay. I'll handle the ferry records. And, Alex…don't mention this around, all right?"

She frowned curiously at him. "But—"

"Don't you dare go alarming the guests with a wild story," Jay said.

"Actually, I was thinking that if there was a corpse and someone's hidden it, it might be a very dangerous topic of conversation," Nigel told her.

"He's right," Jay said. He pointed a finger toward Alex. "No mention of this. No mention of it for your own safety."

"Oh, yeah, right."

Nigel turned around, looking at the beach. He shook his head and started away.

"Where you going, Nigel?" Jay asked.

"To check on the ferry records," Nigel called back.

He reached his launch, gave it a shove back to the water and waded around to hop in, then gave them a wave.

Jay stared at Alex and Laurie again. "Not a word, you understand? Not a word. It doesn't matter if there were a dozen corpses on the beach, Alex, they're not here now. So keep quiet."

"Fine. Not a word, Jay," Alex snapped, walking past him.

"Hey! I'm your boss, remember?" he told her.

She kept walking, Laurie following in her tracks.

"I'm still your boss," he called after her. "And you owe me a new pair of shoes."

They were soon out of earshot. "Alex, there really was a corpse, wasn't there?" Laurie asked. But she sounded uncertain.

"Yes."

"Perhaps...I mean...couldn't you have been mistaken?"

"No." She turned. "I'm going to go take a hot shower and a couple of aspirin. I'll see you later."

Laurie nodded, still looking uncertain. "I'm sorry. Jay has a way of twisting things," Laurie said apologetically.

"I know. Forget it. I'll see you later."

She lifted a hand and turned down a slender trail that led through small palms and hibiscus, anxious only to reach her little cottage.

She slid her plastic key from the button pocket of her uniform shorts and inserted it into the lock. The door swung open.

The air was on; the ceiling fan in the whitewashed

and rattan-furnished living-room area was whirling
away. The coolness struck her pleasantly.

She walked through the living area and into the small
kitchen, pausing to pull a wine cooler from the refrigerator. She uncapped it quickly and moved on, anxious
to flop down on the sofa out on the porch. She opened
the floor-to-ceiling glass doors and went out, actually
glad of the wave of warmth outside, tempered by the
feel of the night breeze and the hypnotic whirl of another ceiling fan.

But even as she fell into a chair, she tensed, sitting
straight up and staring across to the charming white gingerbread railing, too startled by a figure looming in the
shadows of coming twilight to scream. Then she took a
deep breath of relief when she recognized who it was.

It wasn't just anyone planted on her porch.

It was David.

He was wearing nothing but swim trunks, broad,
bronzed shoulders gleaming, arms crossed over his chest
as he leaned against the rail. He was very still, and yet,
as it had always been with him, it seemed that he ema-
nated energy, as if any moment he would move like a
streak of lightning.

Her heart lurched. He was so familiar. How many
times had she seen him like this and walked up to him,
wherever they were, sliding her fingers down his naked
back, sometimes feeling the heat of the sun and sometimes just that of the man? She had loved the way he
had turned to her in response and taken her into the
curl of his arm.

How many times had it led to so much more? There
had been those days when, just in from the water, he
had been speaking to a TV camera, holding her as he

talked, then had suddenly turned to her, and she had seen a sudden light rise in his eyes. She could remember the way he would move, his attention only for her, as he excused himself, smiled and led her away. By the time they reached a private spot, they would both be breathless, laughing and pulling at the few pieces of clothing they were wearing. He could move with such languid, sinewy power; the tone of his voice could change so easily; the lightest brush of his fingers could evoke a thousand rays of pure sensuality. And she had been so desperately, insanely eager to know them all.

But then, that had been in the days when it had mattered to him that she was with him.

He didn't smile now. His deep blue eyes were grave as he surveyed her. She'd seen him cold and distant like this, as well, the light in his eyes almost predatory.

"David," she said dryly, pushing away the past, forcing herself to forget the intimacy and remember only what it had been like once she had determined to pursue her own career and he had begun to travel without her. Days, weeks, even a month…gone. Not even a telephone call, once he was with his true love. The sea.

And those who traveled it with him.

"Alex," he responded. "I've been waiting for you."

"So it appears. Well, how nice to see you. Here. On my porch. My personal porch, my private space. Gee, this is great." Her tone couldn't have held more acidity.

"Thanks." Her welcome hadn't been sincere. Neither was his gratitude. But there was no mistaking the seriousness of his next words.

"So," he said, "tell me about the body you found— the one that disappeared from the beach."

CHAPTER THREE

"What?" SHE SAID SHARPLY.

"You heard me. Tell me about the body." He uncoiled from his position, coming toward her, taking a chair near hers. He was close, too close, and she instantly felt wary and, despite herself, unnerved. They'd been apart for a year, and she still felt far too familiar with the rugged planes of his face, the bronzed contours of his hands and fingers, idly folded now before him.

She managed to sit back, eyeing him with dignity and, she hoped, a certain disdain.

"What the hell are you doing on my porch? There's a lobby for guests."

"Get off it. You must have been in a panic. And Jay probably behaved like an asshole."

"I don't know what you're talking about."

"I'm trying to help you out."

"If you want to help me out, get off the island."

"Am I making you uneasy?"

"You bet," she told him flatly.

That drew a smile to his lips. "Missed me, huh?"

She sat farther forward, setting her wine cooler on the rattan coffee table, preparing to rise.

"I assume you have a room. Why don't you go put some clothes on."

"Ah, that's it. Can't take the sight of my naked chest. It's making you hot, huh?"

"More like leaving me cold," she said icily. "Now go away, please."

His smile faded for a moment. "Don't worry. I know you want me to leave. I haven't forgotten that you had the divorce papers sent to me without a word."

"What was left to say?" she asked with what she hoped was quiet dignity.

"Hmm, let me think. Maybe your reasons for leaving me?"

She got to her feet. "You want the truth? I couldn't take it. I was so in love with you, it hurt all the time. You were all that mattered to me. My dolphins were far too tame for you—and far too unimportant. Our agreement that we'd spend time dedicated to my pursuits didn't mean a thing—not if a sunken ship turned up or a shark-research expedition was formed. Then it came to the point when I said you were welcome to go off even when you were supposed to be helping me—and you went. And then that became a way of life. There's the story in a nutshell. You were gone long before I sent those papers. And sometime in there, I got over you. I love working with dolphins. No, it isn't like finding a Spanish galleon, or even locating a yacht that went down ten years ago, maybe. But I love it. What you apparently needed, or wanted, was a different kind of wife. Either a pretty airhead who would follow you endlessly, or... someone as fanatic about treasure as you are. So go to your room and put some clothes on, or take a stroll over to the Tiki Hut and give someone else a thrill."

She started inside, hoping he would stop her. Not because she wanted to be near him, but because he knew about the body.

Her back to him, she suddenly wondered how he knew. The question left her with a very uneasy feeling.

"Alexandra, whatever anger you're feeling toward me, whatever I did or didn't do, I swear, I'm just trying to help you now."

She spun around. "How do you know about the body, anyway? Jay gave me very direct orders not to mention it to anyone."

He cocked his head slightly. "Jay's assistant talks."

"What did you do? Flirt with Len, too?"

He arched an eyebrow, curiously, slowly. She wished she could take back the comment. It made it appear as if…as if jealousy had been the driving factor in her quest for freedom. And it hadn't been.

Thankfully, David didn't follow up on her comment. "I don't think Len could contain himself. He tried to be smooth and cool, but I guess he feels he knows me and that I'm intelligent enough not to repeat what he said. He told me you'd all gone off in search of a body, and then it turned out to be gone. I overheard Jay tell him that part."

She stood very still, watching him for a long moment. "You know, I came back here to be alone."

"So talk to me, then I'll leave you alone."

"You know, this is very strange. Most people would scoff at the idea immediately. Bodies don't turn up on a daily basis. And yet…it sounds as if you think that there…should have been a body."

"No," he corrected. "I didn't say I thought there should be a body."

Alex pressed her fingers to her temples. "I can't do this," she said.

She was startled when he suddenly moved close to her. "Alex, please. If there was a body, and you saw it—you could be in danger."

She sighed. "Not if no one knows about the body."

"But I know, so others could, as well."

"You said Len only told you about it because he trusts you."

"Others might have overheard."

"Just what do you want?"

He was no more than an inch from her. He still carried the scent of salt and the sea, and it was a compelling mixture. She looked away.

"I don't want anything. I'm deeply concerned. Alex, don't you understand? You could be in danger!" His hands fell on her shoulders then. It was suddenly like old times. "You have to listen to me."

She'd heard the words before. Felt his hands before. Memories of being crushed against that chest stirred within her. She didn't want to believe that she had once been so in love with him just because he was so distinctively male and sensual. There had been times when they were together when his smile had been so quick, and then so lazy, when just a finger trailing across her bare arm or shoulder had...

"David, let go of me," she said, stepping back.

His eyes were narrowed, hard. She'd seen them that way before, when he was intent on getting to the bottom of something.

"Talk to me, Alex."

"All right. Yes, Jay acted like an asshole. Yes, I'm convinced I saw a body. A woman. A blonde. Other than that...I couldn't see her face. The angle of her body was wrong, and she was tangled in seaweed. When we went back, she was gone. Even Laurie, who saw the body first, wasn't sure we'd seen it anymore. She didn't actually go near the body even when it was there. Anyway, there was no corpse. So, are you happy?"

He didn't look happy. Actually, for a moment, he appeared ashen. She wanted to touch his face, but he was still David. Solid as rock.

"Please, will you leave me alone?" she asked him.

His voice was strange, scratchy, when he spoke. "I can't leave you alone. Not now," he said. And yet, contrary to his words, he turned and left her porch, disappearing along the back trail that led, in a roundabout way, to the other cottages and the lodge.

She stared after him, suddenly feeling the overwhelming urge to burst into tears. "Damn it, I got over you," she grated out. "And here you are again, driving me crazy, making me doubt myself...and not doubt myself," she finished softly.

She realized suddenly that twilight was coming.

And that she was afraid.

David had almost made her forget. No matter what anyone said, she'd seen a body on the beach. That was shattering in itself, but then the body had disappeared.

She slipped back inside, locking the sliding-glass door behind her. Then she looked outside and saw the shadows of dusk stretching out across the landscape.

She drew the curtains, uneasily checked her front door, and at last—after opening and finishing a new wine cooler—she managed to convince herself to take a shower.

DAVID SAT AT a table at the Tiki Hut, watching Alex. Not happily. He had been sitting with Jay Galway, who hadn't mentioned Alex's discovery, naturally. There might be a major exodus from the lodge if word got out that a mysterious body had been found, then disappeared, and Galway would never stand for that.

During their conversation, David had asked Jay casually about recent guests, and any news in the world of salvage or the sea, and Jay had been just as cool, shrugging, and saying that, with summer in full swing, most of their guests were tourists, eager to swim with the dolphins, or snorkel or dive on the Florida reef. Naturally—that was what they were set up to do.

David had showered, changed and made a few phone calls in the time since he'd left Alex. He'd still arrived before her.

If she'd seen him at the table, she'd given him no notice, heading straight for the table where John Seymore was sitting with Hank Adamson. They were chatting now, and he had the feeling that part of Alex's bubbling enthusiasm and the little intimate touches she was giving Seymore were strictly for his benefit, her message clear: Leave me the hell alone, hands off, I've moved on.

How far would it go?

All right, one way or the other, he would have been jealous, but now he was really concerned.

A woman's body had been found on the beach, and he had not heard back from Alicia Farr—who was a blonde.

David couldn't stop the reel playing through his head.

From what he'd overheard, Jay was convinced a trick had been played, or that Alex had assumed a dozing sunbather was a corpse. David didn't see that as a possibility. Alex was far too intelligent, and she wouldn't have walked away without assuring herself that the body no longer maintained the least semblance of a vital sign.

A trick? Maybe.

Real corpses didn't get up and walk away, but they could be moved.

If there had been a real corpse and it had been moved, it had been moved by someone on the island. That meant Alex could be in serious danger. After all, Len had told David what was going on, so who knew who else he might have told?

An ex–navy SEAL, maybe? The perfect blond hero— but was that the truth behind John Seymore being at Moon Bay?

Hopefully he would find out soon enough.

"So?"

"I'm sorry, what did you say?" David said, realizing that Jay had been talking away, but he hadn't heard a word.

"Well? Is it a photojournalism thing or a salvage dive?"

"What…?"

"Your next excursion," Jay said.

"Oh…well, I was looking into something, but my source seems to have dried up," David told Jay. My key source either dried up, or was killed and washed up on your beach, and then disappeared, he thought. Then his attention was caught by Alex again.

The band was playing a rumba. She was up and in John Seymore's arms. Head cast back, she was laughing at whatever he had to say. Her eyes were like gems. She was beautifully decked out in heels and a soft yellow halter dress that emphasized both her tan and her tall, sinewy length. Her long hair was free and a true golden blond, almost surreal in the light of the torches that burned here by night.

The lights were actually bug repellents. There was no escaping the fact that when you had foliage like this, you had bugs. But the glow they gave everything, especially Alex, was almost hypnotic.

David turned to Jay. "Sure you haven't heard about anything?" he asked him.

"Me?" Galway laughed. "Hell, I'm a hanger-on. The big excitement in my life is when I get a taste of something because of the big-timers—like you."

"Well, I'm looking at the moment," David told him. "So, if you do get wind of anything, anything at all, I'd like to know."

"You'd be the first one I'd go to," Jay assured him solemnly.

"Interesting that you'd say so—with Seth Granger here and ready to pay." And in the Tiki Hut at that moment, David realized. Granger was a big man and in excellent shape for his sixty-odd years. He was speaking with Ally Conroy, mother of Zach, at the bar. She was at least twenty years his junior, but he'd gathered from their bits of conversation before the swim that she was a widow, worried about rearing her son alone. Seth wasn't all that well-liked by many people, yet Ally seemed to be giving him the admiration he craved. Maybe they were a perfect fit.

"Seth…well, you know. He's always looking for something to bug his way into. Hell, why not? He's rich, and he loves the sea, and he'd like to make a name for himself in his retirement years. Don't you love it? Tons of money, no real knowledge, yet he wants to be right in the thick of things. Executive turned explorer."

"Why not?" David said with a shrug. "Most expeditions need financial backing."

"Yeah, why not? It's what I'd love to do myself. I've got a great job here, mind you—but I sure wish I had his resources. Or your reputation. Every major corporation out there with a water-related product to sell is willing to finance you—even on a total wild-goose chase."

"You know me—game for anything that has to do with the water," David murmured absently.

Alex was leaning very close to John Seymore now. In a moment she'd be spilling out of her dress.

"Excuse me," he said to Jay, rising, then went up to the couple on the floor. Alex wouldn't be happy, but if John Seymore was really such an all-right kind of guy— or even pretending to be one—he would show him the courtesy of allowing him to cut in.

A tap on Seymore's shoulder assured him that he had correctly assessed the situation. The other man, his eyes full of confident good humor, stepped back.

Alex gave David a look of sheer venom. But she wasn't going to cause a scene in the Tiki Hut. She slipped into his arms.

"What are you doing?" she asked him.

"Dancing."

"You know I don't want to dance with you."

He ignored her and said, "I guess you haven't had a chance to talk with Seymore yet."

"John and I have done lots of talking."

"Well, I happened to mention to him one of the reasons I'm here."

"And it has something to do with me?"

"Definitely."

She arched a delicate eyebrow. "I guess you're going to tell me—whether I want to know or not."

"We're not divorced."

"Don't be ridiculous," she said sharply. "I filed papers, you signed them."

"I don't quite get it myself, but apparently there was some little legal flaw. I must not have signed on all the dotted lines. The documents were never properly filed, and therefore the decision was declared null and void. I know what a busy woman you are, but I need to ask you when would be a good time to get together with my lawyer and rectify the situation."

She wasn't even pretending to dance anymore. She just stood on the floor, staring at him. His arms were still around her, tendrils of silky soft, newly washed blond hair slipping over his hands, teasing in their sensuality. He knew he needed to move away, but he didn't.

"That's impossible!" she exclaimed.

"Sorry."

She stared at him, still amazed. "I don't…I…can't…"

"Look, Alex, I know how eager you are to be completely rid of me. I'm sorry. But as of this moment, we are still married."

He wondered if lightning would come out of the sky to strike him dead.

It didn't.

God must have understood his situation.

"It's…it's impossible," she repeated.

He shrugged, as if in complete understanding of her dismay. "I'm sorry."

Something hardened in the depths of her ever-changing, sea-green eyes. "I'll make time to see your attorney."

"Great. We'll set it up. Well, lover boy is waiting, so I'll let you go in a sec. But first I need you to listen to me. Alex, I'm begging you, listen to me. You've got to be careful."

She pulled back, searching his eyes, then shaking her head. "David, I understand why you're here, and frankly, I'm surprised you took the time to actually ask what would be convenient for me. But I don't quite get this sudden interest. Where's Bebe whats-her-name? Or the thin-but-oh-so-stacked Alicia Farr, the Harvard scholar?"

Her question sent an eerie chill up his spine. *I think she's your disappearing body.*

"Alex, I'm afraid you're in danger." His words, he realized, sounded stiff and cold.

She shook her head. "No one else believes I discovered a corpse. Why should you?"

He hesitated for a minute. "I know you," he told her. "You're not a fool. You would have looked closely enough to know."

"Well, thanks for the compliment. I wish Nigel Thompson felt that way. I couldn't get through to him that though it's improbable that a body was really there and somehow moved, it's not impossible. So if you'll let me off the dance floor...?"

He released her. But as she started to step past him, he caught her arm. She looked up, and for a moment, her eyes were vulnerable. Her scent seemed to wrap around him, caress him.

"Don't trust anyone," he said.

"I certainly don't trust you."

He pulled her back around to face him. "You know what? I've about had it with this."

"Oh, you have, have you?"

"I got a long lecture. You can have one, too. You read

a lot that just wasn't there into a number of situations. You never had the right not to trust me. It was just that, to you, the minute a phone or a radio didn't work, I had to be doing something. With someone. And you know what, Alex? That kind of thing gets really old, really quick."

"Sorry, but it's over anyway, isn't it? You received the divorce papers and said, 'Hey, go right ahead.' You were probably thankful you didn't have to deal with any annoying baggage anymore. And now you're suddenly going to be my champion, defending me from a danger that doesn't exist?"

"Alex, you know me. You know what kind of man I am. Hell, hate me 'til the sun falls from the sky, but trust me right now."

"There are dozens of people here. I don't think I'm in any danger in the middle of the Tiki Hut. And trust you?" She sounded angry, then a slow smile curved her lips.

"What?"

"I just find it rather amusing that you're suddenly so determined to enjoy my company. There were so many times when...well, never mind."

He stared at her blankly for a moment. "What are you talking about?"

"It doesn't matter anymore. It's over."

"Actually, it's not," he said. Again he waited for lightning to strike. Not that it should. He was doing this out of a very real fear for her life.

She waved a hand in the air. "All over but the shouting," she murmured.

"Maybe that's what we were lacking—the shouting."

"Great. We should have had a few more fights?"

It was strange, he thought, but this was almost a conversation, a real one.

And then John Seymore chose that exact moment to return, tapping him on the shoulder. "Since you're on the dance floor and not actually dancing…?"

"And it's a salsa," Alex put in.

"Salsa?" John murmured. "I'm not sure I know what I'm doing, but—"

"I do," David said quickly, grinning, and catching Alex in his arms once again. "I'll bring her back for the next number."

"Since when do you salsa?" Alex demanded as they began to move.

"Since a friend married a dance instructor," he told her.

She seemed startled, but he really did know what he was doing. He'd never imagined the dance instruction he'd so recently received from a friend's wife would pay off so quickly. Alex was good, too. She'd probably honed her skills working here, being pleasant to the guests in the Tiki Hut at night.

After a minute, though, he wasn't quite sure what he had gained. They looked good together on the floor, and he knew it. But the music was fast, so conversation was impossible. At the end of the song he managed to lead her into a perfect dip, so at least he was rewarded by the amazement in her eyes as they met his.

In fact, she stayed in his arms for several extra seconds, staring up at him before realizing that the music had ended and the gathering in the Tiki Hut was applauding them.

He grinned slowly as she straightened, then pushed

against his chest. "The dance is over," she said firmly, then walked quickly away.

"You really are a man of many talents."

Turning, he saw Alex's assistant, the pretty young blonde. She was leaning against the edge of the rustic wood bar.

"Thanks."

"Do you cha-cha?" she asked, smiling.

"Yes, I do," he said.

"Well, will you ask me? Or are you making me ask you?"

"Laurie, I would love to dance with you," he said gallantly.

As they moved, she asked him frankly, "Why on earth did you two ever split up?"

"Actually, I don't really know," he told her.

"I bet I do," she told him. "You must be pretty high maintenance."

"High maintenance? I'm great at taking care of myself. I may not be a gourmet, but I can cook. I know every button on a washing machine. I usually even remember to put down the toilet seat."

She laughed. "Well, there you go."

"Excuse me? How is that high maintenance?"

"You don't need anybody," she said. "So it's high maintenance for someone to figure out what they can do for you."

She wasn't making any sense, but she was sincere, and she made him smile.

Then the music came to an end, and he regretted that he had been so determined on proving his mettle with Alex, because he found himself being asked to dance by almost every woman in the Tiki Hut.

And somewhere, in the middle of a mambo, he realized that Alex had slipped away—and so had John Seymore.

SOMEHOW, JUST WHEN things had begun looking a little brighter, David had walked back into her life, and now he was ruining everything.

John's arm sat casually around her shoulders as they strolled toward her cottage. "Hate to admit it," he said casually, "but you two looked great out there. Did you spend a lot of time out dancing while you were married?"

"No. We didn't spend much time together doing anything—other than diving for treasure or facing great whites or experiencing some other thrill."

"Strange," he said.

"What?"

"The way you sound. You love the sea so much, too."

"Actually? I'm not into sharks. I was terrified every time I went into the water with them, but with the crew of hard-core fanatics that always seemed to be around, I didn't want to look like a coward. I love the sea, yes. But I'm into warm-blooded, friendly creatures, myself."

"You really love your dolphins, huh?"

She shrugged, liking the way his arm felt around her, but feeling a sense of discomfort, as well.

David. Telling her that they were still married. But they weren't; they hadn't been for a year. Not in any way that mattered. All he was talking about was legality. His words shouldn't mean a thing.

Except that...

She was traditional. She'd been raised Catholic.

Damn David. He would know her thought process,

that she would feel that she shouldn't be with another man, that it wouldn't be right, and...

Just how many women had he been with in the last year? What was wrong with her that she couldn't see how ridiculous it was for her to be concerned over anything he had to say? Why had seeing him again made her uncertain, when she knew that an easy confidence and charm were just a part of his nature?

"I do love my dolphins," she said, realizing she had been silent for too long after his question. "They are the most incredible animals. What I like most is that they seem to study us just as we study them, and just as we learn their behavior, they learn what our behavior is going to be. Sometimes their affinity for man, especially in the wild, can be dangerous for them, but still, the communication we can share is just amazing."

"They are incredible," he agreed. "I've seen them used in the navy in the most remarkable ways. Never worked with them myself," he added quickly. "But I've seen what they can do."

They had reached her porch. Strange, her thoughts had been filled with David's behavior—she wished she could begin to understand the male of her own species half as well as she understood her dolphins—and then with John's company, which, she had to admit, she had found all the more intoxicating just because she knew that it disturbed David.

Now, despite the light burning on her back porch, it seemed that the shadows of night were all around her, and she remembered the body on the beach. It wasn't that she had ever forgotten, but despite her determination, the doubts of others had crept into her mind.

Was she insane, thinking the woman had been dead?

Or was she more insane now, trying to do what Jay had demanded, keep silent about the possibility of a body on the beach?

John had escorted her up the two wooden steps to her little back porch, with its charming, gingerbread railing. They were standing by her back door.

He was probably waiting to be invited in.

And just this morning, she had thought that if this moment came, she would invite him in.

She mentally damned her ex-husband again. Her almost-ex-husband.

She smiled up at John Seymore. His dimple was showing as he offered her a rueful smile.

"You're really something," he said.

"So are you," she murmured. Blond hair, handsome face, shoulders to die for, arms that were wonderfully secure...

She slipped into them. He lowered his mouth to hers, and she allowed herself the kiss, but she couldn't stop herself from analyzing it. Firm mouth, coercive, not demanding, fingers gently suggestive in her hair, tongue teasing at her lips, slipping into her mouth, warm, very warm, definitely seductive...

On a physical level, he was incredible.

So if she could just forget about David...

She couldn't. Not when he was here, on the island, so irritatingly in-her-face.

She stepped back, stroking John's cheek.

"You're around for a little while longer, right?" she inquired softly, hoping he understood her signals. I'm interested, but it's been a very long and strange day....

"I can arrange to be around for a very, very long time," he told her. Then he grinned. "I'd like to come in. But I understand perfectly. Okay, well, not perfectly, and I am disappointed, wishing I could be sleeping with you tonight."

She felt a flush touch her cheeks. "I didn't mean to… lead you on, to suggest…"

"You didn't. You're just the most fascinating woman I've met in aeons, and…hell, good night. I'll be around."

"I—well, I know you've been talking to David. We are divorced. There's just some ridiculous technicality."

"I'm not worried about a technicality," he told her.

"Neither am I."

"But I will step back if the technicality isn't just on paper, if it's something a lot deeper."

His words made her like him all the more. He wasn't about to step into the middle of a triangle, or be second-string to any other man.

"It's only a technicality—really." She meant to sound sincere. She wasn't sure if she really was or not. And she wasn't sure what he heard in her denial.

"Well…" he murmured.

He drew her to him, kissed her forehead. Then he walked down the steps, and started back along the foliage-bordered path.

She watched him disappear, realized she hadn't opened her door, and felt the pressure of the night and the shadows again. She quickly slid her key into the bolt for the glass doors, then stepped inside, feeling a rise of anger. She had never felt afraid here before, ever.

And now…

Though the image had faded for a moment due to skepticism and doubt, she could now vividly recall the corpse on the beach. A corpse that had disappeared.

She locked the door, making certain it was secure;

then, still feeling an almost panicky unease, she walked through the little Florida room, kitchen and living room, assuring herself that windows were tightly closed and the front door was locked.

Damn David a million times over for both the trials haunting her tonight. If it hadn't been for him, John Seymore would be inside with her. Then she wouldn't be afraid of the shadows, or the memories stirring in her mind.

She slipped through the hallway to the first of the two bedrooms in the cottage, the one she used for an office area. She checked the window there and even opened the closet door.

David's suggestion that she might be in danger seemed to be invading her every nerve. But the office was empty and secure.

Finally she went to her own room, found it safe, then prepared for bed and slipped under the covers. The nightlight she kept on in the bathroom had always provided her with more than enough illumination, but tonight it only added to the shadows.

Usually the sound of the waves and the sea breeze rustling through the trees was soothing, but tonight...

She lay there for several seconds. Waves...breeze... palms. Foliage that seemed to whisper softly in the night, usually so pleasant...

A sudden thumping sound startled her so badly that she nearly screamed aloud. She did jump out of bed.

She'd heard a thump, as if something heavy had just landed on her roof.

She stood dead still, waiting. And waiting....

Nothing, no sound at all. Had she been deceived? The sound might have come from elsewhere....

Or might not have come at all.

She almost let out a loud sigh of pure frustration, but swallowed it back, and slowly, silently, tiptoed from her bedroom.

Into the hall…through to the kitchen. From there she could see both the living room and the little Florida room and the glass doors that led out back. The curtain was partially open. Had she left it that way?

The noise had come from the roof. There was a fireplace in the living area of each of the cottages. Despite the fact that this was sunny Florida, in the winter, during the few days that dipped into the forties or even the thirties, a fire was incredibly nice. But the chimney was far too small for a man to slip through.

So she was safe. There was nothing.

She was letting the simple sounds of nature slip into her psyche and scare her because she was still so unnerved by the happenings of the day.

A coconut had probably fallen off a palm. Still, just to be sure…

She walked to the back, trying to stay behind the curtain, then peeked out the glass. She pulled the drape back just a little more….

And screamed.

CHAPTER FOUR

EVERYONE WAS GONE, Laurie thought. First Alex and John, then David. There were people around, but the Tiki Hut seemed empty. The band had reverted to calypso, very pleasant but also, in her current state of mind, sleep inducing.

Alex was crazy. She'd been married to David Denham and divorced him.

Alex had never been to Date Tournament. Had she realized what was out there, she would undoubtedly still be married.

Maybe Alex thought that nights spent at a place like Date Tournament were simply not in her future. Then again, maybe she would never have such a night—because there was something about Alex that attracted men.

Laurie wished she had that innate…thing, whatever it was. Maybe it would come with age, but Alex was only three years her senior. Well, maybe things weren't as perfect as they seemed for Alex, either.

"You're up late, aren't you?"

She started. It was Hank Adamson. She hadn't seen him before, but the Tiki Hut had been hopping, earlier, so he could have been lost in the crowd.

She saw Jay Galway on the other side of the bar, conversing with Seth Granger and a few of the other guests.

He was staring at her—glaring, really—and giving her a big smile. Sign language, Jay Galway style. She was supposed to be as nice as possible, suck up big-time.

She gave an imperceptible nod to Jay and smiled as instructed at Hank. He slid out the chair opposite her and sat. "Okay if I join you and ask a few questions?"

"Sure."

In his lanky way, he was actually very attractive, she realized.

He grinned. "You look so wary."

"Do I? Well, we all know that the pen is very powerful."

"Update to computer," he said dryly.

"Okay, the written word—no matter how it's written."

"Honestly, you don't have to be so cautious. I didn't come to do a simple review. I'm going to do a whole piece on the place."

"A good piece—or a bad piece?"

"Good, bad…truthful."

"We're a good place," she said.

His grin deepened. "Actually, yes, Moon Bay does seem to follow through on every promise it makes. That's what's important. A little mom-and-pop establishment can get a great write-up, as long as it delivers on what it offers."

"Um, we're not exactly mom-and-pop," Laurie murmured.

"No, but so far, I've gotten a good bang for my buck, and that's what matters."

Laurie smiled. "That's great. I love Moon Bay. It's not just that I work here—I really love it. It's a wonderful place for a vacation."

"With the happiness and well-being of the guests foremost in everyone's mind at all times?"

"Yes, of course…" Laurie murmured, looking down at her hands suddenly. Was that true? What if that hadn't been a prank on the beach today? If Alex had been right, and a woman had been dead—and what if the killer had come back, aware that the body had washed up, and moved it?

"What is it?" She suddenly knew why Hank Adamson was considered so good. He asked casual questions; people gave casual answers. So casual you didn't realize that your mind was wandering off and that you were about to betray your real thoughts.

"What is what?" she asked innocently.

"You were about to say something. Do you feel that maybe, just sometimes, management isn't as concerned with safety as they should be? I'd never quote you by name."

Laurie stared at him and smiled slowly. "Well…" She leaned on the table, edging closer to him.

He did the same, anxious to hear whatever dirt she had to dish.

She leaned back. "Sorry, I don't have a bad thing to say about the place."

Adamson sat back, as well, obviously disappointed. He shook his head. "If there was something going on… something big, do you think that the employees would get wind of it?"

"Like what? The president arriving, or something like that?"

"No…like Moon Bay being involved in…something."

"Drugs? Here? Never," she assured him.

"I wasn't referring to drugs," he assured her.

She laughed softly. "Illegal immigrants? Not with Jay around. He wouldn't hire an illegal if his life depended on it."

"Not illegals," Hank said.

"Just what are you getting at?" she demanded.

"I don't know," he said. "I was hoping you did."

"That makes no sense. This is a resort, specially licensed for work with sea mammals. What could be going on?" Other than a body that appeared on the beach, then disappeared.

"Have you ever heard of a woman named Alicia Farr?" Adamson asked her.

"Sure. She's almost like a young, female Jacques Cousteau."

"Have you ever met her?"

"Nope. I think she's friends, kind of, with Alex. She's worked with David Denham. I'm pretty sure Jay Galway has worked with her, too."

"She hasn't been here, then, in the last couple of weeks?"

"Not unless she's been hiding in the bushes." Laurie was actually enjoying her conversation with him now. She'd had a few Tiki Hut specials, but she always watched her drinking here. And she could stand up to a grilling by a man like Hank Adamson. "Is she supposed to be here?"

"There was a rumor she was going to be, but I guess it wasn't true."

"I guess not."

"You're sure she's not here?" he persisted.

"There are private cottages here, twenty of them. Eight of them belong to the staff, and twelve are rented out. But this is an island. Room service is the only way to get food. There's a little convenience shop in the lobby, a boutique…but, honestly, I think it would be pretty hard for someone to hide out in one of the cottages. Maid service is in and out, engineering…. I'm pretty sure she wasn't here. We're off the Middle Keys, and there are lots of secluded places on the other islands. Maybe she's on one of them. I'm sorry to disappoint you—were you really trying to get a story on her?"

"I am doing an article on Moon Bay," he told her. "You know how it is, though. Lots of times, reporters get wind of a bigger story while they're in the middle of something more routine."

"So if you'd run into Alicia Farr here, that would have been nice, right?"

"It would have been interesting," he said. "You do know what she looks like, right? You'd know her if you saw her?"

"Sure. I've seen lots of articles on her. And I've seen her on television," Laurie said with a shrug.

She yawned suddenly, and quickly covered her mouth with her hand. "Sorry." She was. He was appealing in his lanky way, but he wasn't interested in her—only what she might know. And she had no intention of telling him anything. She'd been ordered not to mention Alex's certainty that she'd seen a corpse, and she wouldn't.

She rose. "Please excuse me. Saturdays are very long here. People coming down from Dade County, locals who just like to come eat at the restaurant. The place is always busy."

He had risen along with her. "Thanks," he told her quietly.

"Sure. This place really is wonderful. I'm not lying,

or just trying to keep my job by saying that. And Alex... well, there's no one better."

"So they say," he murmured, then asked politely, "Can I walk you to your cottage?"

"I don't rate a cottage—not yet," she told him with a shrug. "I just take the trail back to the fork in the road and head for the staff quarters. I'll be fine." She grinned to take the sting out of her next words, moved a step closer to him, and whispered, "Feel free to go question another employee. You'll find out every word I said was true."

He had the grace to flush. She gave him a wave and made her way past two couples on the dance floor, both a little inebriated, but heck, they weren't driving anywhere. If you were going to feel the influence of alcohol, this was the place to do it.

She could hear the band long after she had left the Tiki Hut behind. She started off thinking nothing of the night or the shadows, the trails were lit by torches—not like the ones at the Tiki Hut, which were real, but electrical torches made to give the grounds an island feel. Still...

Once the Tiki Hut was well behind her and the noise from it had dimmed, she thought the night seemed especially dark. Strange, because her dad had shown her once before how the glow that radiated from Miami— sixty or seventy miles away, still extended this far when the sky was clear. But clouds were out tonight. It was storm season, of course. They'd had several nice days in the last week, though, she mused.

Nice days. A few with calm seas, a few others when the water was choppy. But then, the water didn't have to be wild to carry something—like a corpse—to the shore.

She stopped dead suddenly and instinctively, some inner defense aware of a rustling noise. She felt the hair rising at her nape.

She spun around. Nothing. But the bushes seemed to be very, very dark.

She had a sudden, vivid and ridiculous image of a corpse stalking her along the trail....

"Don't be ridiculous," she said aloud to herself.

But then...a rustling in the bushes...

She stared in the direction from which the noise had come, her heart racing a million miles an hour. Slowly, she made a circle where she stood, looking around.

The noise came again. She spun sharply, staring into the brush once again.

Then...a fat possum waddled out from the bushes and moved slowly across the path.

She let out her pent-up breath and giggled.

Then she turned, ready to set out along the path again. Instead she plowed into something dark and solid, and before her numbed mind could react, arms reached around her.

"ALEX, FOR THE love of God!"

David's voice was muted by the glass, but his impatience was evident. She was so relieved to realize that he was the figure on the porch that she didn't really think. She opened the sliding-glass doors, but she had to yell.

"You son of a bitch! What the hell are you doing out there? You nearly scared the life out of me."

He pushed his way in. It was dark, only the lights in front of the house illuminating the area around them. She could see that he still looked like a million bucks, dressed in dark chinos, a red tailored shirt and a light jacket.

She rued the fact that she was wearing a tattered T-shirt with the words "Moon Bay" embroidered in powder blue against a deep aqua background. She was equally sorry that it was very short. Silly. Even if they hadn't been married and she didn't have every inch of his anatomy etched into her memory forever, they spent their lives in bathing suits. She wondered why the T-shirt made her feel so naked. And vulnerable.

He walked through the cottage, checking the front door, looking around. "Is there any other way in here?" he asked, turning around slowly and studying the living room.

"Abracadabra?" she suggested.

"Cute, Alex. Is there any other way in here?"

"Front door, back door, as you can see."

He ignored her and headed for the small hallway that led to the bedrooms and bath.

"Hey!" she protested. She started to follow him, then paused, determined that the last place she wanted to be with him was a bedroom.

A moment later, he was back.

She frowned slightly, realizing he looked as if he had been running his fingers through his hair. She turned on the kitchen lights and stared at him once again. He looked tense. He reminded her of a shark, giving the impression of deceptive ease, while eyeing his prey to strike.

"What the hell are you doing?" she demanded.

"There was someone walking around your cottage, looking in the windows. I chased him around one side... and lost him," he told her.

"If there's anyone slinking around here," she said softly, "it's you."

He threw up his hands. "Alex, I'm serious."

"And I'm serious, too."

"Get this straight—I'm concerned."

Crossing her arms over her chest, she said firmly, "David, get this straight. You don't need to be concerned about me. I don't care about a technicality. We're not married anymore. I might not have been here alone."

"Actually, knowing you, you do care about a technicality," he informed her.

He was far too relaxed. "You followed me," she accused him. "You followed me when I was with another man, who was more than capable of taking care of me if I'd been in any danger."

"Alex, I don't really know that guy, and neither do you, and most important," he said very softly and seriously, "we are talking about a life-and-death situation."

She suddenly saw the man she knew from television, interviews and even, once upon a time, her personal life. The ultimate professional. Reeking of authority and command. Absolute in his conviction.

And for some reason, she shivered.

The woman on the beach had been dead. No matter what anyone tried to tell her. There had, beyond a doubt, been a corpse.

And it had disappeared.

"Maybe you'd like to explain it to me," she said.

He stared at her for a long moment. "I keep thinking you're better off, the less you know," he said quietly.

"Why? You already think I'm in some kind of danger."

"Yes, I do."

"Why?"

"You found a body on the beach. A body that disappeared."

She shook her head, watching him warily. "We've been through this. Jay and the sheriff were both certain I was duped."

"But you know it was real."

She wished so badly that she didn't feel such a desperate desire to keep her distance from him at all costs. Because she did know him. And she knew that he believed her. It wasn't necessary for him to have been there—he believed her.

"If you're so convinced, there must be a reason," she said flatly.

"Want to put some coffee on?" he suggested.

"No."

"Mind if I do?"

"Yes." Even as she spoke, she knew he would ignore her. He gave her a glance as if she was behaving like a spoiled child and moved into the kitchen. His arm brushed hers as he strode past her, and she felt as if she'd been burned.

Apparently he hadn't even noticed. He was heading for the cupboard above the coffeepot.

"Would you stop making yourself at home here, please?" she said, walking past him and shoving him out of the way. "I'll make coffee. You talk."

"What did she look like? The woman on the beach. What did she look like?"

She turned around and stared at him. "Like…a woman. Blonde."

"You didn't recognize her?" He stepped past her, impatiently taking the carafe and starting the coffee.

IN THE DARK

"Recognize her?" Alex said, startled.

"Yes, did you know who she might be?"

"No. She was at a strange angle. And she had long…
or longish hair. It was covering her face. I touched her
throat, looking for a pulse. And then…I don't know how
to describe it exactly, but there was no way not to know
she was dead."

"But you let them convince you that she couldn't
have been, that you were wrong, and she just got up
and walked away?" he demanded.

There was a note of disappointment in his tone.

"The sheriff was there," she told him sharply. "He
doubted me. There was no body. What the hell was I
supposed to do?"

He turned his back on her, opening a cupboard door.

"Cups are over here," she said impatiently, producing
two from another cabinet.

He poured the coffee. He drank his black, so she was
startled when he went to the refrigerator, absently taking out the milk to put a few drops into hers.

She accepted the coffee, watching him, feeling again
an embarrassed awareness of his crisp, tailored appearance and her own tattered T-shirt. Ridiculous to think
about such things when they were talking about a corpse,
she told herself.

"Did you mention your discovery to lover boy?" he
inquired, sounding casual as he put the milk back in
the refrigerator.

"I don't like your tone," she told him.

"Sorry, I don't like what's happening."

"Are you actually jealous?" she demanded.

"I'm not trying to run your life, if that's what you

mean," he assured her. "I just don't like what's happening here."

"You haven't explained a damn thing yet, David."

"Did you tell him?" he persisted.

She let out a sigh of irritation. "No, but that doesn't mean I won't. For tonight…tonight I'm waiting. The sheriff will get back to us, let us know if anybody's missing from one of the ferries or the Middle Keys. He and Jay might have made me feel a little foolish today, but Nigel Thompson is a good man and no fool. And I could accuse you of many things, but being a total idiot isn't one of them. So get to it. What's going on?"

"I'm afraid I might know your corpse," he said quietly, his eyes a strange cobalt by night, and steady upon her.

Her heart seemed to skip a beat.

"Who?"

"Alicia Farr."

"Alicia?" she exclaimed. "Why…why would she be around here? There's not much to attract a woman of her reputation at a place like Moon Bay…but then again, there's not much here for you." She stopped speaking suddenly, staring at him. "I see. Great. You would have told me about this 'technicality' in the divorce, but only because it would have been convenient while you were here. You came to meet Alicia."

"No," he told her.

"You liar," she accused him softly. "Get out—now."

"I didn't come here just to meet her."

"David, I'll call security if you don't leave."

He arched an eyebrow, fully aware that "security" at Moon Bay meant two retired cops who were happy to putter around the grounds at night in retooled golf carts.

There had never been serious trouble at Moon Bay—
until today. And then they hadn't bothered with security;
they had called the sheriff's department immediately.

"David, get the hell out."

"Alex, will you listen to me—I think Alicia is dead."

An eerie feeling crept along her spine. How could she
be jealous of a corpse?

But she had been jealous of Alicia. The woman
was—or had been—a free spirit, intelligent, beautiful
and filled with knowledge, curiosity and a love of dangerous pursuits that nearly equaled David's own.

Could she be dead? That would be terrible.

But it wasn't sinking in. At the moment, Alex felt betrayed. She had to admit, it had felt nice to have David
following her as if he was desperate.

"Alex?" he said, and his tone seemed to slip under
her skin, no matter how numb she was suddenly feeling.

Then he walked over to her, put his cup down, and
his hands went to her shoulders again, the whole of his
length far too familiar against her own, his eyes piercing
hers in a way she remembered too well. "Damn it, Alex,
believe this—I don't want you ending up dead, as well."

They were talking about life and death, and all she felt
was the texture of his jacket, the heat emanating from
him. She breathed him in and remembered the way his
hands could move. He was almost on top of her, and she
felt a physical change in herself, a tautness in her breasts,
with way too much of her body pressed there against his.

She wanted to shove him away—hard.

She managed to get a hand between them and place
it firmly on his chest, pushing him away from her, and
slipped from the place where she had been flush against
the counter.

"Talk, David. Do it quickly. I have a nine o'clock dive in the morning, which means I have to be at the docks at eight."

Her voice sounded tight and distant. She wasn't sure if it was the effect she wanted or not. She should have been concerned, she knew, about Alicia. She had known the woman, after all, even admired her. But she hadn't liked her.

But that didn't mean she would have wanted harm to come to her. So why wasn't she more emotionally distressed? She was just too numb, unable to accept the possibility.

"Alicia called me a few weeks ago. Do you remember Danny Fuller?"

"Of course. He came here frequently, and he was charming." He had been. An octogenarian, the man had been in on the early days of scuba diving and helped in the later development of some of the best equipment available. He had loved dolphins, and that had naturally endeared him to Alex. "Yes, I knew Daniel fairly well. I was very sorry to hear he died about a month ago, at a hospital in Miami. Of natural causes."

"I know."

"They were natural causes, right?"

"Yes. But Alicia was with him a lot at the end."

"I can see it—him dying, and Alicia quizzing him about everything he knew until he breathed his last breath," Alex murmured. She hesitated. Alicia Farr was—or had been, if any of this was true—everything that she had not been herself. She found herself remembering the woman and the times they had worked together. Alicia was the epitome of a pure adventuress, courageous beyond sanity, at times. She was also beautiful.

Even before the last year, she had frequently appeared at David's side on TV and in magazines. He, naturally, thought the world of her.

He'd slept with her, certainly. But before or after the divorce? Alex had never been certain.

That must be why she was feeling so icy cold now. Good God, she didn't want the woman to be dead, but still...

"It's probably true that she pursued him mercilessly," David admitted. "But he also sent for her, so I guess she was the one he wanted to talk to in the end. At any rate, soon after he died, she called me. She said she was on to the biggest find of the century, and that she wanted me with her. And something she discovered had to do with Moon Bay." He seemed to notice the way Alex was staring at him. "Actually, I had already been toying with the idea of coming here, so it sounded fine to me. She set a date, and said that she would meet me here. Whether she made that same arrangement with anyone else or not, I don't know. But when I tried to get back to her, to confirm, I couldn't reach her. Then, when I got here, she was a no-show. I figured she'd gone ahead to check things out. You know Alicia when she's got the bit between her teeth. I still thought she'd show, though. But I did notice that the place seemed to be crawling with a strange assortment of visitors, including Seth Granger, Hank Adamson and your new friend—John Seymore. And then...I heard that you'd found a body on the beach."

For several long moments, Alex just stared at him, not at all sure what to think, or where to start. She felt chilled. She had found a body, and it could have been Alicia's.

No. Easier to believe Jay had been right. That she'd seen someone playing a sick—and very convincing—trick on someone else.

"Maybe Alicia just decided that she didn't want you in on her fabulous find after all. Maybe she's already off on her expedition," Alex said, her voice sounding thin.

"And maybe someone else found out what she had and killed her to get it—or before she could set up an expedition to recover the treasure, so they could get it for themselves."

"If there was really a body, it's gone now," Alex said. "And Sheriff Thompson—"

"I've spoken with him. He hasn't seen Alicia, and your corpse hasn't reappeared."

"Then…then you don't really have anything," Alex said.

"What I have is a tremendous amount of fear that a friend and colleague is dead—and that someone may now be after you. Alex, maybe there's someone out there who thinks you saw something, and that could put you in danger."

Alex shook her head. "David, I'm not going to start being paranoid because of the things that might be. If Alicia is dead, and someone was willing to kill her for what she knew, wouldn't you be in far more danger than I am? What about your own safety?"

"I can handle myself."

"Great. Handle yourself doing what? Waiting? Watching people?"

"I have friends looking for information now."

She stared at him. He had friends, all right. P.I.s,

cops, law enforcement from around the world. And he was serious.

A slight shiver raked along her spine. If all this was true...

"All right, David. I appreciate your concern for my welfare. And I'm very sorry if Alicia is...dead. I know what she meant to you."

"No, actually, you don't."

He walked up to her, angry again, and she tensed against the emotion that seemed to fill him, though he didn't touch her.

"There was never anything intimate between Alicia and me. She was a good friend. That's all."

She didn't look up at him as she raised her hands. "Whatever your relationship...was, it's none of my business. As I said, thanks for your concern. I'll be very careful. I'll keep my eyes open, and I swear, if I hear anything, I'll tell you. Now, may I please go to sleep? Or try, at least, to get some sleep?"

"I can't leave you."

"What?"

"I can't leave you. Don't you understand? If someone out there thinks you can prove that Alicia is dead, that you might have seen...something, you're in danger of being murdered yourself."

She shook her head. "David, my doors lock. Please go away."

They were both startled when his phone suddenly started to ring. He pulled it from his pocket, snapping it open. "Denham," he said briefly.

She saw him frowning. "Sorry, say again. I'm not getting a great signal here."

He glanced at Alex in apology and walked out back, opening the sliding door, stepping out.

She followed after a moment. He was on the porch rocker, deep in conversation. She hesitated, then shut and locked the glass door. She was going to try to get some sleep. But how? Her mind was spinning.

Before she could reach the hallway, she heard a pounding on the glass. Then David's voice. "Damn it, Alex, let me in!"

"David, I'm fine. We'll talk tomorrow. Go away!"

"I won't leave you."

"Well, I won't let you in."

"I'll have to sleep on the porch then."

"Feel free."

She let the curtain fall closed. He slammed the glass with a fist. She was afraid for a minute it would shatter, despite the fact that it was supposedly hurricaneproof.

She stared at the drapes a long time. He didn't speak again, or hit the glass.

Maybe he had actually gone away. She forced herself to walk to her bedroom, lie down, close her eyes.

At some point, she finally slept.

Her alarm went off at six. She nearly threw it across the room. She felt as if she'd never actually slept, as if her mind had never had a chance to turn off.

After a second, she jumped out of bed and raced to the back, hesitated for a second, then carefully moved the curtain to look out.

David was just rising. To her absolute amazement, he had spent the night with his tall, muscular form pretzeled into the rattan sofa on the porch.

Suddenly she was afraid. Very afraid.

CHAPTER FIVE

DAVID WASN'T FEELING in a particularly benign mood toward Alex, even after he had showered, gone back to his own cottage, downed nearly a pot of coffee, shaved and donned swim trunks, a T-shirt and deck shoes for the day. She'd really locked him out.

And gone to sleep without letting him back in.

He should have slept in his own bed. His cottage was next to hers—it just seemed farther because of the foliage that provided privacy and that real island feel that was such an advertised part of Moon Bay.

He hadn't gone to his own cottage, though, because he had seen someone snooping around her place. And the phone call he'd gone out to take hadn't been the least bit reassuring.

With that in mind, he pocketed his wallet and keys, and left his cottage. Wanting to get out on the water ahead of the resort dive boat, he hurried down to the marina to board the *Icarus*.

As he started to loosen the yacht's ties, he heard his name being called.

Looking up, he saw John Seymore walking swiftly down the dock toward him. Hank Adamson and Jay Galway were following more slowly behind, engaged in conversation.

"Hey," he called back, sizing up Seymore again. For

someone who had been spending his time diving the Pacific, he was awfully bronzed. That didn't mean anything in itself. The water on the West Coast might be cold as hell, but the sun could be just as bright as in the East.

"You're heading out early," John Seymore said. "Anywhere specific?"

"Just the usual dive sites," he replied. He realized that Seymore was angling for an invitation. Why not? "Are you booked on the resort's boat?"

"Couldn't get in—she was full," Seymore said cheerfully. "Hank had the same problem. We tried to weasel our way in through Jay, but he suggested we come down here to see what you had in store."

Just what he wanted. Jay Galway, Hank Adamson and Mr. Surf-Blond All-Around-Too-Decent-Guy out on the *Icarus* with him.

On the other hand, maybe not such a bad idea. He would know where the three of them were, and he might just find out what each of the men knew.

He shrugged. "Come aboard."

"I really appreciate the invitation," Seymore said. "Guys!" he shouted back loudly. "We're in!"

"Hop in, grab a line," David said.

John Seymore came on first, followed by Jay Galway, who hurried ahead of Hank Adamson. "Hey, thanks, David. Sincerely," Galway said. David nodded, figuring that Jay hadn't been happy about having to tell the writer that he couldn't get out for the day, even though it must look good for the resort's programs to be booked.

"This is damn decent of you," Adamson said, hopping on with agility. "Need some help with anything?"

"Looks like Jay has gotten the rest of the ropes. Make yourself at home."

"Want me to put some coffee on while we're moving out?" Jay asked.

"Good idea," David said.

"Sorry, I should have thought of that," John said, grimacing. "I always think of being on a yacht like this and drinking beer and lolling around on the deck."

"Oh, there's beer. Help yourself to anything in the galley." Just stay the hell out of my desk, he thought.

David kept his speed low as he maneuvered the shallow waters by the dock, then let her go. The wind whipped by as the *Icarus* cut cleanly through the water. Adamson and Seymore had remained topside with him, and both seemed to feel the natural thrill of racing across the incredible blue waters with a rush. When they neared the first dive spot on the reef, he slowed the engine.

"Trust me to take the helm?" Seymore asked him.

"Sure," David said, giving him the heading briefly, then hopping down the few steps that led to the cabin below.

He glanced around quickly, assuring himself that his computer remained untouched and it didn't appear Galway had been anywhere near his desk, which was in the rear of the main cabin in a mahogany enclave just behind the expansive dining table and the opposing stretch of well-padded couch.

"Good timing. Coffee's ready," Jay told him. Jay knew the *Icarus*. He'd once gone out with David on a salvage expedition, when he'd been going down to the wreck of a yacht lost in a storm, the *Monday Morning*. The boat had been dashed to pieces, but she'd carried a strongbox of documents her corporate owners had been anxious to find. It had been a simple recovery, but Galway had been elated to be part of the process.

"Thanks," David said.

Jay handed him a cup of black coffee. "For a good-looking son of a bitch, you look like hell this morning," Jay told him.

"I didn't sleep well."

Jay poured himself a cup. "Me neither."

"Dreaming about corpses?"

Jay didn't look startled by the question. "There was no corpse," he said flatly.

"Not when you got there," David suggested.

Jay shook his head. "I asked Alex not to say anything—since we didn't have a body."

"She didn't."

"Then?"

"It's an island, a very small one," David reminded him.

"I was sure Laurie would have the good sense to keep quiet when I asked her to," Jay said disgustedly.

"Laurie didn't talk. Things…get around."

"So you're not going to tell me where you got your information?" Jay asked.

"Nope."

"Like I said, there was no body," Jay told him. He frowned. "How far do you think it's gotten around?"

"Who knows?"

Jay groaned. "If the guests start to hear this…"

"I don't think it'll get around to the rest of the guests," David assured him. God, the coffee was good.

"It was Len, wasn't it? And don't deny it."

"Doesn't matter how I know. And I haven't said a word to anyone else. I know Alex hasn't either, and I'd almost guarantee Laurie hasn't. I do have a question for you. What makes you so convinced Alex was duped?"

Jay looked at him. His surprise seemed real. "There was no body there. And corpses don't get up and walk."

"They can be moved."

"I'm not an idiot. I was looking around just like the sheriff. The sheriff. We didn't just call security and forget it. We called the sheriff. There was no sign of a body ever having been there or being taken away. There were no footprints and no drag marks."

"What the hell does that mean? Someone strong enough could throw a woman's body over his shoulder—and there are palms fronds around by the zillions. Footprints on a beach could easily be erased."

"There couldn't have been a body," Jay said.

David watched him for a few minutes. Jay wasn't meeting his eyes. Instead he seemed intent on wiping the counter where nothing had spilled.

"You look like you're afraid there might have been. And worse, you look as if you're afraid you know who it could have been," David said softly.

Jay stared at him then. "Don't be insane! I'd never kill anyone."

"I didn't say you would. You know, I asked you before about Alicia Farr. You assured me that she hadn't checked in to the resort."

"She hasn't," Jay protested.

"She was supposed to be here."

"She called about a possible reservation, but she never actually booked. I didn't think she would. It's not her cup of tea. Anyway, that was it. She called once, made sure I had the dates available that she wanted, then said she'd get back to me. She didn't. That's the God's honest truth. She never called back."

It sounded as if Jay was sincere, but David couldn't be certain.

Jay gasped suddenly, staring at David. "I know what you're thinking! Believe me, there couldn't have been a corpse. And if there was…it couldn't have been Alicia. I mean, she didn't check in. She was never on the island."

"Well, if there wasn't a corpse, it couldn't have been anyone, right? But I should tell you, Alicia was in Miami a week ago, where she rented a boat and said she was heading down to one of the small private islands in the Keys."

"Do you know how many small private islands there are down here? Maybe she intended to come here but changed her mind. She must have arranged to go somewhere else—maybe a place that belongs to a friend or something." His eyes narrowed. "Were you…with her? In Miami?"

David shook his head.

"How do you know what she was doing, then?"

"She called me. Then when I called back and couldn't reach her I had a friend do a trace on her."

"Alicia is independent. She knows her way around."

"When she called me, she asked me to meet her here, at Moon Bay. The way she talked, she was excited about seeing Moon Bay. She seemed very specific. When she called you, she didn't say anything about her reason for coming?"

"I swear, she didn't tell me anything. She was pleasant and asked about available dates, and that was all," Jay assured him, then frowned. They could both see Hank

Adamson's deck shoes, then his legs, as he descended into the cabin.

"Mind if I take a look around her?" he asked David.

"Hell no. I'm proud of my girl and delighted to give you a tour. Jay, how about relieving John at the helm, so he can get a good look at the *Icarus*, too?"

"Sure. I already know my way around," Jay told Adamson. There was a note of pride in his voice. David watched him thoughtfully as he headed topside.

Jay Galway had been sweating when they talked. A little sheen of perspiration had shown on his upper lip.

So...

Either he was afraid, or he was lying.

Or both.

ALEX HAD EXPECTED Zach to be a problem.

He wasn't. The teenager duly handed her his dive card, then sat through her reminders and instructions like an angel. His mom had decided to stay on shore, despite the fact that they were going to make a stop on one of the main islands before returning that night.

Doug Herrera was captaining their dive boat, and Mandy Garcia was Alex's assistant. They all switched between dive excursions and the dolphins. Gil and Jeb were dealing with the morning's swim, and Laurie was taking her day off. Actually, Alex had expected to see her friend at the docks anyway—Laurie loved to dive, and she especially loved a day when the boat was scheduled to make a stop on one of the main islands when she wasn't working. It was a chance to check out the little waterside bar where they had a meal and after-dive drinks, for those who chose, before returning to Moon Bay.

But Laurie had still been at the Tiki Hut when Alex left, so maybe the late night and the excitement of the day had caused her to sleep in. And maybe she had decided not to come because Seth Granger was on the dive, and he always made things miserable.

At Molasses Reef, their first dive, Alex noted that the *Icarus*, David's yacht, was already anchored nearby. They never anchored on the reefs themselves. Most divers were aware of the very delicate structure of the reef and that it shouldn't be touched by human hands, much less bear the weight of an anchor, and wouldn't have moored there even if there hadn't been laws against it. David was close though, closer than they went themselves.

"Now that's a great-looking yacht," Seth commented, spitting on his mask to prep it.

"Yes," she agreed. The *Icarus* was a thirty-two footer, and she looked incredible under full sail. Today, however, David wasn't sailing her. He'd apparently used the motor. The yacht moved like a dream, either way. Inside, the mahogany paneling and rich appointments made her just as spectacular. The galley had every possible accessory, as did the captain's desk. She was big enough to offer private sleeping facilities for up to three couples.

"You should have asked for the yacht," Seth said, eyeing the *Icarus*.

"I beg your pardon?"

"In your divorce settlement. You should have asked for the yacht. She's a beauty. But, hey, you've got another chance to ask for her now. Heard you're not really divorced," Seth said.

"Where did you hear that?"

He laughed again, or rather, bellowed. "People talk,

you know. Moon Bay is an island. Small. People talk. About everything."

He stared at her, which gave her a very uncomfortable feeling. What else was being discussed?

"I don't want her. She belongs to David. Now, if you'll excuse me, I have to get in the water. And so do you. The tour group is waiting."

Her people were buddied up the way she'd arranged them after she'd duly studied their certificates and discussed their capabilities. She'd decided to buddy up with Zach herself.

In the water, leading the way, even though she was checking constantly to assure herself that her group indeed knew what they were doing and how to deal with their equipment, she found a certain peace. The sound of her own air bubbles always seemed lulling and pleasant. As yet, no cell phones rang here.

Zach stuck with her, amazed. A Michigan kid, he'd gotten his certificate in cold waters and was entranced by the reef. It was a joy to see his pleasure in the riot of tropical fish, and in the giant grouper that nosily edged their way.

This was an easy dive; most of it no more than thirty feet. When she counted her charges again, she saw that Seth Granger had wandered off. His "buddy," the mother of the girls from the day before, was looking lost.

Alex motioned to Zach, then went after Granger. He seemed hostile, but, to her relief, he rejoined the group.

Back on deck, he was annoyed. "I saw David out on the reef. I was just going over for a friendly underwater hello."

"Mr. Granger—"

"Seth. Come on, honey, we've seen enough of each other."

"Seth, if you'd wanted an unplanned, individual dive, you should have spoken with David earlier—and gone out on the *Icarus* with him. I'm sure he'd have been happy to have you."

"Don't be ridiculous. You know I know what I'm doing in the water."

"Guess what, Seth? I don't go diving alone. Too dangerous. Now, I can have the skipper take the boat back in and drop you off at Moon Bay, or you can stay with the group and abide by our rules."

He pointed a finger at her. "I'll be talking to your boss tonight."

"You do that."

At the next two stops, he still wandered, but not as badly as the first time, pretending he had become fascinated by a school of tangs and followed them too far, and then, on the last go-round, that he had seen a fantastic turtle and been unable to resist.

When the last dive was completed, Alex allowed herself a moment's pleasure. Zach was in seventh heaven, and her other divers were exuberant over the beauty they had witnessed. They were ready, when they reached the main island and the little thatch-roofed diner, to eat, drink and chat.

"Good job, boss lady!" Jeb commented to her, a sparkle in his eye, as they went ashore themselves. "How about you have a nice dinner, and I'll keep Seth out of your hair?"

Jeb was great. A college senior, he was only hers for the summer. He was a thin kid, with flyaway dark hair, and a force and energy that defied his bony appearance.

He never argued with her, watched her intently all the time, and was one of those people who seemed intent on really learning and absorbing all the information they could. When she wasn't working with Laurie, she was happiest with Jeb, though all her assistants were hand-picked and great.

"You're on," she told him gratefully.

Leaving the dive boat to her captain, Alex made certain all her charges were comfortable at the Egret Eatery, as the little restaurant was called.

Zach had already found the video games located at the rear of the place. The adults had settled in at various tables.

She saw Jay, Hank, John and David at a table and felt a moment's wary unease. The four of them had obviously spent the day out on the reef together. She'd known the *Icarus* was a stop ahead of her all day. She just hadn't realized how full the yacht had been.

She was about to venture toward their table, but then she saw Seth Granger moving that way, so she steered clear.

"Hey, guys," Seth bellowed. "Mind if I join you? Drinks on me. What'll it be?"

"A pitcher of beer would be appreciated," Hank told him.

"Coke for me," David said.

"Come on. You're not going to crash after one beer, buddy."

"No, a Coke will do fine for me." David looked up and caught Alex's eyes across the room. She felt a chill leap across the open space. For a man so determined to see to her safety, he looked a lot like he wanted to throttle her. Apparently he hadn't enjoyed his night on the porch.

But he had stayed there. And he believed her, believed that the body she had discovered was Alicia Farr's, and that she herself might well be in real danger.

But from who?

Since she wasn't captaining any boat, she turned to the bar and asked Warren, the grizzled old sailor who owned the place, for a beer.

"Sure thing, Alex. How's it going over there? It's been a little slow around here."

"Really? I'm not sure about the hotel, but the dives and swims have been full," she told him.

Setting her glass down, he pointed at the television. "Storm season."

"Summer is always slower than winter. Northerners stay home and sweat in their own states during the summer," she reminded him.

He grinned. "Maybe, but we usually get a bigger Florida crowd around here than we've been getting lately."

She glanced at the TV above the bar. "Is something going on now? I haven't seen any alerts. The last tropical storm veered north, right?"

"Yep. Now there's a new babe on the horizon. She just reached tropical-storm status, and she's been named Dahlia, but they think she's heading north, too. They think she might reach hurricane status sometime, but that she'll be off the Carolinas by then. Still, people don't seem to be venturing out as much as usual. Thank God you bring your guests over here. Right now, frankly, you're helping me survive."

"Don't worry. I'm sure business will pick up," she assured him.

"I see your ex is here. It's always good for business when he shows up here. Word gets out, makes people feel like they're coming to a real 'in' place. Still, it's kind of a surprise to see him. You all right?"

"Of course. We're still friends on a professional level," Alex said.

"You know what I think?" Warren asked her.

"What?"

He leaned low against the bar. "I think he came here for you."

"Mmm," she said. Me, and whatever excitement and treasure Alicia had in store, she thought, but she remained silent on the subject.

Then she asked, "Warren, you know who Alicia Farr is, right? Has she been around?"

"Nope, not that I've heard about."

"Well, thanks."

"Who's the blond Atlas with your ex?" Warren asked.

"Tourist."

"Not your typical tourist," Warren commented, wiping a bar glass dry.

"No, I agree." She shrugged. "Thanks, Warren," she told him. The place was thatch-roofed and open, but she suddenly needed more air. She took her beer and headed outside. She walked along the attached dock, where the dive boat had pulled in, came to the end and looked out at the water, studying the *Icarus*.

She wasn't docked; David had anchored her and come in by way of the dinghy. A moment's nostalgia struck her. She had really loved the *Icarus*, and she did feel a pang that the beautiful sailing vessel wasn't a part of her existence anymore.

She had fair compensation in her life, she knew. Diving, here off the Florida coast, would always be a joy, no matter who was on the tour. And she had her dolphins. They might actually belong to the corporation that owned Moon Bay, but they were her babies. Shania, especially. Wounded, just treated and beginning to heal when Alex had come on board, the adolescent dolphin was her favorite—though, naturally, she'd never let the other dolphins know. But she felt as if she and Shania had gained trust and strength at the same time. She had noticed that Shania followed her sometimes. One night, sipping a drink at the Tiki Hut, she had looked up to find the dolphin, nose above the surface, watching her from the lagoon.

And she had learned to live alone. By the end of her whirlwind one-year marriage to David, she had been alone most of the time anyway. Her choice, she reminded herself in fairness. But he never wanted to stay in one place, and she had longed to establish a real base, a real home. Too many times, he had been with a woman who shared his need for constant adventure. Like Alicia Farr. And she had let the doubts slip in and take over. When she had filed the papers and he hadn't said a single word, she had forced herself to accept the truth— she wasn't what he wanted or needed. He had Alicia, and others like her.

He had been planning on meeting Alicia at Moon Bay. And now he suspected she was dead.

With that thought, she dug into the canvas bag she'd brought ashore, found her cell and called the sheriff's office. She was certain she was going to have to leave a message, but Nigel Thompson's assistant put her right through.

"Hey, Alex."

"Hey, Nigel. I'm sorry to bother you, but...I'm concerned."

"Of course. But listen, I checked all the ferry records. No one's missing. Everyone who checked into Moon Bay is alive and well and accounted for. And all the day-trippers and people who checked out of Moon Bay were on the ferries out. Usually there are people in their own boats who come by way of the Moon Bay marina, but not yesterday."

"Thanks, Nigel," she murmured.

"Alex?"

"Yeah."

"I don't think you're easily fooled. I sent some men out last evening to walk the grounds. But they didn't find anything."

"Thank you, Nigel. I guess...I don't know. Thank you anyway."

"Sure thing."

She snapped the phone closed.

She nearly jumped a mile when a hand fell on her shoulder. She spun around, spilling half her beer.

It was just Jeb.

"Sorry," he said quickly. "I didn't mean to startle you. I saw you go out, so I followed. Want to wander into a few shops with me? I need a tie."

"You need a tie?"

He grimaced. "A friend is getting married up in Palm Beach next week. I've got the makings of a suit, but I don't own a single tie."

Her own thoughts were driving her crazy, but she couldn't think of a rational step she could take to solve any of her dilemmas. Might as well go tie shopping.

"SO...WHERE'S THAT NEW girl of yours, David?" Seth asked.

They hadn't been there long; but Seth Granger had already consumed five or six drinks—island concoctions made with three shots each.

David had never particularly liked the guy to begin with, and with a few drinks in him, he was pretty much completely obnoxious.

"New girl?" David asked.

"Alicia Farr. Fair Alicia. Since the wife threw you over after all those pictures of the two of you came out, I figured the two of you were an item. She isn't here with you, huh? I heard tell she had something up her sleeve and was going to be around these parts. Word is she learned something from that old geezer who died a while back. Danny Fuller."

David wondered if Seth Granger was really drunk or was just pretending to be. He'd spent the day listening, waiting for one of his guests to ask the right question, make the right slip. No go. They might have been any four good old boys out for a day on the water.

But now...

"Sorry, Seth. Alicia and I were never an item. We team up now and then for work. We have a lot of the same interests, that's all. There's no reason for her to be at Moon Bay."

"Actually, there was an article about her in the news a few weeks back. Of course, it was in one those supermarket tabloids, so... Anyway, the headline was something like Dying Mogul Gives Secrets to Beauty Who's a Beast. The writer seemed to think she'd been hanging on him hoping to get news on any unclaimed treasure he might know about. There was a definite suggestion that she was coming to the Keys."

Jay Galway thumped his beer stein on the table a little too hard. "So why do you think she was headed for Moon Bay? There are two dozen islands in the Keys."

"That's true enough," David said, eyeing John Seymore. "So you're up on the movements of Alicia Farr, too, huh?" he inquired, forcing a bit of humor into his voice.

"I'm a wannabe, I admit," John said ruefully.

"I know what it takes to be a SEAL," David commented. "I can't imagine you're a wannabe anything."

"Not like me, huh?" Seth Granger demanded, giving David a slap on the back that caught him totally unaware and awakened every fighting reaction inside him.

He checked his temper. "Hell, Granger, with your money? I doubt you're a wannabe anything, either."

"The wannabe would be me," Jay said dryly.

"Jay, you're running a four-star resort, and your vacations are pure adventure," David assured him.

"Yeah, but I bust my butt for all of them—and I'm still on the fringes. But you know…I spent a lot of time with Danny Fuller. I'm sure he had a dozen treasure maps stored in his head, things he learned over the years, and Alicia had the looks—and the balls. So…"

"Looks like we're all here looking for Alicia," Seth said. "And she's blown us all off."

"I don't actually know her," John Seymore reminded them.

"That's right—Seymore's just here to get warm and cuddly with the sea life," David said.

"And your ex-wife," Seth commented.

A tense silence suddenly gripped the table.

Then David's phone rang, as if on cue. "Excuse me, will you?" he said to the others. "Reception is better outside."

He rose, flipping open the phone as he walked out, then paused in the alleyway outside the little restaurant, shaded by a huge sea grape tree.

"Can you talk?" his caller asked.

"You bet," David said. "I've been hoping to hear from you."

"I spent some time at the hospital where Danny Fuller died. Seems Alicia was in on an almost daily basis. One of the nurses heard her swearing to Danny again and again that she wasn't after money, just discovery. And whatever Danny told her, it had to do with dolphins. Apparently the words *dolphin* and *lagoon* came up over and over again. And there was one more thing I think you'll find of interest." The man on the other end paused.

"What's that?" David asked after a long silence. Dane Whitelaw didn't usually hesitate. An ex–special-forces agent, he had opened his own place in Key Largo, where he combined dive charters with a private investigation firm. Sounded a bit strange, but it seemed to work out well enough. He avoided a lot of the big city slush and came up with some truly interesting work, a lot of it to do with boats lost at sea and people who disappeared after heading out for the Caribbean.

Some of them wanted to disappear.

Some of them were forced to do so.

But if he needed information of any kind, David had never met anyone as capable as Dane of finding it out.

Dane was still silent.

"You still there?" David asked.

"Yeah."

"Well?"

"Apparently, according to the old guy's night nurse, your ex-wife's name kept coming up, as well."

"What?"

"She said the two kept talking about an Alex Mc-Cord."

David digested the information slowly. Finally it was Dane's turn to ask, "Hey, David, you still there?"

"Yeah, yeah. I need another favor."

"What's that?"

"Look into a guy for me. If he's telling the truth at all, you should be able to dig up some stuff on him."

"Sure. Who's the guy?"

"An ex–navy SEAL. John Seymore."

JEB HAD HIS TIE. Alex wasn't certain what it was going to look like when combined with a dress shirt and a jacket, but it was certainly a comment about the life-style he loved. Light blue dolphins leaping against a cobalt background.

Alex had purchased one of the same ties. Reflex action, she decided. The darker color was just like David's eyes, and she used to buy all kinds of little things just because they might appeal to him.

"Damn," she murmured as they walked back to the restaurant.

"What?"

"Oh…nothing. I guess I don't really want to go back in and see our…group." Nor did she want to pass the alley. She could see David. He was bare chested, wearing deep green trunks and deck shoes, leaning against the wall. He hadn't noticed them yet, because he was too deeply engrossed in a telephone conversation.

"Our group? Oh, you mean Seth Granger," Jeb suggested.

She shrugged. "Right. Seth." Seth was just a pain in the butt, though. Annoying to deal with, but once she was away from him, she forgot all about him.

She really didn't want to see David. She was furious with herself for having instinctively bought the tie.

"Just walk on by then, Alex. The boat is at the end of the dock. Wait there. I'll go in and gather up the forces. Hopefully anyone who wandered off shopping is back. And hopefully those who did more drinking than eating won't be too inebriated."

She smiled and thanked him, then started down the dock. The sunset was coming in, and she believed with her whole heart that nothing could compare to sunset in the Florida Keys. The colors were magnificent. If there was rain on the horizon, they were darker. On a bright day like today, the night came with a riot of unparalleled pastels.

It was her favorite time of day. Peaceful. Especially when she had a few moments alone, as she did now. The dock was empty. The other boaters docked nearby were either on shore or in their cabins. The evening was hers.

She strolled the length of rustic wood planks and, at the end, stretched and sat, dangling her feet as she appreciated the sky and tried not to think about the corpse she had seen.

Or the husband she had so suddenly reacquired.

"WHO'S MISSING HERE?"

David had just reentered the restaurant in time to hear Jeb Larson's question.

"Mr. Granger," Zach called out helpfully.

"Mr. Denham," Jeb asked, spotting David. "Have you seen Mr. Granger?"

"Sorry, I went out to make a call. He was at the table when I left."

Jay Galway came striding in at that moment, a bag bearing the name of a local shop in his hand. He arched an eyebrow at Jeb. "Got a problem?"

"Just missing a diver," Jeb said, never losing his easy tone. "Mr. Granger."

Jay seemed startled as he looked around. "He was here twenty minutes ago," he said. "David?"

"Don't know. I was on the phone."

"He said something about going out for a smoke," Hank Adamson called. He was standing at the end of the bar. David was certain he hadn't been there a minute ago.

He looked around. John Seymore seemed to be among the missing, as well, but just then he came striding in from around back.

"Excuse me, Mr. Seymore," Jeb called. "Have you seen Mr. Granger?"

"Nope," John Seymore said.

"Leave it to Granger."

The words were a bare whisper of aggravation, but David was close enough to Jay Galway to hear them.

"Well, relax…we'll find him," Jeb said, still cheerful.

"Maybe he went shopping," Zach suggested.

"Yep, maybe," Jeb said, and tousled the boy's hair.

"You know," David said quietly to Jay, "they can take the dive boat on back. We can wait for him."

Jay cast him a glance that spoke volumes about his dislike for the man, but all he said was, "We can wait a few minutes."

ALEX STARED AT the lights as they played over the water. The lapping sound of the sea as it gently butted against dozens of hulls and the wood of the dock pilings was lulling. The little ripples below her were growing darker, but still, there was a rainbow of hues, purple, deepest aqua, a blue so dark it was almost ebony.

She frowned, watching as something drifted out from beneath the end of the dock where she sat.

At first, she was merely puzzled. What on earth…?

Then her blood ran cold. She leaped to her feet, staring down. Her jaw dropped, and she clenched her throat to scream…caught the sound, started to turn, stopped again.

No. This body wasn't disappearing.

And so she went with her first instinct and began to scream as loudly as she could.

"We all have to wait here for just one guy?" one of the divers complained.

"My Mom will be getting worried," Zach said.

"Don't worry, you can use my phone," David assured the teen, handing it to him. "Don't you have a cell phone?" he asked the boy.

Zach grinned. "You bet. But Mom wouldn't let me take it on the boat. Said I might lose it overboard. She doesn't dive," he said, as if that explained everything about his mother.

"Leave it to Seth Granger," Jay said, and this time, he was clearly audible. "Go ahead," he instructed Jeb. "You and the captain and Alex get our crew back. David has said he doesn't mind waiting for Granger." He turned to David. "You're sure?" he asked.

"Sure. We'll wait," he said, and he hoped to hell it

wasn't going to be long. Now, more than ever, he didn't want Alex out of his sight.

The others rose, stretched and started to file out.

And that was when they heard the scream.

Somehow, the instant he heard it, David knew they weren't going to have to wait for Granger after all.

CHAPTER SIX

EVERYONE CAME RUNNING.

Alex wasn't thrilled about that, but after her last experience, she'd had to sound an alarm—she wasn't letting this body drift away. Before the others came pounding down the dock, though, she dived in. Though the man was floating face downward and sure as hell looked dead, she wasn't taking any chances.

The water right by the dock was far from the pristine blue expanse featured in tourist ads. She rose from a misty darkness to grab hold of the man's floating arm.

With a jolt, she realized it was Seth Granger.

By then the others had arrived. David was in the lead and instantly jumped into the water to join her. He was stronger and was easily able to maneuver the body. John Seymore, with Jeb at his side, reached down as David pushed Seth upward; between them, they quickly got Seth Granger lying on the dock, and, despite the obvious futility, Jeb dutifully attempted resuscitation. Alex heard someone on a cell phone, telling a 911 operator what had happened. By the time she and David had both been fished out of the water and were standing on the dock, sirens were blaring.

Jeb, youthful and determined, kept at his task, helped by John, but Seth was clearly beyond help.

He still reeked of alcohol.

Two med techs came racing down the dock, and when they reached Seth Granger, Jeb and John stepped aside. The men from Fire Rescue looked at one another briefly, then took over where John and Jeb had left off.

"Anyone know how long he's been in the water?" one of them.

"Couldn't be more than twenty minutes," John Seymore said. "He was definitely inside twenty minutes ago."

"Let's get him in the ambulance, set up a line…give him a few jolts," one of the med techs said. In seconds, another team was down the dock with a stretcher, and the body was taken to the waiting ambulance.

Then the sheriff arrived. He didn't stop the ambulance, but he looked at Seth Granger as he was taken away, and Alex noted the imperceptible shake of his head. He took a deep breath and turned to the assembled crowd.

"What happened?" Nigel Thompson demanded.

"Well, he was drinking too hard and too fast, that's for sure," Hank Adamson commented.

"We were at a table together," Jay told Nigel. He pointed around. "Seth, John, Hank, David and myself. David's phone rang, and he decided to take it outside. I needed to pick up a few things, so I headed down the street, and then…" He looked at the other two who had shared the table.

"I went to the men's room," John Seymore said, and looked at Hank Adamson.

"I walked up to the bar."

"When did Granger leave the bar?" Nigel asked.

His answer was a mass shrugging of shoulders.

"Hell," Nigel muttered. "All right, everyone back inside."

David was already on his feet. He reached a hand down to Alex, his eyes dark and enigmatic. She hesitated, then accepted his help.

She realized, as she stood, that John Seymore was watching. He gave her a little smile, then turned away. It seemed that day suddenly turned to night. She shivered, then regretted it. David slipped an arm around her shoulders. "You all right?" he asked.

"Of course," she said coldly.

"Alex, you don't have to snap," he said softly.

She removed his arm from around her shoulders and followed the others. She meant to find wherever John was sitting and take a place beside him.

Too late. Zach was on John's left, Hank Adamson on his right. There was one bench left, and there was little for her to do other than join David when he sat there.

She suddenly felt very cold, and, gritting her teeth, she accepted the light windbreaker he offered. She instantly regretted the decision. It felt almost as if she had cloaked herself in his aura. It wasn't unpleasant. It was too comfortable.

The sheriff's phone rang. "Thompson," he said briefly as he answered it. A second later, he flipped his phone closed. "Well, it's bad news but not unexpected. He was pronounced dead at the hospital."

"Mind if we go over Mr. Granger's movements one more time?" Nigel asked.

"He came, he drank, he fell in the water," a businessman who'd been on the dive said impatiently.

"Thanks for the compassion, sir," Nigel said.

"Sorry, Sheriff," the man said. "But the guy was rich and being a rude pain in the you-know-what all day."

"Well, thank goodness not everyone who's rude ends up drowning," the sheriff said pointedly. "I'd have myself one hell of a job," Nigel commented.

"Sorry," the man said again. "It's just that…we're all tired. I only met the man today on the dive, and he wasn't the kind of person to make you care about him. And I'm on vacation."

"Well, then, I'll get through this just as fast as I can. First things first—those of you from Moon Bay. Anyone checking out tomorrow?"

No one was, apparently. Or, if so, they weren't about to volunteer the information.

"Good. Okay, I'm going outside. One by one, come out, give me your names, room numbers and cell-phone numbers, and I may have a quick question or two. Then you can reboard and get going."

Squeaky wheels were the ones oiled first, Alex determined. Nigel asked her whining diver to come out first.

"This is kind of silly," a woman who had been on the dive complained. "A pushy rich man got snockered and fell in the water. That's obvious."

"Nothing is obvious," David said, his eyes focused on the woman. Alex felt the coiling heat and tension in his body before he continued. "Nigel Thompson is top rate. He's not leaving anything to chance."

The woman flushed and fell silent.

Alex felt as if she were trapped, so aware of David in the physical sense that she was about to scream. In this room full of people, in the midst of this tense situation, she found herself focusing on the most absurd things. Like her ex-husband's toes. His muscled calves. Legs that were long and powerful. When he inhaled, his flesh brushed hers.

She forced herself to look across the room at John Seymore, instead.

In the room, conversations began. David turned to Alex suddenly. "You all right?" he asked softly.

"Of course I'm all right," she said. He was studying her gravely. Then a slight smile curved his lips. "Why?" she asked cautiously.

His head moved closer. His lips were nearly against her ear. When he spoke, it seemed that his voice and the moisture of his breath touched her almost like a caress. "You've been undressing me with your eyes," he told her.

"You are undressed," she informed him. "And what I'm thinking about is the fact that a man drowned."

"Did he?"

"Of course! Damn you, David, we were both there."

"We were both there to pull the body out of the water, but we weren't there when he died."

"He drowned," she insisted.

"Isn't this getting to you just a little bit?" His voice lowered even further. "You're in danger."

"And you're going to protect me?" she demanded.

"You bet."

"Are you going to keep sleeping on my porch?"

"No, you're going to let me into the cottage."

"Dream on. I don't know what this absurd obsession with me is, but do you really think you're going to scare me into letting you back in my bed?"

"Only if you insist, and if it will make you feel better."

In that moment she hated him with a sudden intensity, because she had been so secure, so ready to explore a relationship with another man, and now…

David had played on her mental processes. She knew he could make her feel secure…that his flesh against her own could feel irresistibly erotic, compelling…. She wanted to curl against him, close her eyes, rest, imagine.

"You've got some explaining to do, too," he informed her. Suddenly his eyes reminded her of a predatory cat.

She stiffened. "I have to explain something to you?"

"About Danny Fuller."

"Danny Fuller?"

They both fell silent.

As more people filed outside, those waiting to be questioned began to shift around. Alex saw her opportunity and rose, placing as much distance as she could between herself and David.

And then, with nothing else to do, she found herself pacing the room. Danny Fuller? What the hell was he talking about?

She was idly walking in front of one of the long benches when she nearly collided with Jay. He caught hold of her shoulders to steady her, then she sighed, turned and took a seat on the bench right behind him.

She gazed at him where he sat. His hands were steepled prayer fashion in front of him, and he was looking upward. "Thank you, God," he barely whispered. "Thank you for making this happen here and not on Moon Bay."

"Jay!" she gasped, horrified.

He looked up at her and flushed. "Well, he was a mean old bastard, and he'd lived out most of his life," Jay protested. "He liked to drink way too hard, and never believed the sea could be stronger than he was. Well, you can't turn up your nose and think you're better than the Atlantic."

"This is still horrible."

"Yeah, I'm sure all his ex-wives are going to be crying real hard," Jay murmured.

She started to say something, then fell quiet. Without her noticing, the room had been emptying out.

It was just her and Jay left to speak with the sheriff, and Nigel was coming toward them.

"Well, it's a miracle, but no one in this place saw Seth Granger walk out. No one. Not the bartender, not a single waiter, waitress, busboy, cook or floor scrubber, none of the locals, and certainly none of your guests from Moon Bay."

"Nigel, the guy was drunk," Jay said wearily.

Nigel shook his head. "Seth Granger was always drinking, from what I've heard. Strange that he would just walk into the water, though. Stranger still that no one saw him do it. Never mind." He pointed a finger at Alex. "I want to talk to you at some length. Tomorrow. Got it?"

"Me?"

"Two days, two bodies," Nigel said.

"But...you told me there was no second body. Or first body. Other body."

"Alex, I already told you, I did all the checking I could—and I sent men out to walk the grounds. You know I didn't discount your story entirely. Anyway, we'll talk. I'll be out to see you tomorrow. For now...well, I've got some crime-scene people taking a look around here. At this point, it looks as if Seth got a bit too tipsy, took a walk, met the water and then his maker. There's going to have to be a hearing, though, and an autopsy. The medical examiner will have to verify that scenario."

Jay nodded glumly. "Still," he murmured, "at least it happened here, not at Moon Bay." The other two looked at him. "Hey, I'm sorry, but it matters."

"Well, take your guests home, Jay," Thompson said. "You." He pointed at Alex. "I'll see you tomorrow."

"Sure," she murmured.

They left, bidding Warren goodbye. Alex hoped the restaurant wouldn't end up paying for Seth's alcohol consumption. She knew Warren usually watched his customers and had been known to confiscate keys from any driver he thought shouldn't be on the road. His staff was equally vigilant.

From what she had seen, there had been a pitcher of beer on the table. Seth had probably been downing pitcher after pitcher himself, but the waitress had undoubtedly assumed the beer was being consumed by a party of five.

As they walked along the deck toward the boat, Jay stopped Alex. "I'll go back on the dive boat," he told her. "Damage control," he said with a wince.

"There's room for us both," she said.

"Take a break. Go back on the *Icarus*," he said. "That's okay with you, right, David?" Jay asked, turning slightly.

She hadn't realized that her ex—or not quite ex—husband had been right behind them. "Sure," he said.

Great. A ride back with David, John Seymore and Hank Adamson.

Still, she didn't want to make a draining evening any worse, so she shrugged. At least the ride wouldn't take long.

Along with a sympathetic smile, John Seymore offered her a hand down into the little dinghy that would take them back to the *Icarus*. She wound up sitting next to Hank Adamson, while David and John had the oars. Once again, it was John who gave her a hand on board the *Icarus*, but once there, she hurried aft, hoping to make the journey back alone.

No luck.

She had barely settled down on the deck, choosing a spot she had often chosen in years past, when David joined her.

She groaned aloud. "Don't you ever go away?"

"I can't. Not now."

She stared at him. "You know, I'm trying to have a relationship with someone else."

"I don't know about him yet."

"What don't you know about him?"

He looked at her, blue eyes coolly touching hers. "I don't know if he's in on what's going on or not."

She groaned again. "David, he hasn't been out of the military that long. He's from the West Coast. He's not into salvage."

"He's into things connected with the sea, that's for certain."

"So?"

"So I still don't know about him."

"How about letting me make a few judgments on my own?"

"Did you see a corpse on the beach or not?" he demanded.

She looked away, silently damning him. "Yes."

"And are we absolutely positive that Seth Granger just got up, left a bar, fell into the water and drowned?"

"No," she admitted after a moment. "But it's the most likely scenario."

"'Most likely' doesn't make it fact," he said flatly. "The body that you found—and yes, I'm convinced you found a body—was Alicia's. I'm certain of it."

"How do you know that?" she demanded, but then she knew. One of his best friends, Dane Whitelaw, worked in Key Largo, leading his version of an ideal life, running a dive service and an investigations business. "Never mind. You've had Dane looking into it."

"Yup. So do you understand now?"

"Understand what?"

"Why I need to keep you under my wing for the time being."

"Under your wing?" she snapped.

"Don't get bristly," he protested. "After all, we're still married."

"A technicality."

"Even if we weren't, I'd be damned if I'd allow anyone to hurt you."

"John Seymore doesn't intend to hurt me," she said. Then she couldn't resist adding, "Unless I want him to."

He glared at her, eyes hard. "You just won't take this seriously, will you?"

"How do I know you haven't suddenly turned into a murderer in your quest for treasure?"

"Quit fighting me, please. I really don't want to sleep on your porch tonight. It will just make me harder to get along with. And if I'm cranky, I won't go to see a lawyer with you. And once I find out what's going on here… well, I could just take off again and leave you in limbo for a very long time."

"You wouldn't!" she said.

"I didn't file the papers in the first place," he said with a shrug, then rose. "We're nearly back. I've got to go dock her."

Left alone, Alex felt her temper rising, but she wasn't as furious with him at that moment as she was with herself. She shouldn't be making a terrible problem out of things. Let the idiot sleep on the couch. Under the circumstances, she needed to take everything slow. If John Seymore was really interested in her, he would wait around.

Even with her ex-or-almost-ex-husband in the cottage?

They had docked. She rose slowly, all too aware of why she was so upset. Having David on the couch should be no big deal.

Except she would know he was there. And now, with each passing moment, she was more and more aware of why she had been so attracted to him from the beginning, why she felt a strange flush of excitement when he was around, and why she found herself so annoyed that he ran around shirtless so often.

"We really do need to talk," David murmured as they went ashore, following Hank Adamson and John Seymore off the *Icarus*.

"I really need to see to my dolphins," she told him, and purposely walked as quickly as she could along the docks, aiming straight for the dolphin lagoon and praying, for once, that she wouldn't be followed. By anyone.

"COME TO THE Tiki Hut with me?" Jay said to David. He'd waited at the end of the deck. He was trying to sound casual, but there was an edgy note in his voice.

Damage control, David thought.

"I really need a shower," David told him.

"And I don't think anyone actually wants a drink," Hank Adamson said.

"What the hell, I'll go for a few minutes," John Seymore said.

"We'll all go," David determined. He wanted to keep an eye on the guy. He wasn't sure if he was suspicious because a man like Seymore was in a place like this, or because he was interested in Alex. Interested in her? He'd had his tongue halfway down her throat the other night.

"Apparently the sheriff doesn't believe that Seth Granger just fell in the water and drowned," Hank said as they walked.

"What makes you say that?" Jay asked him sharply.

"He questioned everyone pretty closely."

"He's the sheriff," Jay said uneasily. "He has to cover all bases. Why the hell would anyone want to kill Seth Granger?"

The silence that followed his question was telling.

"For being a crass, overbearing windbag, for one," Hank offered dryly.

They reached the Tiki Hut. The employees rushed for Jay as he appeared, and he calmly explained the situation. No one seemed to be terribly sad, David noted. They were amazed, though, and maybe even a little titillated. The drowning of such a wealthy man was bound to excite gossip.

The four men took a table. David admired Jay's determination to deal with the situation. He wanted to be visible, to answer any questions. That was damage control, yes, but at least the guy wasn't shrinking from his responsibility.

Zach's mother, Ally Conroy—the one person who had seemed to be getting on with Seth the night before—was in the bar without her son, and it appeared she'd had a few herself. She rose, walked to the table and demanded, "Are they really saying he just…got up and drowned?"

"That's what they think right now, yes," Jay told her.

"I don't believe it. I didn't know him that well, but I don't believe it," she said, slurring her words. "Everyone was there, right with him. How come no one saw?" Ally demanded. Her voice was strong, but she was shifting from foot to foot as she spoke.

"Probably because none of us was expecting anything to happen," David told her, rising. "Mrs. Conroy, you seem…distraught. Would you like me to walk you to your room?"

"Why? Because I might fall into the water and drown?" she said with hostility.

"Because I wouldn't want you to hurt yourself in any way," David said.

Suddenly her eyes fell. She sniffed. "He liked me. Liked Zach and liked me. You don't know how hard it is to raise a kid by yourself. And he was…not the kind of man who'd get drunk, fall in the water and drown."

"The sheriff will be investigating," David assured her gently. "In fact, he'll be here tomorrow. You can talk to him yourself."

She suddenly seemed to deflate, hanging on David's arm. She looked up at him, a little bleary-eyed. "Hey, you're all right, you know?"

"I'll walk her to her room," David told the others.

They nodded.

Ally Conroy was definitely stumbling as she clung to David. "We've got one of the cottages," she said. "It was an Internet deal. Cool, huh? I'm paying a lot less than most people. Have to watch my money, you know?"

"Of course. I'm glad you got a good deal."

By the time they reached her cottage, he was ready to pick her up and throw her over his shoulder, she was stumbling so badly. He damned himself for taking the time to go with her, was even now missing something being said at the Tiki Hut, some piece of the puzzle that had to come together soon.

Because he didn't believe, not for a minute, that Seth Granger had just fallen into the water and died.

They reached the cottage at last. She couldn't find her key, so David knocked on the door, hoping Zach would hear.

"He was onto something. Onto something big," Ally said suddenly.

"What?"

"He told me about some ship."

"What ship?"

"Where is that damn key?" Ally Conroy said.

David strove for patience and an even tone. "Mrs. Conroy, what ship? Please, think for me."

"The…ship. He was going after a ship. Said he had a friend who needed help, and he intended to help her, because it might be the best thing he'd done in his life. Will you look at this purse? It's an absolute mess."

"Don't worry, there's a key in there somewhere, and if not, Zach will open the door. Mrs. Conroy, you could really help me out here. Did Seth know the name of the ship he wanted to find?"

"The name of the ship…" she repeated.

"The name."

"Oh…yes! The *Anne Marie,* I think he said." Her eyes

brightened, and she smiled, forgetting her quest for her key for a moment. "He was very excited about it. He said there was more fantasy written about her than fact. That the legend had it all wrong. No, history was wrong, legend was right." She shook her head and gave her attention back to her purse. "Where is that damned key?"

The door opened. Zach looked at them anxiously.

"I thought I should walk your mom to your cottage," David said.

Zach looked amazingly world-weary, understanding and tolerant. "Thanks, Mr. Denham."

"No problem, and call me David."

The kid nodded, taking his mother's arm.

"I'm okay," Ally said, steadying herself. She cupped Zach's face, then gave him a kiss on the forehead. "I guess we have to take care of each other, huh? I'm sorry, hon."

"It's okay, Mom."

"I'm going to lie down," Ally said.

"Good idea," Zach told her.

Ally paused, looking at David. "I...thank you," she said.

"Not at all."

"I'll try to remember anything else I can," she told him. "After an aspirin and a night's sleep," she added dryly.

"Thanks again."

Ally walked inside. Zach looked at David. "She liked Mr. Granger," he said with a shrug. "I was sorry, but...I didn't want her getting all tied up with him. I know she was thinking it would be great for me to have a dad, but he was a loudmouth. And rude. I didn't want my mom with him. I didn't make him fall in the water, though."

"I never thought you did, Zach," David said.

"Thanks," Zach said. As David started to walk away, he called him back. "Hey, Mr. Denham? David?"

"Yes?"

"Maybe sometime, if you're not too busy, you could show me the *Icarus?*"

"I'd be glad to," David said. "Maybe tomorrow. Ask your Mom. Maybe we can have coffee together, or breakfast, and I'll take you both out on her."

In all honesty, he liked the kid. Especially after tonight.

And he damn sure wanted to talk to Ally Conroy when she was sober.

Before anyone else did.

CHAPTER SEVEN

LEN CREIGHTON WAS off work, and he considered his free time as totally his own. He sat nursing a double stinger at the Tiki Hut. He needed it.

He'd been behind the desk when a news brief had interrupted the television program in the lobby with the stunning information that millionaire tycoon Seth Granger was dead, apparently by drowning. There was little other information at the time, but he'd heard more about it once the boats had returned to Moon Bay. It had been pretty much the only topic of conversation in the Tiki Hut.

He was still hearing the buzz about it from other tables when Hank Adamson sat down in front of him.

"Long day, huh?" Adamson said, indicating Len's drink.

"Longer for you, I imagine, Mr. Adamson."

"You can call me Hank, please. Yeah, we were there a long time. The sheriff asked everyone if anyone had seen Seth go out or fall in the water. No one had."

"No one saw him? How sad," Len said.

Hank lifted a hand to order a drink. After giving his order, he told Len, "Sad thing is, I don't think anyone cared."

"I care," Len said in protest. He shrugged sheepishly. "He always tipped well."

"He was rude as hell to the waitress today. You don't think she pushed him into the drink, do you?"

Len smiled, but knew he had to be careful with Hank Adamson. "I'm sure he was just tipsy and fell in himself."

"That old sheriff…he's something, though. Ever had a homicide in this area?"

"Not since I've been here."

"Well, there you go. A local-yokel sheriff just trying to make a name for himself."

"Nigel's a good guy," Len defended.

"So you think he really thinks there was foul play?" Hank asked, smiling at the waitress and accepting a beer from her.

"He's no yokel," Len said.

Adamson leaned toward him. "Why would someone murder Granger? They aren't going to be blaming it on any ex-wife. If he was killed, it had to be someone who was with us at that bar. Someone on the staff at Moon Bay?"

"No way!" Len protested.

"Your boss admits he wants in on a lot of action," Hank said. "He'd love to get into the salvage operations business."

Len stood up. Writer or no, Hank Adamson had crossed the line.

"Jay is as honest as the day is long," Len said firmly.

"Hey, an honest man can be driven to murder," Hank said, smiling as he took another sip of beer straight from the bottle. "Sit down. I like your boss. In my opinion, the jerk just fell off the pier. Finish your drink, and I'll buy you another."

Len hesitated. Then, looking across the dance floor,

he noticed Jay, who saw him, and motioned that he'd be over momentarily.

Len smiled. "Jay will be joining us in just a minute," he told Hank. He sipped his drink, then was embarrassed to experience a huge yawn before he could suppress it. "Sorry. It's been a long day."

"Way too long. I don't guess many of us will be hanging around here too late tonight," Hank said.

A few minutes later, when Jay came over, Len rose, stifling another yawn, and bade the two good-night.

THERE WAS NO sign of Laurie Smith at the lagoons, but she wasn't required to be there—it was her day off, for one thing. Still, Alex was surprised. Laurie really loved the dolphins and tried to spend time with them every day.

She hesitated, then pulled out her cell phone and tried Laurie's room. There was no answer. She dialed Laurie's cell-phone number next, but got voice mail.

Strange.

Mandy and Gil were both there, though. They'd already heard what had happened but she gave them the full story of how she'd found him.

"Man, imagine that. A guy can have everything in the world, and still…" Gil said, shaking his head. "Just last night, he was flirting and drinking half the beer in the place. He had one hell of a capacity for liquor."

"I guess so. That seems to be what everyone says," Alex said.

"Tragic when anyone dies like that," Mandy said, shaking his dark head. "He was coming on to that Ally woman last night, and she was eating it up. He was boasting about something really big he was into. I thought the guy was a jerk, myself."

"Hank Adamson was there when it happened, right?" Gil said, rolling his eyes.

"He was there. One of the last to see him alive," Alex said.

"Bet he'll love telling that story," Gil said. "Anyway, I know you want to hear about these guys," he told her, indicating the dolphins.

Mandy showed her the log book for the day. "We were bringing them their good-night snack," Gil said. "Didn't know when you'd be back. But you can take over."

"That's all right," she said.

Mandy laughed. "No, it's not. We know you like to tuck them in."

She smiled. "You two do fine without me," Alex said.

"Hell, the swim was a piece of cake next to your day," Mandy said. "Seth Granger dead. Go figure." He made a face. "And you found him floating. I'm glad it wasn't me."

"You look all done in. We'll take off and leave you to your babies," Gil said. "I'm sure you don't want to replay the afternoon anymore."

"It's okay, but you're right. Truthfully, I don't want to talk about it anymore. Not now, anyway," she agreed.

"Good night, then," Gil said.

"Hey, wait!" she called. They stopped, looking at her expectantly. "Has either of you seen Laurie today?" she asked.

"I haven't," Gil said, looking at Mandy.

"I haven't either. But it is her day off," Mandy said.

"I haven't seen her since last night. She left the Tiki Hut kind of late. She'd been talking to Hank Adamson. She was holding her own against him, too, and the guy can be a real pain," Gil said.

"Yeah, he can. Did he grill either of you?" Alex asked.

"Nope," Gil said. "I was at the Tiki Hut after she left, but…I don't remember seeing Adamson after that, either, actually. But hey, I'm a bald guy with a gold earring, and Laurie is a cute girl. I'd grill her, too, if I were Adamson." He frowned suddenly. "Are you worried about her?"

"No. Not really. It's her day off. She's free to come and go as she pleases," Alex said.

"Actually, come to think of it, Len was looking for her earlier, too," Mandy said.

"Why?"

"I think he had mail for her. Or maybe he just knew that she'd been talking to Hank Adamson, and wanted to make sure she hadn't said anything she shouldn't." He shrugged.

Gil let out a snort. "Adamson is going to write what he wants, no matter what any of us say. Only thing is, now he's going to have an awful lot more to write about, having been there when Seth Granger bit the big one."

"Gil…" Alex said with a groan.

"I'll take a walk by Laurie's room and knock," Gil said. "But maybe she just doesn't want to be disturbed."

"Yeah. She could have a hot date," Mandy agreed.

"You think?" Alex said. She shook her head. "She would have told me. She hated that Date Tournament thing she went on."

"Yeah, but…she sure was impressed by your ex-husband," Mandy said.

"And the blond guy chasing you around the last few days," Gil commented.

"Well, they were both there today when Seth—as you so gently put it—bit the big one," Alex said.

"I'm sure she's fine," Gil said. "I'm sure she'll turn up by morning. Maybe she's somewhere right now, hearing all about Seth Granger. Jay must be having fits. That kind of publicity, connected to his precious Moon Bay."

"Haven't you heard? There's no such thing as bad publicity. We'll probably get more people hanging around. In another year, Warren will be advertising that he has a ghost," Mandy said.

"Hey, the guy is barely cold!" Alex protested.

"Sorry," Mandy told her.

"Let's get out of here and let the boss have her private time," Gil said to him. "'Night, Alex."

The two walked off. Alex suddenly felt very alone.

For a moment she felt a chill, but then realized that the Tiki Hut was blazing with light and music, and she was just across the lagoon from it. She didn't need to feel alone or afraid, she assured herself. And she wouldn't.

The time was now. And there wouldn't be much of it.

Using the pass key he'd obtained, he slipped it into the front door of the cottage, quickly closing it behind him, then locking it again.

If someone should arrive, there was always the back door.

Where to look...?

The bedroom. He'd been there before.

He went straight for the dresser, staring at the things on top of it. He picked up the dolphin again, studying it, shaking it. Perfume sprayed out at him. Choking, he put it down.

There was a beautiful painting of a dolphin on the

wall. He walked over to it, lifted it from its hook, returned it.

Anger filled him. He didn't have enough information, and despite all he'd done, he couldn't get it. Hell, everywhere he looked, there were dolphins around this woman. Live ones, stuffed ones, ceramic ones.

He heard footsteps coming toward the cottage and hurried for the back door. As long as he wasn't caught, he could come back and take all the time he wanted to study every dolphin in the place.

And he wasn't going to be caught. He would make sure of that this time.

Outside the cottage, he swore. He could have had more time right then. It was just one of the damn maids, walking down the trail.

He smiled at her, waved and kept going.

Back toward the lights and the few people still milling around at the Tiki Hut.

David's phone rang as he headed back along the path. When he saw Dane Whitelaw's name flash on the ID screen, he paused, taking the call.

"What did you find out?"

"I'm fine, thanks," Dane said dryly. "How are you?"

David paused. "Sorry, how are you? The cat, the dog? Wife, kids…the tropical fish?"

Dane laughed on the other end. "I researched your navy boy. Seems he's telling you the truth. He left the military a year ago May. Was married to a Serena Anne Franklin, no kids. They split up right about the time he left the service. He's in business for himself, incorporated as Seymore Consultants—there are no other consultants listed, however. There is one interesting thing. He was in Miami for a month before coming down here."

"So…it's possible he met up with Alicia Farr there?"

"It's possible, but there are millions of people in the area."

"Great. The guy may be legit—and may not be."

"I'll tell you one thing, he has degrees up the kazoo. Engineering, psychology, geography, with a minor in oceanography."

"Don't you just hate an underachiever?" David muttered.

"Bet the guy made a lot of contacts over the years. Men in high places. Foreign interests, too, I imagine."

"So just what are you saying? Does that clear him, or make him more suspicious?" David asked.

"In a case like this, I can tell you what I'd go by. Gut instinct."

"What does your gut instinct say?" David asked.

"Nothing. You have to go by your own gut instinct. You know him. I don't. Hey, by the way. I see it's getting even more tangled down there. I saw it on the news."

"Seth Granger?"

"You bet. Millionaire drowns and it's on every channel in the state. What happened? What aren't they saying?"

"I don't know."

"You were there."

"I was talking to you when he walked out and went swimming."

"Curious, isn't it? A guy who could—and would—have financed the whole thing goes down."

"Yeah, curious," David agreed, then added slowly, "Unless someone knows more than we do."

"Like what?"

"Like the ship being somewhere easy to reach. Where someone in a little boat could take a dive down and get a piece of the treasure before the heavy equipment—and the government—moved in. For someone who isn't a millionaire, grabbing a few pretty pieces worth hundreds of thousands before the real discovery was made could be an enticing gamble."

"You might be on to something," Dane agreed. "I'll keep digging on your navy man. Keep me posted. And be careful. There's a storm out there, you know."

"Small one, heading the other way, right?"

"Who knows? Small, yes, but still tropical-storm status. And they think it might turn and hit the Keys after all. Anyway, give a ring if you need anything else."

"Thanks."

David closed the phone, sliding it back into his pocket. The tangles were definitely intensifying. And there was only one person he could really clear in Alicia's disappearance and probable death.

Seth Granger.

Who was now among the departed himself.

Hearing a rustling in the trees, he turned, a sharp frown creasing his forehead. Long strides took him straight into the brush.

There was no one there.

But had there been? Someone who had been walking along, heard his phone ring...

And paused to listen in on the conversation?

ALEX SAT AT the edge of the first platform with her bucket of fish and called out, though she knew the dolphins were already aware she was there. "Katy, Sabra, Jamie Boy!"

They popped up almost instantly, right at her dangling feet. They knew the time of day and knew when they got treats. She stroked them one by one, talking to them, giving them their fish. Then she moved on to the next lagoon and the platform that extended into it. "Shania, get up here," she said. "You, too, Sam, Vicky."

She gave them all the same attention, her fingers lingering just a shade longer on Shania's sleek body. The dolphin watched her with eyes that were almost eerily wise. "You're my children, you know that, guys? Maybe I shouldn't be quite so attached, but, hey…when I had a guy, he was at sea all the time anyway."

"Was he?" The sound of David's voice was so startling, she nearly threw her bucket into the lagoon.

She leaped up and spun around. "Must you sneak up on people?"

"I didn't sneak up, I walked," he told her.

"You scared me to death."

"Didn't mean to. Still, I couldn't help hearing what you said. So…was that it? I was away too much?"

"David, there wasn't one 'it.' My decision to ask for a divorce was complicated. Based on a number of things."

"Was one of them Alicia?"

"No. Yes. Maybe. I don't even know anymore, David."

"I asked you to go on every expedition I took," he said.

"But I work with dolphins. They know when I'm gone."

"So you can never go anywhere?"

"I didn't say that. I just can't pick up and leave constantly. And I don't want to. I like a trip as much as the next person, but I like having a home, too."

"You had a home."

"We had a series of apartments. Several in one year. There was always a place that seemed more convenient. For you."

He was silent for a minute, then asked, "Was I really that bad?"

"Yes. No. Well, you're you. You shouldn't have changed what you were—are—for me. Or anyone else. It just didn't work for me."

"There is such a thing as compromise," he reminded her.

"Well, I didn't particularly want to be the reason the great David Denham missed out on the find of the century."

"There are many finds—every century," he told her. "Are you through here? I came to walk back to the cottage with you."

"What makes you think I don't have other plans?" she demanded.

He grinned. "I know you. There's nothing you adore more than the sea—and your children here, of course— but you're also determined on showering the minute you're done with it."

"Fine. Walk me back, then. I definitely don't want to get dragged into the Tiki Bar," she said wearily, aware that she no longer felt alone—or afraid.

"Want me to take the bucket?"

"Wait—there's one more round for these three."

"May I?" he asked.

She shrugged. David sat on the dock. As she had, he

talked to each of the dolphins as he rewarded them with their fish. Spoke, stroked.

She was irrationally irritated that they seemed to like David so much. Only Shania hung back just a little. It was as if she sensed Alex's mixed feelings about him and was awaiting her approval.

David had a knack for speaking with the animals. He understood that food wasn't their only reward, and that they liked human contact, human voices.

Shania, like the others, began to nudge him, asking for attention.

Traitor, Alex thought, but at the same time, she was glad. Shania was a very special creature. She needed more than the others, who had never known the kind of injury and pain that Shania had suffered.

When the dolphins had finished their fish, Alex started down the dock. He walked along with her in silence. She moved fast, trying to keep a bit ahead. No way. He had very long legs.

"If you're trying to run away, it's rather futile, don't you think?"

She stopped short. "Why would I be running away?"

"Because you're hoping to lose me?"

"How can I lose you? We're on a very small island, in case you hadn't noticed."

"Not to mention that my legs are longer, so I can actually leave you in the dust at any time."

"Go ahead."

"You have the key."

"You have your own place here."

"But I'm not leaving you alone in yours."

His tone had been light and bantering, but the last was said with deadly gravity.

"This is insane," she murmured, and hurried on. She knew, though, that she wasn't going to lose him. And in a secret part of herself—physical, surely, not emotional—she felt the birth of a certain wild elation. Why? Did she think she could just play with him? Hope to tempt and tease, then hurt…?

As she felt she had been hurt?

No, surely not. Her decision to file the papers hadn't been based on a fit of temper. She had thought long and hard about every aspect of their lives.

But wasn't it true, an inner voice whispered, that jealousy had played a part? Jealousy, and the fear that others offered more than she ever could, so she couldn't possibly hope to keep him?

Despite his long legs, she sprinted ahead of him as they neared the cottage. She opened the door, ignoring him. She didn't slam it, just let it fall shut. He caught it, though, and followed her in.

Inside, she curtly told him to help himself to the bath in the hallway, then walked into her own room. She stripped right in the shower, then turned the water on hard, sudsing both her hair and body with a vengeance. Finally she got out, wrapped herself in a towel and remembered that the maid never left anything but hand towels in the guest bath.

Cursing at herself, she gathered up one of the big bath sheets and walked into the hallway. He was already in the shower. She tapped on the door. No answer.

"David?"

"What?" he called over the water.

"Here's your towel."

"What? Can't hear you."

Why was she bothering? She should let him drip dry.

No, knowing David, he'd just come out in the buff, dripping all over the polished wood floors.

"Your towel!" she shouted.

"Can't hear you!" he responded again.

Impatiently, she tried the door. It was unlocked. She pushed it open, ready to throw the towel right in.

The glass shower door was clear, and the steam hadn't fogged it yet. She was staring right at him, in all his naked glory.

"Your towel," she said, dropping it, ready to run.

The glass door opened, and his head appeared. He was smiling. "Just couldn't resist a look at the old buns, huh?" he teased. "Careful, or you'll be too tempted to resist."

She forced herself to stand dead still, slowly taking stock of him, inch by inch. She kept her gaze entirely impassive. Then, her careful scrutiny complete, she spoke at last.

"No," she said, and with a casual turn, exited the bathroom. She heard his throaty laughter and leaned against the closed door, feeling absurdly weak. Damn him. Every sinewy, muscle-bound bit of him. But as she closed her eyes, it wasn't just the sleek bronze vision of his flesh that taunted her.

It was all the ways he could use it.

The door opened suddenly, giving way to her weight as she leaned against it. She fell backward, right into his very damp, very warm and very powerful arms.

CHAPTER EIGHT

IT PROBABLY WASN'T strange that he refused to release her instantly.

"You were spying on me!" he said.

"Spying—through a closed door?" she returned.

"You were listening at the door."

"I wasn't," she assured him. His arms were wrapped around her midriff, and they were both wearing nothing but towels. "I was leaning against it."

"Weakened by the sight of me, right?" he whispered huskily, the sound just against her ear and somehow leaving a touch that seemed to seep down the length of her neck, spread into a radiance of sun warmth and radiate along the length of her.

"I divorced you, remember?" she said softly.

"I've never forgotten. Not for an instant." There was something haunting in his voice, and his hold hadn't eased in the least.

"Would you please let me go?"

"Damn. You're not charmed, standing there, me here, my body, your body…memories."

She fought very hard not to move an inch, certain he was just taunting her, and afraid she was feeling so much more than she should.

"I never denied that you could be incredibly charming," she said, trying for calm, as if she were dealing with a child. "When you chose."

"I'm choosing now."

"Too late."

"Why? We're still technically married, remember? Here we are…together, you know I won't leave this cottage, and I think you believe my concern for you is real. And you are my wife."

In a minute she would melt. She might even burst into tears. Worse, she might turn around and throw herself into his arms, then cry out all her insecurities and her belief that they'd never had a chance of making it.

"David, let me go," she said.

"Whatever you wish." He released her. The minute he did, she lost her towel.

She turned to face him, deciding not to make a desperate grab for it. Standing as casual and tall as she could, she shook her head. "That was a rather childish trick."

"It wasn't a trick. I let you go and your towel fell off. Not my fault."

"Well, thank God you still have yours."

He grinned and dropped his towel. And his smile, as well.

For a moment he stood there, watching her, with no apology at all for the visible extent of his arousal.

He took a step toward her, reaching for her, pulling her into his arms, hard and flush against his length. She knew, though, that if she protested with even a word or a gesture, he would let her go again.

She meant to say…something.

But she didn't. His fingers brushed her chin, lifting her face, tilting her head. Neither of them spoke. His eyes searched hers for a moment; then his mouth met her lips with an onslaught that was forceful, staggering. It took only the touch of his lips, the thrust of his tongue, the simple vibrant crush of his body, and she felt the stirring of sexual tension within her so deeply that she thought she would scream. If he had lowered her to the tile floor then and there, she wouldn't have thought of denial.

But he did no such thing. His lips and tongue met hers with a flattering urgency, and his hands moved down the length of her back, fingers brushing slowly, until they had cleared the base of her spine, curved around her buttocks and pressed her closer still. She felt the hard crush of his erection against her inner thighs, equal parts threat and promise, a pulsing within, creating a swirl of pure sensuality that possessed some core within her. Weakened, shaking, she clung to him, still intoxicated by the movements of his lips, teeth and tongue.

And his hands, of course, pressing, caressing...

She drew away as his lips broke from hers. She needed to say something. Married or not, they shouldn't be here now. She had moved on. For the first time she had felt chemistry with another man. With...

She couldn't even recall his name.

David's mouth had broken from hers, only to settle on her collarbone, where his tongue drew heated circles, then move lower.

"David," she breathed. He didn't answer, because the fiery warmth of his caress had traveled to the valley between her breasts, and with each brush of flesh, she felt the need for the teasing to stop, for his lips to settle, for his body to...

"David..."

Her fingers were digging into his shoulder then. His

tongue bathed her flesh, erasing any little drops that remained from her shower. Everywhere a slow, languid, perhaps even studied caress, everywhere, until those areas he did not touch burned with aching anticipation. Her abdomen was laved, thighs caressed, hips, the hollows behind her knees, her thighs…close…closer….

"David…"

"What?" he murmured at last, rising to his full height, still flush against her, yet meeting her eyes. "Don't tell me to stop," he said, gaze dark and volatile. "Alex, don't tell me to stop."

"I—I wasn't going to," she stuttered.

He arched an eyebrow.

"I was going to tell you that I couldn't stand, that…I was about to fall."

"Ah," he murmured, watching her for the longest moment as heat and cold seared through her, heat that he held her still, cold, the fear that had come before, that he would leave her, that her life, like her body, would be empty.

"I—I don't think I can stand," she said, swallowing, lashes falling.

"You don't need to," he said, and he swept her up, his arms firm and strong, his eyes a shade of cobalt so dark they might have been pure ebony. He moved the few steps through the hall, eyes upon her all the while, pressed open the bedroom door and carried her in. And still he watched her, and in the long gaze he gave her, she felt the stirring in her quicken to a deeper hunger, urgency, desperation. It was almost as if he could physically stroke her with that gaze, touch every erogenous zone, reach inside her, caress her very essence.

She breathed his name again. "David."

At last he set her down, and though she longed just to circle her arms around him, feel him inside her, he had no such quick intent. He captured her mouth again, kissed her with a hot, openmouthed passion that left her breathless. And while she sought air in the wake of his tempest, he moved against her again, mouth capturing her breasts, tending to each with fierce urgency. She felt the hardness of her own nipples, felt them peaking against his mouth and tongue, and then the cold of the air struck them and brought shivers as he moved his body against hers. This time he didn't tease, but parted her thighs and used his mouth to make love to her with a shocking, vital intimacy, until she no longer arched and whispered his name, but writhed with abandon and desperation, unable to get close enough, unable to free herself, ravenous for more and more.

Sweet familiarity. He knew her. Knew how to make love to her. Time had taught him to play her flesh and soul, and he gave no quarter, ignored the hammering in his own head, the frantic pulse in his blood, a drumbeat she could feel against her limbs. She cried out at last, stunned, swept away, crashing upon a wave of physical ecstasy so sweet it left her breathless once again, almost numb, the beat of her own heart loud in her ears. But before she could drift magically back down to the plane of real existence, he was with her, as she had craved, body thrusting into hers, their limbs entangled. The roller coaster began a fierce climb once again, driving upward with a frenetic volatility that made all the world disappear and, in time, explode once again in a sea of sheer sensual splendor, so violent in its power that she saw nothing but black, then stars…then, at last, the bedroom again, and the man still wrapping her with his arms.

Shudders continued to ripple through her, little after currents of electricity, and as they brought her downward, she couldn't help but marvel at the sheer sexual prowess of the man and the almost painful chemistry they shared.

He rose up on his elbow, slightly above her, and used his free hand to smooth a straying lock of damp hair from her face. She was startled to see the tension that remained in his eyes as he studied her. And she was more startled still by the husky tone in his voice when he suddenly demanded, "Why?"

"Why?" she repeated.

"Why did you do it? You didn't call...you didn't write. You sent divorce papers."

She stared back at him. Why?

Because I couldn't bear the thought of you having this with any other woman—ever. Because I was losing you. Losing myself. I was happy at your side, but I needed my own world, as well. And I was sure that one day you would realize I wasn't the kind of woman you could spend forever with.

She didn't speak the words. It wasn't the time. She was far too off balance. She moistened her lips, desperately seeking for something to say.

"Sex doesn't make a marriage," she managed at last. He frowned slightly, staring at her still.

She pushed him away from her. "David...you're heavy," she said, though it wasn't true.

But he shifted off her. She rose and sped into her bathroom, where she just closed the door and stood there, shivering. Finally she turned the shower on and stepped beneath it. If they had really still been married, he would have followed her. He could do absolutely incredible things with a soap bar in his hands, with suds, with water, with teasing, laughing, growing serious all over again, heated....

He didn't follow her. She didn't know how long she stayed in the shower, but when she emerged, he had left her bedroom.

She found a long sleep shirt and slipped into it, then paused to brush out the length of her now twice-washed hair. She realized that she was starving, yet opted not to leave her room.

She set the brush back down on her dresser and noted that her array of toiletries was out of order. The women in housekeeping never touched her dresser, which she kept in order herself, or her desk and computer, in the spare bedroom. Had David been going through her things?

She had a dolphin perfume dispenser. It wasn't valuable, but it was pretty and meant a lot to her, because her parents had given it to her for her tenth birthday. It was porcelain, about five inches high and beautifully painted. She always set it in the middle and arranged the rest of her toiletries around it. Now the dolphin was off to the side and a fancy designer fragrance was in the center. By rote, she rearranged the perfumes, talcs and lotions.

No big deal. Just...curious.

She shrugged, still thinking about making love with David. One part of her wondered how the hell she had lived without him, without being together like that, for an entire year. The other part of her was busy calling herself the worst kind of fool in the world.

Then she reminded herself that she shouldn't be dwelling on personal considerations at all. A man had died today. This time there was no doubt that she had found a body.

In her own mind—and, apparently, in David's—there was no doubt that she had found a body on the beach, as well. And in David's mind, that body had belonged to Alicia Farr. His friend? His sometime lover? Either way, it had to disturb him deeply, and yet...

And yet, there they had been tonight.

She set her brush down, completely forgetting that the toiletries on her dresser had been rearranged.

Then she crawled into bed. Somehow, she was going to make herself sleep.

Alone.

SHE REALLY COULD look like an angel, David thought, opening the door to her bedroom. She was sound asleep in a cloud of sun-blond hair, her hand lying on the pillow beside her face. Just seeing her like that, he felt both a swelling of tenderness...and a stirring of desire.

Determinedly, he tamped down both.

He had the coffee going; he'd returned to his own place in a flash for clothing, and then put out cereal and fruit for breakfast. He hadn't forgotten that he'd promised Zach that he would show him—and his mother—the *Icarus*, and mentioned to the boy that they might meet for breakfast, but it was too early to meet them, and if Alex had maintained her old habits, she would forget to eat during the day, so she needed to start out with something.

And he needed to talk with her.

He walked into the room, ripping the covers from her and giving her shoulder a firm shake. She awoke instantly and irritably, glaring at him as if she were the crown princess, and he a lowly serf who had dared disturb her.

"Breakfast," he said briefly.

She glanced at her alarm. "I don't have to be up yet," she told him indignantly.

"Yes, you do."

"No, I don't."

"Trust me, you do."

She groaned, resting her head in her hands. "Really, David, this is getting to be too much. Listen, last night was…nothing but the spur of the moment. You need an ego boost? It was just the fact that you do have nice buns and you've managed to ruin my one chance for a nice affair here. At any rate, you can stay here if you want to, so knock yourself out. But I've just about had it with you acting like a dictator."

"Then maybe you should quit lying to me."

"About what?" she demanded, looking outraged.

"Danny Fuller."

She groaned. "Now I really don't know what you're talking about."

"Get up. There's coffee. That always seems to improve your temper."

"I don't have a temper."

"I beg to differ," he told her, and added, "Come on, out here, and you can eat while you talk."

He didn't let her answer but exited the room. Just after he had closed the door, he heard the pillow crash against it.

He turned and opened it. "No temper, huh?" he queried.

She still wasn't up. Tangled blond hair was all around her face, and she was in a soft cotton T-shirt that didn't do a thing to make her any less appealing. It should have been loose, but somehow it managed only to enhance her curves.

He closed the door quickly before she could find something else to throw.

In the kitchen, he poured two cups of coffee, then hesitated where he stood, tension gripping his abdomen in a hard spasm.

What the hell had gone so wrong between them? He'd never met anyone like her. He loved everything about her, from her eyes to her toes, the sound of her voice, her passion when she spoke about dolphins, teaching, the sea, and the way she looked when they made love, the way she moved, touched him, the smell of her, sight, sound, taste....

He'd never fallen out of love with her. When he'd received the divorce papers, he'd been stunned. She hadn't said a word. But it was what she had wanted, so, bitterly, silently, he had given it to her.

He started, putting the coffeepot back as she stumbled into the kitchen, casting him a venomous gaze and reaching for the coffee he had poured for her. She took a seat on one of the counter bar stools, arched an eyebrow to him and poured cereal into a bowl and added milk.

"All right, let's get to it. What was my relationship with Danny Fuller supposed to have been? Did I have a thing going with the old guy or something?"

"Don't be flippant."

"I don't know what the hell else you want me to be. Of all the stuff you've come up with since you've been here, this is the most ridiculous. I don't know what you're talking about."

"All right, I'll tell you. Alicia Farr spent all the time she could with Danny Fuller during his last days at the hospital. And in their conversations, two things kept coming up, dolphins—and your name."

She stared at him. He couldn't believe she had been hiding anything, not the way she was looking at him.

She shook her head at last. "Danny Fuller came here, yes. I liked him. He really liked dolphins, and you know me, I like anyone who likes my dolphins. Sometimes we talked casually in the Tiki Hut. He told me about some of his adventures, but if there was something he wanted to do but never attempted, I swear to you, I don't have the faintest idea what it was."

"Did he ever mention a ship called the *Anne Marie* to you?"

Staring at him, she gave it a moment's thought, then shook her head slowly. "No. He never mentioned it, and I never heard any stories about a ship named the *Anne Marie* from anyone else."

David lowered his head. Too bad. It would have helped if Alex had known something.

He gazed up at her again thoughtfully. Either she really didn't know anything or she had added acting to her repertoire of talents. Which might be the case. He had just about forced his presence here. And last night...

Well, according to her, it had been the situation, nothing more. Too many days spent on an island.

"So?" she said. "Is that all you wanted? Is that why you were so insistent on 'protecting' me? If so, honest to God, I can't help you."

"No. You're in danger. If two corpses haven't proven it to you, nothing will."

Her eyes narrowed. "Forget that. You, apparently, have heard about a ship called the *Anne Marie*."

"Yes."

"Well?"

"She was an English ship that went down in the dying days of the pirate era, in 1715. Records have her sinking off the coast of South Carolina. But the story of her sinking was told by a pirate named Billy Thornton— a pirate who apparently expected a reprieve and didn't get one. As he was about to be hanged, he shouted out, 'She didn't really—'"

"She didn't really what?" Alex demanded.

"Well, people have mused that he was about to say she didn't really go down anywhere near South Carolina. You see, before he was caught, he claimed to have seen the ship go down in a storm that ravaged the Eastern Seaboard, but some historians believe he attacked the ship himself."

"He couldn't have attacked the ship alone," Alex pointed out.

"Some legends suggest that since he was off the Florida coast, it would have been easy for him to go ashore, and kill his own men with the intent of going back himself for the treasure."

"And what was the treasure?" Alex demanded.

"There are full records in the English archives somewhere," he said, "but basically, tons of gold bullion, and a cache of precious gems that would be worth millions today."

Alex shook her head. "I don't understand. There must be hundreds of ships with treasures that sank in the Atlantic and are still out there to be found. Why would people kill over this one?"

"Most people wouldn't kill over any treasure. But the bounty to be found on this particular ship would be just about priceless."

"Did Alicia think she knew where to find the *Anne Marie?* If so, she should have announced an expedition and gathered people around her. No matter what, she'd have to go by the laws of salvage."

"Yes. But she was afraid, I think, of letting out what she knew. Afraid that someone would beat her to it."

"Why would Danny Fuller have hidden whatever information he had for so many years? If he knew something, why wouldn't he have gone after it himself?"

"I wondered about that myself. Maybe he just found out. It's my assumption that Alicia learned something from Danny Fuller about where the *Anne Marie* went down. She intended to set up an expedition, and that's why she wanted to meet me here. But she must have talked to other people, as well. And I think someone she brought in on her secret decided that they wanted the secret—and the treasure—for themselves.

"The thing is," David said, hoping he was making an impact on her, "someone is willing to kill for that treasure. And I don't think this person wants the government involved in any way. If he—or she—thinks he can bring up a fortune without the authorities getting wind of it, then I'm assuming whatever information Danny Fuller had, suggested the vessel went down in shallow waters, and that the tides and sand have obscured her. You know, kind of like time itself playing a joke, hiding her in plain sight."

"So…you believe Seth Granger was involved—invited here to meet Alicia, too, and that he didn't just drown, but was killed?" Alex asked.

"It's a possibility," he said. "A probability," he amended.

"How? He was in the bar with everyone else. And

he'd clearly been drinking too much. And if someone did kill Alicia, and it was her body that I found…how in the hell did it just disappear?"

"Obviously it was moved."

"Have you talked to Sheriff Thompson about this?"

"Not directly. I haven't had a chance. I had Dane call him, though, and give him all the information he acquired when I asked him to check into things."

"Great," Alex murmured. "Do you have any idea who this person is?"

"Someone with an interest in the sea and salvage. I thought at first that it might have been Seth, but now… apparently not."

"Who else might Alicia have invited here?" Alex asked. "Or who else might have gotten wind of what was going on?"

"Well, Seth was rich—he could have provided the funding she would need for the expedition. She invited me for my expertise. I'm not sure who else she might have invited."

"So who might have found out something?"

"Your boss, for one."

"Jay? But he isn't an expert salvage diver. As far as I know, he's competent enough on a boat, but he doesn't have the kind of money you'd need for an expedition like this and…" She paused and shrugged. "I see. You think he'd like to have that kind of money. And he would love to be respected for a discovery of that kind." She shook her head. "I can't believe it. Not Jay."

"There's Hank Adamson," David said.

She stared at him incredulously. "He's a reporter."

"And he's very conveniently here right now."

"I think you're reaching," she said.

"Maybe."

"Is there anyone else on your list of suspects?" she asked.

"Just one."

"Who?"

He hesitated before answering. "Your ex–navy SEAL," he told her quietly.

She rose, pushing her cereal bowl away. "I have to go to work," she said curtly, turning her back on him.

He went after her, catching her arm, turning her around to face him. "Please, Alex. Honestly, I'm not trying to run your life, much less ruin it, but for now… just until we get to the bottom of this, don't be alone with anyone, okay?"

"Except for you?" she asked, and her tone was dry.

"Except for me, yes," he said flatly.

She tried to pull away.

"Alex, please?"

"I have to go to work, David," she said, staring at his fingers where they wrapped around her arm. She met his eyes as he let her go and added bitterly, "You really don't have anything to worry about. Last night might have been…unintended, but still, I'd never switch around between men with that kind of speed. I like John, yes. I admire him, and I certainly enjoy his company. But I have a few things to settle with myself before… Under the circumstances—let's see, those being that we're not legally divorced and we may have two murders on our hands—I'll be taking my time getting to know anyone. Will that do?"

He hated the way her eyes were sharp and cold as they touched his. But she had given him the answer he needed from her. He nodded. She turned and headed for the bedroom, and a few minutes later, wearing the simple outfit she wore to work with the dolphins, she came back out, heading straight for the door.

She turned back and said, "Don't forget to lock up when you leave." A slight frown creased her forehead.

"What is it?"

"Nothing. Just don't forget to lock up before you leave. My keys are by the door. Please make sure you pick them up."

She walked out, and he felt as if an icy blast passed by.

Alex's actual degree had been in psychology, with a minor in marine sciences. But as far as her work went, she had learned more from an old trainer when she had interned in the center of the state. He had pointed out to her that the same theories that worked with people also worked with animals. Most animals, like most people, responded best to a reward system.

With dolphins, a reward didn't have to be fish. Like people, they craved affection.

Take Shania. She accepted fish and certainly had a healthy appetite. But she also seemed to know that her vets and the workers here had given her life back to her. The best reward for her came from free swims with the people she loved, mainly Alex and Gil. That morning, after feeding her charges with Gil, Alex entered the lagoon with them, one at a time, for a play period.

At eight, an hour before the first swim was due to begin, there was still no sign of Laurie Smith. Concerned, she called Laurie's cottage, then her cell phone, and received only her voice mail. Worried then, she called Jay.

"I don't know where Laurie is," she told him. "She isn't here, and she isn't answering her phone."

"Give her fifteen minutes, then we'll start a search. She's been talking about taking a few days to visit her family in St. Augustine, but I can't believe she'd just leave without asking for the time. Unless…she's just walking out on us," Jay said over the phone.

"She loves her job. She wouldn't just walk out," Alex told him.

"I'll send someone around to her cottage," Jay promised. "By the way, we may be evacuating our guests and the majority of our personnel soon."

"Evacuating?" she said, stunned.

"Don't you ever watch television?"

"Sorry, I just haven't seen the news lately," she murmured.

"That storm stalled. The forecasters still believe she's heading for the Carolinas, but at the moment she's standing her ground. She's still not a monster storm, and this place is equipped with an emergency generator, but we can't keep the whole place running if we lose electricity and water. We'll move everyone inland for a few days if the storm doesn't take the swing she's supposed to by tomorrow. Along with most of the staff."

Alex hesitated. "I'm not leaving," she said, and added a hopeful, "Am I?"

She heard his sigh. "No, Alex, if it's your choice, you get to stay."

"Thanks."

"You know a lot of people would want to be out of here in the blink of an eye," he cautioned.

"This place has weathered a few storms already. The storm room is perfectly safe."

"I knew you wouldn't leave your dolphins unless

someone dragged you off," Jay said. "All right, let me go. I'll get someone out to check on Laurie."

"Thanks."

Alex returned to the main platform area, where all guests met before breaking into two parties, no more than eight swimmers in each lagoon. Guests began to trickle in to get flippers and masks, and she and Gil started to handing them out. She was somewhat surprised to see that Hank Adamson had joined the swim again—she'd gotten the impression that he was doing each of the resort's activities just once so he could give an assessment of it.

He shrugged sheepishly when she smiled at him. "I actually like this a lot," he told her.

"I'm glad."

"Getting close to the dolphins...well, it's a whole new experience for me. Their eyes are fascinating. It's almost as if they're amused by us. They're kind of like...wet puppy dogs, I guess."

"Much bigger and more powerful when they choose to be," she said.

"Your dolphin swim is the best program here," he told her.

"Thanks."

That day, she let Gil give the introductory speech. In the middle of it, she saw Laurie Smith at last, hurrying to the platform.

A sense of relief swept over her. She realized that, deep in her heart, she had been secretly fearing that Laurie had disappeared—that she, too, would float up somewhere in the water as a corpse.

She frowned at Laurie, but Laurie looked chagrined

enough already. And Alex wasn't about to question her here.

"You're all right?" she asked Laurie briefly as her friend came up next to her.

Laurie nodded, but the look she gave Alex was strange.

"What's wrong?" Alex demanded.

"Nothing. Well, everything. Not with me, though. And we've got to be quiet. People are looking at us. And what I have to tell you... We need to talk alone."

Alex couldn't help but whisper, "I was worried about you. Where have you been?"

Laurie gave her a look again, indicating that it wasn't the time or the place. "You have to swear to keep what I say quiet."

"You know I will, if I can."

"Not if you can. You have to listen to me. And you can't say a word," Laurie whispered. "I mean it. Not a word."

"As long as you're all right. And you're not about to tell me something that will endanger the dolphins or anyone else. Where have you been?"

"Hiding out," Laurie said.

"Why?"

"There was a corpse on the beach that day. Definitely."

"How do you know?"

"Because there's an undercover Federal agent on the island."

"What are you talking about?"

Laurie didn't get a chance to answer.

"All right," Gil announced loudly. "Time to split into groups. Those of you who received green tags with your flippers, head off with Alex and Mandy. Mandy, give a wave, so your people see you. Those of you with red tags, you're with Laurie and me."

"Later," Laurie whispered. "We've got to talk. People are being murdered here." She hesitated, seeing that the groups were forming and she needed to hurry. "You've got to watch out for David, Alex."

"Watch out for David? I thought that you liked him."

"Yes, I do, but…he has a lot at stake. He…he might be the murderer."

"What?" Alex said.

"Shh! We'll talk," Laurie said. "Alone, Alex. We have to be alone."

Before Alex could stop her, she was up and heading off with Gil. Without creating a scene, there was nothing Alex could do.

Stunned, she watched Laurie walk away and pondered what she'd said. David? A murderer? It couldn't be.

Could it?

CHAPTER NINE

"THIS WAS REALLY kind of you," Ally Conroy told David. "I hadn't realized what a big deal you are until I started talking with Seth the other night. That you would take time for us...well, it's very kind of you." She was sitting at the helm by David. Zach, filled with excitement, was standing by the mainsail, looking out at the water as they skimmed over it.

"Not a problem. Zach is good kid."

She sighed. "Yeah, at heart. I've had some trouble with him at school. I'm a nurse, and gone too often. But...we've got to live. Anyway, thank you. I was horrible last night, and you were great. It's just, Seth might have been a blowhard to others—I've heard that term a dozen times from people talking about him—but he was very sweet to me. I was just stunned and upset. He really had a high regard for you, by the way. He was going to speak to you about something important. He said that he was waiting for the arrival of one more professional friend, then you'd all be getting down to business."

"And he talked about the *Anne Marie?*" David pressed gently.

She sighed. "He asked me not to say a word to anyone, but I guess it doesn't matter now. He told me that all his life, he had been interested in treasure hunting. People always wanted his money for their expeditions, but they didn't want him to be a part of them. The woman he was expecting was going to let him go along, not just foot the bills."

"Ally, did he know anything more about where this friend he was waiting for obtained her information?"

"An old man who died. He told her he'd hidden a copy of an old pirate map on this island."

David arched an eyebrow. "You're certain? There's an actual map, and it's hidden here?"

Ally sighed. "I'm not certain of anything, but that's what he said. That the ship went down off Florida, and that the map, the proof, was hidden here."

"Thank you, Ally, for telling me," David said gravely.

"Seth didn't know where the map was," she said. "That's part of why he was so concerned that his friend hadn't arrived yet. He didn't want to talk about it with you until she did arrive." She hesitated. "Do you think maybe…someone thought he knew more about the map than he did, so they killed him? Wouldn't that put you in danger, as well?"

"Ally, we don't know how Seth died yet. And I'm a pretty big boy, but I'll watch out, okay? Thanks to you."

She smiled, turning to watch her son. "Maybe you're right."

"Ally, if you think of anything else that Seth said before he died, will you please let me know?"

"Of course."

"And watch out for yourself, too. You haven't mentioned this to anyone else, have you?"

She shook her head.

"Don't—unless you're speaking with Sheriff Thompson. He'll be over here sometime today."

"I won't say a word," she promised.

He nodded and slowed the *Icarus*, shouting to Zach that he was going to lower the anchor, because they were out of protected waters and could do a little spearfishing.

Moments later, he stood aft with Zach, assuring himself that the boy could handle the speargun without skewering either himself or David. "We come back on board after every fish," he told Zach.

"Right. Because of the blood and sharks. And there are a lot of sharks out here, right?"

"Yup. They usually mind their own business, but…" He shrugged. "I had a friend once who liked to stay down and try to get a lot of fish at once. He used his swim trunks for a storage area. If a shark did smell the blood, the first place it would attack would be…"

"Ouch!" Zach said, laughing.

He tousled the kid's hair, pressed his own mask to his face and made a backward dive into the water.

He meant to give Zach his day out on the boat. He was anxious, however, to return to the dock at Moon Bay before noon. Before Alex would be out of the public eye.

Before she could be alone anywhere…

With anyone.

When the swim was over, Alex rewarded her dolphins with some pats, praise and fish, then stood, anxious to hurry over to the next platform and accost Laurie.

She didn't get a chance to. Jay, in another one of his handsome suits, came hurrying along the dock.

"We're starting evacuation proceedings now," he told her.

"Now?"

She looked at the sky. It was an unbelievably beautiful day, the sky an almost pure blue.

"Don't even bother looking up. You know how fast things can change."

"The storm turned toward us?"

"The Middle Keys may get a direct hit as early as late tonight or tomorrow morning. She's not a big one, but…well, you know. A storm is a storm. The ferry is here, and the guests are packing up. I'd like you and Gil to take a walk down to the beach and make sure we haven't missed anyone."

"Sure."

"The others can rinse down the equipment and get this part of the operation closed down. Later, if the storm keeps on coming, you can go down and open the lagoon gates so the dolphins can escape to the open sea if necessary."

She nodded. The lagoons were fairly deep; her charges could ride out a storm much better than people could. Still, the facility had been planned with escape routes for the animals, should they be needed.

"Did they act strangely today?" Jay asked.

"No."

"Then I'd say we've still got plenty of time."

Jay didn't have a particular affinity for the animals, but he knew enough about them to know that the dolphins would know when the storm was getting close.

"I see that Laurie arrived fine," Jay said.

"Yes."

"She told Len she forgot to charge her cell phone."

"Well, yesterday was her day off, and she wasn't that late this morning," Alex reminded him. Until she had a chance to listen to Laurie, she certainly didn't intend to tell Jay that anything was wrong in any way. She turned around, looking toward the next lagoon. Irritated, she realized that both trainers were already off the platform.

"Where's Gil? Does he know we're going on a beach hunt?"

"I just passed him. He's at the Tiki Hut, grabbing a sandwich."

"Is Laurie with him?"

"I don't know," Jay said. "Don't worry, you'll have a chance to talk to her when you get back. You know the island better than anyone else, so I appreciate you doing this yourself with Gil."

"Sure, I'll go find him."

Alex looked around for Laurie as she walked the path to the Tiki Hut, which was almost dead quiet, despite the time of day.

"Grilled chicken," Gil announced to her, lifting a wrapped sandwich. "I got you one, too, and a couple of bottles of water."

She arched an eyebrow, amused. "The beach isn't that far."

"Yeah, but we've got a lot of trails to check, just to make sure. The ferry's already picked up anyone who planned to check out today. It will be returning soon."

"Where did Laurie go so quickly?" Alex demanded. "She should be cleaning the equipment and battening down with Manny and Jeb."

"I don't know. She was with me right after the swim. She was pretty upset, though. She couldn't believe Jay had us finish the swim when there had been an evacuation notice. But she knows her responsibilities, and we've still got hours to get out, though I'm sure the roads will be a mess. We'll find her when we get back.

Jay said you're staying, but that the rest of the dolphin team has to be on the next ferry."

"Amazing, isn't it?" she said, looking at the sky, despite the fact she knew it didn't really mean anything.

"Always a calm before a storm. Didn't your folks teach you that?" Gil teased.

"I suppose."

They reached the beach. As far as the eye could see, it appeared to be empty.

"Well, I'm sure Jay will make sure all the guests and employees are accounted for," Gil said. "But I guess we have to comb the trails anyway, huh?"

She smiled. "You go to the left, I'll go to the right, and we'll circle around and meet in the middle. How's that?"

Even as she spoke, she felt a lift in the breeze. It was subtle, but there. "I guess the storm really is coming in," she said.

"You never know. They can predict them all they want, but that doesn't mean they're going to do what they're supposed to. Had it reached hurricane status yet?"

"I don't know," she said ruefully. "I wasn't really paying attention. Yesterday was quite a day, if you'll remember."

They'd reached the fork in the trail. "You go your way, I'll go mine," he told her.

She nodded and started off.

The trails were actually really pretty. She didn't know how many of the trees were natural and how many had been planted to give the feel of a lush rain forest. Great palm fronds waved over her head, allowing for a gentle coolness along the walk and, she noted, a lot of darkness and shadow.

The fronds whispered and rustled, and she felt as if the darkness was almost eerie, all of a sudden. There was a noise behind her, and she spun around, then felt like a fool. The noise was nothing more than a squirrel darting across a path.

Still, she felt as if she had come down with a sudden case of goose pimples, and then she knew why. David had told her not be alone.

And certainly not alone walking down an isolated trail.

She was suddenly angry. She'd never been afraid here before. She had enjoyed the solitude that could be found on the island.

But that had been before people started dying.

She quickened her steps, anxious to get back to Gil. "Hello? Anyone out here?" she called. There was no reply.

Birds chattered above her head.

She looked all around herself. Not much farther and she would meet back up with Gil.

She reached the farthest point, seeing the sand on the southern tip of the isle, and stepped off the trail to look around and call out. Nothing.

She turned back, noting that the breeze was growing stronger. In the shelter of the trees, though, she could barely feel it. The dive boat hadn't gone out that morning, she thought, but pleasure craft had probably been rented out. She hoped all the guests were back in.

"Hello?" she called out again, and once more paused to look around. She quickened her pace, then stopped suddenly.

And it wasn't a sound that had caused her to stop. It was a stench. A horrible stench.

And she knew what it was. The rotting, decaying, stench of death.

She started walking forward again, shouting now. "Gil! Gil!"

She started to run, and the smell grew stronger.

There was no denying it. Very near them, hidden in the foliage, something—or someone—lay dead.

"Gil!"

She nearly collided with him.

"What the hell is it?" he asked.

"Something dead," she told him.

"Yeah...that's what I thought. But where is it coming from?" Gil asked.

"It's gotten stronger as I've come toward you," Alex told him.

"Then it's here somewhere."

She stood still, surveying their immediate surroundings.

"Alex."

"What?"

"Let's get out of here," Gil said.

"Gil, we can't. We have to find out what it is."

"Or who it is," he said uneasily. "Alex, this is a matter for the sheriff."

"No! Yes, I mean, but not now. I am not letting anyone else disappear."

"What are you talking about?"

"We have to find out what it is, then call the sheriff. Gil, please?" Alex said. She took a few steps in the direction of a large clump of trees.

"Alex..." Gil said.

"It's here," she whispered. "There are a bunch of palm

fronds on the ground, fallen leaves…and the smell is really strong. It's here."

He looked at her, then sighed. "All right. I'll lift the fronds."

"We'll do it together," she said.

They steeled themselves against the smell of death and set to work.

And after a moment, it was Gil who let out a sick croak of sound.

DAVID HAD LISTENED to the radio warnings and decided it was time to head back in. The water where they were was about seventy feet deep, and he'd snagged a few snapper. Zach, proudly, had speared his first fish ever, and it had been a beauty. Someone would be enjoying his catch tonight, one big beaut of a dolphin—or mahimahi, as the restaurants called it, afraid that otherwise diners would think they were serving big cuddly marine mammals.

They hadn't taken the spearguns down this time; they'd just gone for a last look around. Far below them, a few outcrops of coral welcomed all manner of sea life.

David was just about to motion Zach back to the boat when he saw something that caused him to pause. Anemones could create the appearance of heads with waving hair, and that was what he was certain he was seeing at first. But then…

David thought there was something beneath the skeletal arms of the coral.

He surfaced, and Zach did the same, lifting his mask and snorkel. "We have to go back, huh?"

"Yes. Head on to the *Icarus*. I'll be right with you."

He watched Zach swim back to the *Icarus,* which wasn't more than twenty feet away. Then, taking a deep breath, he jackknifed in a hard, clean dive toward the depths.

He reached the coral, saw the outstretched arm, and…

Horror filled him so completely that he almost inhaled a deadly breath.

There she was.

Alicia. Or what remained of her.

Hair billowing in the water…

Features partially consumed.

Feet encased in concrete.

"THAT HAS TO be the biggest, fattest, deadest possum I've seen in my entire life," Gil said, turning aside. "Phew."

"Thank God it's just a possum," Alex said fervently.

Gil looked at her, puzzled. "Okay, I know I was acting a little weird, but you seemed convinced we were going to find a person."

She shrugged, remembering that Gil had no idea she'd already found one body on the beach. "I guess I'm just spooked because of yesterday. Let's head back."

DAVID DOCKED THE *Icarus* just long enough to drop off Ally and Zach, then headed for dry dock on the Gulf side of Plantation Key.

There he waited for Nigel Thompson to pick him up in his patrol car.

David slid into the passenger seat, meeting Nigel's gaze.

"You're a fool, you know, going back when everyone else is evacuating. Actually, I think it's about to become mandatory. You could have taken that yacht of yours and sailed her straight north," Nigel said.

"And wound up chased by the storm anyway," David said. "And you know damn well I would never leave Alex—or Moon Bay, for that matter—until this thing is solved. I hope this storm comes in and out fast."

"I'd have divers out there now, if I could," Nigel said. "But I've got every man on the evacuation route, and since we're talking about a corpse, I can't risk living men on a recovery mission. The water is getting rougher by the minute."

"I'm afraid that by the time the storm has passed through, the body might have…hell, it might have been ripped apart," David said.

"You know there's nothing I can do right now," Nigel said firmly.

David was silent, then said, "I know. But damn the timing. There was no way to get her to the surface, and then, hell, I had a kid on the boat."

"You know the location. You won't forget?" Nigel said.

"Oh, you bet I know it. And I gave you the coordinates."

Nigel glanced at him. They were on the main road at last, just miles from the ferry platform that serviced Moon Bay, but they were creeping along. There was one road down to the Keys, and one road back, so with the exodus going on, traffic was at a crawl.

"You know, Jay Galway can refuse to let you stay," Nigel warned him.

"He won't," David said with assurance.

"And you're certain you want to stay?"

"More so than ever," David said firmly.

Nigel was quiet again, then said, "Just because you found Alicia Farr today, that doesn't mean that her remains were ever at Moon Bay. I questioned everyone about the woman yesterday, when I was asking who might have seen Seth Granger leave the bar. And not a one of them saw her, any more than they did Seth."

"Which just goes to show you that no one in the place is observant. And that someone is lying," David told him. "Did you get the M.E.'s report back on Seth, yet?"

Nigel nodded.

"And?"

"The man drowned."

"I still think someone helped him do it."

Nigel twisted his head slightly. "Maybe."

"You know more than what you've said," David accused him.

"There are some bruises on the back of his skull," Nigel said. "The M.E. hasn't determined the source of them. He might have hit his head or something. Look, they took him up to Miami-Dade. One of the best guys they've got there is working on him, all right? They deal in fact, not supposition."

"Yeah. Well, there's one dead man for certain, and I know for a fact that Alicia is dead and rotting. And fact. She didn't just drown or have a boating accident. Not unless she lived long enough to cast her feet in cement and throw herself in the water."

"All right, David, I swear, the minute I've got an all clear on the weather, I'll be out there myself with the boys from the Coast Guard, hauling her up. All right?"

"I don't know if that will be soon enough," David muttered.

"For what?"

"She was murdered—there's a murderer loose. On Moon Bay. Can't you do something? I need to get back there fast."

"What do you want me to do, plow down the cars?"

"Put your siren on."

"This isn't an emergency."

"Maybe it is."

Nigel sighed, turned on his siren and steered his patrol car onto the shoulder of the road. "If I get a flat, you're fixing it."

David shook his head, offering him a half smile. "If you get a flat, I'm going to hitch a ride in the first Jeep I see."

STILL ON EDGE, Alex and Gil returned to the resort area just as the ferry was about to leave with the last of the guests and personnel. Dismayed, Alex ran to the dock, looking for Laurie.

"Alex, you're coming?" Jeb called to her from the crowded deck.

"No, but I need to see Laurie," she called from the dock.

"She's inside somewhere," he said. "I'll find her."

Gil had run up behind her. "Damn, I hope someone got my stuff." He turned to her. "You sure you want to stay? The dolphins will be just fine. Think about it, alone in that little place with Jay, Len and a handful of others? C'mon! Just hop on board the ferry. We'll have fun in Miami."

"No, no, I can't leave," she told him.

"It's going to be like a paid vacation."

Jeb came back to the rail. "Hey, Gil, I got your wallet and an overnight bag for you."

"Great."

"Where's Laurie?" Alex asked.

"She said she was coming," Jeb said.

Alex watched nervously as the ferry's ties were loosed and she prepared to depart. She scanned the vessel for Laurie. Gil barely made it to the gangplank. An impatient seaman yelled at him, "I called an aboard five minutes ago!"

"Sorry," Gil said.

The plank was up. Alex stared at the ferry in disbelief, ready to throttle Laurie herself. How could she say what she had—then disappear without a word?

Then, just as the ferry moved away from dock, Laurie appeared at last. She looked distressed. "Alex, stick with Jay, all right? Stick with Jay and Len and…whoever else."

Alex stared back at Laurie, then whipped out her cell phone, holding it up so that Laurie would see her intention.

Laurie gave her a smile, digging in her bag for her own phone.

Then she frowned and put her thumb down. "No battery!" she shouted.

"Jeb, give her a phone!" Alex shouted.

Jeb did, and a minute later Alex's phone rang. She answered it. "Laurie, what the hell's going on?"

"Alex, don't hang around David, okay?"

"Why?"

"Because something is going on. Something that has to do with salvage. Listen, you should be all right. Hank Adamson is staying on—he wants to write a story about battening down for a storm, and John will be there, too."

"John Seymore? Why?"

"I told you about him."

"No, you didn't."

"He's the agent I told you about. He's FBI. Well, I assume he's FBI. Or working with them or something."

"Laurie, how do you know this? Please, explain before the weather comes in and the phones go completely."

"All right, I'm trying. I ran into him, so we went to his cottage and talked. Just talked. That was it. I swear."

"I believe you," Alex said. "Please, get to the point."

"John said he liked you a lot, but he wasn't stepping in when there was obviously something still going on between you and David. He was concerned, though, and wished you weren't still emotionally involved with David. John's afraid that Alicia Farr has disappeared. And that she's met with foul play. He was worried about me, and he's very worried about you, because apparently there's a nurse in Miami who heard Daniel Fuller talking about you, a treasure and the dolphins. Honestly, Alex, I can see why you had such a crush on John—before David showed up again. John is wonderful. I stayed at his place—just in case anyone knew I'd seen the body you discovered and thought that I might know who it was or talk. That's why you couldn't get hold of me. I stayed there even when he was out on David's boat. And last night…he told me about Seth Granger, and that he didn't think Granger died by accident. So…he knows I was going to talk to you. Alex…Alex…are you there?"

"Yes, I'm here. Why does he suspect David?"

"Who else was close to Alicia Farr? Who else is famous for his treasure hunting expeditions? Really, you should have gotten off the island. Maybe you still can. Oh, and, Alex…"

Her voice faded, and there was a great deal of static on the line.

"Alex, did you hear me? Watch…" Static. "I know because…" Static.

Then the line went dead completely.

An arm slipped around her shoulders, and she nearly jumped a mile.

"Hey!" It was Jay. He'd actually doffed his suit and was in simple jeans and a red polo shirt so he could help batten things down. "You all right?"

"Yes, of course." She wasn't all right at all, but she sure intended to fake it. "Jay, who is still on Moon Bay?"

"There's Len and me, you, the reporter—Hank Adamson. He's been incredibly helpful, and he wants to write about the storm. It's not going to be that big a hurricane, at least."

"Right. Hopefully, she'll stay small. But who else is here, Jay? Anyone?"

"John Seymore—and your ex–old man."

"You let those two stay—and made your staff evacuate?"

"David has hit storms like this at sea, he can surely weather it. And John Seymore was a SEAL. They both wanted to stay. I had the power, and I said yes. Do you have a problem with this?"

Yes.

But she couldn't explain that she doubted both men— or why. She couldn't forget her conversation with Laurie. John Seymore claimed to be some sort of agent, but was he really? Had Laurie seen any credentials?

And what about David? David, who kept warning her that she was in danger.

Had he known she had found a body on the beach because he had been the one to murder the woman?

No, surely not. She winced, realizing that she was refusing to believe it because she was in love with him. She had been since she had met him. The divorce hadn't really meant anything, and she would probably be in love with him the rest of her life.

However long, or short, a time that might be.

WHERE THE HELL was Alex? John Seymore wondered. Jay Galway had said that he'd sent her and Gil out to check the trails, but they should have been back long ago.

He went out in search of them himself.

For a small island, there were an awful lot of trails. He began to understand what had taken them so long.

As he walked, he was easily able to assure himself that everyone else had gotten off the island. He called out now and then, looked everywhere and didn't find a soul.

But, returning, he smelled a foul odor on the air and instantly recognized it. The smell of death.

As he hurried forward, his heart shuddered hard against his chest. He stood still, looking around for any sign of company.

After a moment, convinced he was alone, he stepped forward to examine the source of the odor.

A moment later, he stepped back, relieved to have discovered only a dead possum, then hurried along the rest of the trails. When he reached the Tiki Hut, it was empty. Walking around to the docks, he saw no one, and far out to sea, the last ferry was just visible.

He turned, hesitating for a moment. Alex might have gone to the lodge. But though the winds had picked up a great deal, growing stronger by the minute now, so it seemed, they were still hardly in serious weather.

He heard a distant splash.

The dolphin lagoons.

With quick steps, he hurried toward them. He arrived in time to see Alex on the second platform, talking to her charges and handing out fish. He started along the path to the platforms. Halfway there, she met him, empty fish bucket in her hand. She stopped short, staring at him.

"Alex." He said her name with relief.

She still looked at him suspiciously.

"Alex, you…you have to be careful."

"Yes, I know," she said, sounding wary. Then she stiffened. "I hear you're an agent."

"You hear I'm what?"

"An agent. A government agent. An FBI man—or so Laurie assumes."

"I'm not on the payroll, but yes, I work with the FBI."

"If you're working for the government, then why not just announce it?"

"Because there are those who shouldn't know—just yet. Because I don't know what has really happened—or might happen."

"So you're accusing David of being willing to kill to get what he wants?"

John Seymore sized her up quickly and shook his head. "I'm not accusing anyone of anything. Not yet. But Alicia Farr has disappeared. And a man died under mysterious circumstances yesterday. Your name was mentioned by a dying man who supposedly held a secret worth millions."

"I see…. So I shouldn't trust David, and your only

interest in me was because a dying man kept saying my name?" she asked skeptically.

He sighed, feeling his shoulders slump. "I want to protect you."

"Gee, everybody wants to protect me."

"Alex, you know that my interest in you was real."

"What I know is that there are six of us together here for a storm. Together. I won't be alone. And by the way, I don't know a damn thing about the treasure, where it is, or what it has to do with dolphins, so you don't need to draw me into casual conversation about it."

"Alex, I really am with the authorities."

"Want to show me some credentials?"

He pulled out his wallet, keeping his distance, showing her his identification.

"Consultant, right," she said with polite skepticism.

"I'm a civilian employee, working special cases."

"This is a special case?"

"I was a navy SEAL. This is a sea-related investigation."

"Well, as we both know, IDs can be easily faked."

"I'm telling the truth," he said.

"So you went after Laurie?" she said, still polite, but her tone conveying that she didn't believe a word.

"I didn't go after Laurie. There was nothing personal between us. Besides, you were back with your ex-husband," he said flatly, then added a careful, "And far too trusting of him, far too quickly."

"Well, rest assured, I'm not sure if I trust anyone anymore. And now I see Jay. I have to lock up a few things and get up to the lodge. Excuse me, please."

She walked by him as if she had all the confidence in

the world. His eyes followed her, and he could see that she hadn't been lying. Jay Galway was there.

Was he to be trusted?

There was little else he could do but hurry back for his own things and get to the storm room to join the others.

He looked at the sky just as the rain began.

CHAPTER TEN

As soon as David got back to Moon Bay, he raced to look for Alex at the dolphin lagoons. The dolphins were swimming around in an erratic manner, but there was no sign of Alex.

He decided that she might have gone to her cottage. Jay had ordered that the six of them remaining on the island had to gather in the storm room by ten that night, when the worst was due to hit, but it was nowhere near that late, and she might well have gone to her cottage for a bath, clothing and necessities.

But she wasn't at the cottage when he arrived. Running his fingers through his hair and taking long, jerky strides, he went through the little place, room by room.

Then he heard the door open and close. He hurried from her bedroom, relief filling him.

"Alex!"

"Hey," she murmured. She didn't sound hostile, just tense—and wary.

"Are you all right?" he demanded.

She frowned. "Of course." She eyed him up and down. "You don't look too good."

"Yeah, well, I've been worried about you. I told you to stay in a crowd."

"I was with someone all day," she said, still watching him carefully. "I've been busy...just opened the lagoon gates. Uh, I think I need a shower. So if you'll excuse me..."

Was she suggesting that he leave her? Not on her life. Maybe literally.

"I'll be right here. Hey, want coffee? Tea? The electricity will probably go out soon. Of course, there's a generator in the storm room. I guess it's not like you can't have tea later, if you want. But I think I'll make some coffee, anyway." He turned his back on her, walking to the kitchen area, reaching into the cupboard. He could feel her watching him. It wasn't a comfortable feeling.

After a minute, he heard her walk to the bedroom. Her behavior was disturbing. She wasn't fighting him or arguing with him—it was almost as if she were afraid to.

She reappeared just a minute later, obviously perplexed.

"When did you get here?" she asked him.

"About two minutes before you walked in. Why?"

"Did you...move things around in here today?"

"No, why?"

"Oh, nothing. The maids seem to be getting a little strange, that's all. The maid's been in, right? Bed is made, towels are all fresh," she said.

"Then the maid must have been in. I didn't clean up," he said without apology.

She shrugged and stared at him. Studied him. As if she could find what she was looking for if she just kept at it long enough.

"All you really all right?" he asked her.

"I'm fine. But you really look like hell."

"I need a shower, too. I took Zach and Ally out on

the *Icarus*. Then I took her around to the dry dock on the Gulf side and had to get back here."

"You didn't have to get back here," she corrected him. "You don't work here."

"I knew you'd be staying with your dolphins, and I wasn't about to leave you here alone with... Alone."

She nodded. Suddenly, to his surprise, she walked up to him, put her arms around him and pressed against him. Instinctively, he embraced her, smoothing back her wet hair. "What is it?" he asked, at a loss.

"I do know you, don't I?" she whispered.

"Better than anyone else," he said. "Alex, what is this?"

She pulled away slightly, a strange smile on her lips. "You're not good husband material, you know."

That hurt. "You were the best wife any man could have," he told her.

"You do love me, in your way, don't you?"

"In my way?" he said, finding it his turn to seek an explanation in her eyes. "In every way," he said, passion reverberating in his tone, his words vehement. "I swear, I never stopped loving you, Alex. Never. I would die for you in a heartbeat."

She slipped from his arms. "I have to shower," she murmured. "Get a few things together."

She walked into the bedroom. Five minutes later, he couldn't stand it anymore and followed.

The water was streaming down on her. Here, as in the other bath, the glass doors were clear. He should give her space, so that she wouldn't decide to send him away. Now, when he needed so desperately to be with her.

You look like hell, she had told him.

Hell yes. Because I found your disappearing body,

and it is Alicia Farr, and, oh God, what the sea can do to human flesh...

There was no way he would tell her about his discovery now. Not until the storm had abated and the sheriff had come. They were all alone here now, at the mercy of the storm. And maybe of a murderer.

Her head was cast back as she rinsed shampoo from her hair. Back arched, limbs long, torso compelling in its clean-lined arc. He felt the sudden shudder of his heart and the iron tug on his muscles.

Taking a step forward, he opened the glass door. She looked at him and waited.

"I told you, I need to shower, too."

"There is another shower."

"But you're not in it."

He was startled to see her smile. Then her smile faded and a little shudder rippled through her. She backed up, inviting him in. He stripped in seconds and followed her.

"Shampoo?" she offered.

"That would be good."

"On your head?" she asked.

"Where else?"

"Should I show you?"

Her tone was absolutely innocent, and still strange.

And then he realized that she wanted him—and was afraid of him.

He set the shampoo down on a tile shelf and took her into his arms, ignoring the blast of the hot water on his shoulders. "Alex, what's wrong?"

"I'm in danger. You told me so yourself," she assured him, eyes amazingly green in the steamy closeness of the shower.

"But not from me," he whispered.

She stared back at him. Then, suddenly, she shuddered once again, moving into his arms. He held her there while the water poured over them. He felt the delicious surge of heat sluicing over his body, felt himself becoming molten steel, abs bunching, sex rising, limbs feeling like iron, but vital, movable....

She knew his arousal. Knew it, sensed it, touched it. Her fingers slid erotically down the wet length of his chest and curled around his sex. She ran her fingers up and down the length of him, creating an abundance of slick, sensual suds. Spasms of arousal shuddered through him, and he lowered his lips to her shoulder, her throat, then caught her mouth with his own, tongue delving with sheer erotic intent. He ran his hands down her back, massaged his fingers over the base of her spine, cupped them around her buttocks and drew her hard against him. He was only vaguely aware of the pounding of the water. He was keenly cognizant of the feel of her flesh against his, and the heat rising between them. Catching her around the midriff, he lifted her, met her eyes and slowly brought her down, sheathing himself inside her, and finally, when her limbs were wrapped around him and they were completely locked together, he pressed her back against the tile and began to move. She buried her head against his neck, rocking, riding, moving with his every thrust, her teeth grazing his shoulders, the water careening over them both. It wasn't enough.

Without letting her go, he used one hand to reach for the door. Opening it, he exited the slick shower with her still enfolding him and staggered to the bedroom, then fell down on the bed with her, drenching the neat spread and not caring in the least. They rocked together in a desperate rhythm that seemed to be echoed by the rise of the wind and spatter of the rain beyond the confines of the cottage. He moved, and his lips found her throat, her breasts, her mouth, once again. He brought them both to a near frenzy, withdrew, and then, despite her fingers in his hair and her urgency to bring him back, he kissed the length of her soap-slicked body, burying himself between her thighs, relishing her words of both ecstasy and urgency, at last rejoining her once again, his force rising with his shuddering thrust, until they climaxed in a sweet and shattering explosion.

They lay together afterward, damp and panting. His arm remained around her, but strangely, she suddenly seemed detached. So passionate, so incredible…

And then…

"It's getting late. I've got to get dressed. Grab a few things…did you want to go to your cottage? You could do that while I pack a few things."

He stared down at her, definitely taken aback. "Wham, bang, thank you, sir?" he inquired politely.

She flushed. "There's a storm on the way."

"Of course, excuse me, let me just get out of the way."

He rose, baffled, heading for his clothes. Then he stopped, turning back to her. "Alex, there's always a storm on the way."

"What are you talking about?"

"You—there's always something. You won't talk."

"There is a storm out there!" she exclaimed.

"If you'd ever called me, ever talked about the thoughts going through your mind—"

"I called you a number of times, David. There was always someone there to say that you'd get back to me, you were in the water, you were working with a submersible…you were…well, God knows what you were doing," she told him.

He started to walk back toward her. Strangely, she backed away from him.

"David, there is a storm out there. And worse," she added softly.

"We both should have gotten off the island," he said angrily, and started to leave again. Then he spun back on her, letting her edge away from him until she came flat against the bedroom wall. Then he pinned her there.

"Get this straight. Whatever you're feeling, whatever I did, whatever you think I did, I would defend you with my last breath, I would die to keep you safe, and I will love you the rest of my life. Turn your back on me and never see me again when this is over, hell, don't even send a Christmas card, but for the love of God, trust me now!"

He didn't wait for a reply. She had been too passionate, then too stubborn and distant, for him to expect a response that made sense. It was as if she had suddenly decided that she didn't trust him.

He was dressed before she was, wearing the swim trunks and T-shirt he'd had on all day. In a few minutes she was dressed as well, a small duffel bag thrown over her shoulder. "I thought you were getting your things?" she said.

"I'm not leaving you," he told her. "Come on; we've got to stop by my place."

The wind had really picked up, and rain was pelting down. Alex started out, then stepped back, telling him she had macs in the cabinet. They were bright yellow. They certainly wouldn't be hiding in those, David thought grimly.

When he opened the door again, the wind nearly ripped it from its hinges. "Let's go!" he shouted. "This thing is coming in really fast."

They ran along the path. Thankfully, David's cottage was close. Inside, he didn't bother dressing, just grabbed fresh clothing and toiletries, then joined Alex again in minutes. They started along the trail toward the lodge. Just as they neared the Tiki Hut and the lagoons, a flash of lightning tore across the sky, almost directly in front of them.

They heard a thunderous boom. Sparks seemed to explode in the sky.

The island went dark, except for the generator-run lights from the lodge.

In the dark, David took her arm. Together, they began to hurry carefully across the lawn to the main lobby, where Jay was waiting for them impatiently.

He led the way through the reception area, the back office and through a door that led down several steps. It wasn't a storm cellar, since it would be impossible to dig on an island that had been enhanced by man to begin with. Rather, the ground had been built up, so they were actually on a man-made hill.

The storm room was just that—one big room. There were ten cots set up in it, others folded and lined up against a wall, and doors that were labeled "Men" and "Women." There was a large dining table, surrounded by a number of upholstered chairs, and a counter that separated a kitchen area from the rest of the room. A battery-operated radio sat on the counter.

"Nice," David commented.

"Very nice," Hank Adamson said, rising from where

he'd been sitting at the foot of one of the cots. "It's great, actually."

"If you like being closed in," Len said, shrugging. It was clear that he had remained only out of deference to Jay. But he offered a weak grin.

"The kitchen is stocked, we've got plenty of water, and as you can see, the generator has already kicked in," Jay said. "The brunt of the storm is due at about 4 or 5 a.m. She's still moving quickly, which is good. And her winds are at a shade less than a hundred miles an hour, so she's not a category four or five."

"With any luck, it will be all over by late tomorrow morning," Len said.

"And the damage, hopefully, will be minimal," Jay said. "The trees, though…and the foliage. They always go. No way out of it, we'll have one hell of a mess."

"But here we all are," Hank said cheerfully. "So… what do we do?"

John Seymore had been in one of the plush chairs, reading a book. His back had been to them. He rose. "We can play poker," he suggested. "Someone saw to it that there are cards, chips, all the makings of a good game. There's even beer in the refrigerator." He was speaking to everyone in the room, but he was staring at David.

David assessed him in return. "Poker sounds good to me," he said.

"Right," John said. "We can see just who is bluffing whom."

"Sounds like fun," Hank Adamson said. "Deal me in."

OUTSIDE, THE WIND howled. The sound of the rain thundering against the roof was loud, and Jay had turned the volume high on the radio to hear the weather report.

The poker game continued.

It might have been any Friday night men's crowd—
except Alex was playing, too. She liked poker and played
fairly well. But in this group…?

They'd set a limit, quarter raises, no more. And yet it
seemed that every round the pot got higher and higher.

Neither John nor David ever seemed to fold, or even
to check. Between them, they were winning eighty per-
cent of the time. When one of them dealt, there were
no wild cards, and it was always five-card stud. Their
faces were grim.

Thank God for Len and Jay. As the deal came around
to Jay for a second time, he shuffled, calling his game.
"Seven cards. One-eyed jacks and bearded kings wild."

"One-eyed jacks and bearded kings?" John Seymore
said, shaking his head.

"What's wrong with that?" Len asked defensively.
"Adds some spark to the game."

"I think our friends are used to hard-core, macho
poker," Hank Adamson said, grinning at Alex across
the table.

"Sounds like a fine game, right, John?" David asked.

"You bet," John said.

There was a slight discrepancy over one of the
kings—whether he actually had a beard or if it was only
five o'clock shadow. It was Alex's card, and she said she
didn't need for it to be wild. For once, she had a hand. A
royal flush, with the king being just what he was.

It seemed to be the only hand she was going to take.
Watching David and John, she had a feeling they would
both do well in Vegas.

It was difficult to sit there. She wondered how she
could have spent the time she had with David, how

she could have gone to her cottage, felt the overwhelming urge to make love, while still feeling that little tingle of doubt. But watching John Seymore and the subtle—and not so subtle—ways he challenged David, she had a difficult time believing that he could be an out-and-out liar or a murderer, either.

Jay's third turn to deal, and he called for Indian poker.

"What?" David asked.

"You must have played as a kid. We all get one card and slap it on our foreheads. We bet on what we think we have," Jay explained. "You can try to make faces, bluff each other out."

"It's fun, do it," Alex advised.

The cards went around, and they all pressed them to their foreheads, then stared at one another.

"Hey, there aren't any mirrors in here, are there?" Hank Adamson asked.

"Don't think so. And no one is wearing glasses, so we should be all right."

"What do we do now?" John asked.

"You're next to me. You make the first bet," Alex said.

John shrugged and threw in a quarter chip.

He had a three on his forehead. Jay had a seven; Len had the queen of diamonds, Hank a ten, and David the queen of hearts. "Big bet, buddy, for a guy with your card," Len warned him.

"Oh, yeah?" John said. "You should fold right now."

"You don't say? My quarter is in."

"You really should fold," David told John.

"You think? I'm pretty sure you shouldn't even have bothered to ante," John told him.

Betting went around twice, with each of them saying some things that were true and others that weren't.

In the end, Len folded, followed by Hank, and then Jay. The pot rose, and Alex was amazed in the end to find out that she'd been sitting with the queen of spades on her head, enough to beat David's queen of hearts.

"I don't think I should play against you guys. You're going to lie about every hand, and I'm going to fall for it," Len said.

"Len, at most, you're going to lose about twenty-five dollars tonight," Alex told him. "Start bluffing yourself."

"I never could lie," he murmured, shaking his head.

"Ah, an insinuation that the rest of us can lie with real talent?" Hank asked him.

"Careful—anything you say can and probably will be used in a column," Alex warned Len.

"Hey, I'm wounded," Hank protested. "Seriously, I'm having a blast, and I'm going to write this place up as the next paradise."

"Let the man win a few, will you, guys?" Jay said, pleased.

"Yeah, Alex, quit winning," Len said.

"Me? Look at those two," she said, indicating the piles of chips in front of David and John.

"Right. Quit winning, you two," Jay said.

"Hey! I can bluff with the best of them. Don't anyone dare let me win," Hank protested.

"Storms are funny, huh?" Len said a few minutes later, passing the cards to John. "My sister's in-laws all have boats and live right on the water. Years ago, Andrew was supposed to hit the coast. They all asked to come in and stay with my sister inland. Well, that's where the storm came in, and they all got mad at her when their cars were flattened and they had to spend the night praying in a bathtub! This is better, huh?" he said to no one in particular.

"Who would have figured we'd be here tonight?" Jay said, shrugging.

"Who'd have figured?" David echoed. He was staring at John.

"Yeah, odd isn't it, how the best-laid plans can be interrupted by nature?" John Seymore responded.

It was enough for Alex. She had to get away from the table and all the dueling testosterone or she was going to scream.

She yawned. "I'm going to beg out of this. I'm going to make a cup of tea, and then I'm going to sleep."

"But you just won a huge pot. That's not legal," Len said.

"You can split my pot among you. I think I can spring for the ten bucks," she told him, pushing her pile of chips toward the center.

"I can cash you out," Jay said. "That's not a problem."

"And not necessary. Quit worrying and take the chips." Grinning, Alex left them. She walked to the kitchen area, amazed that the storm could be raging all around them, the electricity was out—probably all through the Middle Keys, at the least—but thanks to the generator, she still had the ability to see and make tea. She turned up the radio and heard the newscaster. They were taking a pounding. It could have been much worse, if the storm had been able to pick up more speed.

"Anyone else want anything?" she called, expecting them to ask for a round of beers.

"Naw, thanks," Jay said.

His polite refusal went all around. Alex found it very strange. Poker and beer always seemed to go together, along with an assortment of snacks. None of these guys wanted anything.

It was as if they were all determined to keep a totally clear head.

The game continued as she made her tea. Though on the surface it appeared as if they were just playing cards, she had a feeling that for John and David, it was much more. They challenged one another at every turn.

She sipped her tea, half listening to the game, half to the radio. In a minute, she was going to try to sleep. When she woke up, the storm would be over. The islands would be in a state of wreckage, but hopefully, it would be more trees and foliage than homes and buildings.

But what then? Would she finally get a chance to talk to Nigel? Would they find the truth behind Seth Granger's death?

And what about Alicia, the treasure and the dolphins?

She finished the tea and stretched out on one of the cots. Her eyes closed, then opened suddenly.

Because someone in the room was doing a great deal more than bluffing at poker. Alicia Farr was dead. And Seth was dead, and...

Very likely, someone in the room had committed murder.

David.

No.

Why would he kill Alicia? He had plenty of money from his own enterprises. Of course, he spent it, too. His excursions were costly, and not everything he did was financed by a major corporation. But why kill Alicia? He couldn't go after treasure alone.

And she herself was still in love with him. No matter what had happened, she'd been eager to sleep with him again. Even now, she was sure he was using her. She was apparently the key to something, somehow. Damn Daniel Fuller, even if he had passed on! Why had he dragged her into this?

Then there was John Seymore. Claiming that he, too, had come to protect her. Said he was working with the FBI, even had a great-looking ID. And hey, why not try to seduce the woman he was there to protect? He'd used her, too. But until she'd talked to Laurie tonight, she had liked him, really liked him. And she'd believed he was genuinely interested in her, too, because her instincts had said so.

So much for instincts.

And now…

How could she trust either of them?

She was never going to get to sleep.

"Hey!"

She jumped at the sound of Jay's voice. She rolled over to look at him. He was listening intently to the radio.

"We'll be in the eye of the storm in about half an hour."

He was right. Listening, Alex realized that the brutal pounding of wind and rain was easing somewhat.

"When it comes, I wonder if I should take a peek at the damage," Jay said.

"It's going to be the same damage in the morning," David advised him.

"Yeah, but we'll have at least twenty minutes before it starts up hard again," Jay said.

"This storm is a fast mover," David reminded him.

"He's losing. He just wants to opt out of the game himself for a few minutes," Len said.

"I think we'll all be opting out in a few minutes," Hank said. "Looking at our sleeping beauty over there, I'm feeling the yawns coming on myself."

"We should all get some rest," David said. "I have a feeling it's going to be a real bitch around here after it lets up."

"It will take a few days to get our little piece of the world up and going again, sure," Jay said. "Depending on the damage the main islands face. They'll have electric crews out first, then road crews...we'll have people out next. It's just a matter of repair and cleanup. We've done it before, we'll do it again."

"Actually, I wasn't referring to the storm damage," David said.

"Oh?" Jay said. "Then what?"

"Nigel was supposed to be coming out today to talk to people about Seth Granger," David said.

Len exhaled a snort of impatience. The others must have stared at him, Alex thought, because he quickly said, "Look, I'm sorry. I don't know if it's the right term for a man or not but he was one hell of a prima donna. He thought money could buy him anything, and he was rude to anyone he thought was beneath him. He drank like a fish. If he hadn't drowned, he would have died soon of a shot liver anyway. I'm sorry a man is dead. But I can't cry over the fact that he got drunk and fell in the water."

"But what if he didn't just fall in the water?" David said.

"You were all there with him. What the hell could have happened? He stepped out for air, lost his balance and fell into the drink. Case closed."

"I'm not sure Nigel sees it that way," David said. "Besides, there's more."

"And what would that be?" Jay asked, groaning.

"Oh, come on, Jay. We all know Alicia Farr was supposed to be here. I have the feeling Hank never really came here to do a story on the island. He was hoping to find Alicia and get the lead on whatever she knew," David said.

"You certainly came here to find Alicia," John told him politely.

"Yeah?" David said. "You supposedly didn't even know her—but I'm willing to bet you came here because of her, too. And maybe you actually found her."

"What the hell does that mean?" Len asked.

No one answered him.

"You know, David, you've sure as hell been acting strange today. Starting out your day with the mom and the kid, then dropping them off and moving your yacht."

"He dry-docked his yacht," Jay put in. "If I had a vessel like the *Icarus*, I'd damn sure do the same thing."

"But he came back," Len noted, his tone curious, as he studied David.

"Did you find something out in the water today?" Jay asked. "Is that why you're acting so strange?"

Hank's voice was eager. "Oh my God! You did. You found…oh my God!" he repeated. "You found the body! The body that disappeared from the beach."

"No!" Len exploded. "You couldn't have! This is getting scary. Bodies everywhere."

"Where did you find the body?" John Seymore asked sharply.

"Another drowning victim?" Jay asked, sounding confused.

"I don't think so," David said. "I sure as hell didn't mean to bring this up during the storm, but since it seems you're all going to jump to conclusions, anyway, I might as well tell you the simple truth. No, not a drowning victim. Drowning victims aren't usually found with their feet encased in cement."

Where she lay, Alex froze.

"This is quite a story," Hank said.

Jay groaned. "You just had to bring this up in front of Hank, right, David?"

"I didn't bring it up!" David said sharply. "But maybe it doesn't matter. When the storm is over, the news will break anyway. As soon as he can, Nigel is sending someone out to bring her up."

"Where did you find the body?" Hank asked.

"Out beyond the reefs. I was spearfishing with Zach. Couldn't bring it up myself, because I didn't have the equipment to bring up any weight. Plus I'd already pushed the envelope on getting the kid and his mom back in, and the *Icarus* out of the storm. Nigel couldn't send anyone right away, because his people were all involved in the evacuation, and the water was growing too dangerous, too fast. But once the storm has passed, he'll get the Coast Guard in and bring her out."

"Jeez," Hank breathed.

"Did you know her?" Jay asked.

"Yes, I did. It was Alicia Farr," David said.

The moan of the wind outside was the only sound then as every man at the table went dead silent.

"Alicia Farr—dead," Hank Adamson said at last.

The others turned to stare at him, and he continued, "All right! I did come out here to get a story on her. I'd heard she was on to some incredible find."

Alex heard something make a clunking sound. She turned to look, but quietly, not wanting them to know she was awake, not when she was chilled to the bone just listening.

The clunking sound had been made by Jay as he allowed his head to fall on the table. She was sure it wasn't an emotional response to a woman being dead, though, and maybe she couldn't blame him. He hadn't really known Alicia Farr.

He was worried about Moon Bay.

David had known Alicia, and now Alex understood why he had been so tense.

He'd found Alicia's body.

Someone hadn't wanted the body to be found, so that someone had gone back for her, hidden her, then packed her in cement and thrown her back in the water, sure that this time she wouldn't wash back up.

Had that someone been David, and was he saying this now just to cover his own actions? Of course, he could find the location of the body, because he had put it there himself. The timing was certainly in his favor if he had. The storm could move the body, hide it, even destroy it. The cause of death might become almost impossible to discern. Any physical evidence could be completely compromised.

No, David couldn't be a killer. She wouldn't believe it. He had his talents, but he had never claimed acting to be among them.

And yet, at that table, they had all been bluffing.

Anger against herself welled in her heart. No, how could she believe in her soul that she loved someone so much that she had been so afraid of losing him that she had pushed him away, and then believe him capable of deception and murder?

"On that note, I think the game is over," John murmured. "Hell, I can't believe you kept quiet until now."

"I meant to keep quiet all night," David said irritably. "There's nothing anyone can do until the storm passes. Then the body will be brought up, and Nigel will get to the bottom of what's going on."

"Maybe," Jay said dully. "And maybe he won't find out a damn thing and we'll all be walking around afraid forever."

"I don't think so," David said. "I'm pretty sure that whoever killed Alicia might have helped Seth Granger into the water. And that person will, eventually, give himself away. Until then, just be careful."

"Great, David, thanks a lot," Len said. "Now none of us is going to be able to get any sleep."

"Why?" David said. "Hey, it's just the six of us on the island. We stick together, nothing goes wrong," he said flatly.

A strained silence followed his words.

"No one sleeps, that much is evident," Len said at last.

The sound of the wind suddenly seemed to die out completely.

The eye of the storm was just about on them.

"Hell," Hank Adamson swore. "This is ridiculous. I'm going to sleep. Alicia Farr is dead, and you found her," he told David. "That doesn't make any of us guilty of anything. You're right. Tomorrow, or as soon as he can, Nigel will come out and take care of things."

He pushed his chair away from the table. Alex kept her eyes tightly closed, not wanting any of them to know she had heard their conversation.

"We're in the eye," Jay said suddenly. "Len, come with me. I'm going out. Just for a minute. Just to take a quick look around." He sounded strained.

"You shouldn't go out, Jay," David said.

"I have responsibilities here. I have to go out," Jay said. "The rest of you stay here. Len will be with me. Everyone will have someone keeping an eye on them."

"Just you and Len together?" John said.

"All right, then. Three and three. Hank, you come with us for a minute," Jay said.

Hank groaned.

"Please. Three and three," Jay repeated.

With a sigh, Hank rose and joined them. Jay unbolted the door, stepping out into the dim light of the world beyond the shelter. "We'll just be a minute."

Alex didn't believe for a minute that he was going out to check on the damage. They kept a gun in a lock-box behind the check-in counter. He was undoubtedly going for it.

"What the hell are you doing on this island?" David asked John.

"The same back to you," John said.

Then, out of the blue, the radio went silent as the room was pitched into total blackness.

CHAPTER ELEVEN

THE HUM OF the generator was gone.

Something had gone terribly wrong.

For a moment David sat in stunned silence, listening to the absolute nothing that surrounded him in the pitch darkness. Then he heard a chair scraping against the floor.

John Seymore. The man was up, and Alex was sleeping on a cot just feet away. Seymore could be going after her. Fear—maybe irrational, maybe not—seized him. He couldn't seem to control his urge to protect Alex, no matter what.

He sprang up, hearing the scrape of his own chair against the floor. He heard movement, tried to judge the sound, then made a wild tackle, going after the man.

He connected with his target right by the row of cots. His arms around his opponent's midsection, together they crashed downward, onto the cot where Alex had been sleeping.

Dimly, as Seymore twisted, sending a fist flying, David became aware that the cot was empty. Alex had fled. She might still be in the storm-shelter room somewhere, or she could have found the door and escaped.

Seymore's fist connected with his right shoulder. A powerful punch. Blindly, David returned the blow. He thought he caught Seymore's chin. The man let out a grunt of pain, then twisted to find David with another blow.

They continued fighting for several minutes with desperate urgency, until suddenly an earsplitting gunshot rocked the pitch-dark room.

Both of them went still. The shot had come from the doorway.

Instinctively, they rolled away from one another.

"Alex!" David shouted.

There was no answer.

After the explosion of sound, silence descended again. He wasn't sure where Seymore had gone.

With a sudden burst of speed, he picked himself up and raced toward the open door. Insane or not, instinct compelled him to do so.

ALEX WAS CERTAIN that John and David were going to tear each other apart. Damn Jay! They were supposed to stay together, watching one another, and instead he'd gone for a weapon. What the hell did he intend to do? Hold everyone at gunpoint until the authorities came? Shoot them all?

Could Jay be the killer? No! She refused to believe it. And yet... As soon as he'd left, the generator had gone off.

What the hell had happened?

She had no idea. All she knew for certain was that David and John had suddenly become mortal combatants. Did they know something she didn't? Was one of them telling the truth—and the other not?

She had to get away, in case the wrong man triumphed. Not that she had any idea which one was the wrong one.

She'd already deserted her cot before they toppled over on it. She immediately made a dash for the door, nearly killing herself in the process, the darkness was so complete. She burst into the office and stood dead still, listening. Once she was certain the office was empty, she made her way to the reception area, inch by inch, using the furniture as a guide.

She meant to head for the lockbox herself, just in case she'd been wrong and Jay hadn't gone for the gun after all. Then became aware of breathing near her. She held dead still, holding her own breath.

Waiting, listening.

Aeons seemed to pass in which she didn't move. She nearly shrieked when she realized someone was moving past her, heading for the storm room. Once he had gone and her heartbeat had returned to normal, she tried to move around the reception counter.

Her footsteps were blocked. She kicked against something warm. Kneeling, feeling around, she realized that she hadn't stumbled against a thing but a person.

She recoiled instantly, fought for a sense of sanity, and tried to ascertain what had happened—and who it was. The form was still warm. She moved her hand over the throat, finding a pulse. Feeling the face and clothing, she decided she had stumbled upon Jay Galway, and he was hurt!

Either that, or...

Or he was lying in wait. Ready to ambush the unwary person who knelt down next to him to ascertain what had happened.

Fingers reached out for her, vising around her wrist. She screamed, but the crack of a gunshot drowned out the sound. She wrenched her wrist free and rose, determined to get the hell out of the lodge. The storm might be ready to come pounding down on them again, but she didn't care. There had to be a different place to find sanctuary.

As she groped her way out of the lodge, tamping down thoughts of Jay and whether or not he was hurt or dangerous, she was certain that her survival depended on escape. She lost several seconds battling with the bolts on the main door, then got them open and flew out.

Everything in her fought against believing Jay was the killer. He definitely hadn't been the one shooting the gun.

If Jay was on the floor, where were Len and Hank?

This was all insane!

The night was dark. Thick clouds covered the sky, even in the eye of the storm. Still, once outside, she could see more than she had before.

She hurried along the once manicured walkway, heading not toward the dock but around to the Tiki Hut, on the lodge side of the dolphin lagoons.

As she rushed forward, she was aware of a few dark dolphin heads bobbing up.

She never passed without giving an encouraging word to her charges. Despite the darkness, she was certain the dolphins could see her, and they would instinctively know something was wrong when she didn't acknowledge them.

She should say something to them.

She didn't dare.

She was determined to make her way to the cottages. Not her own—that would be the first place anyone would look for her—but she was sure she would find a door that hadn't been locked. The cottages were nowhere near as secure as the storm room, but at least they'd been built after Hurricane Andrew and were up to code.

But as she veered toward the trail that led toward the cottages, she saw another form moving in the night ahead of her.

Panic seized her. There was no choice. She had to head for the beach.

She turned, then heard footsteps in her wake.

She was being pursued.

DAVID WAS DESPERATE to get to Alex. He damned himself a hundred times over for the announcement he had been forced to make. For not beating the crap out of Jay, rather than letting him leave the room.

But had Jay—or anyone—destroyed the generator? Or had technology simply failed them when it was most desperately needed?

Didn't matter, none of it mattered.

Out of the room, he stumbled, swearing, as he made his way through the inner office and out to reception.

He hesitated. Somewhere on the wall was a glass case that held a speargun. It was a real speargun, one that had been used in a movie filmed on the island a few years earlier. He'd passed it dozens of times, giving it no notice.

Now he wanted it.

Groping along the wall, he found the case. He smashed the glass with his elbow, grabbed the weapon, then heard movement behind him.

David streaked for the front doors, praying that nothing would bar his way.

He found the door, which was slightly ajar.

Yes, Alex had definitely gone outside.

He swung the door open, leaving the lodge behind.

It occurred to him to wonder just how much time had passed since the eye had first come over them.

And just how much time they had left.

THERE HAD TO be a way to double back and find a place to hide and weather the storm.

Alex ran along the path toward the beach, then swore. There was no branch in the trail here, but if she crawled through the foliage, she could reach one of the other paths. All too aware that someone was following and not far behind, she caught hold of an old pine tree and used it for balance as she entered into the overgrowth.

Already, much of it was flattened. Even if she had found a path, it wouldn't have been worth much. The storm had brought down hundreds of palm fronds already. Coconuts, mangoes, and other fruits littered the ground. She tried to move carefully, then paused, wondering if she had lost her pursuer.

She stood very still, listening.

She could hear the sea. The storm might not be on them again yet, but the water was far from smooth. She could hear the waves crashing, could imagine them, white capped and dangerous. And beneath the water's surface, the sand and currents would be churning with a staggering strength.

Had the wind begun to pick up again yet?

Footsteps.

Whoever had been behind her was pursuing her now with slow deliberation, as if he was able to read the signs of her trail in the dark. Maybe he could.

Who was he? Had Jay been an enemy, just waiting in the darkness, or a victim? If not Jay, who could it be?

She froze in place, stock-still with indecision. Which way to go?

There was a rushing in her ears. Her own pulse. She ignored it. She had to listen above it.

Yes, there was another sound in the night. Footsteps, not the beat of her own heart.

Her pursuer. Close. Too close.

As silently as possible, she edged forward, then came to a dead stop once again. There was a new noise, coming from in front of her.

Where to go?

Only one choice.

She headed toward the beach.

SHE WAS AHEAD of him, so close it was as if he could still smell her perfume, on the air. And still she was eluding him.

She knew the island, and he didn't.

David didn't dare call out her name. Someone else might hear him. Once again, he damned himself for the bombshell he had dropped that night. Now the killer knew. He had hidden Alicia's body and now he knew he'd failed a second time. For a moment his mind wandered to the spot where he'd found the body. It wasn't an area where he had believed it would be found, where dive boats brought scores of people daily, but it wasn't impossibly far from the beaten path, either.

So what did that mean? What did the placement of the body mean?

He couldn't worry about it now. He had to use every one of his senses to find Alex.

Before it was too late.

He paused and listened. The rustle of the trees was

eerie in the strange breeze that gripped the island. It was as if the storm was gone…and yet still there.

She was moving again. The sound was so slight, he nearly missed it. He started tearing through the bushes again, following.

She was heading for the beach.

He saw her as she raced forward, then stumbled and fell. Seconds later, he burst out of the bushes behind her.

"Alex!"

He saw then what she was seeing. Just feet from her, Len Creighton was facedown in the sand. In the night, David couldn't make out anything else, whether the man was injured, unconscious…dead.

He couldn't see Alex's reaction to her discovery, but he could tell she'd heard him. She was on her feet again, and she was staring at him, and even in the dark, he could see the fear in her eyes.

"Alex!" he cried. "Alex, come here."

She kept staring at him. As he waited, afraid to move closer, lest she run again, he surveyed the area as best he could in the dark.

Where had Len come from? How had he gotten here?

Where was the danger?

He stared at Alex again. "Alex, you've got to trust me. Come with me—now. Quickly!"

He was dimly aware of leaves rustling nearby; he knew someone else had reached them even before he heard a deep voice protest, "No!"

John Seymore. Damn. He'd been on his trail the whole time. Now, David realized, he'd led the bastard right to Alex.

John Seymore stared at David with lethal promise. He had a gun. Apparently he'd been armed all along and never let on. He could kill the other man, and he knew it. But whether or not he could kill him before David sent a spear into his heart was another matter.

"Alex!" Seymore shouted, keeping a wary eye on David. "Come to me. Get away from him."

"Alex!" David warned sharply.

It seemed as if they stood locked in the eye of time, just as they were locked in the eye of the storm, forever.

Alex stared from one man to the other, and back again. Her gaze slipped down to Len Creighton, who was still lying on the beach, then focused on the two men once again.

Then she turned and dived straight into the water.

"Alex, no!" David shouted.

He couldn't begin to imagine the undercurrents, the power of the water, in the wake of the storm. And he didn't give a damn about anything other than getting her back. He even forgot that a bullet could stop him in his tracks in two seconds. He dropped the speargun and went tearing toward the water.

A dim line barely showed where water and sky met. As he plowed into the waves, he saw something shoot through the water. For a moment he thought Seymore had somehow managed to move quicker than he had and had gotten ahead of him in the violent surf.

Then he realized that whoever was ahead of him was huge, bigger than a man. David plowed on, fighting the waves to reach Alex, heedless of who else might be out there. He broke the surface.

Then he saw.

Alex was being rescued. And not by a man, not by a human being at all. One of her dolphins had come for her. Where the animal would go with her, he didn't know.

"Alex!" he screamed again.

But she had grabbed hold of the dolphin's dorsal fin, and the mammal could manage the wild surf as no man possibly could.

She was gone.

He treaded the water, watching as the dolphin and the woman disappeared in the night. The danger hadn't abated in the least; it was increasing with every minute that went by. He was losing to the power of the water himself. Fighting hard despite his strength and ability, he made it back toward the beach. When he reached the shore, he collapsed, still half in the water.

A second later, someone dropped by his side.

Seymore. Apparently he had ditched his weapon, as well, equally determined to rescue Alex from the surf.

Both men realized where they were and jerked away from one another. Then both looked toward the weapons they had dropped. David could see Seymour's muscles bunching, and he knew his were doing the same.

But Seymore cried out to him instead of moving. "Wait!"

David, wary, still hesitated.

"You had plenty of time to kill her," Seymore said.

"You could have shot me," David noted warily.

"You'd have shot back. But the point is…you dropped the speargun and went after Alex."

"Of course I went after her! I love her."

Seymore inhaled. "Listen to me, I didn't kill anyone. I know you think it's me, but I'm working with the FBI—"

"Yeah, yeah, sure. Now you're a G-man."

"No, I'm a special consultant. I thought *you* were killing people—until two minutes ago."

David found himself staring at the man. His basic reaction was to distrust him, but there was something about the man he believed. Maybe the fact that the Glock had been a guarantee, the speargun a maybe.

Seconds ticked by. Alex was in the care of a creature that could survive the darkness and the elements better than any man. But she was still out there somewhere. And the greatest likelihood was that the dolphin would bring her back to the lagoon. It wouldn't take the animal long.

There was also the matter of the man lying on the beach just feet away from them, possibly dying.

"I'm not the killer," Seymore said.

"And neither am I," David said harshly. More seconds ticked by.

Gut reaction. Dane had told him to go by his gut reaction.

He let another fraction of time go by. Then he moved.

Ignoring Seymore, he got to his feet quickly and walked over to the prone body of Len Creighton. There was blood on the man's temple, but he still had a pulse.

"He's alive," David said. Hunkered down, he tried to assess the man's condition quickly. Concussion, almost certainly. Shock, probably.

If they left him there, he would certainly die in the next onslaught of the storm. But if he was burdened with the man, Alex could die before he got back to her.

David's back was to Seymore. The man could have picked up the gun and shot him, but he hadn't.

David turned back to him. "He's got to be taken to shelter."

Seymore picked up the gun, shoving it into his belt. He stared at David, but, like him, he knew that time was of the essence.

"Alex is out there," John said.

"Yes."

"She'll trust you before she trusts me, though she doesn't seem to have much faith in either of us at the moment," he said at last. "Go after Alex. I'll take Len." Then, true to his word, he bent down, lifting the prone man as if he were no more than a baby.

David hoped to hell the guy was really on his side. As an enemy, he would be formidable.

Was he wrong? Was this all part of an act? Were they all supposed to die tonight, but on Seymore's own terms? He might be leaving Len to face instant death.

There wasn't time to weigh the veracity of John Seymore's words.

"Cottage eight was Ally and Zach's. It's probably open," David said.

"Meet me there," John Seymore said briefly.

There was nothing left to do. David turned, scooped up the speargun, and started running back toward the Tiki Hut and the dolphin lagoons.

AT FIRST ALEX had thought she had signed her own death warrant. It wasn't that she didn't know the power of the waves. She'd been out in bad weather before. She'd seen people flounder when the waves were only four feet. She couldn't begin to imagine how high they were now, but desperation had driven her into the water.

Even with everything she knew, she still hadn't imagined the battering she was going to take, the impossibility of actually swimming against the force of the sea.

She had thought she was going to die.

Then she had felt the smooth, slick, velvet sliding by her. Her mind had been too numbed at first to comprehend. The animal had made a second glide-by, and then she had known.

When Shania returned for her that time, she was ready, catching hold of the dorsal fin, just as she taught tourists to do on a daily basis.

She caught hold, though, and knew that she was doing it for her life. Still, despite her fear and panic and the waves and the desperation of the situation, she was awed. She had heard stories about dolphins performing amazing rescues. She worked with them on a daily basis, knew their intelligence and their affection.

And still...she was in awe. For a moment she wondered where the dolphin would go, and then she knew.

Safe haven.

The dolphin lagoon. Shania's home, the place where she found shelter. Where she had gone when she had been sick and injured. Where she had been nursed back to health.

The dolphin moved with astounding speed. As they neared the submerged gates to the first lagoon, Alex was afraid that she would be crushed against the steel. Shania had more faith in her own abilities. She dove low with her human passenger and raced through the opening, and they emerged in the sheltered lagoon.

"Sweet girl, sweet girl, thank you!" Alex whispered fervently to the dolphin, easing her hold and stroking the creature. "I owe you so many fish. I won't even slip vitamins into any of them," she promised.

Soundlessly, Shania moved off. Alex swam hard to the platform, crawling out of the water, shaking.

She was cold, soaking wet, barefoot, and no better off than when she had begun.

The winds would whip up again, and she had not found shelter.

Out there, somewhere, were two armed men. David and John.

And then there was Jay…. Would he have left Len to die on the sand? Oh God, she'd forgotten in her panic. And Hank? Where had he gone?

Her heart felt as numb as her fingers. There was nowhere to go, and no one to trust.

What the hell to do now? She started to rise, but a sudden wind gust nearly knocked her over. The storm was on its way back.

She headed back around the lagoon, creeping low, her goal now the Tiki Hut. The bar was solid oak. If she wedged herself beneath it, with any luck she would survive the winds and get only a minimal lashing from the rain.

Another gust of wind came along, pushing her forward. She was going to have to wedge herself tightly in. She could and would survive the night, she promised herself.

But when morning came…what then?

DAVID RACED ALONG the path, pausing only when he neared the lagoons, trying desperately to see in the darkness. The rain was becoming heavier; the wind had shifted fully and was now beginning to pick up speed.

Trying to utilize the remaining foliage for cover, he searched the area surrounding the lagoons, then the water. The darkness was deceptive, but he thought he saw dark heads bobbing now and then.

He had no idea which animal had come for Alex, how it had known she was in trouble, or where to find her. Dolphins had excellent vision; he knew they sometimes watched people from deep in the water. But how a dolphin had known where to look for Alex, he would never know.

Even though he couldn't see Alex, he was certain the dolphin had brought her back to the lagoon. Unless something had happened along the way.

He wouldn't accept such a possibility.

David sprinted around the lagoons to the platforms. He felt he was being watched. He searched the closest pool, then the farther one. At the second lagoon, one of the dolphins let out a noise. He brought a finger to his lips. "Shh. Please."

Assuming that John Seymore had told him the truth, and taking into consideration the fact that Len Creighton was definitely out, there were still two more men on the island, one of whom obviously posed a deadly threat. "Where did you bring Alex, girl?" he asked the dolphin. Intelligent eyes stared back at him, but the animal gave no indication of Alex's direction in any way.

As he retraced the path back toward the resort, David thought he saw a movement in the Tiki Hut.

Alex?

He set the speargun down against the base of a palm, knowing that for the moment, he needed his hands free.

What if the person seeking shelter in the hut wasn't Alex?

It had to be.

And if not...he had to take the chance anyway.

Slowly, crouching low, he started to move in that direction. He crept with all the silence he could manage and with the cover of a growing wind.

There she was, seeking shelter under the bar of the Tiki Hut. A good choice.

Still, he didn't show himself. She would scream, run, perhaps make it to the lagoons, and with her animals certain she was in danger, they would protect her once again. They were powerful animals, and knew their power. They could be lethal, taking a man to the bottom of a pool, keeping him there.

He moved very, very slowly. Then froze.

There was a sound from the brush nearby.

A bullet exploded, the sound loud even against the howl of nature.

David made a dive, crashing down against Alex and clasping a hand over her mouth before she could scream.

She panicked, tried to fight him. "Shh, Alex, it's me. You have to trust me," he mouthed as her eyes, luminous and huge, met his. She remained as tense as a stretched rubber band, staring at him.

Then another shot sounded in the night. He felt her flinch, but he couldn't release her mouth nor so much as shift his weight. If she drew attention to them now...

Forcing his weight hard against her, his hand still pressed against her mouth, David remained dead still. Listening. Waiting. It was so difficult to hear over the storm, to separate the natural moan, bend and rustle of the foliage from the sounds that were man-made.

He waited.

Then...yes. Someone was going off down one of the paths. He could hear the barely perceptible sound of receding footsteps.

He eased his hand off Alex's mouth. She inhaled fiercely, staring at him with doubt and fury and fear.

"Please, Alex," he begged. "Trust me."

Her lashes fell. "Trust you?" she whispered. "What about John Seymore? Did you kill him?"

She sounded cold, almost as if she were asking a question that didn't concern her.

"No."

"So you're not the killer? He's not the killer?"

"I don't think so."

"You don't *think* so?" she said, her voice rising.

He clamped a hand over her mouth again. "Shh."

She stared up at him with eyes of pure fire. He eased his hand away again. "Damn you, Alex, I love you. I'd die before I'd cause you any harm. Don't you know that about me?"

Her lashes fell again. "Actually, it's hard to know anything about you," she said.

That was when the lightning flashed. Struck. The boom of thunder was instantaneous, as the top of the Tiki Hut burst into flames.

For split seconds, they were both stunned.

Then David made it to his feet, seizing her hand, dragging her up. "We've got to move!" he urged. Without waiting for her assent, he dragged her quickly through the debris of branches and foliage that now littered the floor.

They headed down the trail toward the cottages as the rain began to pelt them.

"Where are we going?" Alex gasped, pulling back. "Our cottages are the first place anyone would look."

He didn't answer; the night had grown so dark again

that he was barely able to make his way through the trails. All his concentration was on finding their way.

"David?"

"Shh."

He longed to pause, to listen.

He dared not.

Moments later, they reached the cottage where he had delivered Ally Conroy the night before. The door was closed, but when he set his hand on the knob and turned, David found it unlocked.

Then he paused at last.

Seymore could have been lying. The guy was military, experienced. He could kill them all off, one by one. He would never be found. Before relief crews could make it to the island, he could head out, move Alicia Farr's body once again, then disappear. He would know how to do that.

Gut instinct.

And no choice.

David opened the door.

CHAPTER TWELVE

ALEX BLINKED, COLLIDING with David's back as he entered the cottage, then stopped dead.

She peered past him.

The darkness was broken by the thin beam of a flashlight in the kitchen area of the cottage.

They heard the click of a trigger, and a face appeared in the pale light.

John Seymore.

For a moment his features were as macabre as the eeriest Halloween mask. And for a moment she and David were as frozen as ice.

John Seymore took his finger off the trigger, shoving the gun back into his belt. "Alex. You're all right," he breathed.

"Yes," she said stiffly.

"Where's Len?" David asked.

"I've got him on the floor in the kitchen. I cleaned the wound. He's got a concussion, I'm sure. There's nothing else I can do for him now," John said.

"He's alive?" Alex breathed.

"Barely. His only chance is for us to get him across to medical care the minute we can," John said.

Alex moved around from behind David, still wary as she passed John Seymore, heading for the kitchen.

Len was stretched out there. John had covered him

with blankets from the beds and set his head on a pillow. She touched Len's cheek and felt warmth. His pulse was weak but steady, his breathing faint, but even.

She sat back, leaning against the refrigerator, allowing herself the luxury of just sitting for a minute, appreciating the fact that she was alive.

Then her mind began to race. The wind was howling again. She could hear it rattling against the doors in the back. She winced, afraid they would give way, then reminded herself that they were guaranteed to withstand winds up to a hundred miles an hour.

She began to shiver, then started as a blanket fell around her. She looked up. David was standing there; then he hunkered down by her side. A minute later John Seymore sat down across from them, on Len's other side.

"Who did this to him?" Alex demanded, looking from one man to the other.

David stared directly at John Seymore as he answered. "Either Jay Galway or Hank Adamson," he said.

She shook her head. "Jay cared about Len too much."

"Did he?" John asked dryly. "Jay is the manager here. If Alicia had ever shown up, he'd be the one to know it. Especially if she wanted to arrive in secret. Jay could have met her on the beach and killed her."

"No," Alex said. "Jay's hurt—I nearly tripped over him up at the main building, and then he—never mind. It had to be Hank."

"A reporter? Without any special knowledge of boats or the sea?" David asked quietly.

She stared across Len's still form at John Seymore. "So...you're FBI but not exactly an agent?" There was wariness in her voice, and she knew it.

John sighed. "Look, if I hadn't been so suspicious of

David, I would have identified myself from the beginning. But I didn't know who could be trusted. For all I knew, you were in on it somehow, Alex."

"What I want to know," David said, "is how the FBI became interested in Alicia Farr, and why?"

"The government always wants its cut," John said simply. "Different agencies, at different times, had their eyes on Daniel Fuller. He liked to talk. According to his stories, the ship went down in American waters. No way was the government going to let a treasure hunter get to her secretly."

"So...you followed Alicia?" David said.

John shook his head. "I'd been in Miami. We knew Daniel Fuller was dying, but he refused to see anyone but Alicia. I'm sorry she lost her life over this, but she was a fool. She didn't exactly hide her visits. She was overheard calling Moon Bay. So I came to see what would happen when she arrived. My job was just to find out what she knew about the *Anne Marie*. But Alicia didn't show up. You did, David. And Seth Granger, who talked way too much. And the reporter. Then Alex found the body on the beach."

Alex felt David's fingers curl around hers. She swallowed hard. There was something so instinctively protective in that hold.

For a moment, the gravity of their situation slipped away.

If John Seymore suddenly pulled out his gun, she knew David would throw himself between them. He *did* love her.

Maybe he had always loved her.

But the sea would always come first.

"How did you know Alex found a body on the beach?" David demanded sharply.

John shrugged. "I made a point of meeting up with Laurie Smith. She's a very trusting individual. Too trusting, really. It was risky, telling Laurie the truth. But it also seemed important that she lie low, since someone might know she had been with Alex and seen the body."

"Laurie is on the mainland, or at least the main island, if she didn't head out of the Keys entirely," Alex murmured. "So she knows. She knows everything that's going on. It's insane for someone to be trying to kill us all now. The authorities will know."

David was staring at John again. "Maybe not so insane. Whoever killed Alicia also helped Seth Granger to his death. That means they didn't care about financing. We've got someone on our hands who means to get to the wreckage of the *Anne Marie*, bring up the treasure without equipment or an exploratory party, then disappear."

Alex looked from one man to another. "All right, for the sake of argument right now, David, you've decided it isn't John, and, John, you've decided it isn't David. And it's obviously not Len or Jay." She frowned. "I told you, when I ran out of the storm room, I tripped over Jay."

"He was dead?" David asked sharply.

Both men were staring at her.

She shook her head. "No," she admitted. "He...he tried to grab me."

Their silence told her that they both believed Jay was guilty.

"He was the one who insisted on going out," David said to John.

"He'd know how to kill the generator," John agreed.

"Wait!" Alex protested in defense of her boss. "He

didn't attack me. I was afraid, so I ran, but…but he could have been hurt," she said guiltily, "and just trying to get me to help him."

"Alex," John said seriously, "you know that you're the one the killer really wants. It was your name Daniel Fuller mentioned over and over again. Are you sure you don't know why?"

She felt David's tension, his fingers tightening around hers. She knew what he was thinking. If you actually know something, for God's sake, keep quiet now!

He might have decided to trust John Seymore, but John's question had set off sparks of suspicion in his mind once again.

So why did she trust David so implicitly? Maybe he had been so determined to save her because he, too, believed she knew something.

"I don't have a clue. He never talked to me about the *Anne Marie*. Ever. He rambled on, told lots of stories about the sea, and he loved the dolphins. That's all I know," she said. Her words rang with sincerity, as they should have. They were true.

"Well, hard to hide anything on a dolphin," David said. He was staring at John Seymore. Sizing him up again?

"What do we do now?" she murmured.

As if in answer, the wind howled louder.

"Wait out the storm," John said.

"You have a gun," Alex said, pointing at John. "The doors lock. We can just wait until someone comes from the main island, until the sheriff gets here. Even if the killer comes after us, well…there are three of us, not counting Len, and one of him."

"Or two," David said grimly.

John cocked his head toward David. "You think Hank and Jay are in on this together?"

"I don't think anything. I'm just trying to consider all the possibilities," David said.

"Once the storm is over, we can't really sit around waiting to be attacked, anyway," John said.

"Why not?" Alex asked.

"Because," David said, not looking at her but at John Seymore, "even if Nigel was the first one to show up after the storm, he could be shot and killed before he ever got to us. If only one man is behind this, it's likely the other one is dead already. And we know the killer's armed."

"We need a plan," John murmured.

"Whatever the plan, Alex stays here," David said. "Locked in, when we go out."

"Great. I'll be a sitting duck," Alex murmured.

"Locked in," David repeated sternly.

"And what are you two going to do?" she demanded. "This isn't a big island, but there are all kinds of nooks and crannies where someone could hide. How are you going to find him—or them?"

"Well, we've got a few hours to figure it out," John said grimly. "No one will be moving anywhere in this wind."

TOWARD DAWN, ALEX actually drifted off, her head on David's shoulder. He was loathe to move her, not just for the silky feel of her head against him, but for the trust she had displayed by allowing her eyes to close while she was next to him.

Trust, or exhaustion.

"It's over," John said.

Seymore hadn't dozed off. Neither had David. They had stared at one another throughout the night. Now it was morning, and the storm was over.

They had their plan.

David roused Alex. "Hey," he said softly.

She jerked awake, eyes wide.

"We're going," he told her. "Remember, you don't open the door to anyone once we've gone. Not John, and not me."

"I don't like this," she protested. "The sheriff could be far more prepared than either of you think. He's not a bumpkin. You should both stay put, right where you are. That leaves us as three against one, remember?" She was pleading, she realized.

"You'll be all right if you just stay locked in," David said.

"I'm not worried about me, you idiot!" she lashed out. "I'm worried about the two of you. Going out as if you—"

"Alex, let us do this," John said.

"Don't forget, no one—*no one*—comes in," David warned her sternly again. This was going to be difficult for Alex, he knew. She was accustomed to being the one in charge, accustomed to action.

And they were asking her to just sit tight.

"I've got it," she said wearily. "I heard you. But I still don't understand what the two of you are going to do."

"We're going back together for the speargun," David said. "Then John is going to watch the trail, and I'm going to wait at your cottage."

"You know, whoever this is could come here and we could ambush him. Or them," she tried.

"Alex, he—or they—may never realize we came to

this cottage," David said. "In fact, we're praying that he doesn't."

He got to his feet. John joined him. He reached a hand down to Alex, drawing her to her feet and against him. His voice was husky when he said, "No one." He moved his fingers against her nape, sudden paralysis gripping his stomach.

Seymore looked away.

David kissed Alex. Briefly. But tenderly.

"Follow us to the door and bolt it immediately, don't just lock it," John told Alex. "If it's Jay, he's got a master key."

"Bolts, on both doors," David said. "Front and back."

"Yes, immediately," she said.

They stepped out cautiously.

The world seemed to be a sea of ripped-up palm fronds and foliage. Small trees were down all over.

"Close the door," David told Alex.

Her beautiful, ever-changing, sea-colored blue-green eyes touched his one last time. She went back in, and he heard the bolt slide into place behind them.

"This way for the speargun," he told John Seymore.

The other man nodded grimly and followed his lead.

ALEX'S DIVING WATCH was ticking.

Five minutes, ten minutes.

Fifteen minutes.

By then she was pacing. Every second seemed an agony. Listening to the world beyond the cottage, she could at first hear nothing.

Then, every now and then, a trill.

Already, the birds were returning.

Her stomach growled so loudly that it made her jump.

She felt guilty for feeling hunger when David and John were out there, in danger, and Len Creighton still lay unconscious on the kitchen floor.

With that thought, she returned to his side. He hadn't moved; his condition hadn't changed. She secured the blankets around him more tightly.

That was when she heard the shots.

She jumped a mile as she heard the glass of the rear sliding doors shatter.

Alex didn't wait. She tore through the place, closing doors so that whoever was out there would be forced to look for her. Then she raced into the front bedroom, opened the window and forced out the screen, grateful they hadn't boarded up the place. As she crawled out the window, she wondered if the shooter was Jay Galway or Hank Adamson.

Then it occurred to her that maybe they didn't know the truth about John Seymore.

And he was the only one of them who she knew had a gun.

In the stillness of the morning, the bullets hitting the glass, one after another with determined precision, sounded like cannon shots.

David had been waiting by the door of Alex's cottage. He'd left it ajar, standing just inside with the speargun at the ready as he watched the trail. No one would be coming through the back without his knowledge—he'd dragged all the furniture against it.

But at the sound of the gunshots, he started swearing. What if John Seymore was the shooter?

No, couldn't be. Gut instinct.

Someone was shooting, though, and David felt ill as

he left the cottage and raced dexterously over the ground that was deeply carpeted in debris.

What if his gut instinct had been wrong?

He'd left Alex at the mercy of a killer.

Heedless of being quiet, he raced toward Ally's cottage, heading for the back door.

Instinct forced him to halt, using a tree as cover, when he first saw the shattered glass. He scanned the area, saw no one, heard no one.

Racing across the open space, the speargun at the ready, he reached the rear of the cottage.

He listened but still didn't hear a thing.

The broken glass crunched beneath his feet, and he went still. Once again he heard nothing. Slowly, his finger itchy on the trigger, he made his way in and moved toward the kitchen.

There, lying under a pile of blankets, just as they had left him, was Len Creighton. Then, before he could even ascertain whether Len was still alive, David heard a noise, just a rustling, from the front bedroom.

Silently, he moved in that direction.

The door to her cottage was open.

Alex had run like a Key deer from the other cottage and, without even thinking about it, had come here.

Because David would be here.

The front door was ajar.

She hesitated, found a piece of downed coconut and threw it toward the open doorway. Nothing happened.

Cautiously, she made her way to the door. She peered inside. No one. Logic told her that once he'd heard the bullets, David would have run to her assistance.

She entered her cottage, thinking desperately about

what she might have that could serve as a weapon. The best she could come up with was a scuba knife.

She kept most of her equipment at the marina, but there were a few things here.

She raced into her bedroom, anxious to pull open the drawer where she kept odds and ends of extra equipment, reminding herself to keep quiet in case she had been followed. But she was in such a hurry that she jerked the entire dresser.

Perfumes and colognes jiggled, then started to topple over. She reached out to stop them from crashing to the floor and instead knocked them all to the floor with the sweep of her hand.

The sound seemed deafening.

She swore, returning attention to the drawer, but then something caught the corner of her eye.

She paused, looking at the pile of broken ceramics and glass.

The little dolphin had broken, and she could see that a piece of folded paper had been hidden inside the bottom of the ceramic creature.

Squatting down, she retrieved it.

Ordinary copy paper.

But as she opened it, she realized just what had been copied. A map. The original had been very old, and there was an X on it, and next to that, three words: *The Anne Marie.*

She stared at it numbly for a second, then remembered the day when she had found her things out of order. Someone must have hidden the map that day. Returning her mind to her predicament. Rising, she opened the drawer, heedless now of making noise. She found the knife she had been seeking and quickly belted it around her calf.

Then she heard a noise as someone came stealthily toward the front of the house.

Once again, she made a quick escape through a bedroom window.

DAVID BURST INTO the bedroom of Ally's cottage, spear-gun aimed.

But no one was there.

He immediately noticed the open window and the punched-out screen lying on the floor.

Silently, he left the bedroom, then the house, and hurried on toward Alex's place.

Now the door was wide open. Cautiously, he entered.

He hurried through the cottage.

This time, it was her own bedroom window that was open. A punched-out screen lay mangled on the floor.

He heard a shot.

The sound had come from the area of the Tiki Hut.

He raced from the house and toward the lagoons.

"Stop, Alex. Stop!"

She had simply run when she left her place. Away from the front door. Her steps had brought her to the lagoons and the Tiki Hut. She made it to the lagoon on the outskirts of the Tiki Hut, which was little more than a pile of rubble now. She spared a moment's gratitude that she hadn't spent the night under the bar after all.

The voice calling to her gave her pause.

It was John Seymore. And she knew he had a gun.

She turned, and he was there, closing in on her.

"Wait for me," he said. But as she stared at him, another man burst from the trees.

It was Hank Adamson. And he, too, was armed.

"Alex, it's all right!" Adamson called out. "I've got him covered. Seymore, put down the gun or I'll shoot you."

"Alex, let him shoot me," John said. "Get the hell away from him."

"Alex, don't be an idiot. Don't run," Hank Adamson insisted.

At that moment, David burst from the foliage, his speargun raised. "Alex, get the hell away from here!" David roared, but then he paused, seeing the situation.

"Hey, David," Hank Adamson called. "I've got him!"

"Yeah, I see that," David said. For a moment his eyes met hers. Then they turned toward the lagoon before meeting hers again. She realized that he was telling her to escape. Shania had helped her once. The dolphin would surely take her away again.

But she didn't dare move.

"Yeah, you've got him, all right," David said, walking to Seymore's side. "Hank, where's Jay?" he asked. "It's all right, Alex. It's okay…Hank has got this guy covered."

She knew from his eyes that he didn't mean it.

But how was he so sure that John Seymore wasn't the bad guy?

"Hank, where's Jay?" David repeated.

"This guy must have gotten him during the night," Hank said, indicating John.

And then Alex knew. Amazingly, David looked dead calm, and earnest, as if he were falling for every word Hank Adamson said. He was gambling again, she realized. Bluffing. In a game where the stakes were life or death.

His life.

She could see what he was doing. He was going to go for Hank Adamson and take the chance of being shot. He was risking John Seymore's life, as well, but she could see in that man's eyes that he was willing to take the risk. The guy was for real.

"Now!" David shouted.

His spear flashed in the brilliant morning sunlight that had followed the storm.

John Seymore made a dive for her, and they crashed into the lagoon together.

As they pitched below the surface of the water, Alex was aware of the bullet ripping through it next to them. She heard the concussion as another shot was fired.

In the depths of the lagoon, the bullets harmlessly pierced the bottom. She and Seymore kicked their way back to the surface. Heads bobbed around them. Dolphin heads. Her charges were about to go after John.

"No, no...it's all right!" She quickly gave them a signal, then ignored both them and John Seymore as she kicked furiously to reach the shore.

Two men were down.

"Careful!" John was right behind her, holding her back when she would have rushed forward.

He walked ahead of her.

Hank Adamson, speared through the ribs, was on top. Blood gushed from his wound.

"David!"

She shrieked his name, falling to the ground, trying to reach him as John Seymore lifted Hank Adamson's bleeding form.

"David!"

He opened his eyes.

"David, are you hurt? Are you shot?"

"Alex," he said softly, and his voice sounded like a croak.

"Don't you die, you bastard!" she cried. "I love you, David. I was an idiot, a scared idiot. Don't you dare die on me now!"

He smiled, then pushed himself entirely free of Hank Adamson and the pile of leaves and branches that had cushioned them both when they fell. He got to his feet.

"She loves me," he told John Seymore, smiling.

Seymore laughed.

Alex couldn't help it. She threw a punch at David's shoulder. "That doesn't mean I could live with you," she told him furiously.

"Actually, we have another worry before we get to that," David said, looking at John. "We've got to find Jay. And pray that help gets here soon, or we'll lose Len for certain."

They found Jay near where Alex had stumbled into him the night before. He was groaning, obviously alive. From the doorway, they could see him starting to rise. When he heard them, he went flat and silent once again.

"It's all right, Jay," Alex said, racing to his side. "It's over."

He sat up, holding his head, fear still in his eyes as he looked at them.

"It was Hank," he said, as if still amazed. "It was Hank…all along."

"We know," Alex told him.

"Len?"

"He's alive. We have to get him to a hospital as soon as possible," John said.

"Thank God," Jay breathed. He looked at them all. *"Hank,"* he repeated. "How did you figure it out?"

John looked at David. "How *did* you figure it out?"

Alex stared at David, as well.

David shrugged. "Two things. Seth Granger was killed. The man with the money, and Hank would fit into that category. That meant it had to be someone who didn't need money or backing. Someone who meant to get what he could, then get out."

"You said two things," John Seymore told him.

David stared at John. "Gut instinct," he said at last. He angled his head to one side for a moment, listening, and said, "There's a launch coming. Thank God. Nigel Thompson can take over from here."

EPILOGUE

SHE HURRIED ALONG the trail. She knew she was being pursued, but now, the knowledge brought a smile to her face.

They would be alone. Finally, after all the trauma, all the hours.

Still, there was something she had to do first.

Hank Adamson wasn't dead; he, like Jay and Len, had been taken aboard a helicopter and airlifted to Jackson Memorial in Miami. All three men were expected to make a full recovery.

It was chillingly clear that the reporter had intended to use the storm as cover to kill them all, Alex last, so that he could find out what she knew by saving one victim for the end and pretending he would let him live if she would just talk.

He would never have believed that she didn't know anything. Until the end, of course. Before Nigel arrived, she had given the map to David, then smiled in relief when he had turned it over to Nigel Thompson.

She didn't give a damn about the whereabouts of the *Anne Marie*. And even if David did, people were still more important to him than any treasure.

She reached the first platform, and fed Katy, Sabra and Jamie-Boy, aware she was being watched.

As she sat down at the next platform, David, who had

come after her, sat down beside her. "I have to butt in here," he told her. "I owe Shania, too. I owe her everything. Do you mind?"

Alex shook her head, and watched him for a moment as he fed and touched every dolphin, talking to them all, giving Shania special care.

"You know," she said softly, "I was jealous of Alicia, but I'm truly sorry that she's dead."

"So am I." He looked at her. "You were wrong, though, to be jealous. We never had an affair."

"She was just so...perfect for you," Alex said.

"No, she wasn't. I was always in love with you. *You* were perfect for me. I was an ass. I didn't show it. You loved your training, I loved the sea. I didn't know how selfish I had gotten."

"Well, since we're still married," she mused, "I guess we'll just have to learn how to compromise."

"Alex?"

"What?"

"I lied," he admitted. "I saw you with Seymore, and I had to think of something. Because this much is true. I love you, more than anything on earth, with every bit of my heart, my soul, and my being."

"You lied to me?" she said.

He shook his head, looking at her. "Alex, I've learned to never, ever take someone you love for granted. We can compromise. I don't need to be in on the find of the century. For me," he added softly, "*you* are the find of the century. Any century. Don't throw us away again, please."

"David, that's lovely. Really lovely. But are you saying we're not still married? That's what you lied about?"

"Forgive me. I didn't know what else to do. Well?"

She smiled. "Actually, I'm thinking that we should be remarried here. Right here. By the lagoons. A small ceremony, with just our closest friends here. I mean, we did the big-wedding thing already."

He gazed at her, slowly giving her a deep, rueful grin.

Then he pulled her into his arms and kissed her.

* * * * *

We hope you enjoyed reading

LAW AND DISORDER
&
IN THE DARK

by *New York Times* bestselling author
HEATHER GRAHAM

HARLEQUIN®

I N T R I G U E

EDGE-OF-YOUR-SEAT INTRIGUE,
FEARLESS ROMANCE.

Look for six *new* romances every month from
Harlequin Intrigue!

Available wherever books and ebooks are sold.

SPECIAL EXCERPT FROM

Join FBI agent Craig Frasier and criminal psychologist Kieran Finnegan as they track down a madman who is obsessed with perfect beauty.

"Horrible! Oh, God, horrible—tragic!" John Shaw said, shaking his head with a dazed look as he sat on his bar stool at Finnegan's Pub.

Kieran nodded sympathetically. Construction crews had found old graves when they were working on the foundations at the hot new downtown venue Le Club Vampyre.

Anthropologists had found the new body among the old graves the next day.

It wasn't just *any* body.

It was the body of supermodel Jeannette Gilbert.

Finding the old graves wasn't much of a shock—not in New York City, and not in a building that was close to two centuries old. The structure that housed Le Club Vampyre was a deconsecrated Episcopal church. The church's congregation had moved to a facility it had purchased from the Catholic church—whose congregation was now in a sparkling new basilica over on Park Avenue. While many had bemoaned the fact that such a venerable old institution had been turned into an establishment for those into sex, drugs and rock and roll, life—and business— went on.

And with life going on…

MEXP1987

Well, work on the building's foundations went on, too.

It was while investigators were still being called in following the discovery of the newly deceased body—moments before it hit the news—that Kieran Finnegan learned about it, and that was because she was helping out at her family's establishment, Finnegan's on Broadway. Like the old church/nightclub behind it, Finnegan's dated back to just before the Civil War, and had been a pub for most of those years. Since it was geographically the closest place to the church with liquor, it had apparently seemed the right spot at that moment for Professor John Shaw.

A serial killer is striking a little too close to home in the second novel in the
NEW YORK CONFIDENTIAL *series,*
A PERFECT OBSESSION
coming soon from New York Times *bestselling author*
Heather Graham and MIRA Books.

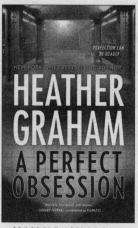